UNDERCOVER IN A NIGHTMARE

They bundled Steiner out, slamming the door, and a heavy silence descended on the hut. Tully held his breath, counting the seconds.

Suddenly the night was rent by a horrifying scream, a noise too high and grotesque to be identified as human. It came again, one volley following hard upon the other, gliding up the entire scale of recognizable sound. Loud and shrill, it filled every POW's head with the injustice of its pain until Tully wanted to yell out in unison.

Then, as abruptly as it had started, the screaming stopped, and silence flooded the hut, bringing solace to their ragged responses.

Tully lay in silence, staring at the ceiling. For him, the suffering still lingered, like a dark force that could not be assuaged. For the first time, the true nature of his predicament impressed itself upon him. If Strahle's bully boys would break a man's legs for insulting the Führer, he thought, what in hell's name would they do to an enemy spy?

AUTUMN TIGER

AUTUMN TIGER

卐

BOB LANGLEY

BANTAM BOOKS
TORONTO • NEW YORK • LONDON • SYDNEY • AUCKLAND

All the characters and events portrayed in this story are fictitious.

*This edition contains the complete text
of the original hardcover edition.*
NOT ONE WORD HAS BEEN OMITTED.

AUTUMN TIGER

*A Bantam Book / published by arrangement with
Walker & Company*

PRINTING HISTORY
Walker & Co. edition published July 1986
Bantam edition / April 1988

ISBN 0-553-27113-X

Published simultaneously in the United States and Canada

Bantam Books are published by Bantam Books, a division of Bantam Doubleday Dell
Publishing Group, Inc. Its trademark, consisting of the words "Bantam Books" and
the portrayal of a rooster, is Registered in U.S. Patent and Trademark Office and in
other countries. Marca Registrada. Bantam Books, 666 Fifth Avenue, New York,
New York 10103.

PRINTED IN THE UNITED STATES OF AMERICA

KR   0 9 8 7 6 5 4 3 2 1

AUTUMN
TIGER

1

For J.A. Tully, director of Section III (Science and Technical Affairs) of the Central Intelligence Agency, the morning of Monday, 4 August, began like any other. He rose at 6.30, donned a tracksuit, and went for his customary run round the streets of his fashionable Georgetown home. Tully had been advised to run at the age of thirty-one by his doctor Francis Summers, three days before Summers had died of a heart-attack while making love to his secretary, a muscular but luscious Seminole Indian woman who had once made her living wrestling live alligators for the tourists in Everglades National Park.

Tully had taken to running with the single-minded dedication he applied to everything else, and though he was now fifty-nine years old and five days off his retirement as Section III director, he could never suppress a certain malicious satisfaction at the sight of panting young executives staring in disbelief as he overtook them with the ease of a born athlete.

He passed the university and turned towards the Potomac, the warmth of the August sun slanting across clumps of scarlet hibiscus and blue thurnbergia. The roar of a helicopter split the air, harsh and discordant above the little white period homes and lawns glistening with dew. Tully sometimes felt Washington was a city of helicopters, and was glad he lived no closer to the river, which the pilots used as a flight route to and from the White House.

He was not, by any stretch of the imagination, a striking

man to look at, a fact which had afforded him much unease during the long years of his early youth, and had had a profound effect, in both an oblique and direct sense, upon his later life. He was neither short nor tall, lean nor fat, dark nor fair, weak nor strong. As his mother had been fond of saying, Tully was infuriatingly ordinary. His ordinariness was phenomenal. He was so ordinary that for the first twenty years of his life, scarcely anyone had recognised his existence, not even his father, who had spent most of his days in a state of alcoholic incognizance and who had mistaken Tully at various times for the grocery boy, the garbage man, the Internal Revenue inspector (who, Tully's father claimed, had been snooping on him since 1936), a Pinkerton detective (employed by the Internal Revenue), Quanah Parker, chief of the Comanches, General Philip St George Cooke, and Lawrence of Arabia. This lack of recognition by his own parent did not do a great deal for Tully's self-esteem, and he grew up with a terrible awareness of his anonymity, a trait which would not in itself have been such a hard burden to shoulder had he lived in any other society but the most aggressively competitive one in the world, the United States of America.

Tully hated the whole idea of being ordinary. He took correspondence courses to improve his brain power. He studied yoga, Buddhism, memory retention, and astronomy. He read the *Encyclopaedia Britannica*, twenty-four volumes in all, from cover to cover. He built up his body with dynamic tension exercises, and for a while his musculature did seem to gain an impressive degree of bulk and definition, but because of his ordinariness no-one ever bothered to kick sand in his face, which instilled the project with a certain air of purposelessness.

When he left college in September 1942, World War Two was at its height, and he returned several years later with a Certificate of Merit from the Office of Strategic Services and a series of livid scars on his cheek that would have imbued any other man with an air of mystery and danger. But such was the aura of mediocrity surrounding Tully, that everyone merely assumed he had walked into a streetlamp someplace.

When the war ended, Tully remained with the American intelligence network, joining the ranks of the embryo CIA under its first director Allen Dulles. For a short time his ordinariness was put to some practical use in such clandestine activities as surveillance and the bugging of hotel rooms, but eventually he had to be dropped from covert action operations because his superior officers kept sending him out on missions and forgetting he was there.

Amazingly, in spite of all this, Tully was not an unattractive man. As Pauline Steinberg, who worked for AOI, once remarked, after three joints of Popo Oro smoked in swift succession and interspersed with an equal number of shots of Jim Beam Kentucky Bourbon, Jack Tully, if viewed through dark glasses with the light falling in a certain direction, was indisputably handsome. It was simply that for no reason anyone could surmise, Tully was a nonentity, a hole in the air, a creature whose existence might have had some conceivable purpose on this earth if only somebody could have figured out what it was.

His single talent lay in the fact that he played the piano like an angel, and could, everyone felt, have been a distinguished musician if he had only applied his mind in that direction. Every morning before breakfast, he played for an hour, generally fugues by Bach. He felt he had an almost personal communion with Bach, and liked to improvise, taking off on flights of fancy in precisely the way Bach himself had done with the work of earlier composers.

It was this inherent and undeniable musical flair which stopped the CIA ignoring him altogether, and after he'd been dropped from Section IV (Operations) he was funnelled into administration, through whose ranks he rose with remarkable rapidity. There was something definitely advantageous about being ordinary in administration, Tully discovered, for while everyone else was jostling, elbowing and manoeuvring for position, he was promoted from one department to the next for no other reason than that nobody considered him a threat. Suddenly, people were saying 'Good old Jack,' where before they had merely said, 'Who?'

His second marriage, to a lady attorney from Shreveport, turned out to be satisfying and harmonious, and though he had not, he knew, married Louisa for love, nevertheless, no woman could have made him a better wife. Though their relationship was founded less on passion than expediency, Tully sometimes felt its very staidness made it more secure, and in a curious way more fulfilling, too. They respected each other, and out of the respect had grown a deep and lasting affection.

At fifty-six, Louisa was still an attractive and desirable woman. Of their two boys, one was a lawyer in Abilene, Texas, the other a doctor in San Francisco, and at the end of the week, after his retirement dinner, he and Louisa were putting their home on the market and moving out west to live in California.

Tully never understood why Louisa had chosen him as a mate in the first place, for she was a formidable lady in both character and temperament; not merely alluring (she carried about her an air of physical magnetism that even a eunuch would have to acknowledge) but intelligent too, and while Tully was by nature reticent and introspective, Louisa was articulate, witty, and often brilliantly sardonic. Between her marriage to her first husband and her meeting with Tully on a Hudson River steamboat one rainy Sunday afternoon, she had at various times been squired by some of the most attractive and enterprising men in the world, including a week-long interlude with young Jack Kennedy (long before he had aspired to the White House) which had culminated in a stormy quarrel in the back of an old Chevvy parked above Lincoln Boulevard. Throughout the Kennedy administration, Tully had often experienced a quiet sense of pride at the thought that his wife was probably the only woman in America who had ever said no to the President.

Nevertheless, Tully was genuinely puzzled as to why this woman, with her undeniable vivacity, her striking good looks, and her inherent sense of panache, should have displayed such dubious taste in choosing as her partner through life, himself. As earlier girlfriends had constantly pointed out, he was a far from exciting catch in the marriage-stakes, and to find his destiny united with that of a woman of beauty, intellect, and wit, produced in Tully occasional bouts of mental disorientation, which, when his brain found the enigma too complex to encompass, resulted in chronic attacks of dandruff.

The extraordinary thing was that Louisa unquestionably loved him. At first, he had doubted the sincerity of that love, unable to believe that such a woman could experience genuine emotion toward a jerk like himself, but as the years went by, the realisation penetrated even Tully's sceptical skull that the affection and tenderness she expressed were no lie.

It would have surprised Tully to learn that Louisa had acquired, at an early age, a simple distaste for men of power and ambition, sensing in them a conceit that not only repelled her mentally, but also made her frigid. She was attracted to Tully by, of all things, his mediocrity. She liked his gentleness, his tolerance, his sympathetic nature, and above all, the one quality he hated most about himself, the fact that he was ordinary. She loved him with a passion that was both spiritual and sensual. He could not match the intensity of that love. Despite his outwardly passive air, for the greater part of his life Jack Tully had been filled with a sense of deep dissatisfaction, a feeling of unrest he attributed to something that had happened in the early part of his career. There were times he dreaded the prospect of retirement, for he knew that without work to sustain him he would be faced with the company of a woman he barely understood, and of whom (though he loved her implicitly) he often felt secretly afraid.

On the morning of 4 August, eight days from his sixtieth birthday and five from his retirement as head of Section III of the CIA, Tully arrived at the office and found his secretary Denise in a state of high excitement.

'I've been calling you for the last half-hour,' she said. 'Charles Schulman's here.'

Tully frowned. Charles Schulman was head of FOCB, the CIA Foreign Operations Co-Ordination Board, the department that handled secret intelligence work overseas. Though Tully knew Schulman socially, their paths seldom crossed in a professional sense. He felt a mixture of curiosity and unease. 'Where is he?' he asked.

'I put him in your office,' Denise said. 'I had to do something. He's got some other guy with him. A Mr Guichard.'

'Harry Guichard?'

'That's right.'

Tully's tenseness mounted. Harry Guichard headed the Operations Special Research Board, the department that planned and executed undercover missions at home and abroad. Guichard belonged to that section of the Agency everyone knew existed but no-one ever quite believed in, the murky area of international espionage.

Tully felt his pulse racing. For more than thirty years he had sat among his filing cabinets writing reports, compiling data, and apart from a short period at the start of his career, the true nature of his business had never touched him. Now, five days from his pension, he found the intrusion slightly alarming.

He tapped on the door and entered his office, blinking in the morning sunlight. Schulman rose to greet him, a solid man, medium-sized, with sleek black hair and a pair of large brown eyes that seemed to fill his entire face. He smiled affably. 'Jack.'

'Hello, Charles. This is a surprise.'

'Couldn't pass up a chance of welcoming you on your final week, Jack. How does it feel to be into the home-stretch?'

'A little weird, I guess.'

'You know Harry Guichard of OSRB?'

Tully nodded to Guichard, a lanky Texan with a sandy crewcut who smiled politely. Flecks of grey decorated Guichard's temples, but his face looked young and fit. 'We've met a couple of times, I think,' Tully said.

Inside, he felt a kind of delayed panic, thinking, my God! here am I nearing the end of my career and I still can't keep my cool in the presence of these guys. His palms had started to sweat, his shirt collar to dampen. Being met at nine o'clock in the morning by Schulman and Guichard had thrown him out of gear. 'Do you gentlemen drink this early?' he asked, remembering his manners.

'Not right at the moment, Jack,' Schulman murmured.

'Coffee, maybe?'

'Later. First, it's important we have a talk.'

He paused and added, 'Undisturbed, Jack.'

Tully walked behind his desk and sat down. His stomach felt as if it had lost its substance and was undulating somewhere beneath his breastbone. 'Sounds kind of secretive,' he said.

'Secretive is right. What we're about to tell you his classified. We want it kept under wraps.'

'Okay.'

Schulman sat down and drummed his fingertips lightly on his knee. He had a reputation for ruthlessness that belied his affable exterior, and never in his life had Tully seen him display the slightest sign of unease. But he was nervous now, that was apparent.

'I know covert action operations are a little outside your sphere these days,' Schulman said, 'but I'm afraid your name's come up on this one, and there's no way we can avoid it.'

Tully stared at him, his pulses quickening. He was nearly sixty years old, for Christ's sake. Retiring on Friday. There had to be some mistake.

Harry Guichard guessed what was going through his mind.

'I know it sounds crazy, Mr Tully, particularly on your last week with the Company. But one of our operatives came out of East Germany yesterday. The hard way, over the wire. He could have used his cover and left with the Perisco Trade Delegation at the end of the month, but he had a piece of information that just couldn't wait.'

'What kind of information?'

Guichard hesitated. He looked at Schulman, and then back at Tully. 'Stapius wants to defect,' he said.

Tully heard the rumble of traffic from the street outside. He stared at them helplessly. 'Is that supposed to mean something?'

Schulman sighed. 'Stapius is head of the HVA section of the East German Intelligence agency, MfS,' he explained. 'He's masterminded some of the most brilliant coups ever conducted against the West, and he's operated so successfully that not a single photograph of the man exists on company files. He's been a thorn in our flesh for nearly forty years now. His defection could set the whole European network on its ears.'

Tully clenched his fists below the desktop. This was not the kind of information he was normally party to. He tried to respond intelligently. 'Did Stapius say why he wants to defect?'

'No.'

'But you believe him?'

'Well, we didn't in the beginning. However, our man is convinced he means what he says, and our man's been a field operative long enough to discern the difference between fact and fiction.'

'Did he actually talk to Stapius?'

'Nobody's talked to Stapius, Jack. Nobody's even seen Stapius. Our operative is working through a mediator, a guy called Skow. Skow wants to defect too. We get them both for the price of one, though of course Stapius is the big cigar.'

'But I can't see what it's got to do with me,' Tully muttered, 'I'm a desk man. I tot up accounts, sift through files. I never even heard of this guy Stapius before.'

'Well, he's heard of you, Jack, that's for sure,' Schulman said. 'He's laid down no conditions for his defection. He's asked for nothing, no money, no guarantees, not even a respectable pension. Just one thing.'

'What's that?'

'He wants you to receive him when he comes over.'

Tully looked at him in amazement. 'That's crazy,' he whispered.

'That's what we thought, Jack.'

'I'm an administrator, you know that Charles.'

'Believe me, Jack, we've gone over this thing again and again, and damn my ass if I can spot the connection. At first, we figured Stapius must have made a mistake, but our operative confirmed the name: J.A. Tully, Section III, Science and Tech.'

Tully rose to his feet and strolled to the window. He tried to look cool and authoritative, tried to keep his shoulders square and his stomach tense, like Henry Fonda as the young Abe Lincoln.

'Nothing like this has ever happened to me before,' he said.

'I know, Jack. I know how crazy it all seems. But we want you to think hard. Can you pinpoint any reason, anything at all that might give us a clue as to why Stapius chose you?'

Tully shook his head. 'Nothing.'

'Think Jack. Please try. You used to be a field operative in your youth. Maybe at some point in the past . . .'

'It was thirty-odd years ago, Charles. Everyone I met you'll find in my reports.'

'We've checked them all, Jack. Most of the agents you encountered are known to be dead.'

'Then that's it. I can't turn back the clock like it was yesterday.'

He turned to look at them. 'When's Stapius coming over?'

'Tomorrow night in Paris. He's promised to deliver himself to our embassy at nine.'

'Why Paris?'

'We can't tell for sure. There's an East German study group at the United Nations, and the Kirov ballet is appearing at the Palais des Congrès. It's just possible he's accompanying one of them.'

Tully moved away from the window and sat back in his chair.

'It could, of course, be a trick,' he said.

Schulman nodded. 'That's right, Jack. But what would he have to gain?'

'Maybe he wants to kidnap me?' Tully murmured.

'For what reason? You said yourself you've been behind a desk for the past thirty years. Hell, Jack, there's nothing you can tell Stapius about the Company he hasn't got on his files already. If he wanted to grab a key man, why didn't he specify Harry here? Or Joe Galazka? Or even me? And why choose Paris? Why not pick someplace on his own side of the wire? In Paris, he's four hundred miles inside neutral territory.'

'Revenge then?'

'What are you talking about?'

'Maybe at some time in the past I stepped on Stapius's toes unwittingly.'

'And he wants to pay you back after thirty years, Jack? Be your age.'

Tully paused, hesitating to ask the next question.

'What d'you want me to do?' he queried softly.

Schulman took a deep breath. 'Jack, I hate to involve you at this late stage in your career, but Stapius is too big a mackerel to ignore. We want you to fly to Paris and meet him. Nothing complicated. Our man Thiedeck will be there to keep an eye on things. We'll stick you in a good hotel, you'll trot along to the embassy and make the appropriate noises on Stapius's arrival, then you'll come home. As easy as that.'

Tully considered for a moment. 'What if it turns out to be just another Stapius manoeuvre?'

'We'll have so many SS men around, not even your own wife could get within kissing distance without a signed statement in triplicate from me.'

'And the French?'

'We're keeping them out of it. Stapius is too big, Jack. If he's on the level, we have a chance of grabbing the intelligence prize of the century. I give you my word your personal safety will be our number one concern. At no time will you be in the slightest danger. And once it's over, we'll fly you back to Washington in time for your retirement dinner on Friday. What d'you say?'

'You make it sound so simple.'

'It's our ballpark Stapius is playing in, Jack. Nothing can go wrong. Nothing.'

Tully was silent for a moment. He was not a brave man, he knew that. Fit maybe, still capable of functioning when he had to, but he had no illusions about his character. Schulman and Guichard belonged to a different world, they were different in every respect: in temperament, intellectual disposition, experience.

And face it, he was no spring chicken. Okay, when you were fresh out of high school maybe being sixty seemed more ancient than Methuselah, but as the years went by you got a new slant on things, time took on a new perspective, you realised as you passed from one decade to the next that your hopes and dreams didn't change all that much. And there was no fool like an old fool, he mused.

Dummy. What do you want to play the hero for?

He had never sought glory, never, not even in his earliest days, and he had, if the truth were known, endeavoured consciously and assiduously to remove himself from any element of physical danger. Now, like a middle-aged man who attempts to prove his virility by chasing wildly after women, he found the prospect of active service strangely alluring.

It's crazy, he thought. Kid's stuff.

But something started up inside him, an unaccountable excitement that wouldn't be ignored and couldn't be denied.

'The last time I was in Paris,' he said, 'Louisa and I stayed at a little hotel in St Germain des Prés. It had a terrace right on the sidewalk, with red-checked tablecloths and wine they sold at a quarter a litre.'

Schulman peered at him, puzzled. 'What about it, Jack?'

'You think they might still have a room free, even in August?'

Schulman smiled. He glanced at Guichard, chuckling good-humouredly. 'Jack,' he said, 'if I have to, I'll rent every damned room in the hotel.'

The stewardess said: 'Ladies and gentlemen, in a few minutes we'll be landing at Charles de Gaulle Airport. Please fasten your seatbelts and extinguish all cigarettes. Thank you.'

Tully stared through the window at the bank of cloud below. It had been a smooth flight; no turbulence in the air, no hiccups on the ground. As an omen, it was a good start. Even the movie had been new. His only complaint was that his muscles were stiff and sore from the long hours of inactivity, but you learned to accept such things as you grew older.

He had to admit he was edgy. His conversation with Schulman had taken place less than twelve hours before, and it was quite a switch moving from ordinary run-of-the-mill stuff to active operations, especially at his age. He didn't believe Schulman's assurances that there'd be no danger. With a man as experienced as Stapius, there was bound to be danger.

He hadn't told Louisa. She'd never have sanctioned it if he had. He could imagine her face, taut and worried; that firm set to her chin when she disapproved of something he'd done, or planned to do. Louisa would have taken on the whole CIA to prevent him going, so he hadn't mentioned Paris. She thought it was routine. Los Angeles, he'd said, to make up the numbers at a diplomatic convention. She'd shown some surprise, but hadn't suspected. He could have said no. Now there was no turning back.

It took less than an hour to clear customs, and as he entered the airport lounge he spotted a tall young man with reddish brown hair and a thick moustache. They had never met, but Tully recognised his face from a photograph in his pocket.

'Mr Tully?' the young man smiled.

'You're Thiedeck,' Tully grunted as they shook hands.

'Welcome to Paris, Mr Tully. I hope your stay will be an uneventful one.'

'I'll second that,' Tully said.

They pushed their way through the milling crowd and stepped on to the mobile walkway leading to the ground floor. A party of nuns passed them by on the opposite side, going up. One of the nuns was trying to comfort a small boy who was sobbing hysterically.

'August is a dead month in Paris,' Thiedeck said. 'The residents move into the country and the city fills up with tourists. You can't move for coach parties.'

'I'm not here for the sightseeing,' Tully murmured. 'The faster I'm on the plane home, the better I'll like it.'

Thiedeck looked at him curiously. 'They tell me you're due to retire soon.'

'End of the week. This is kind of my swan-song.'

'Well, don't worry, you'll be in no danger here, I'll see to that.'

Tully studied Thiedeck as he led the way to the underground parking lot. He looked capable enough, strong as an ox, judging by the width of his chest and the set of his shoulders, and with a bright intelligent face that probably denoted a quick brain. But against a man with Stapius's record, he was still a novice. Let Thiedeck enjoy his illusions. Tully intended to look after himself.

'What's our schedule?' he asked.

'First, we go to the Tuileries.'

'The Tuileries?'

'Skow wants to take a look at you. I chose the Tuileries because it's so open. There'll be dozens of people around. Less chance of anything going wrong.'

'Skow is Stapius's man.'

'Right.'

'And after he's looked at me?'

'He reports back to Stapius that you've arrived in Paris, and we go to the embassy and wait.'

'This guy Skow, did he give any indication what part I play in all of this?'

'Skow's like all those bastards from the MfS,' Thiedeck said bluntly, 'tighter than a peacock's ass.'

Tully was silent as they drove into town. He watched the city building up around him and a strange excitement coursed through his veins.

A thin drizzle began to fall as Thiedeck took the exit road and cruised down the Rue Lafayette towards the Opéra. Tully peered out at the bustling sidewalks. A gendarme stood chatting to an old lady in a woollen shawl. Oysters lay packed in ice on a fishmonger's slab. Nowhere in the world was quite like Paris, he thought.

Thiedeck swung round the Madeleine toward the Place de la Concorde, dodging in and out of the traffic with a speed that left Tully gasping. Automobiles hurtled at them from every direction. Tully winced as Thiedeck swung between a little Renault and a heavy milk-truck. My God, the MfS he'd face any day, but Paris in the rush-hour was something else.

Thiedeck turned off the Concorde and in typical French fashion parked the car on the sidewalk. Tully clambered out and turned up his collar against the rain. The trees of the Tuileries looked soggy and damp. Tully peered up the Champs Élysées toward the distant frame of the Arc de Triomphe, and Thiedeck, catching his glance, smiled an apology. 'I wish I could turn you loose,' he said, 'but Schulman would have my hide. I don't want you out of my sight for one second. When we've got Stapius and you're safely on the plane back to the USA, then I'll begin to breathe again.'

'You've got your job to do,' said Tully. 'I understand.'

Thiedeck took him by the arm. 'Go through the gates to the goldfish pond,' he instructed. 'Just walk slow and easy. I've got men posted all over the place in case there's trouble.'

Tully felt the tension building up inside him. He strolled dutifully, Thiedeck at his side, holding on to his arm like a guide handling a blind man. For the first time, Tully had the awful sensation of being used. To Schulman and Guichard he was an object. If he died today, they'd forget him in a week.

He realised he was trembling. Silly to feel scared with all this normality about, he thought. Everything looked normal. Water dripped from the lamp-globes. A line of schoolchildren wandered by, shepherded by a priest in a flat-brimmed hat. He looked pale and overwrought.

What could happen, what could possibly happen?

But a chill settled on Tully's neck as he sauntered down the stone stairway and crossed the paddock to the artificial lake. He stared at the water. Goldfish darted beneath its surface.

'Is he here?' he whispered.

'Sure,' Thiedeck said, 'that's Skow with the birdseed.'

Tully peered up at a man feeding the pigeons nearby. He looked pale and undernourished, his shirt collar frayed around the edges. As he reached into his paper bag, Tully saw that his fingernails were rimmed with dirt.

'As soon as he's satisfied,' Thiedeck whispered, 'he'll report back to Stapius.'

Suddenly, the man looked over. Tully stared at him in silence, and for a moment their eyes locked. No sign of emotion crossed Skow's face, but without hesitation he crumpled the paper bag into a tight little ball, pushed it into his pocket, and began to stride purposefully in Tully's direction.

'He's coming over,' Tully grunted.

Thiedeck gave a gasp. 'Jesus Christ!'

Skow slipped his right hand inside his raincoat and Tully felt his heart stand still. My God, he's going to shoot me, he thought.

There was no expression in Skow's eyes. They had the bland indifference of a butcher at a slaughterhouse. He was drawing closer. Another few steps and he couldn't possibly miss. Tully felt a sense of indignation. Why didn't Thiedeck do something? Surely the idiot was armed?

And then, as he watched, a flurry of action broke out on the cindered footpath. People who, until a second ago, had looked like innocent pedestrians—a pair of workmen sweeping up leaves, an unkempt derelict drinking liquor from a dusty bottle, a negro with an expansive umbrella—suddenly, they all converged on Skow in a seething swirl of movement and hauled him to a halt. Tully felt a surge of relief as he saw the affronted look in Skow's eyes and watched the thin lips tighten.

'Please,' Skow snapped in a high-pitched voice, 'release my arms.'

'You miserable bastard,' Thiedeck growled, 'you said you just wanted a look.'

Skow struggled to regain his composure. 'I have a gift for Mr Tully,' he announced, 'from Stapius.'

'What kind of gift?'

'In my pocket.'

Thiedeck nodded to one of the men holding Skow. The man fumbled inside the raincoat and produced a tiny package wrapped in gaudy paper. He handed it to Thiedeck, who studied it suspiciously. He held the package to his ear and gave it a gentle shake. 'What's inside?' he demanded.

'I do not know,' Skow replied. 'Stapius instructed me to deliver it, that is all.'

Thiedeck looked at him. 'Our deal still stands?'

'Of course. Nine o'clock. We will be there.'

Thiedeck nodded to the men holding Skow, and they released him with reluctance. Skow brushed his raincoat in an imperious manner, and with a last furious glance at Thiedeck, turned and began to stroll in the direction of the Louvre.

Tully looked at the package curiously. 'Shall I open it now?' he asked.

'Are you crazy?' Thiedeck grunted. 'How d'you know it won't blow up in your hand? We'll take it back to the embassy and stick it under the X-ray machine. If it's safe, you can have it then.'

He glanced at his watch. 'Four more hours till nine o'clock,' he said. 'The next move is up to Stapius.'

Tully sat in the embassy office and rubbed his forehead. The encounter with Skow had affected him more than he'd imagined. Being older didn't make death any more palatable, he realised; he was just as scared now as he had been in his youth.

Thiedeck watched him from the corner. 'Nervous?' he asked.

Tully shrugged his shoulders. He didn't feel like talking. Already, he regretted his decision to come to Paris. He wasn't built for this, godammit. Clandestine meetings with defecting agents from East Germany belonged to men of a different temperament. A different age, too. He'd been a fool.

The telephone rang and Thiedeck lifted the receiver.

'Yes?' he said in a flat voice.

He listened a moment, then put one hand over the mouthpiece.

'It's Leyton,' he murmured, 'he's got your package.'

'Send him in,' Tully grunted.

Leyton looked puzzled when he came through the door. 'We checked the thing thoroughly,' he said, 'but there was nothing inside except this. No note, no message, nothing.'

'What is it?' Thiedeck muttered.

'A cigarette-lighter. Pretty beat-up.'

Thiedeck took the lighter from Leyton's hand, studied it briefly, then tossed it to Tully. 'Recognise it?'

Tully held the lighter up, frowning. It was old-fashioned in design, and made of solid gold. Its metal was discoloured and in places badly scratched, but staring at it, Tully felt an odd tingling in his stomach. 'My God!' he whispered, 'it's not possible.'

Thiedeck frowned. 'What's up, Mr Tully?'

Tully shook his head in silence, his movements slow and retarded like those of a man recovering from a stroke.

Thiedeck glanced at Leyton and back again. 'Mr Tully,' he said, 'does that lighter mean something to you?'

Tully rose to his feet and moved to the window. He studied the lighter minutely, turning it over in his hands. It can't be the same one, he thought, it can't be.

He slipped his thumb beneath the main screw and found the hidden groove he knew was there. Expertly, he pressed it with his nail, and with a muffled click the outer panel flew open to reveal an inscription engraved upon the gold.

Trembling, Tully took out his glasses and put them on. He held the lighter up to the window and formed the words with his lips. 'To J.A. Tully, with deep affection, from the residents of Avery, Wyoming, April 1943.'

Traffic thundered in the street outside.

'Please,' he said softly, 'will you leave me for a moment.'

Thiedeck hesitated. 'You know my orders.'

'I . . . must be alone. A few minutes, that's all. Please.'

Thiedeck looked at Leyton and slowly, almost imperceptibly, nodded. 'We'll be right outside the door,' he said. 'Call, if you need anything.'

For what seemed an immeasurable length of time, Tully stood in the window peering at the lighter. His body grew light, the oldness fading from his bones, and in his mind he was young once more, and supple, filled with a tense restless energy that stretched and expanded like a flickering flame. The years rushed away and the present faded until only the past remained, and he knew in that moment that, simply by remembering, nothing in his life could ever be the same again.

2

Berlin, February 1945.

The city looked gaunt under the slate-grey sky. Shattered buildings lined the streets, and a heavy pall of dust filled the air, bringing with it the acrid scent of cordite. Traces of frost glistened among the ruined masonry. To the east, the sky looked crimson.

Tully heard the sirens as he cycled home from work. They had become so much a part of his experience these past few months that their wailing produced no sense of fear, only frustration that the nightly broadcast which told his superiors he was still alive was about to be disrupted. He detoured around a sign in red paint which warned 'Danger! Unexploded Bomb,' and spotted among the rubble bicycles parked in orderly rows. Berlin was a city of bicycles, for the majority of motor vehicles had been commandeered by the army.

Somewhere to the west an artillery barrage opened up, sending vibrations along the cratered ground. There was no panic. Air-raids had become a way of life. People scurried to the shelters with an air of urgency rather than alarm.

Tully pedalled harder, glancing at his wristwatch. If he missed the broadcast tonight he would have to wait another twenty-four hours, that was the rule. One broadcast a day, and never at the same time twice—London's idea, to prevent the Gestapo homing in on his frequency.

Bombs exploded in the direction of the Brandenburger Tor, their blasts making a deeper sound than the anti-aircraft guns, like a heavy bass drum being pounded discordantly in the background. A uniformed member of the Kriminalpolizei stopped Tully at a roadblock and studied his *Fremdenpass*.

'Where are you going?' he demanded.

'Home,' Tully told him.

'You know the law. When the sirens sound, you take shelter.'

'But my wife's ill. She can't get out of bed.'

'What difference does that make? You won't be much good to her with your head blown off. Leave your bicycle with the others and get below. Nobody'll pinch it.'

Resignedly, Tully propped his cycle among the rubble. You did not argue with the Kriminalpolizei, he thought. In Tully's position, you did not argue with anybody. The broadcast would have to be jettisoned.

He joined the throng of people flooding down the stairs to the underground railroad station. The subterranean tunnels were still the safest place to hide in the ravaged city. Wooden benches had been arranged along the empty platforms, and though most were already occupied, men and women, with a patience born of painful experience, were busy making themselves comfortable on the concrete floor.

Tully fumbled in his pocket for his cigarettes. At least there were still some pleasures left in life, he thought, even if he had to buy them on the black market.

He found a place against the cold brickwork. Opposite, a wounded stormtrooper, his leg in splints, peered glumly at the dirty floor. In the far corner, someone was singing a popular marching song, but no-one took up the refrain.

Tully heard the shudder of bomb-blasts outside, some so close that the shelter walls seemed to vibrate. When this happened, the singing in the corner faded and the people grew quiet, holding on to each other with an air of grim possessiveness.

Tully smoked in silence, his body trembling. He knew he was a write-off, had known it for weeks. He was like a man with an unspeakable illness. It wasn't fear of death, he thought. Dying was part of the job. It was the loneliness. The strain of living a lie. The fear of discovery and the pain it would bring. For almost four months, Tully had operated in the very heart of Germany. Though the information he sent back was not in itself important, pieced together by the R and A (the Research and Analysis Branch of the OSS) each fragment or observation helped to build up the Allies' knowledge of what was happening inside the Reich. But the four months had left their mark. Tully's face looked older than its years. His eyes were hooded, the hollows beneath his cheekbones sharply defined. Meagre rationing had reduced his bony frame to skeletal proportions, and now his clothes hung on him like limp rags. Worst of all, continual stress had produced inside him a feeling of utter despair. It was not oblivion man feared most, Tully thought, not even pain if he thought there might be an end to it. But destroy the rhythms of his life, obliterate the order of his daily existence, and you ruined his faith in his own species.

Above, the roar of the bombing moved further afield. Tully heard the wail of a fire engine and the clatter of running feet. He wondered if the policeman was still upstairs. Hardly. Not after that hammering. Tully nipped the tip of his cigarette and slipped it inside his pocket. He had to get out. He was too late for the broadcast, but he would rather take his chances in the open than crouch in this miserable hole like a squirrel in a trap.

He straightened and moved toward the door, placing his feet between the lines of outstretched legs. No-one looked at him.

He felt cold air wafting into his face as he climbed the steps two at a time. Gasping, he reached the street and paused to check his bearings. The policeman had gone, and in the spot where the barricade had stood was a smoking crater. The sky had darkened during the short time he'd been below, and now the night was streaked with probing searchlights. In their macabre glow, he spotted artillery flack hanging among the clouds like frozen mushrooms.

He picked up his bicycle and pedalled furiously through the debris. Near the Potsdamer Platz, the *Trümmerfrauen*, the rubble women, were sorting through the refuse where a bomb had fallen. The front of the building had completely disappeared, leaving its ceiling to sag ominously, supported by a network of twisted girders. The interior of the room looked strangely undamaged, as if the blast that had taken out its wall had somehow missed the spindly pieces of furniture, scattering them with dust but leaving them otherwise intact. The people who had lived in the house, however, had not been so lucky. They were being laid out on the sidewalk, an old lady, a younger woman of twenty-four or five, and a boy of about fourteen or fifteen. They were all dead. Smothered with dirt, they looked oddly untouched by the blast. The only sign of injury was a trickle of blood smudging the young woman's mouth. Tully looked away. They seemed so calm, so utterly unmoved. He could have taken blood and gore. A hand loose, a leg tossed casually into the gutter, he was always prepared for that. Unattached limbs did not assume the character and personality of corpses laid peacefully in repose.

He cycled through the Tiergarten and turned up the Kurfürstendamm, trying to ignore the flashes that streaked the sky like summer lightning.

A tinkle of glass reached Tully's ears, and he heard someone shout, 'Hey, give us a hand here, will you?'

A policeman was waving at him from the ruins of a shattered house. An ambulance stood parked at the roadside. Tully dropped his bicycle and hurried across. 'What's up?' he asked.

'Someone's still in here,' the policeman said, hauling at a massive beam of timber. It lifted slightly, shifting the weight of several tons of masonry above it. Two ambulancemen leaned underneath, scooping hard at the rubble with their shovels.

'Alive?' Tully murmured.

'She was a minute ago,' the policeman said.

Tully leaned forward, adding his own strength to the timber. Together, they managed to raise it a further few inches.

'Think you can hold it on your own?' the policeman asked hoarsely.

'I'll try,' Tully promised.

The policeman had already let go, and the immense weight of the timber forced Tully into the earth. He sucked air into his lungs, moaning with effort.

The policeman burrowed into the hole, the ambulancemen

behind him. Tully could hear them rummaging around inside. He gritted his teeth, staring wildly at the sky. The scene seemed oddly unreal—the ruined building, the eerie ballet of the searchlights, the flames billowing out of the windows across the street. He felt his muscles begin to weaken and thrust upwards, the timber biting at his arms, grinding into his skin.

'Easy now,' he heard the policeman say, 'just a few more seconds.'

He was crawling out of the hole, dragging something behind him. The ambulancemen pushed from below, and Tully, glancing down, saw it was the figure of a young woman, the entire front of her dress drenched in blood. As they hauled her clear, she brushed against him, leaving a scarlet smear across his thighs.

Tully let the timber drop with a gasp. He was shaking all over from the effort. He staggered to where the ambulancemen were tucking the girl on a stretcher.

'She looks dead,' he hissed.

'She's still breathing,' the policeman said. 'You never can tell at first glance. Sometimes the blood makes it look worse. On the other hand, I've seen corpses with barely a scratch on them.'

Tully remembered the family dead on the sidewalk and nodded miserably. I hate war, he thought.

The ambulancemen loaded the stretcher into the back of their vehicle, and drove off through the mud and snow.

The policeman turned to Tully, smiling. He was covered with muck. 'Thanks for your help,' he said, 'but oughtn't you to be in a shelter?'

'I have to get home,' Tully lied. 'My wife's ill.'

'Where's your gasmask?'

Tully's stomach jumped. Good God, he'd left the damn thing at the factory. How could he have been so stupid? Everyone, civilians and servicemen alike, were required to carry gasmasks at all times.

'I . . . I must have dropped it somewhere in the excitement.'

The policeman stroked his upper lip with one finger. He

had the flimsy beginnings of a moustache. His eyes narrowed
as a flicker of suspicion crossed his face. 'Shouldn't you be in
uniform at your age?' he asked.

'I'm exempt,' Tully said.

The policeman laughed humourlessly. 'Nobody's exempt
these days. I've seen men in the army with arms and legs off.'

'It's nothing to do with health. It's my job. I work at the
Ehrenfeld arms factory.'

The policeman's frown deepened. 'Let me see your
papers,' he ordered.

Tully fumbled inside his jacket. He had no illusions about
the flimsiness of his cover. On the surface it seemed sound
enough—he had established himself over the past few months,
he had friends at the factory who could vouch for his character
and conduct—but he knew he could never withstand the
rigours of a determined cross-examination. In the OSS training
school, they had taught him to hold out against interrogation
and torture, but that had been fifteen months ago. Now the
very foundations of his psyche were crumbling. Whatever
happened, he couldn't afford to be scrutinized.

The policeman studied Tully's *Fremdenpass* carefully
before handing it back. 'Men are dying by the wagonload in
Russia and France,' he said. 'How did you swing a cushy
number like this? Friends in high places, have you? An uncle
with the Ministry, a cousin in the Security Office?'

'Nothing like that,' Tully said hastily. 'I volunteered for
military service, but they turned me down.'

'We're rooting out corruption at every turn,' the policeman
stated. 'Nobody's immune these days. Your friends won't help
you, if you're lying.'

'I have no friends,' Tully insisted urgently, 'no-one of
influence whatsoever. I'm telling the truth, I swear it.'

For a moment, the policeman's calm eyes seemed to bore
into Tully's skull, and Tully held his breath, struggling to keep
his features straight. Then at last the policeman seemed to
relax. 'Very well,' he said, 'you're free to go, but get off the
streets as quickly as possible. We've enough casualties on our

hands without idiots like you getting themselves blown to bits. Go home at once.'

Tully felt relief flood through his veins. A tiny vein began to throb inside his temple, boring inward behind the left eye. He nodded gratefully.

'Thank you,' he said.

And turning, he ran for his bicycle.

Belgium, February 1945

The men in C-for-Charlie Company felt weary and dispirited. A month before, they had been relaxing in the Huertgen Forest when the Germans had launched their counter-offensive in the Ardennes, smashing across a fifty-mile front. Taken by surprise, the Americans had fought back in chaos and confusion, and by the beginning of January, with the breakthrough finally halted, they had sustained nearly eighty thousand casualties. However, since the Germans had lost a hundred-and-twenty thousand, as well as a thousand planes and five hundred tanks, the battle was diplomatically regarded as an American victory, a fact that did little to reassure the men of C-for-Charlie Company, who had fought in appalling weather conditions and who were now dangerously close to the level of exhaustion.

Corporal Gary Lae, medium-sized, snub-nosed, twenty-three years old, moved with the stumbling gait of a man in whom innumerable hours on the road had wrought distaste for mobility of any kind. He was tired of walking. He felt he had been walking all his life. At the ranch where he had spent his boyhood he had ridden a great deal, and had even, at the age of sixteen, travelled on horseback all the way to Guadalajara in southern Mexico, but he had always regarded walking as something foreign to his nature.

Like snow, he thought. He came from central Florida, and until a month ago had never seen snow in his life. He remembered with dull irony his excitement when the flakes had first begun to fall, how he had rolled down the snowbanks, screaming like a kid fresh out of school. Now, the endless slushy roads filled him with a sense of depression. Snow, he had learned to his cost, was cold and wet. Snow could also kill. That vast blanket of white that looked so pretty in the fields and orchards was as much a part of the enemy as the snipers who hid among the trees and hedgerows to harass the American advance positions.

Gary Lae raised one arm, calling a rest halt, and the men of his platoon sank gratefully down at the roadside. They looked done in, their faces pinched with cold, their eyes glassy with fatigue. The thought of shuffling on over mile after mile of snow-covered roadway was just too awful a prospect to contemplate. Lae knew he had to find transport. It was his God-given duty.

He peered through the plane trees at the ruins of a village ahead. 'Think I'll take a looksee up the road,' he murmured quietly.

Private First Class Clyde Tidyman, a thickset negro from Detroit who had once played point guard for Michigan State, peered at Lae curiously. 'What'n hell for?' he asked.

Lae shrugged. 'Maybe I can find us a set of wheels.'

Private Tidyman took off his helmet and ran his fingers through his curly hair. Seizing his rifle, he climbed to his feet. 'You'll need help,' he grunted.

'Don't you want to rest?'

'Sure. But I want to ride more. When it comes to auto-rustling, man, you're lookin' at the smartest heist merchant on the block.'

Lae nodded in agreement. 'Okay,' he said, 'let's see what we can find.'

The two men entered the village cautiously, splitting up to hug each side of the ruined street, watching the doors and windows for signs of enemy sharpshooters. There was no evidence of the inhabitants. The village had been decimated by artillery, and Lae guessed its populace had long since fled.

Great chunks of masonry cluttered the roadside, and through the gaps in the shattered walls Gary Lae could see the pitiful remains of what had once been family living quarters. He averted his eyes, as if his presence was an affront.

Slowly, the two men picked their way from doorway to doorway, scouring the debris for the sight of an abandoned vehicle. They had almost reached the perimeter of the village square when the sound of a shout halted them in their tracks.

Gary Lae glanced at Tidyman huddled in an alcove on the opposite side of the street. Tidyman's eyes looked bright yellow beneath the canopy of his helmet. For a moment, neither of them moved, and in spite of the cold Lae felt sweat break out beneath his armpit and run in a trickle down his left side.

The shout came again; this time there was no mistake. What the hell, Lae thought, whatever it was the guy was hollering, he wasn't doing it in English, and to Gary Lae of C-for-Charlie Company that was practically a declaration of hostility in itself.

Then a man emerged from the line of distant buildings and began to run toward them, waving furiously. He was dressed in a black mudstained suit, and as he moved, weaving and twisting, his feet slithered wildly in the snow.

Lae was filled with an air of foreboding. Though he could not say why, he felt like a spectator at some grotesque picture show where the film had been deliberately slowed to allow the audience to savour the full sensation of human anguish and impending death.

The man had almost reached the centre of the square, his black suit sharply defined like an ink-stain on a freshly laundered sheet, when suddenly the air was split by the rat-tat-tat-tat-tat of a machine-gun hidden among the rooftops. Lae watched dry-mouthed as the snow spurted in a ragged line. The bullets caught the man in the back of the hip and he seemed almost to take off, his body rising into the air, arcing gracefully in a perfect forward roll as if he had practiced the manoeuvre in some secret gym. When he crashed to the earth, blood streamed from his side into the tyre-rutted slush. Gary Lae felt himself shudder. The wind drove loose snow into his mouth and eyes.

The man peered up at him, his face demented with pain. 'Help,' he hissed in English, 'for God's sake, help.'

Lae shook himself. The man was less than twenty feet away, but to pull him to safety would mean exposure to the machine-gunner in the square beyond. If he moved fast, he could maybe get back to cover before the bastard guessed his range, but it'd be one hell of a gamble. Besides, the guy was done for, any fool could see that. He was damn near cut in half, for Christ's sake.

To Lae's horror, the man began to drag himself toward him, scrambling over the snow and dirt. 'Help,' he croaked painfully, 'for the love of God.'

Lae looked across the street at Private Tidyman. Tidyman, guessing his intention, nodded curtly, then without hesitation leaned around the corner of the building and opened fire in the direction of the machine-gun nest.

Lae dashed forward. Seizing the wounded man by the wrists, he dragged him backwards over the snow, the roar of Tidyman's rifle echoing in his ears and mingling with the hoarse staccato of Tidyman's voice cursing steadily in a furious, impassioned kind of way.

Lae reached the shelter of the building and waved to Tidyman to detour backwards through the ruins and join him.

It was clear instantly to Lae that his rescue attempt had been in vain. The man had been on the verge of death already. The drag across the rubble had almost finished him off. His skin was quivering, and a strange coldness emanated from his limbs. For a moment Lae thought he had faded altogether, but as he struggled to stem the outflow of blood from the man's hip, he saw the thin lips flutter and a faint sound came drifting out.

Lae leaned forward so that the man's mouth was barely an inch from his ear. 'What is it, soldier, what are you trying to tell me?'

The man whispered and Lae frowned, not understanding. 'You'll have to repeat it, mister, I didn't quite catch that.'

But the monumental effort to communicate had taken the man's last ounce of strength, and his pale face settled into a mask of rigid composure. As his eyes glazed and his damp hair fluttered in the wind, Gary Lae realised he was nursing a corpse.

Tidyman found him sitting thoughtfully over the body as he came scrambling through the debris. 'We'd better get out of

here, man, before them bastards get too curious,' the negro
muttered.

Lae looked at him in puzzlement. 'He was trying to tell me
something,' he said.

'Yeah? What kind of something?'

'I dunno. Something that didn't make sense.'

'What was it?'

'He just said: "SSG 300".'

Tidyman frowned. 'That's all?'

'Yeah. But he said it three times.'

'What the hell, the guy was dyin'. He was probably
delirious.'

Lae picked up his carbine and slung it over his shoulder.

'The poor sonofabitch got hisself shot for it,' he said. 'I
think we'd better get back and pass the word to the lieutenant.'

The Generalmajor was very taken with Helga Heiferman. He
was a big man, portly in build, pallid in complexion, and from
the moment of his arrival at the discreet entrance to the house
at number twenty-two Havelstrasse in Berlin, he had scarcely
been able to take his eyes off her. The Generalmajor was not
one of the house's regular customers. He had returned from the
front only the week before, and had come on the recom-
mendation of a boyhood friend, a colonel in the Grenadiers
who had provided him with a letter of introduction. The plush
sitting room with its Teutonic tapestries, delicate furnishings
and innovatory ceiling mirrors was filled with a variety of
ladies dressed, for reasons of practicality and enticement, in
frilly bits of ruffled silk, soft nylon, crêpe de Chine and, as
obligatory accessories, the fashionable suspender girdles so
popular with the new German master race. The girls however
were, with one exception, too strapping and muscular for the
Generalmajor's taste; he had never grown used to the Nazi
obsession with gymnastic womanhood, and had learned to his
cost the impracticality of attempting a liaison with partners
whose physiques in any way matched his own. But Helga
Heiferman was different. Her small elfin body, her face,
scrubbed like a choirboy's and filled with an elusive sweetness,
even an innocence, made it difficult to believe she was a

whore. As a rule, the Generalmajor knew how to deal with whores, but with Helga he found himself reduced to the humiliating state of a stuttering schoolboy. She was so delicate, so incredibly demure, that the mere act of being in her company left him tongue-tied and uncertain, and it took almost two hours before he could summon up the nerve to ask her, in a voice shaking audibly with passion, if she would accompany him to the apartments on the second floor.

That was the Generalmajor's first mistake. What he did not know—was not in a position to know—was that Helga Heiferman was an enemy spy. She had been installed in the whorehouse by Allied inteligence because it was frequented by high-ranking Wehrmacht officers, and she had taken to the rôle with enormous exuberance, for in the hungers which assailed her, her daily search for the consummation of the flesh, Helga was almost insatiable. She had first become aware of this fact after losing her virginity at the age of thirteen in the back of a schoolbus travelling from Leipzig to a folk concert in Dresden.

The Generalmajor's illusions of innocence and purity were rudely shattered when, once upstairs and undressed, Helga, her pert breasts merrily jouncing, leapt upon him with the fury of a wildcat. The Generalmajor had drunk a great deal of champagne immediately prior to his arrival, and what to Helga was merely a zestful encounter was, to the unfortunate figure clasped in the pincer-like grip of her thighs, an experience of such magnitude that long before orgasm his brain had swooned into unconsciousness.

Feeling his hardness turn flaccid inside her, Helga clambered free with a disappointed frown, and peering swiftly at the Generalmajor's eyelids, began to ferret through the pockets of his discarded tunic. Inside his wallet, she discovered a copy of a letter addressed to the Oberkommando der Wehrmacht. The security was listed as 'category one'. The letter said simply:

My dear Hermann,
Of course I echo your optimism for the future. Believe me, I have stated on frequent occasions that the defeatists among us should be hounded with the utmost ruthlessness.

However, on humanitarian grounds I deplore the concept of SSG 300. Such a decision may well lengthen the war in our favour, but could cost us dearly in the future assessments of mankind. My own feeling is that we should concentrate on forging a rift between the Allies themselves. In this way, an honourable armistice might be arranged.

Helga opened a drawer and took out a small camera. Spreading the letter on the dresser top, she photographed it swiftly six times. Three hours later, the roll of film was carried by special courier across the Rhine, passed to a member of the Belgian resistance at Verviezs, and at four o'clock the following morning was delivered into the hands of U.S. Army Intelligence at Montcriel.

Tully lived on the top floor of an ancient apartment house that had been earmarked for demolition long before the war began. It was a dispiriting place, but in a perverse way he felt its squalor matched the nature of his business. He entered by the rear door and, parking his bicycle in the backyard, clambered breathlessly up the darkened staircase. His encounter with the policeman had unnerved him. Four months ago he'd have laughed at the experience. An amusing interlude, he'd have thought, a chance to test his reactions, to pit his wits against the authorities. Now he was filled with a sense of horror. He'd almost cracked back there. He knew the signs, he'd seen them often enough in others. He'd need to watch himself in future.

On the top landing, as he fumbled for his key, Frau Richner, his neighbour, small and pinch-faced, peered at him from her doorway. 'Herr Raderecht,' she murmured, 'are you all right?'

He tried to smile. 'Yes, thank you,' he answered, 'a little breathless from pedalling too hard. Shouldn't you be in the shelter?'

She wrinkled her nose. 'I can't stand being cooped up with all those frightened people,' she said. 'If I'm going to die, I'd rather do it in my own room.'

'Don't talk of death, Frau Richner, you know it's bad luck.'

She stared at his clothes, her eyes widening with surprise.

'Herr Raderecht,' she whispered, 'you're covered in blood. Are you hurt?'

"No, no,' Tully said in confusion, 'it's not mine. I stopped to help with an injured woman.'

Frau Richner clucked sympathetically. 'These dreadful air-raids, night after night. Sometimes I think I'll go crazy.'

'Try to stay calm, Frau Richner. Remember, they can't kill us all.'

He found his key and opened his door. He wanted to escape the tryanny of those beady eyes. He was about to step inside when she said: 'Herr Raderecht?'

'Yes?'

'There was a man here asking about you. He didn't leave his name.'

Tully felt his stomach tighten. 'Did he . . . look familiar?'

'No. I think he was some kind of official.'

'What did he want?'

'Just to know if you lived here, and when you'd be back. I told him you were on shift-work.'

Tully nodded, forcing himself to smile. He mustn't betray himself in front of Frau Richner. They'd taught him that at training school. Be most careful with those nearest you.

'Ah,' he said, smiling more widely as a high-pitched wailing sound reached them from outside, 'there's the all-clear at last. Goodnight, Frau Richner, and thank you.'

He stepped inside and closed the door, holding his breath until he heard her lock click shut. What did it mean? he wondered. Who was he, the man who had called? Gestapo? And then he was angry with himself. For God's sake, he might have been anyone. He couldn't run every time some stranger called.

He crossed to the window, drew down the blind, and switched on the light. His room was cramped and sombre, the furniture grubby and frayed. A bed stood unmade against the far wall. In an alcove perched a solitary gas-ring. There had been no gas for over a week, however, and Tully had finally resorted to a small paraffin stove which he'd borrowed from a friend at work.

He fumbled his way to his battered piano, opened the lid, and took out a half-empty bottle of whisky. His hands trembled as he poured himself a drink. The liquid splashed over his wrist and a wave of nausea swept up from his stomach, blinding his vision, chilling his spine. He leaned forward, placing his forehead against the wall, listening to the muffled voices of people emerging from the air-raid shelters outside. The whine of fire-engines rose above the distant crackle of flames. Then the sounds went away and a strange peace settled over the city. Tully, still trembling, slowly straightened and went about his business. He had to get out, he thought. He couldn't stick it much longer. The very next broadcast, he would ask to be relieved. The call sign was simple. He could tap it out in an instant. He'd wanted to for weeks now, but pride had got in his way. Now he had no pride left.

He made himself some supper, listened to the late news on the wireless and played for a while on the piano. The music soothed him. Feeling better now he had reached a decision, he took off his clothes, switched off the light, and climbed into bed in the dark.

Tully woke slowly, coming out of a deep stupor to the realisation that something was wrong. He lifted his head from the pillow and held his breath, listening hard. Feet clattered on the staircase outside, the noise growing louder, moving from floor to floor. Something in the sound turned his spine to ice. It carried the unmistakable ring of authority.

The radio, he thought, I've got to get rid of the radio.

But before he could move, there was a sudden pounding on the door, and then with a screech the lock gave way and the timber burst inward, swinging wildly on its hinges. Framed between the doorposts stood two men in raincoats. Even in the darkness, Tully could see the dull gleam of revolvers in their fists.

The first man groped for the wall switch and pressed it with his thumb. 'Karl Raderecht?' he demanded.

Tully struggled to assume an air of dignity. 'Who are you?' he asked.

'Get dressed and come at once.'

'Am I under arrest?'

'At once,' the man repeated.

Tully hesitated. Clothed, he would be slightly less vulnerable, he reasoned, and throwing back the blankets he reached for his trousers. While the first man kept Tully covered, the second began to scout round the room, pulling out drawers, shifting furniture, scattering Tully's pitiful possessions in every direction. Tully dressed in silence, his heart thumping. This was the moment he had always dreaded. Confrontation. Arrest. When the questions began, he knew he was bound to crumble.

He saw the pale face of Frau Richner peering in from the landing, and with a conscious effort he tried to look affronted.

'I'm a German citizen,' he stated. 'I demand the reason for this intrusion.'

'Shut up,' the first man growled.

His companion hauled the piano into the centre of the floor, and Tully's heart sank. It took the man less than a minute to locate the loose floorboard and prise it up. With a look of triumph, he reached beneath and lifted out Tully's radio.

The first man scowled. 'German citizen, eh?' he muttered.

Seizing Tully roughly by the arms, they half-pushed, half-dragged him across the landing and bundled him downstairs to the street. A car stood in the roadway, its headlamps dimmed with metal shields. They opened the rear door and pushed him in, one man slithering quickly behind him. His companion climbed into the driving seat, switched on the engine, and swung away from the kerbside.

Tully felt sick as he peered at the streets of the almost-deserted city. A column of smoke hung above the rooftops, but most of the fires appeared to have been put out, and apart from the occasonal bomb-disposal crews they passed few pedestrians.

He wondered where he'd gone wrong. Carelessness, it had to be. But how? He'd covered his tracks with meticulous care.

Nevertheless, somewhere, somehow, he must have slackened. A momentary slip was all it took.

They drove through several roadblocks where field police of the Waffen-SS holding sub-machine guns surrounded their car. Each time, their driver displayed his card of office and they were quickly waved on. They cruised down the Kanstrasse to the Adolf Hitler Platz, and from there to the tip of the Havel Lake. Crossing the bridge, the driver swung south, edging around Kladow.

Tully felt puzzled. He'd expected to be taken at once to Gestapo headquarters on the Prinz Albrechtstrasse, but here they were leaving the city, with dark fields stretching out on both sides of the road.

The man beside him gave a deep sigh and took out a packet of cigarettes. 'Smoke?' he asked, offering one to Tully.

Tully looked at him in surprise. 'Thanks,' he muttered.

He placed the cigarette between his lips and leaned forward to accept the man's proffered light.

'Sorry if we scared you, old boy,' the man chuckled in English, 'had to make it look good.'

His air of menace had completely disappeared, and Tully noticed for the first time that his face was very young and covered with freckles.

'Who are you?' Tully asked.

'Harry Gribbin, Special Operations Executive. Chap in front is Major Michael Thomas.'

'British Intelligence?'

'Sort of. How did you like the performance? I thought it went rather well in the circumstances.'

Tully leaned back against the seat cushion, breathing hard. Jesus Christ! he thought, what are they trying to do to me?

'Where am I going?' he murmured.

'France,' the man said crisply. 'There's something big on, and they need you at the top. I hope your parachuting techniques are shipshape.'

'I haven't been near a parachute in months.'

'Well, they dropped you in here, didn't they?'

'That was right after training.'

'I shouldn't worry, old boy. I'm sure it'll all come flooding back when they shove you out up there.'

The road narrowed and they were forced to slow down, their route blocked by unfilled shell craters. The driver found a gap in a nearby fence and drove cautiously through, bumping over grass clumps and shiny slivers of mud. Tully saw a strip of blacktop gleaming in the starlight. 'What is this place?' he demanded.

'Airfield, used to be. Civilian stuff before the war. The Luftwaffe utilised it for a while till the RAF bombed the runway. Now it's left largely derelict.'

Tully spotted a grey blur taking shape in the darkness. As they approached, it solidified, gathering form and substance. It was a plane of some indeterminate design, its hull coated with camouflage, its flanks and wings disguised with black Nazi crosses.

Tully looked at Gribbin. 'Your lot?' he murmured.

'That's right. A Junkers JU 88A, shot down over Norfolk. We patched it together for special operations.'

'Someone must want me awfully bad.'

'Right again.'

Tully glanced at the airstrip and his heart jumped. The entire surface was strewn with shrapnel holes. 'My God, how did she get in here?' he exclaimed.

'Ask not how she got in, old boy. Worry rather about how she'll get out.'

The car slithered to a halt and a tall man in an RAF flying jacket opened the rear door, smiling brightly. 'Lieutenant Tully?' he asked.

'Yes.'

The man stuck out his hand. 'Flying Officer David Rowe. Welcome aboard.'

Dazed, Tully climbed from the car and followed him to the aircraft. 'You'll find there's not much room, I'm afraid,' the pilot said, 'they didn't build these things for comfort.'

Tully eased through the hatch and nodded to the second crewman who was busy warming up the engine. The pilot rummaged among the rigging and came up with a dark bundle. 'Familiar with these?' he asked.

Tully swallowed. 'I haven't touched a parachute in a hell of a long time,' he admitted.

'Well, there've been a few refinements since the old days, but stick to your training and you'll be okay. We've brought you a flying suit to keep out the cold. Lionel here will be your dispatcher. Follow his instructions and we'll deliver you to mother as safely as a stork with a baby. Good luck, and happy landing.'

Tully didn't answer. The pain in his temple started up again, boring behind his left eyeball. The pilot moved forward and Tully struggled obediently into the fleece-lined flying suit, clipping the parachute harness around his body, and settled down to wait for take-off. No sense fighting it, he thought. They would tell him everything in their own good time.

3

The roar of the engine deadened Tully's eardrums. From where he sat, wedged in the narrow aisle between the navigator and the pilot, he could see the entrance to the nose-cone where the observer lay sprawled across the Plexiglas web peering into the night. The light in the forward section switched to green, and the dispatcher, a small wiry man with a massive moustache, gave Tully the thumbs-up and began to release the catches on the hatch.

Tully's heart thumped wildly. He re-checked his parachute harness, hoping to God he remembered all the things he'd been taught in training school. Legs together. Chin on chest. Fall straight. Count to twenty in case chute didn't open.

The dispatcher eased back the cover and Tully caught a glimpse of the night outside. There was nothing to see, no moon, no lights.

He moved to the opening and sat with legs dangling over the edge, the air-stream pounding his face. The dispatcher checked the static line that would spring his parachute loose. The man's huge moustache made him look slightly absurd, and he grinned at Tully, giving the thumbs-up signal again as if he felt his passenger needed all the reassurance he could get. His eyes were brown and calm; not sad exactly, but commiseratory. The man understood what he was going through, and Tully felt grateful for that. He'd give his last dollar to be standing where the dispatcher was now, sending some other poor fool into the blackness with the sure knowledge that in a few hours' time it would be back to base for bangers-and-mash or whatever the hell it was the damned British ate.

Tully felt the aircraft shudder as the throttle eased back, and his muscles tightened. The light in the forward section changed to red, and the dispatcher tapped him lightly on the shoulder. With a deep breath, Tully leapt through the hatchway, feeling the icy blast of the windstream batter at his face, gasping as his body was buffeted sideways by the eingine wash. He was filled with the sensation of falling, that awful brain-swooning, stomach-plunging emptiness that came in childhood to terrify and derange. He felt a surge of relief as he heard the chute rustling above his head. It billowed out, cascaded backwards into the sky like a roman candle. The great sheet fluttered, took the strain, tugged gently at his armpits and thighs, and suddenly he was floating earthwards like a cruising bird. Tully breathed deeply, his ears still ringing from the engine noise. It was impossible to see the ground, impossible to see the sky even, for the two seemed to blend into an impenetrable fog that had no substance or perspective. Then dimly, like an object glimpsed through a steamy window, he saw the earth taking form beneath his feet. There were fields down there, a road, a line of tall trees, strips of glistening snow. It was difficult to gauge height or distance, and difficult too to judge the speed at which he was falling, for the world was a hazy sprawl of black and grey. Then he spotted a line of telegraph posts, their wires down, and the tall poles gave him a point of reference at last. He braced himself for the impact, gritting his teeth, feet pressed tightly together. His heels hit the crusty snow surface and he rolled expertly. In an instant he was up, uncoupling the parachute harness before the billowing silk had had a chance to settle.

The field in which he'd landed undulated gently to the left, and Tully saw the twisting line of a narrow stream, and further off, a cluster of trees and a high wooden fence that signified the boundary between this field and the next. He unzipped his flying suit and peeled it off, wondering whether to bury it together with the parachute and then deciding, for the sake of expediency, to hide them in the trees ahead. He rolled up the material as best he could and deposited it under a bush; at least it wouldn't be discovered for a day or two, unless the wind got up and blew the chute loose.

He saw a thickening in the shadows, a greyness that turned to black as a man moved into his line of vision. He was tall and lean and dressed in the uniform of an American infantry corporal. A flashlight shone in Tully's eyes, bright and startling.

'Lieutenant Tully?' a voice asked.

'Yes.'

The light switched off, and as he stood blinking, the corporal smiled at him through the darkness. 'Good to see you, Lieutenant,' he said. 'We expected you to land in the next field. Propwash probably blew you off-course.'

'Who are you?' Tully demanded.

'Corporal James Teasle. If you'd like to follow me, sir, I've got transport over by the road here.'

Tully hesitated. 'What about the parachute? Think it's concealed enough?'

The corporal looked amused. 'You've been living behind the lines too long, Lieutenant. You're with friends now. Somebody'll be along to pick up the chute in the morning.'

They clambered over the fence, and Tully spotted an open jeep with a pale star gleaming faintly on its camouflaged hull. The corporal climbed behind the wheel and Tully slithered in beside him. The corporal started the engine and they roared off into the night, the trees whipping by in a dizzy blur.

'Where are we?' Tully asked.

'Near St Lo. If you're wondering about the Heinis, relax, Lieutenant. You're more than two hundred miles behind our advance positions.'

Tully looked at him carefully. The corporal's face carried the healthy air of a cereal advertisement. Clearly his war had been different from Tully's. 'Have you any idea what this is all about?' Tully inquired.

The corporal grinned. 'Sorry, I'm only the hired help. They told me to pick you up, and I picked you up. From here on, you belong to the colonel.'

'Colonel who?'

'Colonel Theodore Reiser. If I was you, I'd sit back and

enjoy the ride. I have a hunch that where you'll be going, this
is the only luxury you're likely to get.'

The road dipped through snow-covered pastureland and Tully
closed his eyes, forcing himself to relax. The air felt
refreshingly chill against his cheeks and throat. It seemed a far
cry from the world he had just left: the food queues, the air-
raids, the inescapable odour of death.

They drove into a village where armoured trucks and tanks
lined both sides of the street, and the sidewalks teemed with
dirty, good-natured GIs. He spotted men of the 5th Infantry
Division and the Canadian Black Watch.

White-helmeted MPs stopped them at a barrier and
checked the corporal's papers, then their jeep swung through
the gates of a sombre-looking château and shuddered to a halt
in a cobbled square. A number of soldiers (mostly American,
Tully noticed, though there were one or two British in flak
jackets and dark berets) stood about chatting aimlessly.

'This way,' the corporal said, and Tully followed him
through a French window and along a wide corridor with an
enormous arched ceiling. The place carried an air of archaic
elegance, and Tully felt slightly ridiculous in his threadbare
suit and cracked muddy shoes.

The corporal opened a door and ushered Tully inside.

'Wait here,' he smiled, 'the colonel will be with you
directly.'

Tully peered around with wonder. The room was huge, its
walls lined with floor-to-ceiling mirrors and ancient portraits
set against dark mahogany panelling. Chandeliers with beads
of malachite and blue glass dangled overhead. An antique
writing-desk stood in front of the marble chimney-piece.

He sat down, fumbling in his pocket for his cigarettes. As
he drew them out, his hand began to tremble again, and with a
sense of fury he realised his convulsions were returning. Then
the door clicked, and a voice behind him said crisply:

'Please don't smoke, Lieutenant.'

He half-turned in surprise as a small thickset man brushed
by. He wore the uniform of a US colonel, and his face looked

bronzed beneath a mop of cropped grey hair. His heavy chin bulged over the rim of his shirt-collar, making his features appear almost Churchillian. He placed a thermos flask on the desktop and smiled at Tully thinly. 'Can't stand cigarettes,' he explained. 'Gave up smoking four years ago, and now the smell of the damned things drive me crazy. How about some coffee instead?'

'I'd like that, sir,' Tully muttered, slipping the packet inside his coat. Then, remembering his rank, he rose politely.

'Sit down, Tully,' the colonel said. 'You don't have to stand for me.'

He pushed back the desk cover and took out two metal cups which he placed on the blotting pad, side by side. He unscrewed the thermos flask and filled each cup in turn.

'They sent me behind enemy lines once,' he said, 'in the last war. I was scared out of my wits, so I know what you've been through. I lasted all of seven days. You've been out there for close on four months, and that's more than we have a right to ask of any man.'

The colonel leaned over the desk and handed one of the mugs to Tully, but as Tully took it, nodding, his trembling fingers splashed the scalding liquid over his wrist, and he winced in pain. He seized his arm with his free hand, holding it steady.

The colonel looked at him with a worried frown. 'You okay, Tully?'

'I . . . . I think I've got a touch of the chills. It's the damp, sir.'

'Take it easy, son. You're with your home team now.'

The colonel stared at Tully in silence for a few moments before drawing out a chair and sitting down. His face looked florid under the lights. 'That bad, huh?' he grunted.

'I'll be okay,' Tully whispered, angry at himself. He was lying and he knew it, but he hated to let the symptoms show. His pride again.

'You look sick, son. You could do with a damned good rest. I wish I could give it to you. Unfortunately, you're needed. You're the only man we've got who speaks German like a German and who's demonstrated he can operate right in the enemy heartland.'

Tully felt his spirits drop. 'You're sending me back to Germany?'

'No. To the USA.'

Tully stared at the colonel in silence for a moment, not daring to believe what he'd just heard. 'Home?' he whispered, and the longing he felt was clearly discernible in his voice.

The colonel's face clouded. 'Sorry, son, it's not the way it sounds. I wish I *could* let you go home. Christ knows you deserve it. You'll be going to the States all right, but you'll be going as a German soldier.'

He took the cup from Tully's hand and quickly refilled it.

'I know how you feel,' he added. 'There are times I think I'd give my right arm for a chance to get back to the farm again. Idaho, you come from, isn't it?'

'Wyoming, Colonel.'

'We're practically neighbours, give or take a thousand miles or so. I come from Washington—Washington State, that is. Up in the Great North-west. God Almighty, I wish I was there now. Were you a ranch-hand, Lieutenant?'

'No, sir. I worked as an interpreter for a law firm. We had quite a German community around Avery. It got to be my second language.'

The colonel nodded. 'That's why we need you, son. You understand the enemy and the way he thinks. You're the only one we've got who can do this job.'

Reiser opened a drawer and took out a brown paper envelope. He slit open the flap and scattered a number of photographs across the desktop.

'I want you to look at these,' he said.

Tully picked them up. They'd been taken at various times and in various places. One was a holiday snapshot showing a man in civilian clothes sitting on a pier at some seaside resort. Another showed the same man, this time in the uniform of a German sturmbannführer, standing on the steps of the Reichschancellory in Berlin. His face was youthful, though Tully estimated him to be in his early forties. His features were rugged, masculine, and pleasant. Heavy scars marred the chin and nose, but there was something appealing in the thin mouth and the humorous grey eyes. He did not look, Tully thought, like someone who took life over-seriously.

'Ever seen that man before?' Reiser asked.

'No.'

'His name's Oberst Otto Graebner, German Military Intelligence. The British have been keeping a file on him since well before the war. He's one hell of an operator. He infiltrated the Russian High Command in 1942 and damn near pulled off a plan to kidnap Stalin.'

Tully looked again at the square muscular face, the crooked smile. 'He looks . . . he looks the type who might do that,' he muttered.

'Reckless?'

'Yes, sir,' said Tully, 'a reckless man.'

'I hate to admit this, Lieutenant, but I wish we had a few like Graebner on our books. He's no ordinary intelligence officer. Even as a boy he was practically a child prodigy. At college, he received the Kaiser Wilhelm Award for the most outstanding thesis of his decade. In civilian life he became a fully-fledged doctor of medicine, the author of a book on meteorological radiation, and a world expert on Eastern culture. Those scars you see on his nose and chin came from duelling at university. He was quite a swordsman, the champion of his corps. When Admiral Canaris fell from grace and the Abwehr was taken over by the Gestapo, Graebner was one of the few high-ranking officers to survive, which shows how highly the Germans regard him.'

'May I ask, sir, why you are telling me all this?'

'Because Graebner's our prisoner,' Reiser said shortly, 'though we're not supposed to know that yet. We discovered him among a shipment of POWs waiting to be transported to the United States.'

'He's surrendered?'

'Not exactly. He was dressed as a private in the Panzer Grenadiers and carrying papers in the name of Franz Mohr.'

'Trying to mask his real identity, I guess.'

'I'm afraid it isn't so simple. You see, there really was a Franz Mohr. We interrogated him right after capture. Now he's disappeared. Somehow, Graebner namaged to infiltrate the transit camp and switch places with the man. The question is: why?'

Reiser reached into the envelope and drew out a sheet of paper. 'Graebner was stripped and searched along with the other prisoners,' he went on, 'the usual practice in transit camps. Stitched inside the lining of his overcoat we discovered this. This is a photo-copy; the original was slipped back in its place so Graebner wouldn't realise his cover had been blown.'

Tully glanced at the paper. It was a letter addressed to Oberst Otto Graebner from SS Reichsführer Himmler. It said simply:

Dear Graebner,
Your concern over the SSG 300 issue is understandable, but you must accept that the final decision rests with the Führer. He feels that if Von Runstedt's offensive breaks down in the Ardennes, we will have no other recourse but to employ every means at our disposal to destroy the threat to our fatherland. I urge you to make the neccessary preparations with the utmost speed. Carry this letter as proof of your authority, and show it to anyone who can offer you assistance. In the name of the Führer, they are commanded to co-operate without question or limitation. Good luck, and Heil Hitler.

Tully looked at Reiser.

'We don't know what it means,' the colonel told him. 'The phrase SSG 300 has cropped up a couple of times in our intelligence reports, but whether it refers to a new weapon or a new strategy we have no idea.'

"Didn't you discover anything at the debriefing, sir?"

Reiser shook his head. 'Graebner hasn't been debriefed. At this moment he's in the hold of a British troopship halfway across the Atlantic, totally unaware that we know his identity. Germany's top intelligence officer doesn't deliver himself into enemy hands unless he's got a damned good reason. We have to discover that reason. We have to discover what SSG 300 stands for.'

'Couldn't you just keep interrogating the guy until he cracks?'

Reiser sighed. 'We daren't do that. He might give us a few scraps of information, but not enough. What's more important, the Nazis could send in another man, and next time we might not be so lucky. He could slip through our security net.'

'I see,' said Tully.

For the first time, he noticed how tired Reiser looked. There were dark shadows on the colonel's face, and his eyes were redrimmed and weary.

'Lieutenant Tully,' Reiser said, 'at this moment there are nearly half-a-million German prisoners-of-war on US soil. Think of it. Half-a-million, spread around five hundred camps throughout the country. They're guarded by green troops and a handful of old men. Everyone else of value has been absorbed into the war effort. In this issue, at least, we've lagged far behind the British. They recognised from the beginning that enemy prisoners would have to be catered for. We've always made winning the war our number one priority. Now we've got a forgotten German army right in the heart of our homeland.'

'Hardly an army, Colonel. Prisoners behind barbed wire.'

'But not as helpless as you think. Their camp guards are understaffed, undertrained, and overstretched. Let's speculate for a minute. Supposing—just supposing—that Graebner managed to mount a concerted escape plan, not just at one camp, but at camps all over the American continent. Let's say he broke loose only a fraction of that half-million, maybe twenty thousand, maybe fifty thousand, what then?'

'Chaos and confusion.'

The colonel laughed dryly. 'Lieutenant, it would be an unmitigated disaster. We haven't the men left in the US to handle that kind of situation. We'd have no choice but to withdraw troops from Europe, and that would give the Germans time to re-group and re-arm.'

'You think that's what he has in mind?'

'No, I'm guessing wildly. But it's just one of a dozen possibilities. We have to figure out the right one.'

'When you say, "we", Colonel, I assume it's me you're talking about.'

Reiser nodded. 'We're sticking you in the pipeline. We have a bunch of prisoners waiting at Cherbourg for transportation to New York. You're joining them.'

'As a German soldier?'

'That's right. You'll be dispatched to the same camp as Graebner. It'll be up to you to make a friend of the man, win his confidence, find out what the hell he's up to and get the word back. It's that simple.'

Tully drained his coffee and put down the mug. He sat for a long moment, staring at the floor. 'With respect, Colonel, simple's hardly the word. If Graebner's as good as you say he is, getting to know him won't be easy. He'll be expecting a plant among his fellow prisoners. It's common practice on both sides.'

'I didn't say it would be easy. You'll be on your own. You'll get no support from us. Even your camp commander won't know your real identity. When you have information, you'll have to find your own way of making contact. I'll give you my Washington number to memorise, but how you get to a phone depends on your own initiative.'

He hesitated. He was not an uncompassionate man, Tully realised. He understood the subtle terrors his orders could create in others, and he cared, which was quite a handicap for a man in Reiser's position.

'Let me level with you, Tully, I want you to know what you're in for. Our War Department hasn't handled the POW situation too well. Some of our guards aren't experienced enough to exercise proper control. There've been escapes, communication problems, even political murders, among the prisoners themselves. In some cases, camp life is controlled by small groups of fanatics who hold phony courts and pretty well run things by their own rules. We try to break them up. We organise reeducation programmes, stuff like that, but the fact is, Nazism has often gained too strong a hold to stamp out. The camp authorities are scared. There's a war on, and nobody's giving them any support. As long as there's no direct threat to their administration, like a riot or an attack on a camp guard, they prefer not to interfere. Which means that if your identity is discovered, your life won't be worth a plugged nickel.'

Tully was silent for a moment. His hands started to tremble again and he clenched his fists hard, pressing them into his knees. 'You don't make it sound an attractive proposition, Colonel.'

'I'm telling it like it is, son,' Reiser said gently. 'We've got less than twenty-four hours to prepare your cover. After that, you'll be like Daniel in the lion's den.'

'Do I get any choice in this?'

'Well, nobody's forcing you to go, but if you refuse, we'll be too damned late to get anyone else.'

'That's the dirtiest trick you've played tonight, Colonel.'

'It goes with the job, son.'

The colonel's face looked grave, as if the act of sending men out to imperilment and possible death wrought in him an indefinable sadness. He opened a drawer, took out a bottle of Scotch, and placed it on the desk.

'I disapprove of booze on duty,' he said, 'but you look like a man who could use a drink.'

'How's it feel?' the tailor asked.

He was a fussy little corporal with service-issued spectacles who came from Santa Monica, California, and who told Tully he had once worked in the costume department of Metro-Goldwyn-Mayer. His hair was sleek, his cheeks chubby, and his voice had the high breathless quality of a choirboy, as if by some accident of generation he had completely by-passed puberty.

Tully tugged at the sage-green tunic, smoothing it straight across his chest. It was the uniform of a private in the Sixth Gebirgsjäger, the German mountain ranger regiment. On the breast pocket was an enamel Edelweiss badge, proclaiming its wearer to be a Bergführer or mountain guide. The outer ring of the badge carried the word 'Heeresbergführer', meaning army mountain leader. Two wound decorations adorned the other pocket, and an embroidered arm insignia depicting oak leaves and an acorn had been sewn onto the left sleeve. The trousers were made of light calico, and the cap was a peaked forage 'Gebirgsmütze' unique to German mountain troops. Though the material was new, it had been expertly weathered to give it the appearance of wear and tear.

'Fits like a glove,' Tully said. 'How did you manage to make it so old?'

'Easy, Lieutenant. We treated the cloth with potassium permanganate and baked it in an oven.'

'Amazing.'

Peering critically at his reflection in the looking glass, Tully had to admit he looked every inch a soldier of the Wehrmacht. Even the weariness under his eyes seemed to reflect the rigours and terrors of battle. 'You've done an excellent job,' he declared.

The corporal beamed happily. 'Hell, Lieutenant, it was nothing. In *The Last Adventurer*, none of the costumes would fit Barrymore's stand-in, and we had to alter the lot, twelve changes in all, inside two hours.'

'War must seem a little dull after the excitement of Hollywood,' Tully said.

'Dull, Lieutenant? No, it ain't dull, but it sure is a hell of a lot safer.'

Tully laughed. He was beginning to relax a little, to accept that for a few short hours he could put aside the lie he lived and indulge himself in the company of his fellow countrymen.

When the kitting-out was over, the long night of study and revision began. For safety's sake, Tully was allowed to keep his German cover name, Karl Raderecht, but the rest of his story had to be absorbed from scratch. He had to memorise the ranks and disposition of the entire Alpenkorps, a grand total of twenty-one divisions, with signal units, engineer battalions, and even police (Polizei) groups. He had to study and remember the theoretical strengths and equipment scales for a typical fully-equipped mountain division, and such irrelevant facts as the uses and values of the MG 34 medium machine-gun, the IG 18 howitzer, and the Geb H40. He had to engrave upon his mind such unconnected fragments as the Gebirgsjäger methods of bridge-building, pontoon-construction and casualty evacuation in high mountain peaks. He had to learn the names and life histories of his imaginary family: his wife (with whose photograph he was dutifully supplied), his baby son (also in the picture), his uncles and aunts, cousins and grandparents; the latest Wehrmacht slang expressions, the current German film stars and bandleaders, the backgrounds of individual soldiers, (particularly those who had distinguished themselves either as heroes in battle or as eccentric, colourful characters), and the regimental traditions and marching songs.

Afterwards, he was interrogated by a young captain with beautifully manicured nails, while Colonel Reiser stood watching from the back of the room.

'Where were you captured?' the captain demanded.

'Houffalize,' Tully said.

'How?'

'We were cut off from the main battalion, forced to surrender.'

'Which group?'

'Sixth Gebirgsjäger.'

'The name of your commanding officer?'

'Oberst Von Kramer.'

'Did you know Unterfeldwebel Steiner?'

'No, sir.'

'Horst Meili?'

'He was our regimental cook.'

'Describe the man.'

'He was portly, dark-haired, thirty-three years old. He had a mole on his left temple.'

'Where were you trained?'

'At Bad Reichenhall.'

'What was the name of the town's most popular café?'

'Feidermuk's.'

'And the head-waiter there?'

Tully hesitated. The captain watched him in silence from behind his desk. 'What's wrong?' the captain asked.

'I . . .' Tully shrugged. 'I can't remember.'

The captain sighed. 'You'll have to do better than that,' he said. 'If I'd been a German officer, we'd have had you cold.'

Tully felt irritated. 'You can't expect me to remember the whole damned town,' he complained.

The captain had the implacability of a Sherman tank.

'Everyone in the Sixth Gebirgsjäger knows the head-waiter at Feidermuk's. You can forget the big things, like troop movements, or even the precise details of your surrender—nobody blames a man for getting confused in the heat of battle—but never forget Frido. In Bad Reichenhall, he's an institution.'

Tully felt unbearably tired. He wanted to rest, to sleep. God Almighty, he'd taken a lot in the past few hours. It wasn't a man they were looking for, it was a godamned machine.

'Something's wrong with that tunic,' Colonel Reiser exclaimed suddenly, moving towards him. He jerked the material sideways, frowning. 'There's a new seam under the armpit.'

'Yes, sir,' answered the captain. 'We had to make a few changes. Tully's lost so much weight in the past few months.'

'For Christ's sake, man, Tully's supposed to have been crawling round the battlefields of Europe. If somebody spots that, it could blow his cover sky-high.'

The captain reddened. 'We'll fix it right away,' he murmured.

The colonel's beefy face slackened, and Tully felt a momentary pang of guilt for being irritable. The severity of the night had left its mark on Reiser too. The colonel, he realised, hated this even more than he did.

'Turn out your pockets,' Reiser ordered.

Obediently, Tully laid everything he was carrying on the desktop, his Wehrmacht *Soldbuch*, a wallet with a picture of his make-believe wife (a dark-haired woman with a tiny baby), a cigarette-lighter, a handful of coins, and a handkerchief. Enough items to avoid suspicion. Not enough to disclose unnecessary information.

The colonel picked up the cigarette-lighter and examined it carefully. 'What's this?' he asked.

'It's my good-luck token, Colonel. It was given to me by the folks of my home town in Avery as a going-away present.'

'Tully, I told you to get rid of all personal property. You're supposed to be a soldier in the German army, for Christ's sake.'

'You don't understand, Colonel. When they dropped me into Germany, the British took every damn thing I had. They even drilled out the fillings in my teeth so they could re-plug the cavities with German dental cement. The only thing they let me keep was that lighter, because it was manufactured in Switzerland and you can buy the same model in any city in the Reich. Sometimes, when things got really bad, when I'd reached the point where I couldn't be sure who the hell I was anymore, I used to take it out and just hold it. I know it sounds crazy, but that lighter was the only thing that kept me sane, Colonel. It was my one link with home.'

Reiser watched him with no expression on his face. 'Made in Switzerland, you say?'

'Yes, sir.'

Reiser tossed it into the air, then placed it on the table. 'Okay, I guess we can make an exception in this case.'

He strolled to the window and drew back the blinds, peering out at the village street. He looked out of place in uniform, Tully thought, and wondered idly what Reiser had done in civilian life.

Turning, the colonel's face was gentle. 'Tired, son?' he asked.

Tully nodded.

'I'd like to let you sleep for a week, but if we don't get your cover straight, it's your ass in a sling, not ours.'

'I understand, sir.'

Reiser smiled. For a moment, he looked almost paternal, or like a favourite uncle from out of town. Then he shook himself, and straightening, strolled to the back of the room.

'We've got four hours left,' he snapped crisply. 'Let's go over it once again.'

'He's not ready,' the captain said. 'Nobody can absorb that much in twenty-four hours, nobody.'

Colonel Reiser stood at the window and watched dawn break over the rooftops. It was a dismal day: the sky was heavy with sleet, the sidewalks coated with thin ice. He felt weary, wearier than he could ever remember. It was almost an hour since the transport had arrived to take Tully away, and Reiser felt sick to his stomach at the thought of Tully going on such a hazardous mission when any damned fool could see the poor bastard was on the brink of collapse.

'He'll slip up,' the captain said. 'Sooner or later he'll get something wrong, he's bound to. If I'd been interrogating him for real, I'd have broken the sonofabitch apart.'

'I know,' Reiser said bleakly, 'I've seen men crack up before. My God, don't you think I'd replace Tully if I could? There just isn't time. Win or lose, he's the only game in town.'

He kept his voice clipped, his manner stubborn. He did not want the captain to guess his real feelings, as if they constituted a weakness somehow, an unforgivable flaw for a man in his position.

He hated this aspect of his business. Danger meant nothing to Reiser. He had never shrunk from it, had even, in his younger days, welcomed insecurity as a penitent might welcome contrition, finding in its discomfiture a curious release and fulfillment. But the act of sending Tully into mortal jeopardy, when all Reiser's instincts warned him the man was ill-equipped to fend for himself, filled the colonel with self-loathing. He dreaded the future, the thought of what discovery would mean for Tully, and the guilt and remorse his end would bring to Reiser himself.

'There must be something we can do,' the captain insisted softly.

The colonel nodded, clearing his throat with a harsh little cough that carried in it a hint of hopelessness. 'Sure there is,' he said, turning from the window. 'We can pray.'

4

Belgium, February 1945

A cold wind blew through the little railroad station, bringing with it a hint of fresh snow. Standing on the platform, Paul Houwer spotted the pilot-light of a great locomotive lunging slowly out of the darkness. He saw the engine taking shape, belching smoke and steam into the chill night air, then the boxcars rolling in behind, their blunt, slightly curving roofs etched against the sky like the undulating spine of a gigantic caterpillar. Houwer felt his pulses quicken as he discerned, perched on the carriage rims, German soldiers with Schmeisser submachine-guns across their knees.

Paul Houwer, short-statured, grey-haired, fifty-two years old, was the railroad dispatch officer for the area surrounding Duisburg, and throughout the occupation of Belgium had proved himself a loyal friend to the Nazis. What the officers of the Wehrmacht did not know, however, was that Paul Houwer was also the leader of the local resistance movement, and the sight of such a heavily-guarded convoy rumbling to a halt at his deserted railroad station in the middle of the February night instantly alerted Houwer's inquisitive instincts. The Allied armies were already within striking distance. Artillery flashes lit the southern sky like summer lightning and the rattle of gunfire had been a constant symphony since the previous afternoon. If the Germans were moving cargo with such secrecy, it had to be something of the utmost significance.

Houwer hurried into the ticket-office and found the station-master, René Krabbe, writing out his evening report.

'Leave that,' Houwer snapped curtly, 'the *Moffen* are here.'

The *Moffen* was a derogatory term he used to describe German soldiers. Krabbe looked at him blankly.

'At this time of night?'

'Something's up. They're moving a special cargo. They've got guards on every carriage, which means it must be bloody important. I have to get a look at it.'

'How?' Krabbe asked.

'Can you divert their attention for a bit?'

The station-master looked doubtful. 'I don't think so, not on my own,' he said.

'Then contact Felix. Tell him all I want is a minute or two. If he can just give them something to think about while I open one of the boxcar doors, that should be enough. He'll have to be quick though. They won't hang about forever.'

The station-master rose from his seat and reached for his overcoat. Houwer heard the scrape of jackboots on the platform outside, and putting on his brightest smile he went out to meet the two SS officers who were strolling towards him, their death's-head cap badges gleaming like pale jewels in the night.

'Herr Houwer?' one of the officers demanded in a haughty voice.

'I am Houwer,' the Belgian answered fawningly. 'You've taken us rather by surprise, I fear. We had no word you were coming.'

'Security,' the officer answered. 'Our cargo carries the highest authority.'

'Then you may rely on my discretion.'

The officer nodded. His cheeks were pale, his eyes lost in a blur of shadow beneath his *schirmütze* peak. 'We've heard good things of you, Herr Houwer,' he said. 'You have been a staunch friend to the Reich.'

'I believe a man should stand by his friends,' Houwer replied easily, 'particularly in such volatile times. What can I do for you gentlemen?'

'We need water for the boiler, and a fresh supply of fuel.'

'I'm sure that can be arranged. Perhaps in the meantime you'd like to step inside the office? It's such a cold night, and I believe I can offer you a little something to aid the circulation.'

For the next ten minutes, Paul Houwer sipped cognac with the two SS officers and waited in a fever of impatience for something to happen. Everything depended on Krabbe and Felix moving quickly.

At last, just as Houwer was beginning to despair, a flurry of shouts reached them through the ticket window. The SS officers grabbed their caps and ran on to the platform, Houwer following in quick pursuit. At the rear of the train, crimson flames were licking into the night. The guard's van had caught fire.

Soldiers ran down the platform and set to work beating out the blazing timber. Houwer watched them for a moment, then with a quick glance in both directions he dropped between the two frontmost carriages and scrambled beneath the wheels. Rising on the other side, he peered at the boxcar above. Chalked on its wall was the slogan: SSG 300. Reaching up, he tried the door. It was locked.

Houwer moved back between the carriages and unhooked the coupling lever. Using it as a jimmy, he sprung open the lock with a muffled click, gently eased back the door, and peered inside. His eyes widened with astonishment. 'Good God,' he whispered softly.

Twenty minutes later, he stood on the platform and watched the train pull out. The world was going crazy, he thought. The last vestige of sanity had finally crumbled in the Nazi High Command, there could be no other explanation. With the Allied armies already on the horizon, some lunatic had detailed a troop of desperately-needed men to safeguard nothing more strategic than a cargo of idiotic tulip bulbs.

The jeep swung to a halt on the Cherbourg quayside and Tully peered around him curiously. French dock-workers in dungarees and berets were busy loading a British merchant ship. Across the railroad tracks, tall buildings fronted the harbour, their walls peppered with shrapnel holes. Barrage-balloons cluttered the sky like frozen swans.

'Okay,' grunted the MP, nudging Tully with his elbow, 'let's move, soldier.'

Obediently, Tully dismounted, wrinkling his nostrils at the scent of rotting garbage from the sea below. It was raining, and the sky seemed to sag above the rooftops like a soggy blanket. He felt drained after the long night of digesting facts and answering questions. Since they'd pulled him out of Berlin, he'd scarcely had a moment to breathe. The parachute jump, the meeting with Reiser, the forced studying, the interrogation, they were too much to take at one go. He was close to collapse, he knew; he needed sleep desperately.

At a point where the railroad track left the dock and moved towards the centre of the town, a barbed-wire compound had been erected. It was guarded by troops with carbines slung across their shoulders. Inside, German soldiers stood about in groups, or squatted wearily against the fenceposts, their bodies stooped in attitudes of indifference and boredom.

The MP gave Tully an impatient shove. 'Over there,' he growled, 'don't keep me out in this rain any more'n I have to.'

Tully's heart began to thump as he moved toward the compound. He saw the prisoners watching him, and realised this would be his first test. Would they accept him now, or would his cover be blown before he'd even started? His chances of discovery were, he knew, less likely here where the prisoners felt disoriented than in the POW camp where they would have a chance to organise, but there was always the possibility.

A guard wearing a rainslicker halted Tully with his rifle.

'His name's Raderecht,' the MP said, 'you'll find him on the list.'

'Okay,' the guard muttered, and unlocked the gate.

Tully stepped into the compound, his pulse pounding. None of the prisoners looked in his direction, but he had the feeling he was being scrutinised nevertheless. He found a place by the fence and stood watching the rain dripping from the wire. No-one approached for a long time, and he tried to appear casual and unconcerned, staring out at the armoured vehicles trundling along the quayside, at the massive crates being loaded into the ship's hold.

After a while, a prisoner detached himself from the main group and strolled across to join him. He was tall and slender, his hair unkempt beneath his battered forage cap. His face was blotchy from the wind and sun. He held out his hand.

'I'm Willi Stroud,' he said. 'Where did they pick you up?'

'Houffalize,' Tully answered cautiously. 'You?'

'Italy, five weeks ago. They've had me kicking my heels around these bloody transit camps ever since. Christ knows what for. Got any fags?'

Tully fumbled in his pocket and gave the German a cigarette.

'Interrogate you, did they?' the German asked as he leaned forward to accept Tully's light.

'Off and on.'

'Heavy?'

'Nothing special. They tried a few tricks to trip me up. I gave them the usual, rank and number. They quit in the end.'

'That's the way to play it. Dumb. Don't let them think you know what they're after. Give them any damn thing and they'll make use of it somehow.'

'That's right,' said Tully.

Stroud looked at his uniform. 'Sixth Gebirgsjäger, eh? We've got one of your mob here already. Hans Schleiben. Know him?'

'No.'

'Well, it's a big army.'

The rain filled Tully's nostrils with the odour of damp clothing. He stamped his feet on the ground.

'What happens now?' he asked.

'We hang about,' said Stroud, smoking his cigarette. 'You'll get pretty good at that, after a while. We're waiting to board that ship over there, just as soon as the cargo's loaded.'

'They're sending us abroad then?'

'Rumour is, America. Redskins and movie stars. I hope to God it's dryer than this place.'

'Where are you from?' Tully inquired.

'Hamburg,' Stroud answered. 'You?'

'Berlin.'

The German pulled a face. 'Hit pretty bad, I hear.'

'It's bad all right.'

Stroud drew on his cigarette, peering through the wire at
the dockfront. 'You know, before the war came along, I'd
never travelled beyond Wittenberge. That was the furthest I
went in my life. Now they're sending me to America. Funny,
isn't it? I guess I've got something to thank the Führer for.'

'How are things on the Italian Front?' Tully asked.

Stroud chuckled grimly. 'They've got us slammed up
against the mountains. I don't care about the Allies so much,
but those bloody Eyeties are blocking off the roads and
ambushing our convoys, and they were supposed to be our
friends. You don't know who to rely on any more.'

'They still say we're winning, back in Berlin,' Tully
grunted.

Stroud gave a thin smile. 'If you believe that, you'll
believe anything. But don't mention it in front of the others.
Some of those sods back there are really political.'

Tully looked at him. 'You're not?'

Stroud shrugged. 'Christ, I never understood what this war
was all about anyhow.'

Tully let himself relax. 'My name's Karl Raderecht,' he
said. 'Have another cigarette.'

'I haven't finished the first one yet.'

'Keep it for later. I feel the need of a friend.'

Stroud grinned. 'Throw your fags around like this and
you'll soon have all the friends you can handle.'

At noon the loading of the cargo vessel was completed, and
twenty minutes later the prisoners were escorted on board by
armed British soldiers. They were divided into groups of
twelve and taken below to their quarters. Tully found himself
in a small overcrowded cabin where bunks had been laid side
by side with barely three inches between each. Hurricane-
lamps dangled from steel pipes overhead, and somewhere near
at hand he heard the throb of the engines.

The Germans selected their bunks and peeled off their
saturated clothing. So far no-one had challenged Tully's

presence. All he had to worry about now was what happened on the other side.

He stretched himself out on the nearest bed and closed his eyes, listening to the diesels pounding. He could smell the salty odour of the harbour and was filled with a pulsing excitement. Prisoner or not, he thought, he was going home.

Louisiana, USA

The jeep bounced along the rutted roadway, raising a cloud of dust that drifted over the fields and meadowlands in a trail that would be visible, Etta felt, for at least five miles or more. Pink plastered-brick farmhouses peeked between the tree-trunks. They passed an ancient plantation home, and Etta saw curving staircases and Doric columns girding its front like some relic out of *Gone with the Wind*. Here in the south you felt an air of timelessness somehow, as if the war, and to some extent the twentieth century, had passed it by.

They crossed a bridge where giant cypresses framed the river's edge, their branches strung with curtains of Spanish moss.

'How beautiful,' she whispered.

The policeman driving grinned. 'Once in a while the farmers collect that stuff,' he told her. 'They hook it off the lower branches with long poles, then send it up north to furniture manufacturers for stuffing chairs and such.'

'Is it a parasite?'

'No ma'am. Spanish moss feeds on air, but if it gets too heavy it can smother them trees to death.'

They came out of the cypresses and Etta saw a rough-hewn fencepost with neat rows of green-leafed plants beyond.

'That's tobacco,' the policeman said. 'It's called perique, and this is the only place in the world you'll find it grown.'

He chuckled. 'The only place in the world you'll find it smoked too,' he added. 'It takes a strong stomach to hold that flavour down.'

She had travelled down by train, leaving Baltimore in the chill grip of winter to emerge in New Orleans to the mild humidity of a Louisiana spring. The change had cheered her.

After the deathliness of snow, slush and ice, she was filled with a sense of emerging life.

They moved from the open fields into a clutter of stiff-leaved pines, duckweed, and bald cypress trees. The road picked its way over scum-coated pools on trestles raised high above the water's surface.

'What is this place?' she murmured.

'Part of the swamp, lady. Not a good place to be unless you keep to the driveway. Only people who know their way about in here are the Cajuns. They're the descendants of the old French Canadian settlers who fled to Louisiana after Wolfe took Quebec. They live on the bayous, catch crayfish in summer, move into the swamps to hunt fur in winter. They claim them shallow-draft boats they paddle are so light they can ride a heavy dew.'

Etta smiled. The policeman's face had a boyish, unlived-in look, and his limbs seemed awkward and ungainly. Sitting in the passenger seat, she felt almost maternal towards him. The coach from New Iberia ran only twice a week, and he had been kind enough to offer her a lift.

'What made you take the Cleator place?' the policeman asked.

'I saw it advertised in the newspaper.'

'But it's pretty damned isolated up there. A girl like you, all on your own, won't you get scared?'

'I'm not alone,' she insisted. 'There's a farm next door.'

'Hell, that's a good quarter mile away. If the river floods again, you'll find it lonely all right. The road to Jimson Hollow gets cut off most every spring.'

Etta watched the trees gliding by. It felt good to be back in the country. She had missed that, had been too long in the dreadful sprawl of sandstone skyscrapers they called Baltimore.

The road forked and they turned to the left, moving out of the marshes and into open countryside. Etta saw green fields, heavy foliage, and the spiky contours of more swamp beyond. Suddenly their route was barred by a massive truck trundling slowly westward, its rear packed with men in tattered uniforms. Spotting Etta, the men began to shout and wave.

There were two sentries with rifles perched on the tailboard. They grinned, but made no attempt to curb this outburst of noisy exuberance.

The young policeman swore and jammed his hand on the hooter.

'Damn Krauts,' he growled.

'Who are they?'

'German prisoners-of-war.'

'You mean Nazis?'

'Sure. They're from the camp on the flats.'

'But what are they doing out here?'

'They work in the fields and lumber camps,' the policeman said. 'It's part of the Labour Programme.'

He swore again. 'Bastards act like they own the goddammed place.'

His cheeks were angry and he looked vindictive. Etta smiled to herself. She knew his venom was not really directed at the prisoners, but at his own uncertainty. Their cheering had made him feel protective towards her, and he didn't quite know how to react.

They pulled out to overtake and the prisoners' voices got louder. Etta watched their grinning faces sweeping by, and instinctively raised one hand in a little wave. The shouting broke up in a chorus of wild whoops, and the policeman swore again beneath his breath.

Etta was annoyed at herself. She wished she hadn't encouraged them. She'd done it without thinking, and now she felt sorry for the policeman and was glad when they'd left the truck behind and the Germans were lost in a maze of fields and heavy woodlands.

'You married?' the policeman asked.

She hesitated. 'My husband was killed at Guadalcanal,' she said.

The memory brought no sense of pain. They had scarcely known each other. A young man, young in his ways, who had never had a chance to establish his identity. They'd been together less than five weeks before he'd gone to the Pacific, and that had been the last she'd seen of him. Now she found it difficult even to recall his features.

'Happened to a lot of good men,' the policeman murmured.

'Were you never in the army?'

'No, ma'am. I wanted to go, believe me. I'd give my eye-teeth for a crack at them Nips, but I got a bum knee. Bust it playing football at high school. It don't bother me none, unless I over-use it, but it took me out of the draft.'

Etta was quiet for a moment. There had been an unmistakable note of regret in the young man's voice. It seemed strange to her that anyone could regard the war as desirable.

He gave her a sidelong glance. 'What brought you to Cannesetego County?' he asked.

'My husband spent his boyhood here,' she explained. 'I thought it might make him seem close again. I'm going to teach music at the school. I have a piano coming down from Baltimore by train. I hope to give lessons in my free time.'

'But a lady like you. I mean, so pretty and all. You'll find it awfully lonesome up there.'

'Well, I couldn't stand the city. When . . . when Clinton died, I felt I had to get away. I grew up in the country, you see.'

'Where was that?'

'Sweden,' she said.

'No kidding? I thought you had some kind of accent.'

'It was a long time ago. My parents emigrated to Canada when I was fourteen. I met Clinton in Vancouver. He was training to be a pilot.'

'Folks still alive?'

'My father is.'

'Well, I guess you can always go back if things get too lonesome at Jimson Hollow.'

She remembered the tall stern man with the beady eyes and autocratic profile. Unlike Clinton, he was etched into her memory in a way she could never forget.

'No,' she said softly, 'I'm never going back.'

The road dipped, then swung to the west, meandering through softly-rolling meadowland and clusters of thick pine forest. Etta spotted a house perched on top of a small rise, a river to one side, a thatch of trees to the other. It looked peaceful and remote, its sloping roofs dipping almost to the ground.

'That's the Cleator place,' the policeman said. 'Not much to look at, but you'll find it's plenty roomy inside.'

He swung the jeep off the road and slithered to a halt at the front door. She climbed out and reached into the back for her baggage. 'You've been very kind,' she said, smiling. 'Thank you so much for the ride. I'm sure I can manage from here.'

A strand of damp hair hung over the policeman's forehead, and he brushed it absently away before switching off the engine and leaping nimbly out.

'Lady,' he said, 'I wouldn't let you hurt them pretty hands carrying such heavy bags. You go on up to the house. I'll bring these along directly.'

She let herself in at the front door, holding her breath as she smelled the musty interior. It was not, at first glance, heartwarming. The walls were bare, the floor uncarpeted, the furniture ancient and drab. There was dust everywhere, and the rain had evidently been leaking in, for there were dark stains on the ceiling.

Etta moved through the house, opening the windows, letting in the air. All it needed was a good clean-out, she thought, someone living here. She'd soon have it looking as good as new.

The young policeman stepped over the threshold and dropped her bags on the floor. He peered about him with a boyish grin.

'She's a bit dusty, I reckon,' he said. 'Been empty for nigh on three months.'

'It'll do just fine.'

He moved inside, wiping his palms on the seat of his pants. He looked awkward and uncertain, and realising suddenly he was still wearing his hat, he plucked it from his head with a gesture of embarrassment. For the first time, she sensed his concern had not been entirely philanthropic. He was attracted to her, despite his youth, and the realisation filled her with a faint feeling of alarm. No complications, she thought; she'd promised herself that.

'Well,' he murmured, 'if there's anything else I can do, anything at all, you only have to say the word.'

'Thank you, officer, I do appreciate your help.'

'I'll be on my way then.'

'Very well.'

'You're sure everything's okay?'

'Everything's perfect.'

He hesitated. She knew he wanted to do something bold and decisive, like touch her, perhaps even take her in his arms, but something held him back, an air of insecurity. He looked younger than ever, his face tense and nervous. In the end, he turned with an awkward shuffle and clumped to the door. She watched as he climbed into the jeep and started the engine.

'Thank you again,' she called.

He waved once, then with a thunder of exhaust fumes he swept across the yard and down to the open road. She smiled as she watched him fade into the distance. Despite his air of perplexity, she had to admit that she liked him. Still, she was pleased he had gone. It was difficult enough for a young woman living alone. No sense inviting trouble.

She moved through the house again, looking it over room by room. Upstairs, she found a full-length looking-glass and stood in front of it, examining herself critically. She wondered what the young policeman had found so appealing. She was not by any means pretty. Not what you could really call pretty. Not like the movie stars, anyhow. But her face was pleasing and attractive, and she had a strong, sensual body that carried an air of warmth and promise. Many men in the past had called her beautiful, and certainly she had never wanted for men when she'd needed them. But then, she had never found a man she'd truly wanted either. Not even Clinton. Poor dear Clinton. He had been drawn to her by her strength, seduced by the very virtues he feared were lacking in himself. For a few brief weeks, she'd made him happy. At least she'd given him that. If only she'd been able to love him too. Love? she thought. What did she know about love? Love was a bag of dirty tricks, a ludicrous idiocy used by men to assuage the hunger that was life itself, and by women to cheat and connive. She had no time for love.

The murmur of voices drifted in from the woods outside, and Etta moved to the window. Across the river, she spotted a highwire fence with watchtowers at each end and a line of low wooden huts beyond. The German POW camp, she realised. The men were singing in the early evening. The sound filled her with a sense of sadness, a need for comfort and light and physical contact. They had so much in common, she and those men behind the wire. She felt a wave of sympathy, of understanding. They were here through the fortunes of war. She was here because she was a hopeless ricochet from the human race. It was an intimacy of a sort. In their separate ways, they were all prisoners together.

5

It was nothing to get concerned about, nothing of any significance, but Tully knew something was different the minute he opened his eyes. The engines, he thought, they had changed their rhythm. They had become so much a part of his life during the past four weeks, purring their way through the North Atlantic gales, that any deviation in their pattern was like a change in the beating of his heart. He listened, holding his breath. There was no mistake. The throbbing was gentler, softer, smoother.

Willi Stroud had noticed it too. Clambering out of his bunk, he shuffled to the porthole and wiped it clean with one elbow. He peered out, and gave a gasp of excitement. 'Hey, Karl,' he said, 'come and look at this.'

Tully threw back the bedclothes and leapt up to join him. He peered through the distorted glass and felt his heart flutter wildly as he stared directly into the familiar green face of the Statue of Liberty.

'My God,' he hissed.

They were in the United States.

The broad lips and blank eyes, the pointed crown, stood etched against a sky the colour of roofslate. To Tully, nothing in his life had ever looked so beautiful. He felt a thickening in his throat and swallowed hard. Pressing his cheek against the cold hull, he squinted sideways through the porthole to where he could just make out huge blocks of concrete rising in columns of white and sandy brown on the Manhattan skyline.

He daren't trust himself to speak. He had dreamed about this so often that now the moment had arrived he was shaken by an emotion almost too powerful to control. All the anguish of the past four months faded from his mind like a terrible dream. Even the boredom of the voyage, the dreary exercise periods on deck, the interminable hours cooped in their overcrowded cabin, seemed nothing more than an irritating interlude. He was home.

In a fever of impatience he waited for the disembarking to begin, but as usual it was the lousy cargo that got unloaded first, and they had to spend another two hours listening to the sounds of movement on the quay above. Men shouted, cranes clanked, wheels rattled, trains whistled. Tully's heart pounded. They could do what they liked to him, he thought, they couldn't change his emotions, his thought processes, they couldn't take away the terrific feeling of actually being home again. Even though he had only been in New York once before in his life (on a forty-eight-hour furlough from Norfolk, Virginia), he felt he knew this city as intimately as his own (which he did, of course, having glimpsed it for years in innumerable cops-and-robbers movies in which automobiles screeched around corners in a blaze of sirens and flashing lights), and he stood waiting, seething with impatience, until at last a British sergeant appeared and unlocked their cabin door.

'Everybody out,' he yelled. 'Top deck, on the double.'

Tully filtered through with the others, trying not to elbow his way to the front, keeping his face expressionless as he strode down the gangplank and stared hungrily at the scene on-shore. The city looked immense in the early morning. He saw massive skyscrapers, high-level concrete piers, grain elevators, great cranes trundling along iron rails. A gigantic billboard perched above the harbour urged him to 'Buy War Bonds'.

Willi Stroud nudged him discreetly. 'Better hide that Bergführer's badge,' he warned. 'These Yanks are bloody souvenir crazy.'

'Thanks,' Tully said, and unclipping the badge from his breast pocket, he concealed it inside his hat. He breathed hard, harder than he had ever breathed in his life, sucking in that good, clean, auto-polluted New York air. It really was amazing how different it smelled from the air he'd left behind, all those salt-and-briny Atlantic gales choking up your lungs with their goddam purity; you just couldn't beat the good old scent of exhaust fumes, rotting garbage, stale cigarettes and—this was the clincher—the unmistakable odour of pastrami drifting in from the street outside.

Home.

He wanted to shout out loud in sheer delirium.

They were lined up on the dock and their names were called by an American sergeant wearing an MP armband, then they were escorted to a large metal warehouse and searched for what seemed to Tully the umpteenth time. A young Pfc with a Kentucky accent took less than two minutes to discover the badge inside Tully's cap. 'Sorry, old buddy,' he said, pocketing it swiftly, 'but I've got to have something to show the folks back home.'

Tully resisted the temptation to answer him in English. He glanced across at Stroud, who gave a sympathetic shrug.

The searching over, they were shepherded to another section of the warehouse to be deloused. Tully hated this procedure. It seemed dehumanising to be lined up like unwashed schoolboys while soldiers with syringes squirted DDT over their bodies and belongings. The entire process was carried out with the bored indifference of men disinfecting a herd of cattle. When at last they emerged from the warehouse, the sky had brightened and the Manhattan skyscrapers stood outlined against a wintry sun.

Tully was feeling calmer now; he had his emotions back under control. He peered at the brownstone buildings rearing into the sky and wondered how the place could seem so damn terrific in the middle of March, with slush all over the streets and the air so cold it sliced through his lungs with every breath he took.

He spotted a railroad track and a locomotive with steam hissing breathlessly between its massive wheels, then armed guards ferried them into the carriage cars behind, and they shuffled down the aisles, choosing their seats.

'Looks like we're travelling in style,' Stroud murmured.

Tully had to agree. The cars were clean and newly-upholstered and despite the presence of armed GIs at each door, there were none of the customary discomforts he associated with troop trains in Europe. Their coach exuded an air of calm civility.

The branch-line on which they stood looked out over a metal grill to the street below, and the Germans clustered excitedly at the windows, peering down at the sprawl of Chinese laundries, liquor stores, second-hand junkshops, and tumbledown bars. Tully was swept by an overwhelming wave of nostalgia. Nothing had changed, nothing. Manhattan looked just the way he'd known it would, and for a moment he wanted to stand there and breathe it all in, as if by some incredible supernatural process he could inhale the very essence of the city.

'Look at those automobiles,' a man murmured. 'I never saw so many automobiles in my life.'

'What about the height of the buildings, for Christ's sake?'

'No sign of bomb damage,' someone observed.

'Hey Gunter,' Walter Schmidt yelled, 'I thought you said the Luftwaffe had flattened New York?'

Gunter Reitlinger, small, wiry, ardently fascist, pulled a sour face.

'*Dummkopf*,' he growled. 'You think the whole city's like this? They brought us this way on purpose as part of their demoralisation exercise. They want us to believe our boys aren't doing any damage over here. Move uptown a few blocks and you'll soon see a difference.'

Idiot, Tully thought.

'I wonder what time they blow the horn for chow,' Stroud said, and Tully suddenly realised that in the excitement of the morning, they'd had no breakfast. He was aware of a gnawing emptiness in his stomach. 'I'm starving,' he admitted.

'Me too,' said Schleiben.

'Well, you'd better get used to doing without,' Reitlinger growled. 'The Americans haven't enough to feed themselves. They can't afford to waste food on the enemy.'

'They look pretty sleek to me,' Walter Schmidt grunted, peering through the window.

'They're damn near starving,' Reitlinger insisted. 'Our submarines in the Atlantic have cut off their supplies from abroad, our bombers have destroyed their warehouses. We'll probably be living on rats and sewer water.'

At that moment, the carriage door opened, and a negro porter pushing a trolley loaded with sandwiches and two large coffee urns entered quietly. 'Mornin' gentlemen,' he said in English.

They stared at each other. Walter Schmidt leaned forward, examining the contents of the trolley with disbelief. For most of them, their front line diet had been composed largely of iron rations and a few paltry provisions scavenged from mobile field kitchens. 'These are all for us?' Schmidt grunted in his halting English.

'Yes, sir,' the negro said. 'Much as you c'n eat.'

With cries of enthusiasm, the Germans seized the food and began to devour it voraciously. Grave and dignified, the porter filled a tray of cups and gave one to each man. Yet Tully couldn't eat, that was the amazing thing; one minute he was hungrier than a lumberjack, the next he was sitting with the sandwiches in his lap and so excited he couldn't get a single mouthful down his throat. He sat chewing and chewing, peering through the window at the street below. It was a beautiful street, really and truly beautiful. Even the drunks sprawled on the sidewalk looked beautiful, freezing their butts off in the snow and slush while pedestrians stepped over them in that quaint American way.

A truck stood parked beneath the arches of their bridge. Its roof was elongated to allow the driver to stand upright when necessary, and painted on its flanks were the words: 'Sprawler's Hot Dogs, Smooth'n Spicy'.

'Hey look,' Schleiben said suddenly. '*Bockwürste.*'

'I didn't think they had those things over here,' Schmidt whispered.

Schleiben moistened his lips. 'Just like home,' he said.

He glanced round. The negro porter had moved to the next car. Schleiben reached up and tried the window, and to Tully's amazement it slid open with a soft creak. My God, what kind of a crappy outfit were they running here? The train was filled with German soldiers and the fools hadn't even locked the carriage windows.

He stared at the guards. They were out on the platform helping the porter load the baggage car.

'Hey, Karl,' Schleiben said excitedly, 'Let's go down there and grab ourselves a bagful.'

Bohmler laughed out loud. 'I'll give you five marks if you do it, Hans,' he shouted.

Schleiben looked at Tully, his face gleaming. 'Are you game?' he hissed.

'Sit down, you bloody fool,' Tully snapped. 'How far do you think you'll get dressed in that *Waffenrock*? They'll grab you before you hit the sidewalk.'

'Like to bet?' Schleiben grinned.

He was already out of his seat, one hand on the window ledge. He looked as if nothing in the world could restrain him.

'Go on, Hans,' somebody urged, 'let's see you do it.'

Schleiben cast a swift glance backward, then before Tully could raise a hand in protest, he'd stepped on to the armrest and slipped swiftly through the open window. Christ, he's gone, Tully thought wildly. Reiser will kill me.

He peered out at the platform. The GIs had finished loading the baggage car but were now chatting amiably to the negro porter.

A ripple of excitement passed among the watching prisoners.

Stroud gave Tully a nudge. 'What about it?' he whispered. 'Shall we give it a try?'

'Are you crazy?'

'Come on, don't be scared.'

Stroud, grinning like a lunatic, leapt up, balanced his foot on the window ledge, and slid quickly to the track outside.

Tully locked his gaze on the opposite wall. He simply wouldn't look, he thought. He kept his eyes straight, his face aloof. He would not be a party to this. Damn fools. Those guards out there were just kids. Kids with rifles in their hands. He wasn't about to take a bullet in the ass for some stupid hot dog, for Christ's sake.

I will sit here and study the posters, he thought.

The words glared back at him: 'Come to Heavenly Humboldt, in the heart of California's Redwoods.'

What a blissful prospect, he mused, but he was not, under any circumstances, going through that window. Not that he wouldn't give his right arm to stand in the streets of New York again. To stand like a free man, instead of trapped in some railroad car with a bunch of crummy Nazi soldiers. But he wasn't going, because he had his duty as an American officer.

Of course, it was only a couple of hundred yards or so, no distance at all if you moved fast enough. And the guards were so dumb they were still deep in conversation with the idiot porter. And down there lay the streets of America, inviting, tantalising, alluring.

But he wasn't going.

That was not what he had come for.

He switched his gaze to another poster. 'Free 196-page Vacation Guide to New York State,' it said. 'Offers a thrilling preview of what your vacation can be . . . helps you make the most of every exciting hour.'

He felt virtuous and unselfish. Certain things in life rose above the yearnings of the individual, he thought. Like duty. Commitment. Integrity.

Okay, so it was—what?—maybe a block-and-a-half to freedom, and the damn fool guards were still not looking, but he wasn't going. No way. His mind was solid on that.

Solid.

But what he wouldn't give to stand down there, unfettered and unencumbered, just for a minute or two. Goddammit, a few seconds would be worth the risk.

'Let me out of here,' he croaked in a strangled voice.

And in one swift movement, he had scuttled through the opening and dropped to the cindered track outside.

My God, he thought wildly, Reiser'll have me shot.

Crouching, head and shoulders pushed hard against the carriage hull, he realised he was invisible to most of the American guards on the train. There was no platform on this side, only the metal grillwork of the bridge, and further down, a line of dark railroad sheds. Stroud was waving at him earnestly.

'This way,' he hissed.

Tully danced over the rails, ducking beneath the grillwork to where Stroud and Schleiben were slithering down a spiral staircase. Tully's breath rasped in his throat. He took the steps three at a time, and as he touched the ground, Stroud and Schleiben began clambering over a high wire-mesh fence. He saw Schleiben reach the top first. Slipping out of his tunic, the German laid it over the barbed-wire on the upper rim, and the two men slid quickly to the other side.

Tully climbed, gasping hard, his muscles quivering with strain and trepidation. At the top he paused for a moment while he retrieved Schleiben's tunic, then he leapt to the ground.

He'd done it.

He was standing in the streets of New York.

Tully wiped his sweaty palms on the sides of his tunic. Seated in his driving seat, reading his morning paper, the hot dog man stared in astonishment as the door was dragged open and three German soldiers glared at him from the sidewalk.

'We want some hot dogs,' Tully snapped curtly.

The driver couldn't believe his ears. 'What are you, some kind of screwball?' he muttered. 'Don't you realise you can be arrested for wearing those outfits?'

'Three hot dogs,' Tully repeated stubbornly.

'Hey listen, buddy, this is my coffee-break, right? You want hot dogs, come back when I'm open for business.'

'*Hau-up*,' Schleiben ordered menacingly.

'*What*?' the man muttered, taken aback at the sound of Schleiben's German.

'*Hau-up*,' Schleiben repeated, and grabbing the vendor by the shirtfront, pitched him into the gutter.

Schleiben clambered in like a breathless schoolboy. He grinned happily as he uncovered the huge metal tubs and found the frankfurter sausages and breadrolls inside.

The driver pounded on the windshield, his sense of shock giving way to indignation. 'Get outta there,' he yelled. 'You want me to call a cop?'

Tully seized the driver by the front of his shirt and lifted him bodily back from the van. 'Get lost,' he growled in a dangerous voice.

The driver swallowed two or three times, then as Tully released him, he turned and trotted down the road, making for a distant telephone booth.

A group of children wandered by in the sunlight, stopping to stare at Schleiben, their eyes dark and sombre. Schleiben grinned, opening up the back of the truck. 'Hey,' he said, *'Willst du eine wurst? Komm rüber.'*

Though his language was unfamiliar, the children grasped his meaning in an instant, and with squeals of delight gathered around the van, reaching out eager hands as Schleiben passed the steaming hot dogs quickly around. *'Mach langsam,'* he yelled, *'Ist genug für alle.'*

On the opposite sidewalk, a group of elderly ladies stopped to stare in approval at the children lunging and jostling like demented savages. They crossed the street, smiling indulgently.

'What a nice gesture,' one of them said.

She turned to Stroud, who was busy brushing dust from his trousers.

'Is that man a friends of yours?''

Stroud looked blank, and Tully stepped in hastily. 'I'm afraid he doesn't understand American, ma'am. He's a . . . a stranger around here.'

'Oh, I can see that,' the lady smiled, her grey curls lifting gently in the wind. 'What is your regiment?'

Tully felt his spirits sink. 'Well, we're not exactly the military, ma'am.'

She looked at him, puzzled. He could see traces of white where her face powder had gathered in the wrinkles on her face.

'Then what are those uniforms you're wearing?'

Tully thought desperately, his brain in a turmoil.

'Salvation Army,' he said, 'Guatemalan Division.'

The lady's smile widened. 'I had no idea the Guatemalans were in New York.'

'Yes, ma'am, we wanted to show our solidarity with the American people in this their hour of need.'

'How charming. Is that why you're feeding these children?'

Tully nodded gravely. 'In times like these, it's so often the innocent who suffer.'

The old lady turned to her friends. 'Doesn't it warm your hearts to see such fine young men displaying the virtues of Christian charity?'

She turned back, nodding her head in an approving kind of way. 'I intend to see that your inspiring conduct is given full coverage by this nation's press.'

'That's kind of you, ma'am,' Tully said.

He felt ashamed of himself for deceiving her. She was kind of nice really, plump and motherly, with bright brown eyes which studied Tully through a pair of thick-rimmed spectacles.

'Young man,' she said, 'would you do us a small favour?'

'A favour, ma'am? If we can.'

'I was just thinking about how the Salvation Army has built so much of its strength on music.'

'That's true.'

'Well, we—that is, the ladies here and myself—belong to a religious order that also believes in the powerful spiritual message of melodic harmony. So I wonder if you'd be kind enough to sing us a Guatemalan hymn?'

Tully felt his stomach sink. He looked at her in silence for a moment. 'A hymn, ma'am?' he echoed.

'You know, the sort of thing you sing at your meetings back home. We'd dearly love to hear you praising the Lord in true Guatemalan fashion.'

Tully took a deep breath. He called Schleiben over from the van. Schleiben was clutching hot dogs in both fists. He looked mildly ridiculous.

'They want us to sing a hymn,' Tully said.

Schleiben stared at him in silence. 'I don't know any hymns,' he muttered testily.

'Well, you'd better think of one fast. They won't understand the words anyhow, but for Christ's sake sing *something*.'

Schleiben looked at Stroud. Stroud's face was blank. He muttered something in a soft voice, then together they took a deep breath and launched into the opening bars of the Nazi Horst Wessel song.

Oh, my God, Tully thought, I'll go down in history as the

biggest traitor since Benedict Arnold. Children will burn my effigy on the Fourth of July.

Stroud and Schleiben's voices strengthened as they warmed to the music, bellowing out the lyrics on the chill afternoon air. The ladies smiled in appreciation, tapping their feet to the rousing melody. The woman who'd asked them to sing seized Tully's arm. 'Wasn't it your founder who said: "Why should the devil have all the best tunes?"' she yelled.

He nodded back furiously with a strained grin. 'Heaven surely wouldn't touch this one,' he answered.

As they launched into the second verse, the ladies picked up the refrain, humming it gently at first, then singing louder as their confidence grew, and Tully stared miserably at the sky as the strains of the Horst Wessel, issuing from a dozen throats drifted across Battery Park over the streets of New York.

Patrolmen Butler and Davis sat parked in a blind alley watching the Staten Island ferry disgorge its usual cargo of servicemen and civilians. They had thirty minutes left before they went off duty, and Butler was damned if he was going to cruise around looking for trouble. His wife's brother was home from the navy, and he'd promised to take them both out to dinner tonight, and though Butler didn't particularly like his brother-in-law, who generally spent the evening spouting about his exploits in the war-torn Pacific, he couldn't face the thought of explaining things to Martha if he turned up late again. It had been a sore point between the two of them since their wedding day, when Butler had been called out on a lousy Signal 13 (a Call for Assistance, the highest priority code in the New York Police Department) and hadn't gotten back until two o'clock in the morning. Though he and Martha were compatible in every other way, she never seemed to understand that a policeman's life was no nine-to-five job, which was why Butler had insisted, in the interests of marital harmony, that the last half-hour be spent in this quiet bunghole where he could clock off the second his shift was over.

Butler spotted a man coming towards them from across the street, and something in the way the man walked struck dismay into Butler's heart. He knew instinctively the guy was looking for a cop. He had that air about him, that flush of urgency. Here goes my peace of mind, Butler thought, Martha will decapitate me for sure.

The man rapped on the side window with his knuckles, and sighing, Butler slid it down.

'Officer,' the man said, 'there's a bunch of old ladies singing Nazi marching songs down by the dock.'

Butler stared at him in silence for a moment, his beefy face cool and appraising. Was the idiot drunk?

'Are you trying to make a dummy out of me?' he growled.

'No, sir.'

'If this is bullshit, buddy, I'm gonna haul your ass right down to the station house.'

'Listen, officer,' the man insisted, 'I know a Nazi song when I hear one. I spent six months in Austria before the war.'

'Shut up, Charlie,' Davis snapped as the radio started to crackle. A voice broke through the static, terse and strained.

'Attention, attention,' it said, 'all cars in the vicinity of the 24th Seaport proceed at once to South Street and Battery Park area and intercept three male Caucasians in German uniforms in illegal possession of stolen hot dog truck.'

Butler felt his senses sway. 'Holy Jesus!' he exclaimed.

Switching on the engine, Davis stabbed the accelerator with his foot and they hurtled out of the alley with their siren wailing. Butler peered through the windshield, moaning audibly.

'Martha'll never believe this if I live to be a hundred,' he groaned.

Tully spotted the patrol car long before it halted. The policemen climbed out, staring towards them with expressions of disbelief; then unholstering their pistols, they approached warily along the sidewalk.

Stroud and Schleiben became aware of their presence, and their voices trailed away.

'What the hell is this?' the first policeman asked.

'Why officer,' smiled the old lady, 'don't look so alarmed. These gentlemen are members of the Salvation Army. They've been feeding our underprivileged children.'

The patrolman stared at her with a perplexed look.

'What did you say, lady?'

'The Salvation Army. They belong to the Guatemalan Division.'

'With the iron cross?' the policeman muttered, peering at Schleiben's tunic.

'They were teaching us one of their best-loved hymns. I must say, going to church in Guatemala must be quite an invigorating experience.'

The policeman looked at his companion, who shook his head in amazement. They had the air of men to whom the vagaries of life provided a constant source of wonder.

'You Krauts get your butts over to the prowl car,' the first patrolman said, 'and don't nobody make a move out of place.'

Tully repeated the order in German, and the three POWs obeyed in silence. Realising their moment of freedom was over, they stood in docile fashion, legs spread, hands on the car roof, while the two patrolmen frisked them expertly and handcuffed their wrists behind their backs.

The old ladies watched this procedure with expressions of horror.

'Officer,' the first one complained, 'these gentlemen are guests in our country.'

'You're damn right there, lady,' the policeman answered, 'and I intend to make sure they remain our guests for a long time to come.'

'I'll report you to the Police Commissioner. This is an appalling misuse of authority.'

'You do that, ma'am. If I ain't home by dinnertime, my old woman's gonna misuse me.'

The three prisoners were bundled into the rear seat, and with a roar the patrol car surged away from the sidewalk. The old ladies stood in the snow and watched it disappear with expressions of dismay.

'Those ppor fine boys,' the first one said. 'We never did get a chance to teach them "God Bless America".'

A great cheer went up from the waiting train as Tully and the others were jostled across the dockside by angry GIs. They had been delivered back to the Military and their handcufffs removed after extensive questioning at the police station.

As the escapees were shepherded into their carriage, the other POWs gathered round to pump their hands and shower them with congratulations. Dazed by the welcome, Tully made his way to his seat and collapsed into it. He was filled with relief that the escapade was over, but he was conscious too of a sense of bitter irony, of inveterate injustice. For the first time in my life I'm a hero, he thought, and it's with the wrong crummy side.

6

The train chugged slowly south across the drab New Jersey flatlands, and for a while the prisoners thronged the windows, exclaiming excitedly as each new panorama hove into view; but when the countryside continued to unfold in a tedious sprawl of industrial complexes and sullen villages, their enthusiasm gradually faded, and by the time they had reached the outskirts of Washington, D.C., each man had resigned himself to a dreary, monotonous journey.

They were fed once more, just before eight; a tray of meatloaf and potato salad and—as a special treat—a bottle of light beer per prisoner. Then the porter distributed blankets, and they settled down in their seats for the night.

Now that the madness in New York was over, Tully dwelled, for the first time in days, on the job ahead. He had put it from his mind during the long Atlantic voyage, concentrating instead on building up his cover. His escape attempt had been a momentary insanity, a fractional lapse of reason, and he hoped to God Reiser never found out. But it was time to earn his keep again.

He thought about Graebner, wondering what he'd be like. Friendly and communicative, or suspicious and aloof? Tully shook his head in weariness. It was dark and he was tired. God only knew how far they had to travel before they reached their destination. He would worry about the future when they got there.

The train stopped often during the night, but though Tully

woke and pulled back the curtain, he was never able to work
out their exact position.

For three whole days, they rattled slowly southward,
passing towns, villages, distant tree-covered mountains, wide
muddy rivers. The afternoons lengthened into evenings, and
still the journey continued. The atmosphere in the crowded
carriage grew strained to breaking point. The men lost their
bantering good humour. Some of them were secretly beginning
to agree with Reitlinger that the damned Americans were
trailing them round in circles just for the hell of it. Tempers
grew short, and once or twice fights flared up, but these were
quickly stopped by the guards who, still smarting from the
New York episode, watched warily from the car doorways.

Then, on the evening of the third day, the train pulled to a
halt at the edge of a small tumbledown town, and Tully saw US
troops waiting at the trackside. A voice shouted: 'Okay,
everybody out. On the double, you guys, we ain't got all
night.'

They were lined up in ranks and their names called. The air
was warm and humid, a blessed relief after the harsh cold of
the New York spring. Across the street, Tully spotted a
drugstore, its windows ablaze with light. Fluffy pastries
perched beneath plastic food covers, and he was shaken by a
sense of longing so intense he thought he would actually faint
from it. He would have given anything in the world, he
thought, to walk right in and sit down at the fountain. But once
the roll-call was over, they were loaded on to heavy trucks and
driven out of town across open fields, heavy pine forest, and
segments of murky cypress swamp.

For several miles they rumbled in convoy, and then, just as
darkness was setting in, Tully spotted a cluster of wood huts
surrounded by a barbed-wire fence. A sign on the gate said:

'Camp Cannesetego,
Cannesetego County,
Louisiana.'

The camp was flanked on three sides by heavy woodland,
and on the fourth by open pastures and a road that ran, Tully
learned later, almost ten miles to the Lomstoun turnpike. There
was only one way in and one way out which, from the security

point of view, made it virtually escape-proof. There were two
perimeter fences, both fifteen feet high, with a twenty-foot gap
between them, and six machine-gun towers dotting the
periphery at evenly-spaced intervals. The upper section of the
enclosure was devoted to the recreation area, a stretch of open
land large enough to encompass a basketball court, while the
lower section held the visitors' parking lot, the Garrison
Echelon, the QM office, the shop, the utility yard, the hospital,
and the heating plant. Between these service areas lay the four
compounds where the POWs were quartered. Each compound
contained six structures so drab and dismal they struck a chill
into Tully's heart the first time he set eyes on them. It was not a
place to inspire warmth and comfort, he thought.

The trucks stopped at the reception hut, and each man was
obliged to disembark and lay out his personal effects for
inspection. Tully's coins were placed in an envelope bearing
his name and identification number.

'You'll get 'em back when the war ends,' he was told with
a grin.

The new inmates were photographed for the camp records,
and a large white PW was stencilled on the back of each man's
tunic.

Then they were introduced to their camp commander, a
small brisk southerner with fleshy features and a protruding
paunch. His initiation speech was cordial but brief.

'Welcome to Camp Cannesetego,' he told them in German.
'My name's Colonel Glusky.'

In clipped staccato tones, he went on to outline the details
of fire precautions, sanitary maintenance, and medical and
dental inspections. They listened in silence, their brains
stunned into apathy by the long punishing journey.

'Under the terms of the Geneva Convention,' the colonel
explained, 'you'll receive a certain percentage of your army
pay throughout your stay here. This will not be delivered in
currency, but in canteen coupons which can be exchanged at
the Inmates Club. However, if any damage is sustained by any
piece of United States property, the prisoners responsible will
pay the cost of repair out of their weekly allowance. Reveille is
at five-thirty, breakfast at six. At seven-thirty you'll begin your

work projects for the day. Under the terms of the Labour Programme you'll be taken to neighbouring farms or logging operations where you'll be expected to earn your keep.'

He paused, his face visibly darkening. 'A word about escape,' he said. 'I understand some of you suffered an attack of itchy feet in New York. Since you're newcomers to the United States we've decided to press no charges, but any similar antics in the future will be handled with the strictest severity. I guess you noticed the barbed wire and machine-guns on your way in. They're merely a precaution. Since this camp functions largely on mutual trust—by that, I mean you will not be heavily guarded—there are those among you who may be tempted to make a break for freedom. Let me emphasise that such a move would be extremely ill-advised. Not a single escapee has ever made it back to Germany. The truth is, gentlemen, there's no place to go. Even if you reach the Mexican border, you'll find the United States has an extradition treaty with the Mexican government and you'll end up right back here. The punishment for escape attempts is thirty days in the pig-pen. If you're wondering what the pig-pen is, it's that little box you'll find at the head of Compound 3. Offenders are shut inside without human contact of any kind. I'm willing to bet that by the end of a month, you'll never ever think of escaping again.'

When the briefing was over, they were taken to the mess-hall for dinner, then split into small groups and distributed among the long rows of prison huts. Tully and Stroud were allocated number 14 in Compound 2. It was long and low-ceilinged, the kind of bunkhouse Tully had lived in during his training at Norfolk, Virginia, and later in Worcestershire, England. Beds lined two sides of the room and pot-bellied stoves perched at both ends. There was a locker between each bed and a small corridor leading to the latrine.

It was not so much the hut itself which worried Tully, however, as the hostility of its inhabitants, who greeted Tully and Stroud's entry with as much enthusiasm as anglers viewing the arrival of a boisterous swimming party. They sat on their beds, writing letters, reading magazines (one man was building a paper aeroplane), and not a word passed their lips as

Tully and Stroud picked their way down the centre aisle, selected the last unoccupied bunks, and began to unpack their things.

This is a hell of a welcome, Tully thought. He glanced at Stroud, who shrugged helplessly. It was inherent in Tully's nature that he felt indifference keenly, having experienced it in others for most of his life, but on this occasion he knew there was too much at stake to take such a rejection to heart.

He walked to the man in the next bed and stuck out his hand. 'Karl Raderecht,' he said.

The man stared at him in silence for a moment, then nodded. 'Okay,' he answered coolly.

'What the hell's wrong with everybody? Are we lepers or something?'

'No,' the man said, 'it's nothing personal. You've not been properly screened yet, that's all.'

'Screened?'

'Well, how do I know you're Karl Raderecht? Maybe you're General George Patton, for Christ's sake. All new inmates have to face the camp interrogation committee. Until you've been cleared by them, nobody's allowed to talk to you. It's kind of an unwritten rule.'

'You mean we've got to walk around as if we'd had our tongues pulled out or something?'

'Only until tomorrow. They'll interrogate you then, just as soon as they get the committee organised.'

'Who does this organising?'

'Same guy who does everything else. Sergeant Strahle. He's a three-tier'd bastard. Sick up here.'

The man tapped his forehead. 'Used to be a sturmbann-führer once. Got busted on the Russian front for executing five infantrymen in a field hospital. He claimed they were malingering. Excess of zeal, the Brass called it. Still, even without his rank, he manages to run things pretty well his own way. He's got a bunch of Nazi hoodlums backing him up, meatballs all of them—brains of rabbits, but muscles like Hercules. Nobody stands against Strahle, not if they intend to stay in one piece, they don't.'

'And the Americans let him get away with it?'

The man laughed humourlessly. 'Damn little they can do to stop him. Old Glusky's understaffed and overworked. All he cares about is keeping things running smoothly. As long as Strahle doesn't step on his toes, the colonel's more than happy to look the other way. Strahle maintains his own kind of discipline, and that suits Glusky down to the ground.'

Tully pursed his lips, running his palms against his combat jacket. 'You think this Strahle'll give us a bad time?'

'Maybe. Maybe he'll take a liking to you. It happens. He can make life very comfortable, if he does. For a price, that is.'

'You mean he likes to be bribed?'

'I wasn't talking about money. He's as queer as a three-dollar bill. Why do you think you're being interrogated tomorrow? Camp security, bullshit. It's so Strahle can give the new talent the once-over.'

'Jesus Christ!' Tully whispered.

He strolled back to his bunk, blinking. So Reiser's prediction was proving correct? The damned camp *was* controlled by a bunch of fanatics.

Crossing the Atlantic had been one thing. That had been easy. Tully's cabin-mates had been as confused as he was. But here, it was different. Here, they had it all worked out. With time on their hands, there was nothing else to think about, goddammit.

Turning back his blanket, he began to undress, his brain racing over the terrors and indignities that were about to be unleashed against him, and it was then, while he was standing inelegantly with his pants off, that he noticed for the first time the man in the opposite bed. He was small and muscular, with a sharply receding hairline and pointed features that looked as if they'd been pinched out of molten wax. But what caught Tully's attention was the fact that the man was dangling over his mattress rim, vomiting on the floor. His whole body was shivering, and as Tully watched, the lights of the bunkhouse glistened in oily diffusion along his sweat-soaked flanks. Tully made to move across.

"Leave him alone,' the man in the next bed said.

'But he's sick,' Tully grunted.

'He's not sick, he's scared.'

'What d'you mean, scared? Scared of what?'

'Strahle court-martialled him this afternoon.'

'Court-martialled!' Tully exclaimed. 'What was the charge?'

'Insulting the Führer.'

Tully almost laughed out loud. 'You're crazy. We're four thousand miles from Germany.'

'Makes no difference. He was found guilty. They're carrying out the sentence after lights-out.'

'What sentence, for Christ's sake?'

'He's been ordered to have his legs broken.'

It was the moment of truth for Tully, the point at which he realised all his worst fears had been justified, and a kind of dull terror surged through him, an oppressive, strangulating force that seemed to emanate from the air itself and settle relentlessly about his skull and shoulders.

'Take my advice and stay out of it,' the man said. 'You can't help the poor bastard, and there's no sense in making an enemy of Strahle unless you have to.'

Suddenly Tully realised why the hut had been so silent. It was not hostility he'd sensed, but dread.

'We've got to stop it,' he declared firmly.

'How?'

'By sticking together.'

The man laughed. 'Strahle likes that kind of thing. He'd send in his torpedoes and bust all our legs. A few extra victims wouldn't worry him in the slightest.'

'Then we'll warn the authorities.'

'Think they'll listen?'

'For Christ's sake, we'll make them listen.'

'Forget it, soldier. Strahle's got this whole damn camp in his pocket, and that includes the guards as well. Believe me, we're sorry for Steiner, but he brought it on himself. Don't try to be a crusader. Just concentrate on keeping your nose clean. You'll soon find out it's the only way to survive.'

He's right, Tully thought wildly, for God's sake he's right. What happens to this German soldier is no concern of mine.

I'm here to do a job. I can't get involved in issues that don't concern me.

He returned to his bed and took off the rest of his clothes, adopting, like the others, a pose of studied nonchalance as he worked hard and laboriously at folding his trousers, straightening his tunic, smoothing out imaginary creases with his fingertips.

As he climbed into bed, he shut his ears to Steiner's sobbing, trying to pretend he was unaware that fifteen feet away a terrified human being lay trembling in his own vomit.

Lights-out came at ten, but even in the darkness the tension in the room remained almost palpable, holding them in a grip that wiped out any possibility of sleep. Though the silence was intense, Tully knew the others, like himself, were lying taut and motionless, staring fiercely into the gloom.

Steiner's sobbing undulated in a series of intermittent waves, sometimes loud and insistent, disturbing their senses with its proclamation of fear, sometimes fading to a gentle whimpering sound as if his body had lost the power to vociferate in the face of such an unthinkable fate. The odour of his vomit filled the room, bringing with it an inescapable awareness of human frailty, a knowledge inherent in each of them that in death and suffering man must ultimately remain alone. Tully wondered if, by closing his eyes and concentrating very hard, he could will himself into slumber. That way, he might miss the awfulness of what was about to happen. Violence was sick, he'd always believed that. But Steiner was the enemy. And Reiser was depending on him. The German would have to look after himself.

The minutes passed and still the air of taut expectancy continued, then—click—Tully's nerves jumped as the door swung open and someone entered the hut at the opposite end. He blinked in the darkness. He could see the man's outline perched in the aisle between the beds, legs apart, hands on hips in the swaggering posture so beloved by Hitler's supermen. The intruder was tall, barely an inch off six feet, and there was no flesh to his bones, as if beneath the calico tunic only the skeletal framework existed, bestowing the wearer with an illusion of sinewy strength.

'Steiner?' the newcomer purred.

The voice was higher than Tully had expected. It carried a breathless girlish quality, unusual for such a big man.

'Time to go, Steiner,' the voice murmured.

The sobbing rose hysterically, no longer a wordless plea for help as it had been earlier, but an inarticulate protest that hung beneath the roof-beams, rebuking them all.

The intruder snorted in disgust. 'Bring him out,' he ordered.

The door swung open and two more figures entered, their outlines bulkier than the first. As they crossed the floor, Tully sensed rather than observed the power in their limbs. Even in the darkness, they had the air of men for whom brute force was the only true strategy of life.

They dragged the sentenced man from his bunk and hauled him towards the latrine, his legs trailing helplessly on the ground. Tully heard one of the newcomers curse as, in a spasm of blind terror, Steiner's sphincter muscle gave way.

'Bastard's shit himself,' the man growled angrily.

'Bring him into the head,' the tall one commanded, 'that's where he belongs.'

They bundled Steiner out, slamming the door, and a heavy silence descended on the hut, a silence so perfect it was almost holy, Tully thought. He held his breath, counting the seconds. All sensation seemed drained from his body and he lay as a dying man might lie, feeling the numbness crawl within him, a cold wave of insensitivity creeping inch by inch along his legs and thighs and lower trunk.

Then suddenly, the night was rent by a horrifying scream, a noise too high and grotesque to be identified as human. It came again, one volley following hard upon the other, gliding up the entire scale of recognisable sound. It was, in a curious way, almost a parody of itself, jarring their senses with its eerie pitch. Loud and shrill, it filled their heads with the injustice of its pain until Tully wanted to yell out in unison.

Then, as abruptly as it had started, the screaming stopped, and silence flooded the hut, bringing solace to their ragged responses.

A long drawn-out sigh rose from the lines of listening men,

and with the tension broken they turned in their bunks and settled down to wait for the peace that sleep would bring.

Tully lay in silence, staring at the ceiling. For him, the suffering still lingered, like a dark force that could not be assuaged. For the first time, the true nature of his predicament impressed itself upon him. If Strahle's bully boys would break a man's legs for insulting the Führer, he thought, what in hell's name would they do to an enemy spy?

Major Miles Wiseman, Medical Officer at Camp Cannesetego, had once been President of the American Association of Medical Practitioners, a post that was not in itself an auspicious one, though it meant a lot to Wiseman and was seen by his friends as an indication of how successful he might have become had he not resorted to the bottle. No-one was more aware of this irony than Wiseman himself, who had always been filled with a burning belief in his own potential and who could never understand how he had managed to become an alcoholic in the first place. His habit had started quite innocently, with a shot or two after surgery hours to relieve the tensions of the day, and then, almost without his noticing it, the size of the shots had steadily increased, until at last he'd been forced to admit that he was inescapably hooked. It was the drink that put paid to his hopes and aspirations. When the war came along, instead of being dispatched to the battle-zones of Europe or the Pacific (where he might have done some good), he was tucked away in this almost-forgotten corner of the earth in a role he bitterly resented, but which, because he was by nature a humane man and a kind one, he endeavoured to fulfill to the best of his ability—during those moments when he managed to remain sober.

On the morning after Tully's arrival, Major Wiseman made his way, bleary-eyed, to the married-quarters home of the camp commander, Colonel Walter Glusky. The colonel's wife let him in at the front door, and he found the colonel himself seated in the kitchen, busily eating a large plate of ham and grits. Major Wiseman felt his stomach react uneasily. He could never understand the colonel's fondness for grits, for the one and only time he had tried them himself (after a hefty session in the officers' mess), he had thrown up afterwards in the head.

Glusky was surprised to see him. He never quite knew what to make of Major Wiseman. Wiseman did not fit into the colonel's experience of army men. Colonel Glusky had been a professional soldier all his life, and it confused and bewildered him that someone like Wiseman, who refused to abide by the rules and regulations, and who sometimes displayed an open contempt for all things military, not only existed but actually survived in this war. He waved Wisemen in with his fork. 'Sit down, Miles,' he said. 'Had breakfast yet?'

'You know I never touch a thing before noon. My digestion.'

'Have some coffee then.'

'No thanks. You go ahead, I'll just sit and watch.'

Wiseman perched himself on a stool on the opposite side of the table. Through the window, he could see the barbed-wire perimeter fence of Camp Cannesetego, and the menacing outline of the machine-gun posts around its rim. He did not care for the colonel much. His feelings were not based on any direct animosity; it was simply that he and the colonel were different animals, and recognising this fact made it difficult for Wiseman to feel comfortable in the colonel's presence.

Colonel Glusky studied him with a thoughtful frown. 'Up early, aren't you, Miles?' he said, spearing a piece of broiled ham. 'I thought you liked to sleep it off in the mornings.'

'We had an emergency last night,' Wiseman told him. 'Steiner in Hut 14.'

'Yeah?'

'They found him in the latrine with his legs broken.'

'Jesus.'

'He says the lavatory cistern fell on him.'

Colonel Glusky chewed in silence for a moment, then took a sip of coffee. 'Somebody ought to have his ass in a sling on that one, Miles. Those huts are barely two years old.'

Wiseman pressed his lips together in a thin line. Nothing irritated him more than somebody playing dumb or stupid. 'Come on, Walt,' he snapped with exasperation, 'you know damn well it wasn't an accident. It was Strahle again.'

'Strahle?'

'Sooner or later, you're going to have to do something about that Nazi bastard.'

The colonel's face was bland. He asked casually: 'Did Steiner actually mention Strahle?'

'Of course he didn't. Nobody ever does.'

'So once again it comes down to your supposition. Every time somebody gets hurt in Cannesetego, you claim it's Sergeant Strahle's fault. Yet none of the casualties ever utters a word to support that theory. They maintain—every last one of them—that their injuries were sustained by accident.'

'Of course they do,' Wiseman exploded, 'Strahle's running this camp like a goddammed slavemaster. Anybody steps out of line, he threatens action against their families in the fatherland. Those thugs of his make the Capone gang look like a bunch of country parsons. He's got swastikas painted all over the place, pictures of Hitler in every damned hut, SS slogans scribbled on the walls. For Christ's sake, Walt, we might as well be living in the heart of Nazy Germany.'

Colonel Glusky's neck seemed to sink into his collar so that his tie fluttered each time he swallowed. His face looked impassive. 'What do you suggest I do about it, Miles?' he asked.

'Well, you could start by getting rid of that Nazi propaganda.'

'Beyond my jurisdiction, Miles. Washington has decreed that German prisoners-of-war are still soldiers, and have a right to display nationalist material in their living quarters if they choose to.'

'And Strahle?'

Glusky shrugged. 'Evidence, Miles, we need evidence.'

'You've got the evidence of your own eyes, for Christ's sake. You can see what he's doing out there.'

Glusky nodded thoughtfully. He cleaned his plate with a piece of bread, then he drained his coffee and immediately refilled his cup. His face carried an air of immeasurable patience.

'Miles, let me tell you something. I hate this job I'm doing. The guys I trained with at officer school are out in Europe and the Pacific winning themselves a war, while I'm stuck in this miserable craphouse playing nursemaid to a bunch of dumb Heinis who actually believe Hitler's invasion forces are on their way to liberate them. I've got close on two hundred and fifty POWs behind that wire, and less than thirty men to keep them in line. In spite of that, I have to comply with the Labour Programme and allow all inmates out of the compound so they can lend a hand in the farms and lumber forests. Have you ever given a thought to what would happen if they decided to break loose? Two hundred and fifty men, Miles. They could be clear across the state before anybody realised they were even missing. Supposing they decided to hold a riot? What do I do, send in my troops? They wouldn't last ten minutes. I simply haven't the muscle to keep order in this camp, Miles. That's why I really don't give a damn what Strahle does to those dummies, just so long as he maintains camp discipline. Order, efficiency, stability, that's all I care about. If Strahle has to crack a few skulls while he keeps things running, well, I'm not about to get my balls in a tangle. Now you go back to your hospital and pour yourself a good stiff drink, because whether you like it or not, Strahle exists, and it's because he exists that you and I are able to sleep nights.'

Wiseman sat looking at him in silence for a moment. He reached for his hat and strolled to the door. 'Walter,' he said, turning.

'What?'

There were tiny blue veins on Major Wiseman's cheeks, but his eyes looked cool and assertive. Rank meant nothing to Wiseman, Glusky thought. He always was an insubordinate sonofabitch.

'You are a grade-A asshole,' the major said bluntly.

And without waiting for Glusky's reaction, he went out and closed the door behind him.

The new inmates stood in line outside the toolhouse, awaiting their turn for screening. They looked shaky and apprehensive; the events of the previous night had wrought in them a strange unwillingness to accept reality, and their faces displayed a pallor that seemed out of place in the morning sunshine. It was

Sunday, and all work had been suspended for twenty-four hours. In the recreation area, prisoners in shorts and sneakers were noisily playing a game of soccer, and nearer, another group had rigged up a volleyball net. The new arrivals watched them with dull uncertain eyes. They still had Strahle to face, and the memory of what had happened to Steiner hung in their minds like a moment of terror carried over from a bad dream.

When the toolhouse door opened and a man stepped out, there were calls of 'How'd it go, Seigi?' but the man, instead of answering, gave a wry shrug and strode off. Tully felt his stomach tighten. He wondered how he would stand up to questioning. No dread was so solitary, so isolated, as that of the spy, he thought.

He still shuddered when he recalled Strahle's handiwork the night before. It had been a gruesome initiation, and had had a profound effect upon the men, for they huddled together, not from a desire for warmth, but out of a simple need for human comfort.

For some reason, Willi Stroud seemed less intimidated than the others. 'This is bloody ridiculous,' he grumbled, thrusting his hands into his trouser pockets. 'How much longer do they expect us to wait? We've been hanging about for nearly three hours.'

'They like to sweat us a little,' Tully said.

'Well, they'd better get a move on, or I'm shoving off back to the barrack hut.'

'Strahle'd only come after you.'

'Screw Strahle. I'm sick to death of hearing about Strahle. He's not God Almighty, for Christ's sake.'

A prisoner, lounging nearby, burst into laughter at the sound of Stroud's irascibility. Stroud turned to glare at the man, his face indignant. 'What's so funny?' he demanded.

'You,' the man said, still chuckling, 'you're new here, you don't understand.'

The side of the man's cheek, above the left temple, had at some time in the past been badly scarred, either by the close passage of a bullet or a shell-blast. The skin looked blue and shiny, as if someone had stuck a thin sheet of plastic between his eyebrow and his hairline.

'Strahle's like a bum leg you have to learn to live with,' he explained. 'There's no clear reason why he functions like he does, it just happens, that's all. Nobody understands what hold he's got over those gorillas of his, but they follow him like a bunch of spaniels. When Strahle gives an order, you should see the bastards jump.'

'Well, he's only a sergeant, for Christ's sake.'

'But he has that air about him, that sense of authority. Giving orders comes natural to Strahle. He's a true aristocrat.'

'You're sure?' Tully asked curiously.

'He comes from one of the oldest families in Heidelberg. Seen those scars on his face? He fought sixteen duels at university.'

Tully frowned, remembering Graebner. Graebner too was an expert swordsman. 'I thought duelling was illegal now,' Tully grunted.

'Well, strictly speaking it is. But Strahle bought a couple of old cavalry sabres from one of the guards and hid them under the floorboards in his hut. Every once in a while, he and his cronies have a practice session in the heating plant. Still, they don't actually duel any more, not since the Führer banned the practice. Whatever else you might say about the sonofabitch, you have to admit one thing—he's a loyal Nazi.'

Instinctively, Tully shuddered. There was something intimidating about the mere mention of Strahle's name, as if his air of menace permeated everything.

Tully peered through the boundary fence at the nearby pine trees. Strange to think safety lay only a few steps beyond. He wished to God he could just walk out of here. Secure and unthreatened. Unshackled and unencumbered. Free.

One by one, the new inmates were called into the toolhouse, and just before noon, Tully's turn came.

'Good luck, Karl,' Stroud said as Tully took a deep breath and stepped through the door.

The hut interior was dark and musty, lit by a solitary shaft of daylight that slid through a window in its roof. Axes, picks, and shovels had been stacked round the walls to make room for a long trestle table behind which sat five men, watching him impassively. Strahle was at their centre, his pale cheeks a milky blob in the filtered sunlight. Strangely, he looked less imposing glimpsed by day. Last night, swathed in shadow, he had seemed to Tully like a demon out of hell itself, but here in the toolhouse, he appeared mild—sensitive even. His eyes flickered over Tully, cool and appraising. 'Sit down,' he ordered.

A metal bucket had been placed on the floor to serve as a stool, and Tully perched himself on its bottom peering at Strahle uncomfortably. He realised the use of the bucket had been deliberate. Seated, his head was the lowest in the room, which made him feel physically and psychologically inferior.

'Name?' Strahle demanded.

'Raderecht,' Tully answered.

Strahle glanced down the sheet in front of him. He wore a pair of small pince-nez spectacles which perched on the bridge of his nose, and Tully wondered if his eyesight really was failing or if, as a resolute Nazi, he was emulating the Führer who, rumour had it, always wore pince-nez for reading and paperwork.

'Number seventeen,' the man next to Strahle murmured.

Strahle found Tully's name on his list and underlined it with a pencil. 'Ah yes,' he said, 'aren't you the man who tried to escape?'

'One of them.'

Strahle looked at him with new interest. There was something disconcerting about the eyes. They were not sharp and direct, but curiously limpid. They lingered with an insistence that was almost a caress. Tully shifted uncomfortably on his perch.

'Where did you expect to get to?' Strahle asked.

'Nowhere,' Tully said.

'You simply . . . ran away?'

'Helps to keep the *Amies* on their toes.'

Strahle smiled thinly. 'You're an idiot, Raderecht. Now they have you down as a marked man. If you want to escape, you've got to prepare. Stunts like yours only make it harder for the rest of us.'

Despite the fact that Strahle was remonstrating, his voice was gentle, and there was a look on his face that Tully couldn't decipher. Jesus Christ, he thought, don't let the bastard take a liking to me.

'Sixth Gebirgsjäger, isn't it?' Strahle asked.

'That's right,' Tully murmured.

'How were you captured, Raderecht?'

Tully went into his rehearsed routine. 'We were at Houffalize when the Americans came in. Most of the regiment pulled back at once, but a bunch of us operating up front with a G 36 got cut off from the main group, and took shelter in a ruined farmhouse. When the farmhouse was surrounded, we had no alternative but to surrender.'

'Can you prove that?'

'No,' Tully answered. 'I didn't realise I'd have to.'

Strahle took off his glasses and smiled at him pleasantly.

'Nobody's calling you a liar,' he said in a conciliatory tone. 'We simply want to check you out, that's all. If the Americans think we're not on our toes, they'll infiltrate our security system. That's why it's important you answer our questions.'

He turned to one of his companions. 'Do we have anyone from the Sixth Gebirgsjäger here?'

'Corporal Lemberger,' the man said. 'He's waiting in the other room.

'Ask him to come in, will you?'

Corporal Lemberger was small and dapper with thin cheeks and a heavy beard shadow. Though he had shaved scrupulously, the lower part of his chin seemed to merge into the semi-darkness, giving his face the curious appearance of having been split in two. He looked at Tully with eyes that were neither friendly nor hostile.

'Do you recognise this man?' Strahle demanded.

Lemberger shook his head. Strahle scribbled something on the sheet in front of him.

'Would you care to ask him some questions?'

Lemberger cleared his throat. He looked far from happy with his role of inquisitor. 'Who was your commanding officer?' he demanded uncertainly.

'Oberst Von Kramer,' Tully answered.

'And his aide?'

'Frederich Koenigsreuter.'

'Did Koenigsreuter display any physical . . . peculiarities?'

'He had a glass eye,' Tully said.

'Which one?'

Tully hesitated only a moment. 'Left.'

Lemberger shifted on his heels. He shuffled constantly, as though uncertain whether or not he ought to stand at attention, and his voice had the flat, monotonous quality of a man reciting something learned by heart.

'Every Gebirgsjäger unit carries a medical chest equipped to deal with certain hazards not encountered in the normal processes of war. What are they?'

'Rope burns, frostbite, snow blindness and altitude sickness.'

For several minutes the questions followed a similar pattern, sometimes technical, dealing with aspects of Gebirgsjäger training, sometimes relating to individual personalities within the regiment. Tully was able to answer them smoothly and accurately, and he thanked heaven for Reiser's meticulous attention to detail. Eventually, however, he was brought to a standstill.

'Were you ever stationed at Bad Reichenshall?' Lemberger asked.

'I was,' said Tully.

'Then you were familiar with Feidermuk's, I take it?'

'Feidermuk's was the most popular café in town.'

'Who was the head-waiter there?'

'Frido Weiss.'

'And his daughter?'

Tully hesitated. He saw Strahle watching him closely. He saw the committee, their faces bathed in shadow.

'The name of Frido's daughter?' Lemberger repeated.

'I . . . I can't remember.'

'What?' Lemberger exclaimed in disbelief.

Strahle frowned, staring at Lemberger with irritation.

'Any reason why he should?' he muttered.

Lemberger gave a helpless shrug. "Anyone who's been to Feidermuk's must know Elsebeth,' he insisted. 'She served behind the bar there. She was, how shall we say . . . very pneumatic. It would hardly be possible to visit Feidermuk's without being aware of her presence.'

Strahle looked at Tully more sharply.

'How is it you do not know Elsebeth?' he demanded in a harsh voice.

Keeping his face calm, Tully asked: 'How long has the corporal been a prisoner here?'

'Thirteen months,' Lemberger replied promptly.

'Then that explains it. I've heard people speak of Elsebeth, though I didn't realise she was Frido's daughter. Her aunt was injured in a bombing raid on Bonn. Elsebeth had to go and look after her. I never saw her in the flesh.'

Strahle studied him in silence for a moment, then he looked at Lemberger. 'Is that possible?' he demanded.

The corporal seemed uncertain. 'I suppose so,' he admitted. 'She never mentioned an aunt in Bonn, but who knows?'

'Proceed with the questioning.'

Tully breathed a sigh of relief.

The examination continued for another twenty minutes, and throughout it all Strahle watched Tully with a steady almost-hypnotic gaze, scrutinising the American's reactions as if each answer offered a penetrating insight into his mind and character. As the questions continued, however, Strahle's concentration began to relax, and presently Tully realised he was satisfied. Once, when Tully looked at him directly, Strahle gave an encouraging smile and Tully felt his spirits sink. A smile from Strahle carried all the warmth of an alligator on the attack. If this sick sonofabitch starts getting romantic, Tully thought, then henchmen or not, I'll break his goddammed neck.

At last, the examination came to an end.

'You are free to use this camp as you wish,' Strahle said, 'but I would like to impress upon you one thing. You are a soldier in the German army, and must think of yourself, not as a prisoner, but as a member of the Führer's liberation forces, do you understand that?'

Tully nodded, keeping his face straight.

'Remember abortive escape attempts serve only to increase

American vigilance and security. No-one is allowed to make a break without first clearing it with the escape officer. Is that understood?'

'Yes, sergeant,' Tully answered.

'Very well, you may go.'

Tully rose to his feet and stepped to the door, his facial nerves twitching.

'Raderecht?' Strahle said suddenly.

Tully looked back. Strahle was smiling. 'We might have a little chat later,' he suggested, 'about friends, interests, that sort of thing. I've a feeling we'll find a great deal in common. I'll send for you when I have a moment.'

Tully stared at him coldly. A ball of dread gathered in his chest, spreading outwards to embrace his entire frame. He remembered the words of the man in the barrack hut. 'He can make life very comfortable, at a price.'

Tully closed the door and walked back to his hut, his heart thumping. As if he didn't have enough problems, for Christ's sake. It was all he needed, an amorous psychopath lousing up the operation. He would have to tread carefully for the next few days, very carefully indeed.

7

The unwillingness of Colonel Glusky to interfere in the internal politics of his camp was not a unique attitude in that spring of 1945. Though the United States had entered the war with her eyes open in almost every other aspect, she was totally unprepared for the 400,000 German prisoners, the 50,000 Italians, and the 5,000 Japanese who arrived from the battlefields of Europe, Africa, and the Pacific to be distributed among the 511 prison camps scattered around the American interior. Serious attempts were made to re-educate the more ardent Nazis, but ideological conflicts among the prisoners themselves led to many non-nationalistic Germans suffering at the hands of fanatical thugs who formed themselves into vigilante groups and ran the camps on fascist lines. The War Department turned a blind eye on these unwholesome activities, not through indifference but out of a genuine concern for American prisoners-of-war in German hands. The dictates of the Geneva Convention were strictly adhered to, and POWs were treated as decently and as humanely as possible. The open display of patriotic material was permitted and, though it seems incredible in retrospect, on special occasions such as Hitler's birthday swastika flags were unfurled above the palisades of American-run stockades.

For the people who lived in the rural communities where the camps were based, their establishment called for a period of considerable adjustment. In 1943, when farmers, loggers, and industrialists were being urged to produce in Herculean proportions to boost the war effort, the first contingents of enemy soldiers arrived at the railroad depots of Colorado, Utah, Nebraska, Oklahoma, Arkansas, and Tennessee. The sight of these foreign invaders was not welcomed by American country-folk. The media had painted the German soldier as a rapacious monster, and the thought of such creatures escaping and rampaging across the landscape produced a wave of alarm that persisted throughout the second and third years of the war. As it happened, though escapes occurred with monotonous frequency, no raping or pillaging ever took place, and after the Normandy invasions, when most of America's manpower had become engaged in the thrust toward the enemy heartland, the flood of POW's provided the perfect solution to the inevitable labour famine.

German prisoners were channelled into lumber production, crop harvesting, and road building. Escapes became less regular. Security grew more lax. POWs were often allowed to wander freely in the surrounding towns and villages. There was even a secret Government proposal to form a German Volunteer Corps to fight the Japanese. Rural Americans began to realise that the individual German was not the savage beast they had been led to suppose, and though actual friendships were few and far-between, the sight of Nazi uniforms, with yellow diamonds sewn on their backs, became commonplace in the streets of small-town America.

For some reason, however, in Cannesetego County, Louisiana, this sense of acceptance took longer to establish. The prison camp on the flats was regarded at best as an eyesore, at worst as a dastardly plot by the damned politicans in Washington to Germanise whole tracts of the American countryside, beginning with the areas which had done least to elect them into their dubious seats of office. But by the spring of 1945, after much fraternisation between prisoners and local inhabitants, a fragile peace had ensued, a peace often threatened by the most illogical incidents, and sometimes by the kind of misunderstandings that are bound to arise between two peoples who share no common language, customs, or culture. As the Labour Programme moved into full swing, individual farmers and those members of the community who could prove they had a reasonable need were allowed to submit requests for the use of German labour. Inevitably this system was often abused.

Eli Glanton, who ran a smallholding on Point Angouleme, was allocated one day a Grenadier corporal by the name of Wilmsdorf to help him clear timber from his bottomland so that he could extend his ploughing the following spring. As events proved, however, Glanton wanted Wilmsdorf to run the whisky still he kept hidden in the swamp, for with his three sons taken by the draft, Cannesetego County had suffered its worst drought of any year since Prohibition. Wilmsdorf himself, always fond of a tipple, regarded this unasked-for chore as a divine labour of love, and all might have gone well had he not, three weeks later, been rushed to the County Hospital suffering from malnutrition, having existed for the past twenty days on virtually nothing except Eli Glanton's moonshine. The police immediately prosecuted Glanton, who observed huffily in court that it was no wonder these damned squareheads were losing the war when they had no stomach for good drinking whisky which had sustained him and his three sons for the past twenty years.

It was this kind of incident that strained relations between Cannesetego's residents and the camp authorities, and that led to innumerable nightmares on the part of Colonel Walter Glusky, who had the delicate job of explaining things to both the local populace and to the authorities in Washington, D.C. No matter how hard he tried to be conciliatory and diplomatic, crisis flashpoints continued to flare with the speed and insistency of an Independence Day firecracker. Perhaps the greatest threat to Glusky's peace of mind lay in the weekly picture show. There was no movie house as such in Cannesetego County, but each Thursday a travelling showman came into town and set up his equipment in a classroom at the local school. No POWs were allowed off-limits after sundown, but after much prompting by the War Department, Glusky agreed to allow prisoners to be taken by coach each week to watch the show with the local inhabitants. The Germans sat in the last three rows, and as a rule the evenings passed without incident, but to the consternation and fury of the American audience, whenever the programme included a war film, the Germans insisted on cheering their own side with lusty exuberance. 'It was not as though they were booing the Allies,' Colonel Glusky pointed out to the delegation from the Citizens' Committee, 'they were simply responding to the sight of their fellow countrymen with the kind of patriotic enthusiasm any true American should be able to appreciate.' But as the cheering went on, American chagrin deepened, and on those evenings when World War Two was being fought on the screen, Colonel Glusky was uncomfortably aware that it might erupt at any second into the confines of Cannesetego County schoolhouse.

It was Jacob Kelner who finally hit upon the solution. On the night they were showing Spencer Tracy in *The Seventh Cross*, he sat with his back to the screen, a loaded shotgun resting across his knees, his cold grey eyes watching the rows of German faces, daring them to launch into their customary applause. Not a sound disturbed the cloistered stillness. The Germans behaved impeccably, and thereafter, with Jacob Kelner riding shotgun, an uneasy peace settled over the makeshift picture house, and over the residents, willing or otherwise, of Louisiana's Cannesetego County.

There was, however, no peace for the men whose job it was to keep the prison functioning, and it was into this complex web of tension and absurdity that Tully and his comrades found themselves delivered in the first week of March, the last year of the war.

The mess-hall was crowded at six o'clock in the evening. Above the long lines of tables rose the clamour of conversation interspersed with the clanking of cutlery and the scraping of wooden stools.

Tully stood with his dinner tray, looking for a place to sit. After two days, he had still not grown used to the nightly circus in the chow-hut. It was like eating in the middle of Times Square, he thought, and he wondered if any race in the world were as vociferous as the Germans.

He felt his heart leap as he spotted a thickset figure in a faded uniform ploughing through a plate of meatloaf and scrambled eggs. The man's hair was trimmed short and brushed straight back from the forehead, and a livid scar ran diagonally from below his left eye to the corner of his jaw. There was a pleasing pugnacity about his features; he looked aggressive, a man who could make trouble, but he carried also an air of humour and warmth. He was older than he'd looked in Reiser's photographs, but there was no mistaking his identity. The man was Otto Graebner.

Tully felt his senses tensing. It was the perfect moment to make contact. What could be more natural than a casual discussion over the dinner-table?

Still clutching his tray, he edged between the long rows of seated figures to where the German was sitting. 'This place taken?' he asked.

Graebner shook his head.

Tully flopped into the vacant chair and began to unload the contents of his tray. He kept his voice light and casual. 'Is it always like this in the evening?'

Graebner's lips twisted into a grin. He speared a piece of bread with his fork and popped it into his mouth. His eyes, Tully noticed, were light grey and startlingly distinctive.

'New here?' Graebner asked.

'Got in two nights ago.'

'Well, you'll get used to it. They're always a bit boisterous when the day's work is done.'

'You sound like an old hand. How long have you been in Cannesetego?'

'Close on a month.'

'Jesus, how do you stand it?'

Graebner looked amused. 'It's a matter of adaptation,' he said. 'You can hammer your head against the wall until your brains drop out, or you can play it their way. Not much sense tearing your guts to shreds over something you can't change.'

'Never thought of running off?'

Though a couple of inches shorter than Tully, the sheer bulk of Graebner's chest and shoulders conveyed the impression of immense size. His throat was corded, and a cluster of dark hair nestled at the vee of his shirtfront. It was not so much his stature that disconcerted Tully, however, as the penetrating sharpness of his eyes. They were the focal point of his entire face.

Suddenly Graebner laughed out loud.

'What's so funny?' Tully demanded, injecting a note of chagrin into his voice.

Graebner shook his head, still chuckling. 'Everybody who comes to Cannesetego thinks the same thing. First chance they get, they'll run for cover.'

'You think it can't be done?'

'Escape? Sure. Escaping from Cannesetego, that's nothing. Staying free is something else again. To reach the highway to the north, you've got to get through the swamp. That's Cajun country. Those Cajuns get a bounty on every prisoner they turn in, dead or alive, and they know that swamp like their own backyard. Even if you did make it—and God knows, your chances are lower than a snowball in hell's, since there's only one road—where would you go? Mexico, maybe? You'd never get there. They'd pick you up long before you reached the border and slam you right back in the pig-pen.'

'Nobody's had the guts to try it?'

'Oh, they break out from time to time. Nobody's managed to stay out though.'

'I'll stay,' said Tully.

'You're pretty damned sure of yourself for a new boy.'

'Not "sure". I'm desperate. I'll never stick it here.'

'Everybody feels like that for the first week or so. Once you get the hang of things, you'll find there are places a damn sight worse than Cannesetego, believe me.'

'Never.'

Graebner studied him. 'Where you from, soldier?'

'Berlin.'

'Well, you ought to feel grateful. Back home, you'd have the kindly attentions of the RAF to worry about. Let me give you a word of advice. Settle down, relax. The war can't go on forever.'

Tully shook his head. 'You don't understand. It's not just the war, it's something else. My wife.'

'She'll be okay.'

'That's not what I mean. It's . . . well, she was always

kind of physical by nature, and I'm afraid if I'm away long enough, sooner or later she might . . .'

He let his voice trail away. He was subtly and deliberately flattering Graebner by offering a personal intimacy.

Graebner lit a cigarette and sat back in his chair.

'Concentrate on survival,' he advised. 'You can sort out your emotional problems when the fighting's over.'

'That's easier said than done.'

'You'd be surprised how easy it can be. The worst things at Cannesetego are boredom and lack of privacy. There's not a hell of a lot you can do about the latter, but the first is easy to fix. See Wilmsdorf over there? He fills in his time drawing up crossword puzzles. He sells them for canteen coupons. Not a lucrative pastime, but it helps to keep him sane. Hochaus is busy building a model of the Graf Spee. He's been on with it for nearly a year now. By the time it's finished, it should be a work of art, except that he's always finding new features he wants to add. Anything to keep his hands and mind occupied. I do Chinese equations. Work them out in my head all day long. Did you know the Chinese are the most patient race on earth?'

'You're a strange character,' Tully said.

'How's that?'

'You talk like somebody with education. You're not like an infantryman at all. What are you, a Bolshevik?'

Graebner thrust back his plate and laughed out loud.

'It's time we had somebody here with a sense of humour,' he cried.

He stuck out his hand. 'My name's Franz Mohr.'

'Karl Raderecht,' Tully murmured, shaking it warmly.

'Well, take my word, you'll find it's not such a bad life here once you settle in. If you get into any kind of trouble, come and talk to me. I'll see what I can do.'

'Thanks,' Tully said, smiling. 'I'll remember that.'

Tully felt good as he left the mess-hall. He'd passed the interrogation test, and made contact with Graebner. Not a bad start in only two days.

The sky looked heavy under the setting sun. A faint drizzle

had begun to fall, and the fenceposts were glistening in the twilight.

Tully saw Scheller and Eyke strolling towards him across the compound. Scheller and Eyke were two of Strahle's most trusted lieutenants. They were big men both, with wide girths and solid hips. They reminded Tully of the cartoon Nazis he'd seen in newspapers before the war.

Tully had forgotten Strahle in the confusion of the past two days. Now the memory of Strahle's smile and that last lingering promise brought a chill to his chest.

Scheller was smiling. 'Strahle wants to see you,' he said.

'What about?' Tully demanded.

Scheller's smile broadened. Moisture dripped from his cap peak and his shoulders were stained dark from the evening rain. In the sultry air, a faint curtain of steam rose above his shirt collar. 'When Strahle summons, you don't ask questions,' he said.

They crossed the compound through the drizzle, Tully walking slowly, the Germans flanking him on either side. At the door of Hut 18, Eyke knocked twice and ushered Tully across the threshold. Unlike the other huts, number eighteen had been divided into separate rooms with clapboard partitions. In a doorway at the head of the corridor stood Strahle. Tully stared at him in astonishment. Strahle was dressed in pink pajamas, a frilly house-robe, and pince-nez spectacles. His face was powdered, his lips rouged, and a pair of pearl earrings dangled from his ear-lobes. He was smoking a cigarette and leaning provocatively against the doorjamb. He smiled when he saw Tully.

'Good of you to come,' he said.

'What is this, Halloween?' Tully asked dryly.

Strahle pouted and moved aside to let him in. The room was small but comfortable. On a mahogany cabinet stood a small vase filled with flowers, and a photograph of the Führer. A massive eagle had been painted on the wall above, with swastikas inscribed on both wings. The bed had been tucked discreetly in the corner, and was not the standard QM-issue but a full-sized double with a spring mattress and brass rails at either end.

'How d'you like it?' Strahle asked, watching Tully closely.

'Not bad.'

'Not bad? It's the finest room in camp.'

'Okay, I'm impressed. How did you pull it off?'

Strahle chuckled. 'My dear Raderecht, I learned a long time ago you can do anything in the world if you use your head. The guards here are more than amenable as long as no-one challenges their authority. Colonel Glusky likes order in his camp. I supply it. It's that simple.'

'Even when it means disabling our own side?'

Strahle looked surprised. 'What are you talking about?' he asked.

'Corporal Steiner,' said Tully.

Strahle delicately tapped ash from his cigarette. 'Steiner was the lowest form of human existence,' he said. 'In Germany, he would have been put up against a wall and shot. I thought we displayed remarkable restraint.'

He eased an armchair up to the coffee-table. 'Sit down,' he murmured, 'I'll get you some wine. It's Californian, I'm afraid, but not at all bad. We have to make *some* allowances for the war.'

He opened the cabinet and took out a bottle of wine with two glasses. Placing one glass in front of Tully, the other in front of himself, he filled them both and recorked the bottle. 'How d'you think you'll like Cannesetego?' he asked.

'I've hardly had a chance to find out yet.'

'You'll soon settle in. Life can be very agreeable here, if you're prepared to compromise. Give and take, that's the secret. I discover to my surprise I quite like the Americans. They're a trifle juvenile, but eminently corruptible.'

He winked. 'Never trust a man who can't be corrupted,' he added.

He pushed a box across the table and opened the lid.

'Chocolates?' he asked.

Tully shook his head. Strahle took one himself and bit into it, holding it delicately between thumb and forefinger. 'They're my greatest weakness,' he admitted. 'I used to eat them by the boxful back home. Nobody understood why I didn't get fat. A question of metabolism, I suppose. Some people are lucky. I stay the same weight month in, month out.'

Tully sat silently in his chair. He felt like a man faced with a dangerous snake.

'I was most impressed by you on Sunday,' Strahle said, 'the way you answered the questions, calmly, authoritatively. You didn't panic like some of your companions. It was almost as if . . . well, it was almost as' if you'd swotted up beforehand. I like a man who knows how to control himself.'

'It wasn't easy,' Tully admitted.

'I know. Nobody likes being cross-examined. But you are a remarkably self-contained fellow, Raderecht. You have a certain . . . sensitivity. That's a word most of the slobs here can't even spell. You've no idea how dreary it gets mixing with clods like Scheller and Eyke. They have their uses, I'd be the first to admit, but they're tanks, both of them. There's nothing inside. No brains. No emotions. If they ever had an original thought in their lives, it probably stemmed from between their legs.'

The powder on Strahle's face had gathered in the creases at the sides of his eyes and his lipstick was smudged. He looked like a clown from some absurd circus.

'Why did you bring me here?' Tully asked bluntly.

'Bring?' Strahle raised his eyebrows. 'I didn't bring you, I invited you.'

'Why?'

'I was impressed, that's all. You struck me as a man who knew his own mind, and I am starved for intelligent company.'

'You puzzle me, Strahle.'

'In what way?'

'Of all the men in this camp, why are you the top dog? How do you control them, the Schellers and the Eykes? It can't be physical strength. You're a fit-looking specimen, I admit, but Scheller and Eyke are big enough to tear you limb from limb. It can't be money, because nobody's got any. And it can't be rank, because even as sergeant you're not the senior NCO. So what is it, Strahle? What makes you so bloody important?'

Strahle chuckled. 'I knew I was right about you, Raderecht. You *are* different.'

He rose to his feet and strolled to the window, drawing back the curtain to peer at the rain. His thin frame looked boyish inside the frilly housecoat. One of his earrings came loose and dropped to the floor with a tiny rattle, but Strahle ignored it.

'I'll let you in on a little secret,' he said, 'something I learned a long time ago. Nobody's quite what they seem. All of us, every last one, are living a lie. We build up masks so nobody will see what we're like inside. But the crazy thing is, because we know how fragile our own masks are, we're prepared to accept other people's at face value. It's a kind of unwritten law of survival. But the mask a man hides behind will tell you more about what's going on inside his mind than he even knows himself. You can discover everything, his motivations, his hopes, his deepest fears. Once you know what he's afraid of, you can control him totally. I surround myself with men I can control. The ones I can't, I smash.'

'And where did you learn this . . . worthy philosophy?'

'Where I grew up. On the Hamburg docks.'

Tully frowned. 'I thought . . .'

'What?'

'I thought you were from an aristocratic family.'

Strahle turned, smiling. 'Who told you that?'

'It's the general word around camp.'

'My God!' Strahle said with a laugh.

'You mean it isn't true?'

'Of course it isn't true. My father was a stevedore. As far back as I can remember, I've hated the aristocracy and everything they stand for.'

He moved to the table to pick up his cigarette. 'Mind you,' he added, 'I've never been a communist. Some of my friends tried to get a union going in the early days. I refused to join. They couldn't understand that although I hated the moneyed classes as much as they did, I was perfectly happy with the system. I wasn't out to save the whole damned world. Only myself.'

He inhaled in silence for a moment, then pulled out the chair with his foot and sat down. 'I recognised there are ways and means of getting the things you want, if you're single-minded and determined enough. I went to Heidelberg University. It wasn't easy. I had to pay my way, and God knows I was no scholar. But I took them on at their own game, those bastards who looked down on me. I learned to be a gentleman the hard way.'

'And the duelling?'

Strahle seemed surprised. 'You know about the duelling?'

Tully nodded at his seamed face. 'It's pretty obvious, even to a yokel like me.'

Strahle touched his scars with his fingertips. 'I discovered I had an aptitude for swordplay, that's all. I fought sixteen duels at university.'

'Wasn't that a bit immoral for a loyal Nazi?'

Strahle sighed. 'I never understood why the Führer banned the practice,' he admitted. 'They were affairs of honour. We didn't actually kill each other. You nicked your opponent's face and the first to draw blood won. Properly handled, duelling is the perfect way for men of refinement to settle their differences.'

'And for you to impose your will on others,' Tully added quietly.

Strahle stared at him, and his eyes lost some of their warmth. 'You're an uncomfortably perceptive man, Raderecht,' he said. 'Do you realise that in a few short minutes I've told you more about myself than I've told anyone in my entire life?'

Tully didn't answer.

'Are you married?' Strahle asked.

'Yes.'

'Idiot. A man who knows his own mind doesn't need women.'

'You disapprove of the feminine sex?'

'They always were—they always will be—inferior. The most important thing in life is friendship, real friendship. That's something no woman could ever understand.'

'I take it you're talking about friendship of the spiritual kind?'

'Well, I'm not averse to fleshly pleasures too. But women cheapen that somehow. They destroy a man's identity. There's not much to be said about being cooped up in this miserable craphole, but at least we've no females to put up with.'

'I feel kind of sad about that,' admitted Tully.

'Then you're a fool. True affection shouldn't follow your basest instincts. When you feel something for another person, it should be a divine thing. Do you know the greatest fighting force in history?'

'The Wehrmacht?'

Strahle smiled weakly. 'Not the Wehrmacht. The Spartans. The reason? They seldom bothered with the opposite sex. They were utterly self-sufficient.'

'I guess that's why you don't see too many Spartans around these days.'

Strahle finished his drink. He was sweating slightly, and the moisture had left feathery streaks through the powder on his face. With one earring missing and the other still intact, his head looked curiously lopsided.

'I was never the type for a quick lay, Raderecht,' he whispered. 'With me, a relationship has to mean something. I want a sense of union, of compatibility. It's something I've never been able to find with a woman.'

Tully was silent. Suddenly, Strahle reached out and seized his hand on the tabletop. The muscles contracted through Tully's entire body.

'I want you to think of me as your friend,' Strahle muttered, 'someone you can turn to, unburden to.'

'Let me go,' Tully snapped.

Strahle didn't release his grip. His cheeks seemed to sag against his skull and his eyes filled with a disconcerting intensity. 'Don't look so fierce, Raderecht. There's nothing shameful in two people caring for each other.'

Tully spoke slowly. 'Strahle, leave go of my hand.'

Strahle's mouth looked slack. His hair lay plastered against the shiny dome of his forehead. 'I could call in Scheller and Eyke,' he hissed, 'but I'm a sensitive man and I prefer compliance to brute force.'

Without hesitation, Tully turned the hand beneath his and cracked it down on the table edge. There was a sharp clunk as bone and flesh collided with wood, and Strahle screamed in pain. He leapt to his feet, tucking the injured member beneath his armpit.

'You damn near broke my wrist,' he shouted.

'Be thankful it wasn't your neck,' Tully snapped. 'Don't ever touch me like that again.'

Strahle nursed his hurt, his eyes glittering with anger.

'I was wrong about you, Raderecht. I took you for a man of sensitivity. Now I find you're as stupid as all the rest.'

'I'm not built your way,' Tully said, 'and nothing you can say or do is going to change that.'

'You ignorant fool. You think you can treat me like a stableboy? I'll make you sorry for what you've just done. I'll make you wish to God you'd never been born.'

Tully glared at him, filled with an irrepressible anger. Then the feeling passed and disgust took its place. 'You poor sick bastard,' he said quietly.

And without another word, he turned and walked out into the night.

8

The sun blazed down in a sickening barrage of heat. Among the trees, the men worked in silence, their bodies half-naked and glistening with sweat, their faces slack with the tyranny of fatigue.

The logging was carried out like a carefully-planned military operation; a portable steel mast known as a 'spar' was erected in the centre of a clearing and used to drag the felled timber out of the underbrush and load it onto massive transport trucks. The Germans worked in twenty-strong teams armed with single-bit axes and push-pull saws. They carved wedge-shaped undercuts into the tree-trunks to control the direction of fall, then followed up with back-cuts to bring the timber hurtling down. When the trees were felled the branches were trimmed off and the logs cross-cut to serviceable lengths, then metal cables were wrapped around their girths and they were hauled out to the loading bay.

In the shade of a twisted sycamore, two guards, carbines resting casually across their knees, watched the workgangs as they toiled. From time to time, the prisoners cast hopeful eyes in their direction, peering at the sun as it lazily traversed the sky, until at last one of the Americans stretched himself and blew a whistle to signal the start of the mid-morning break.

Sighing with relief, Tully moved into the shade, his nostrils clogged with sawdust. The buzz of insects filled his ears. He spotted Graebner sprawled in the brush, his massive body matted with hair. Tully had forgotten Graebner in his meeting with Strahle and the confusion of the past two days. Now he realised it was time to focus his mind on what he had come for.

He walked over and flopped down at the German's side. Graebner's skin flinched as a fly settled on his forehead then took off in search of a less complaining target. He wiped his face with a grubby handkerchief and spread it out in the sun to dry. Tiny salt flecks crusted his eyebrows and tough grey hair.

'Settling in okay?' he asked casually.

'I don't think I'll ever settle in,' Tully grunted.

'What's wrong?'

'It's okay for you, all brawn and muscle. This outdoor life is killing me.'

Graebner smiled with amusement. The gruelling pace of the morning had had no effect on him at all. He looked like a champion relaxing after a brisk warm-up. Again, Tully was uncomfortably aware of the strength that lay in those massive shoulders.

'Why don't you slow down a bit?' Graebner suggested. 'You go at everything like a bull in a china shop. In this sun, you've got to conserve your energy.'

'We ought to feel ashamed of ourselves anyhow,' Tully said. 'I mean, what we're doing is working like coolies to help the enemy war effort, right? Shouldn't we be sort of sabotaging a few things here and there?'

'You mean burn a couple of tree-trunks?' Graebner smiled. 'Think it'll make any difference to what's happening in Europe?'

Tully studied the thick-jowled, sabre-scarred face, the sharp eyes and solid neck. He reflected wryly that if Reiser had offered him any choice in the matter, he'd have given Graebner a very wide berth indeed.

'I can't figure you out at all,' he said.

'Then don't try. When somebody starts intruding on my privacy, it makes me nervous. No questions, agreed?'

'Just being friendly. In a place like this, a man needs all the friends he can get.'

'I heard you already turned down one friend.'

'Strahle?'

Graebner nodded. 'Word's out he's going to break you. It's all around camp. Some of the men are taking bets on your survival. I'm afraid your odds aren't too good.'

'Will he get me the way he got Steiner?'

'No. He'll have to box clever, you've done nothing wrong. Strahle's pretty powerful, but he's not God Almighty. He can only impose his law if you step out of line. However, his boys are experts at the waiting game. They know just how to apply pressure until the victim breaks. I have a hunch you've an unpleasant time ahead.'

'What would you do in my position?'

'Get him first,' Graebner said simply.

'How?'

'How the hell should I know? You're the target.'

Tully hesitated. 'Remember what you said in the mess-hall? How if I got into trouble, you'd see what you could do?'

'I remember.'

'Well, I'm in trouble now. Will you help?'

Graebner chuckled humourlessly. 'I like you, Raderecht, but Strahle's no enemy of mine and I don't intend to commit suicide by going up against the bastard. If it was something else, maybe, but not this. It's up to every man to survive the best way he can.'

He closed his eyes and Tully was filled with deep foreboding. Danger he could face with equanimity, he'd proved that, but the loneliness of his terror was what made it so hard to handle.

A guard came strolling along the line of resting men, his carbine slung across his shoulder. 'Anybody here speak American?' he demanded.

On an impulse, Tully raised his hand. The American shifted his chewing gum to the other side of his mouth. 'See that house up yonder? They're moving a piano inside. Get along there and lend a hand, soldier.'

Tully climbed wearily to his feet. He walked out of the woods, the sun blistering hot on his shoulders. Forget Strahle for the moment, he told himself. He can't do anything openly, so concentrate on Graebner. He's the ace in this deck.

He felt dispirited about Graebner. Despite his approaches, he had failed to gain the German's confidence. He would have to think of something more devious, something more dramatic, to arouse his interest. He needed subtlety. He needed subterfuge.

He would have to use his head.

Etta was standing with the deliveryman when the German soldier arrived. He was bare to the waist, his thick hair tucked beneath a battered forage cap. His skin glistened from the rigours of the morning, and there were traces of freckles on his narrow cheeks. 'Need some help here?' he asked in English.

'It's the piano,' she said. 'It's very heavy, I'm afraid.'

The German wiped his mouth with one hand. He looked at the bulky instrument perched on the truck tailboard, one end protruding precariously. 'Okay,' he said, nodding to the driver, 'you take it from the other side. Move when I give the word.'

There was something curiously decisive in the German's manner. Etta liked men who knew how to take control. Clinton had been like that.

She watched them wrestle the giant piano from the truck rear, and guided them gingerly through the open doorway.

'Please be careful,' she said. 'It's awfully fragile.'

'Lady,' the deliveryman grunted, 'it weighs a ton.'

'Put it against the wall. I've moved the furniture.'

Hissing and grunting, they settled the piano in the spot she had chosen and straightened gratefully, their faces flushed with effort.

'That's just fine,' she smiled. 'Thank you.'

Mopping his cheeks with a handkerchief, the deliveryman followed her into the kitchen while she looked for her purse. He was small and middle-aged, his skin cratered from some ancient skin disease. Sweat droplets gathered on his nose-tip, and he flicked them idly off with one finger, studying her curiously.

'Don't you feel a little nervous living all the way up here?' he asked.

'Why?' she said, surprised.

'I mean with them Krauts across the road.'

'Oh, they're well-guarded, I imagine.'

The man sniffed. 'Lady, they're Nazi soldiers. I'd feel a damn sight happier if they were chained together in steel cages.'

She shrugged. 'Well, somebody has to help with the timberclearing. Most of the local men have been drafted into the army.'

'That's what I mean. What happens if that bunch busts loose? Who's going to track 'em down? The soldier boys in the field there? They're only kids.'

'I don't think the prisoners will try to escape. Where would they go? There's nothing here but swamp. They'd be picked up before they'd travelled ten miles.'

The deliveryman chuckled dryly as he stuffed the money she gave him into his shirt pocket. 'Lady, you're a lulu,' he said, and sauntered to the door.

She stood on the threshold and watched him drive off, trailing dust on the hot morning air. She felt sorry to see him go, for any human contact at all, no matter how flimsy, served as a salve to her loneliness.

A whistle screeched. Peering across the woods, Etta saw the POWs climbing wearily to their feet. Their rest-break was over. She envied them that, the chance to work, to bury oneself in the insensibility of labour. With nothing to fill her days, the futility of her life seemed stronger than ever.

Suddenly she heard a soft murmur drifting on the air. She frowned. Someone was playing her piano.

It was music of a kind she'd never heard before, full of strangeness and isolation. She turned her head, afraid to move in case she disturbed its momentum. It was beautiful, she thought.

The music swelled, lingering like the trace of some indefinable perfume, bringing alive her senses. Mesmerised, she turned and wandered into the parlour.

At the keyboard sat the German prisoner, his fingers dancing over the notes with a strange compulsive frenzy.

With a start, he became aware of her presence and stopped playing. She felt a sense of loss as the music faded.

'Please go on,' she whispered.

The man looked uncertain, rising to his feet. 'I guess I shouldn't have done that,' he said. 'It's just that it's been so long . . .'

'I never heard anyone play so beautifully.'

He smiled. His smile illuminated the narrow face. He was not a handsome man, not in the obvious sense, but something within her responded to his lean cheeks and pale haunted eyes.

'It's what I do when I'm feeling bad,' he said. 'It makes me feel good again.'

'You mean you can't read music?'

'Oh sure. But basically, it's instinctive, I guess. Kind of runs in the family. My old man's the same way.'

'Have you ever played in public?'

'I'm not that kind of musician, ma'am. When I sit down at a piano, it's just a personal thing. I don't think I could play to order just to please a bunch of strangers.'

'You must. You have a rare gift. You've no right to keep it to yourself.'

The smile lingered at the corners of his mouth, and she thought how young he looked, how vulnerable. For God's sake, she told herself, he's an enemy soldier. Keep things in perspective.

She stepped to the piano and rested her forearms on its top.

'Where do you come from?' she asked.

'Berlin.'

'You speak American like a native.'

'I went to an American school. For children of the Embassy staff. My old man sometimes worked as a driver there, so it got to be kind of my second language.'

She smiled. 'You're not at all like I'd expected. I thought all Germans were something out of Frankenstein. Square heads and thick necks.'

He laughed. 'And I thought all Yanks wore cowboy hats and chewed gum.'

She liked him. He was interesting. Gentle and sensitive and appealing in a bony kind of way. She experienced a momentary urge she had thought long forgotten.

'What's your name?' she asked.

'Karl Raderecht,' he said.

'I'm Etta Richardson.'

'Is that "Mrs" Richardson, ma'am?'

'My husband was killed at Guadalcanal.'

'That's too bad.'

'What about you? Have you a family back home?'

'A wife and little boy.'

She felt her spirits drop. What did she expect? she thought. Of course he was married. What difference did it make anyhow? A complete stranger played a few random notes on the piano and she was ready to take leave of her senses. When it came to emotional stability, she was way beyond redemption.

The German fumbled in his hip pocket. Oh God no, don't tell me he's going to show me pictures of the woman.

For some reason, she couldn't bear that. His dutiful spouse. His Germanic offspring. She'd rather not acknowledge their existence.

'Would you like a drink?' she asked hastily.

'Not in the middle of the day.'

'Coffee, then?'

He hesitated. 'Sure, why not? I'm in no hurry to get back to work.'

She made the coffee in a daze. Something had happened to her she couldn't put a name to. Not physical, she thought. Well, not entirely. There was that too, all right, but there was something else besides. It was indefinable, that was the scary bit.

They sat at the table sipping coffee, and she watched him secretively. How sensitive his features looked beneath the sweat and grime.

He talked about music, not in any knowledgeable way, but with an inherent understanding that went beyond knowledge, and she listened in silence, shaken by emotions she scarcely knew how to control.

'Do you miss being home?' she asked.

He shook his head. 'Berlin's no place to be right now with the air-raids and all.'

'What did you do before the war?'

'I worked for my father. He ran a transport service. Mostly limousines. I used to drive wedding guests, that kind of thing. It only lasted a summer though. I'd barely quit school when I got drafted.'

'Is your father still alive?'

'He was when I left.'

'What will you do when the fighting's over?'

'Go home, I guess. Pick up the pieces again.'

'Back to driving?'

'Maybe. I hadn't planned that far.'

'You ought to be a musician.'

He smiled thinly. 'I don't think there'll be much call for music in Germany when it's finally over.'

'Then don't go back,' she said. 'You could apply for an immigrant's visa. A man with your talent would go far in America.'

He stared at her in surprise. 'That's a funny idea,' he said.

She felt suddenly embarrassed. What on earth was she talking about? What this man did after the war was his concern, not hers.

She tried to change the subject. 'Is it bad at the camp?'

'It's okay. You get used to being shut up after a while.'

'Do they feed you enough?'

'Sure. It's not the food. I guess mostly it's the lack of privacy. There's no place to go to be alone.'

She hesitated as a startling thought occurred to her.

'Why don't you come here?' she suggested.

He frowned. 'Here?'

'Wouldn't you like that? You could play the piano.'

He shook his head. 'They'd never allow it.'

'You haven't asked.'

'I'm a prisoner-of-war.'

'And a brilliant musician who needs to practice.'

He sat staring at her. 'You're crazy.'

'Supposing I could arrange things with the authorities?'

Had the music affected her senses? she wondered. Had loneliness at last unhinged her? Yet she sat in silence, willing him to say 'yes.'

'You think you could?' he whispered.

She rose from the table, hiding her confusion in a bustle of movement. She knew only one thing, she had to see him again. Though her cheeks were burning, she kept her face straight, her eyes calm and untroubled, as she gathered the cups together and stacked them on the service tray. 'I'll see what I can do,' she promised.

9

Colonel Walter Glusky sat in his office and thoughtfully studied the woman in front of him. She was slim and exceedingly pretty, with dark hair, brown eyes, and a strange little smile that made the colonel's stomach twitch each time it flitted across her fascinating mouth. Her clothes looked stylish and well-cut. She wore silk stockings too, an improvement on the usual schmuks who inhabited the area. There was, however, something about her he found faintly disturbing; a hint of strength, a streak of wilful determination.

He leaned forward, resting his arms on the desktop. 'This is a most unusual request, Mrs Richardson,' he said.

'I realise that, Colonel.'

'I mean, these men are officially prisoners-of-war. To be truthful, I don't know how the War Department would feel about any further fraternising with US citizens.'

She smiled. 'Fraternising is hardly the word, Colonel. I was thinking of a piano recital, not a cocktail party. It would certainly be an enormous boost to our musical appreciation class.'

Colonel Glusky glanced at his aide, Captain Farrington. Something about this woman unnerved him. He had the impression that once she made up her mind, nothing in the world would stand in her way.

'You realise that under the terms of the Labour Programme, this man is required to help with the local logging operations?'

'We could hold it on a Sunday,' she answered promptly, 'or one evening during the week. The prisoners never work after dinner, do they?'

Colonel Glusky sighed. 'Mrs Richardson, you're a very persuasive young lady. But let me explain something. I have nearly two hundred and fifty inmates in that compound out there, and barely thirty troops to keep them under control. Quite honestly, I haven't the men to spare as escort.'

'That's understood, Colonel. That's why I'm offering myself as a guarantor for Raderecht's conduct.'

'You!' he exclaimed in surprise. Then he chuckled. 'With the greatest respect, young lady, would you mind telling me what you'd do if Raderecht took it into his head to run for the border?'

'Colonel Glusky, you know perfectly well that any one of these men could take off any time he felt like it. They're inadequately guarded and during the day they're spread across several miles of countryside. It's not the fear of your soldiers that keeps them in line. It's the knowledge that there's nowhere to run to.'

Glusky glared at her. The defectiveness of his command was ever-present in his mind, but he preferred not to discuss it with the surrounding populace.

He stared up at Captain Farrington. 'Who is this guy, anyhow?' he demanded.

'One of the new intake, sir.'

'Not even a trustee? you're asking me to take one hell of a chance, young lady.'

'I don't see why,' she replied smoothly. 'The prisoner has given me his word.'

The colonel pursed his lips. 'When would this concert take place?'

'I was thinking about the end of next month.'

'One night only?'

She hesitated. 'Well, not exactly, Colonel,' she murmured. 'You can't expect Raderecht to step on a stage and play before nearly a hundred people without getting some practice first. And you have no piano on camp.'

'Of course we have a piano,' Colonel Glusky exclaimed.

He looked at his captain for support. 'We must have a piano.'

Captain Farrington shook his head. 'No, sir,' he said. 'We've had one on order for months, but there's some kind of snarl-up with Services and Supply Branch.'

Etta smiled. 'However, that's not a problem, Colonel. May I suggest Mr Raderecht be allowed to come to my house for a couple of hours each evening when his work in the woods is finished? My neighbour has agreed to lend me his car so I can deliver your prisoner back to the camp personally, and I will take full responsibility for his conduct and behaviour.'

Glusky stared at her in silence. She had the whole damn thing figured. Piano lessons for the goddamned Krauts. She'd be offering coffee and muffins next.

'Mrs Richardson, are you out of your mind?'

'I don't think so, Colonel. My request may seem a little unusual, but it's certainly not unreasonable. Remember this war can't last forever. The real problems will come after peace has been declared. Then we're all going to have to do a little readjusting. What I'm asking is a chance to create a cultural liaison between one of your prisoners and the people of this county.'

Colonel Glusky sat back in his chair. There was something irritatingly logical about her argument. He could see no way to refute it. The colonel liked to keep things on an even keel. A peaceful life, that was what he longed for. If he was destined to sit out the war in this miserable craphole, he preferred to do it without complications. He hated being confronted with a request he could see no grounds for refusing.

He looked again at Captain Farrington. The captain gazed back stonily. Clearly there would be no help from that quarter. Colonel Glusky sighed.

'Mrs Richardson,' he said, 'I hope to God you never join the army. I have a hunch that if you put your mind to it, you'd have us all fighting for the other side within a week.'

Next morning, Etta rose bright and early. She wanted everything to be just right. She felt excited and expectant, as if never before in her life had she been so aware, never had her emotions been so keen, her senses so alert. Even the sights, sounds, and smells of her familiar household filled her with a curious elation.

The memory of the German disturbed and stimulated her. She recalled with startling vividness the way he'd held his chin, the stoop of his shoulders as he'd perched at the piano, the sight of his fingers dancing over the keyboard. She scarcely knew what it was she wanted; only to have him near, she thought, to look again at his slender face and the dark shadows on his narrow wrists, to feel his presence.

At noon, she borrowed her neighbour's jeep and drove into Lomstoun to do some shopping. She bought vegetables, lamb, pinta beans, and a bottle of red wine. She'd contemplated doing broiled oysters with cream and cheese, one of her specialties, but in the end she decided on Gormeh Sabzi, a spicy Middle Eastern stew. On impulse, she bought two candlesticks, then drove back to the house and set to work preparing the evening meal. Etta had always enjoyed cooking. Her father claimed she had an inherent ability that went beyond the vision of the normal chef. It was one of the few kind things her father had ever said to her, and though she had loathed him for his vulgarity, despised him for the hateful way he had treated her mother, and feared him for those moments when, drunk, he had beaten her mercilessly for misdemeanors real or imagined, nevertheless she'd never been able to suppress a quiet sense of pride at the way he'd responded to her cooking. She wondered if the German would feel the same. She was, in a sense, showing off, she realised. She wanted him to see her in the best possible light. And besides, it was pleasant to cook for somebody for a change. It was no fun sitting alone at the dinner table night after night.

So engrossed did she become in peeling, chopping, and boiling that before long the afternoon had lengthened into evening, and leaving the pot gently simmering, she went upstairs to bathe. She undressed and stood in front of the looking-glass, studying herself critically. She was hardly a beauty, she thought, but men did seem to find her attractive. She saw them watching her out of furtive eyes. Even the colonel, though he'd tried to maintain an air of dignity, had cast sneaky glances at her as she'd sat in his office. She understood men like the colonel. What worried Etta was the thought that the German might be different. He was sensitive, complex. He wouldn't be attracted by the obvious. She would have to tread carefully. You couldn't rush things with a man like that.

Suddenly, she was furious with herself. What on earth was she playing at? She was not some dewy-eyed virgin straight out of high school. The man belonged to another society, a different race. He was the enemy, she had to keep that in mind. In no way could this be anything more than a pleasant interlude, a passing moment snatched from the rigours of war.

Towards five, she heard the sound of the trucks arriving to carry the men back to camp and felt herself grow tense. Any moment now, she thought. Then the front door rattled as someone hammered on it with a fist, and she started. My God! he was here.

She glanced at herself in the looking-glass, straightening her hair. She looked fine. A little pale, but not so anyone would notice.

She went downstairs and opened the door. Raderecht was standing on the porch, his face and shirt covered with dirt. There were dark sweat stains under his armpits and across his chest. She smiled gently to herself. He was hardly the ideal dinner companion.

'Hello,' he said awkwardly.

She stepped back to let him in. He took off his cap and ducked across the threshold. 'How are you?' he asked.

'Very well. Thank you.'

'Good.'

He nodded his head a couple of times, standing in the centre of the floor. Then he cleared his throat and peered around. He seemed to be looking at the room for the first time. She became aware that her heart was thumping.

'I was afraid you wouldn't come,' she said.

'Why's that?'

'I don't know. I just thought you wouldn't, that's all.'

She took his cap and hung it on a hook. She felt tense and uncertain, and needed to do things with her hands.

He was whistling soundlessly under his breath as he moved to the piano and ran one finger along its keyboard. 'They said you'd fixed a concert.'

'No.'

He looked surprised. 'You haven't fixed a concert?'

'It was a lie,' she whispered, 'to get you here.'

'Oh.'

He lifted his hand from the keyboard and drummed his fingers on the piano lid. Then, with a quick awkward motion, he slipped both hands into his trouser pockets. 'I know it sounds silly,' he said, 'but I'm feeling kind of nervous.'

'Me too,' she admitted.

With a smile, she added: 'Would you like to go upstairs and clean up?'

He looked down at his soiled workclothes. 'I guess I'm not fit company for a hound-dog in this mess.'

'Well, the water's hot, and I left some towels out.'

She hesitated. 'There's something else. I bought you some clothes. A pair of jeans and a clean shirt. You can leave them here and change when you come over.'

He frowned. 'Why did you do that?'

'I thought you might like to get out of that prisoner's uniform. Wouldn't you like that?'

'I suppose so.'

'I had to guess at your size, so let's hope they fit.'

His frown deepened. He was staring through the doorway into the kitchen, and she watched his face, holding her breath. She had prepared the table carefully, setting out the wine and the candles for maximum effect.

He turned to her, puzzled. 'What is this?'

She said lightly: 'I . . . I thought since this is your first night, we might leave the piano until later. I'm sure the food at the camp is very good, but it must get tiresome after a while.'

'That's . . . quite a table,' he grunted.

'Aren't you hungry?'

His face looked uncomfortably serious. The awful thought occurred to her that for some reason he might be offended. Then suddenly he grinned, and the tension was over.

'I'm ravenous,' he admitted.

'Get a move on then,' she ordered, her spirits lightening. 'Dinner will be served in twenty minutes.'

Despite the fact that she hadn't eaten all day, Etta barely nibbled at her food. Instead, she sat watching the German, fascinated. She had never seen anyone eat so voraciously, and if she felt mildly disappointed that his attention was riveted upon his plate rather than on her, she was enough of a perfectionist to experience a quiet sense of elation as she watched the Gormeh Sabzi swiftly disappear. He might be a little on the bony side, she reflected, but there was nothing wrong with his appetite.

Over coffee he began to relax, and she felt her own tension quickly disperse. He was comfortable to be with. Frank and pleasant. Not in the least pretentious. If he had designs upon her, other than friendly ones, she saw no sign of it. I was right, she thought. You're a nice man, Karl Raderecht.

She told him about her marriage and about Clinton's death, and he listened in silence, his face calm and thoughtful. She realised she had never talked so much or so intimately to anyone before. It was a curious experience. The German was a total stranger, yet she felt more at ease in his company than with any man in her life.

'Would you marry again?' he asked.

She shrugged. 'I was sorry at the time, dreadfully sorry, but Clinton was hardly a milestone in my life. I ought to feel ashamed of that, oughtn't I?'

'Not at all.'

'It's just that, well, I married him for no other reason than because it seemed the thing to do at the time. Also, I guess, it felt terribly romantic. He was training to be a pilot. He would go off to distant lands and exotic places. I never seriously believed he would actually get killed. That was where reality came creeping in. When the cable arrived, I felt nothing, absolutely nothing. I knew I ought to feel some sense of loss. Pain, grief, horror. But by then, I'd gotten so used to living without Clint, I couldn't even recall his features.'

'I don't think that's so surprising,' the German said.

'I've never stopped feeling guilty about it.'

'You were with him barely five weeks.'

'More like four,' she murmured.

'He must have seemed like a stranger.'

She stared down at her empty plate, filled with sudden uncertainty. She didn't want to ask the next question, but somehow or other she had to know.

'What about you?' she said. 'How long have you been married?'

'Three years,' he answered quietly, 'more or less.'

'And your little boy. How old is he?'

'He's two.'

'Did you . . . did you meet your wife while you were in the army?'

'No. We met at a place called Garmisch in the Bayerische Alps. She was working as a waitress in a café there.'

'Did you marry her right away?'

'Not immediately. We had to put it off for a bit when I got drafted.'

She tinkered with her coffee cup. She wanted to stop but something was pushing her on. She had to know the truth.

'Are you happy?' she asked softly.

'I don't know,' he admitted.

He eased back in his chair and looked at her, his eyes thoughtful. 'You said you lived with Clinton for less than five weeks. I can beat that. Forty-eight hours after we were married, they sent me to France. I haven't been home since.'

She looked at him, surprised. 'You've not seen your wife for nearly three years?'

He shook his head.

'She must . . . my God! She must seem like a stranger too.'

'Or like someone I've seen in a magazine someplace. What worries me is that I've changed.'

He looked down at his fingers toying with the wine glass.

'I'll let you in on a secret,' he said. 'Two days before the Allied invasion, they gave me a furlough. I went to the Riviera and spent a couple of weeks lounging in the sun. I couldn't face the thought of going home to somebody I didn't know.'

'Not even to see your child?'

'Not even for that.'

She was quiet for a moment. She could hear the clock ticking in the parlour. Somewhere outside, a car roared by. She was filled with an inexplicable sadness, like that which in childhood had haunted her on dark summer nights, and she felt her body begin to tremble with a long-deferred need.

'I wonder whether it all matters,' he said suddenly. 'I mean, in the context of history, who cares how many people die this year or next? What difference does it make if your husband comes back or my wife is a stranger? There's only the here and now. The past and the future don't exist.'

'I couldn't have put it better myself.'

'We're two of a kind, I think, you and me,' he said.

'Except that you're luckier.'

'How's that?'

'You have your music.'

He laughed shortly. 'You make it sound something special.'

'It *is* something special,' she insisted, and on an impulse she reached out and squeezed his wrist. The touch of his skin sent shock waves through her body.

'*You* are something special,' she said quietly. 'Very special indeed.'

Tully stood under the shower, letting the water sluice over his face and chest. It was good to feel clean again after the sweat and grime of the day. He lathered his hair with soap, washing the grit from his skull, humming softly as he thought about the young piano teacher. She was quite a girl, that one. Beautiful, there was absolutely no argument on that score. Beautiful the way Merle Oberon was beautiful, or Vivien Leigh. Well, not quite like that, but with the same cool, crazy elegance, that stunning facial symmetry. Her eyes were a knockout. He'd gotten hung-up on her eyes the first time he'd seen her, and next time he knew it hadn't been a lie—they were, undoubtedly, exquisite. She was not smart or intellectual or anything like that, but she wasn't dumb either, and she found him attractive, that was the crazy thing. After all, he wasn't exactly the nation's sweetheart. Good-looking women weren't in the habit of seeking his acquaintance. Goddammit, how he'd hated having to lie about his wife and kid. All that bullshit about going off to France after a forty-eight-hour honeymoon. He hoped to God she'd forgive him when the time came.

What the hell are you talking about, you dummy? he thought. You think she'll care about you once the war's over? The only men around here are over forty and under eighteen. When the competition hots up, you won't get to first base, you sad bastard, so best make the most of it while it lasts.

He turned his face to the faucet, closing his eyes as the water streamed down his brow. What he should be worrying about, concentrating all his energy on, was Graebner. He hadn't done too well with that bastard, he realised. Every time he tried to strengthen their relationship, the German froze him out cold. Not that the guy was openly hostile; he just wasn't friendly, that was all. And Tully couldn't push things without arousing his suspicions.

Still, he'd managed to keep him under observation, that much had been easy. As far as Tully could tell, Graebner had no special friends, and in fact spent most of his time writing letters to which no replies ever came. That was the crazy part. He just kept writing and nothing came back. Who was he trying to contact? Tully wondered. Someone within the United States? Well, whoever the hell it was, time was clearly running out. Graebner was growing agitated. You could see it in the way he moved, the tense way he held his head, the curt brusqueness with which he answered his name at morning roll call. One way or another he would have to make a move soon, and when he did, Tully was determined to be ready.

Willi Stroud hammered on the door.

'Hey, Karl,' he bellowed, 'what the hell are you doing in there? It's nearly time for chow.'

'I'll be out in a minute,' Tully yelled. 'Wait for me at the hut.'

He began to whistle as water bathed his glistening skin. His worrying about Graebner faded. He felt great, he realised. She'd done that. He'd felt good ever since he'd met her. For the first time in years, he was filled with hope for the future. Was that all it took, somebody caring? A girl who until a few days ago he hadn't known existed? Well, he wasn't about to question it, that was for sure. A woman like that, who clearly loved him, who actually cared for a miserable sadsack like J.A. Tully—dammit, it looked like things were going his way for a change.

He heard a movement on the other side of the door.

'You still there, Willi?' he bellowed.

There was no answer. Tully frowned. He hadn't been mistaken. Something had definitely scraped against the woodwork. He slid back the bolt and tried to push the door open. Nothing happened.

'What the hell?' he murmured.

Suddenly he noticed the water was getting hotter. Dense clouds of steam were beginning to gather in front of his face.

'Jesus Christ,' he gasped.

A tremor of fear passed through him as he realised it was impossible to switch the torrent off. The showers were controlled by a central dial on the wall outside. He hammered at the door, thrusting his shoulder against the panel in an attempt to force it open.

'Willi,' he shouted, 'for God's sake, Willi.'

But the roar of the spray drowned his voice.

His skin stung as the heat gathered in intensity, and he rammed his spine against the brickwork, trying to drive the door open with both feet. It wouldn't budge.

Hopelessly, he glanced upward. A metal grille covered the booth top, blocking his way. Strahle, he thought. It had to be Strahle, or one of his henchmen.

Christ, how could he have been so stupid?

Steam was building up, filling the confined space until he could scarcely see the door any longer. He gritted his teeth as the hissing jets seared his naked skin. He tried to block the spray with his hand, but the metal faucet was raging hot and he jerked back with a cry of pain. He had the sensation of being boiled alive, as if his hide had somehow peeled away, leaving his innermost organs naked to the scalding torrent. He heard a sound, thin and almost indiscernible, rising above the thunder of the water, and realised he was screaming.

Reaching up, he hooked his fingers through the metal grille and thrust his shoulders against the tiles, struggling to escape the full fury of the crippling downpour. For a few brief moments, he gained a blessed respite. Hanging there, his skull pressed hard against the bars above, his body missed the main force of the stream, though he knew that when his strength gave out, when he collapsed at last to the floor below, he would be helpless beneath its torrent.

He was able to see the conduit which fed the shower booths reaching away to the opposite wall. A desperate thought occurred to him. Could he break it in two? Could he burst the pipe and siphon off the water before it reached his cubicle? What he needed was leverage. Something sturdy to split the soldered joints. He tried each of the overhead bars in turn. Solid as rock. No joy that way.

He hammered on the shower head with the side of his fist. It shuddered under his blows. Not too secure, he thought. A good steady pressure with his arm might break it. But the metal was burning hot. The question was, could he stand the pain long enough to sever the seam? No other choice, he told himself grimly. It was either that, or boil like a clam.

Gasping at the air, he hooked one arm through the grille above, anchoring himself fast, then, seizing a second bar with his free hand he thrust his wrist against the pipe and pushed with all his might. Waves of pain lanced along his arm, exploding inside his skull. He felt the metal give slightly, but the seal held firm. He pushed again, stifling a scream, trying to shut off the agony of his tortured limb.

The pipe creaked, and scalding water spurted out of the loosening joint. Swallowing hard, he thrust with all his strength. The pipe bent dramatically, but held firm. Break, you bastard, break, he thought.

His forearm felt numb to the elbow, and his brain began to reel. His eye-sockets seemed puffed and unnatural. Tears ran down his cheeks at the sheer injustice of the situation. Four months behind enemy lines only to die in a stinking shower-room. And in the middle of his own country, too. It was a bitter irony. They'd probably call it an accident. Once again, Strahle would get away clean. The thought of those cold anaemic features filled Tully with a fury he hadn't known he possessed. He thrust outwards with the last shred of strength in his body and felt the pipe suddenly burst apart, the feed bending beneath his pressure till the water streamed through the grille and onto the floor outside.

Tully collapsed to the ground, his skin blazing. From somewhere far off, he heard a whistle blow loud and shrill. A voice muttered: 'Say, where the hell's this water coming from?'

Boots scraped on the concrete floor, then the door burst open and Tully felt himself being dragged clear by a pair of startled GIs.

'He's pinker'n a broiled shrimp,' one of them murmured.

'Is he alive?'

'I guess so.'

Tully felt a hand slapping his cheek. He opened his eyes. A pimpled face hung barely an inch from his own.

'What happened in here?' the American demanded.

Tully tried to speak, but nothing came.

'Hey Mitch, somebody jammed this booth with a metal bar,' the other voice said. 'Who'd do a thing like that?'

The first man shook his head worriedly. 'I don't like the way this guy's looking. We'd better get him to the sick bay quick.'

He reached down and hauled Tully to his feet. 'Grab a hold of my arm, buddy,' he said, hooking his grip around Tully's waist. 'If I was you, I'd start playing poker; you're the luckiest man alive today.'

The collecting of intelligence material is, by its very nature, often a confusing undertaking. The men who have the job of sifting through the reports and scraps of data sent in by agents in the field are, in a sense, attempting to fit together the pieces of a gigantic jigsaw puzzle. They have to decide not merely which fragments correspond with which, but what light, if any, each throws on the overall picture. Thus a radio message, indicating nothing more significant than that a spate of fresh oranges have appeared in the Berlin fruitstores could well mean that the Allied bombers in the Mediterranean have not been doing their job efficiently enough.

Of course, this is intelligence gathering at its most simple and primitive. The true role of an intelligence service is not merely to uncover the enemy's secrets, or even to conceal one's own, but also to deceive. By launching a series of sabotage raids on certain plants in Nazi-occupied Norway, the Allies managed to convince the Germans that the key to nuclear power lay in heavy water and not in the production of Uranium 235. This put the enemy on a false trail, and the Germans fell far behind in the field of atomic research, though proof of this was not uncovered until after the war.

Nevertheless, because of this complex web of deceit, the art of intelligence is not unlike a card game in which the slightest signs and body signals of one's opponent are observed and analysed, then fitted together to produce an assessment of what is happening inside his mind. The was the role of the R. and A., the Research and Analysis Branch of the OSS. As information arrived from agents behind enemy lines, it was sifted and appraised in a central control office to determine how it illuminated the grand design.

Throughout the months of February and March 1945, a series of seemingly unconnected incidents on the battlefronts of Europe produced in Washington (where the scent of victory was tantalisingly close) a feeling of vague unease. Out of these incidents, two common denominators arose. One was an irritatingly obscure phrase, SSG 300. The other was more ambiguous; it lay not so much in the information itself as in the attitude of the people who provided it. Each held a curious conviction, rare in those whose nation lay so close to defeat, that the Führer still had one last card to play, a card so devastatingly effective that it could change the tide of war—not carving victory out of defeat (at such a late date, not even the German people were prepared to believe that), but at least laying down the basis for an honourable and negotiated peace.

It is doubtful if, in normal circumstances, the men at the R. and A. would have given credence to these reports, but their superiors were still smarting from their failure in December to assess data from captured German soldiers and anticipate Hitler's desperate breakthrough in the Ardennes. Consequently, when the term SSG 300 began to rise with disturbing frequency, an air of concern accumulated at OSS headquarters in Washington, D.C.

On 22 March, Colonel Theodore Reiser met Presidential aide Harvey Winfield and the Chairman of the Military Intelligence Advisory Group, Warren Degermark, in the Yellow Oval Room on the second floor of the White House. The chamber served as a study for President Roosevelt, and its walls were lined with ship prints and photographs from the early part of the twentieth century. Above the mantelpiece hung Rembrandt Peale's famous portrait of George Washington.

The two aides listened in silence to Reiser's evaluation of the evidence in the folders in front of them. When he had finished, Degermark asked: 'Is there nothing at all to suggest what this SSG 300 might be?'

Reiser shook his head. 'A secret weapon, a code name for a new strategy, who knows?'

'Rockets?' suggested Winfield.

Reiser looked at him. 'What?'

'That's their specialty, isn't it? Rockets. Like the V2.'

'I doubt that,' said Reiser.

'I don't know. SSG 300 sounds like a rocket to me. What d'you think, Warren?'

Degermark shrugged. 'We can speculate till we're blue in the face,' he said. 'The question is, what do we do about it?'

Reiser shifted uncomfortably in his seat. 'There's one possibility I think you should know about. We have a man in custody, a high-ranking German intelligence officer. When he was captured, he was carrying a letter of authority from no less a person than Reichsführer Himmler. The letter referred indirectly to SSG 300.'

'Has he been interrogated?' Degermark asked.

'No, sir.'

Degermark frowned. He glanced at his companion, then back at Reiser. 'Would you repeat that, Colonel?'

'The trouble with a man like Graebner,' Reiser explained, 'is that we can never be sure how much he'll tell. In this instance, half a story might be worse than no story at all. Instead, we've tried a different tactic. We've sent in one of our own people to win Graebner's confidence.'

'A spy?'

'A plant.'

'Isn't that a kind of hit-or-miss arrangement?'

'We figured it was the best strategy in the circumstances, sir.'

'But surely a plan of this sort could take months. I think we should pull the German in for immediate questioning.'

'Do that,' Reiser said, 'and you'll blow everything. Graebner's an officer of considerable substance. He'll certainly be capable of withstanding any of the pressures or persuasions we can bring to bear.'

'But this man of yours, this spy, how can we tell if he knows what he's doing?'

'Tully's the best there is,' Reiser said. 'You have my word on that.'

The two aides did not share Reiser's confidence, but the colonel stood his ground, pointing out that any information gleaned from Graebner under duress might prove to be at best of little value, and at worst, useless. At the end of their discussion they agreed to give Tully another two weeks. If nothing happened within that time, Graebner would be isolated and debriefed in the normal manner.

Reiser felt pleased with himself as he left the White House by the south portico and cruised down Pennsylvania Avenue. He had done his duty, had shared the responsibility. Winfield and Degermark were now as much a part of this as he was. If things went wrong, nobody could lay the blame at his door. Two weeks from today, he'd begin to worry again. Until then, the problem of cracking Graebner would remain strictly Tully's baby.

Tully stood hesitating on Etta's porch. He felt like someone suffering from a bad case of sunburn. The doctor, Major Wiseman, had told him that a few more seconds' exposure to that boiling water would have undoubtedly resulted in severe scalding. As it was, his skin had already completely recovered; all except his face, anyhow. His face, which had taken the initial brunt of the spray had turned an embarrassing scarlet, and when he thought of how close he had been to permanent disfigurement, possibly even death, the conviction lodged coldly inside him, as cold and as hard a conviction as he had ever felt in his life, that somehow or other Strahle had to be stopped.

And yet he had no time for Strahle, he thought, no time for Etta either. His duty was clear. He had to concentrate on Graebner. Nothing in the world was more important than that. Except survival maybe. Without survival he couldn't hope to get close to Graebner, so survival had to be important. And if survival was important, then Strahle and Etta were important too. Strahle because he threatened it, Etta because she sustained it. Graebner would have to wait for the moment.

He knocked gently, and Etta opened the door. When she saw him, her eyes widened in surprise and horror. 'What happened to your face?' she cried.

He tried to grin, but his skin felt like stretched rubber over the raw protruberances of his skull.

'I had a little accident,' he told her.

'An accident?'

'I got locked in the shower. Couldn't turn the damned water off. It was red-hot.'

She hustled him inside, her chest rising and falling rapidly, then, in a calm, carefully-modulated voice, she said: 'Karl, will you sit down a minute.'

Gingerly, he eased into an armchair.

'You say you were locked in,' she murmured. 'Will you explain that to me, please? You mean someone deliberately locked you in there?'

'That's right.'

'Somebody locked the door and turned the water to hot?'

'Yes.'

'Good God, Karl, did you tell the authorities?'

'What could they do?'

'What could they do? They could find out who's responsible and make sure he's punished for a start.'

'I know who's responsible,' he said. 'I'll fix him in my own way, in my own time.'

She stood staring at him with exasperation, and for a moment he thought she was going to cry. The realisation made him feel strange. No-one had ever cried over Tully before, not even his mother, from what he could remember. He found the experience reassuring.

'Karl, tell me the truth. Was it the guards who did this to you?'

'No.'

'Your own countrymen?'

'Yes.'

'Your own countrymen did it?'

'Sure.'

'But what about Colonel Glusky? Does he realise what's going on up there?'

Tully sighed. 'You've got to understand something. Colonel Glusky's walking a tightrope. He's keeping order in that camp the best way he can, and that's by playing ball with the Nazi bastards who are running things. Glusky doesn't like it one bit, but he's got no choice. He hasn't the men or the resources to maintain control, so he has to use diplomacy, and that means looking the other way once in a while.'

'What about the War Department?' she cried. 'Don't they care what's happening at Cannesetego?'

'The main objectives of the War Department lie in Europe and the Pacific. They're happy to leave the Colonel Gluskys of the world to sort out the dirty business of POW management the best way they can.'

'It's outrageous.'

Tully shrugged. 'It's life,' he said.

She went upstairs to the bathroom and came back a moment later patting her cheeks with a facecloth. Tully sat with both hands resting on the chair-arms, staring straight in front of him. He felt guilty at having upset her, and wanted to make amends.

'Would you like me to play the piano?' he asked.

She laid the facecloth over a chair-back. 'Not tonight,' she said. 'I thought . . . I thought we might go out for a change.'

'Out where?'

'There's a hayride down at the village.'

'A hayride?'

'Wouldn't you like that?'

'You're crazy. You can't take me on a hayride. I'm an enemy prisoner, for Christ's sake.'

'Who'll know the difference in your civvies? You talk like an American. You even look like an American.'

'But I'm *not* an American,' he insisted. 'They'll ask questions. They'll want to know why I'm not in the army.'

'Tell them you're on sick leave. One glance at your skin and anyone would believe that.'

'It's too dangerous,' he grunted.

'What can happen?' she asked. 'At the very worst, a few days solitary confinement. Isn't it worth the risk to feel like a real human being again?'

He looked at her in silence for a moment. Then he walked to the piano and absently prodded the keyboard with his finger. When he turned around, he was smiling. 'You're right,' he agreed. 'It *is* worth the risk. Let me go upstairs and get out of these things.'

As it turned out, he was glad she'd changed his mind. They sat together on the haycart creaking gently along narrow lanes, the sky dark and filled with stars. The other couples were friendly and polite, and after the initial introductions were over left him pretty much alone. He told them he'd been wounded in the Pacific, and nobody pressed the point. They peered at his fevered skin, grinned sympathetically, and accepted his reticence as a natural by-product of his injuries.

After a thirty-minute ride, the line of haycarts came to a halt on the foreshore of a narrow bayou, and they built fires, toasted wieners, and listened to the night sounds of the nearby swamp. The air was warm and the sky looked oddly translucent, as if just by reaching up his arm he could sweep away the stars and reveal some blinding truth beyond.

After a while, the guitars came out, and they sang in the darkness. For Tully, it was like returning to a scene from his childhood.

'What are you thinking about?' he asked Etta.

'Home,' she said.

'Sweden?'

'No, Canada. We used to live in Edmonton, up in northern Alberta. My father ran a haberdashery there.'

She stretched out her legs, leaning back on her elbows, the firelight dancing across her cheeks.

'One summer he sent my brother and me to a little fisherman's hostel in the Rocky Mountains. I think it was probably the happiest summer of my life. On nights when the hostel was empty, we'd take the canoes out across the lake till we found some sheltered stretch of shoreline, and there we'd light fires, cook steaks, and sing songs just like this, or maybe listen to the coyotes baying in the distance. They always had such a mournful sound, like the crying of children drifting throught the night.'

Tully stared at her, peering at the shadows in the hollows of her eyes.

'There were bears in the woods,' she said, 'and sometimes in the early morning you'd hear them scavenging around on the roof of the cookhouse, ripping up the shingles, trying to get in. They'd smell the food, you see. We'd have to run out and hammer on an old metal tub to frighten them off. One day, a roebuck came right into the lodge, actually walked inside calm as you please. I took pictures of him, but he bolted when Jamie tried to give him some bread.'

'Jamie?' Tully muttered.

'He's my brother. He's in the navy now. Somewhere in the Pacific.'

'How old were you when all this was happening?'

'Eleven, I think. Maybe twelve. It seems a lifetime ago. I thought the Rockies the most beautiful place I'd ever seen in my life. There were high alpine pastures, and flowers everywhere—and sparkling streams dropping hundreds of feet out of rocky gorges. Some mornings I'd wake up and all the mountains would be shining in the sunlight, and I'd see deer and elk and sometimes maybe a bull moose, drinking quietly, his horns so huge and powerful you'd think no neck could possibly hold them. And sometimes I'd see a whole family of bears, the papa bear, the mama bear, and two or three little baby bears, shuffling through the forest in single file, or maybe perched on the tops of tall saplings, swinging madly from side to side. They thought that was great fun.'

'Where was your father in all this?' Tully asked.

Her face clouded. 'Back in Edmonton,' she whispered. 'I think . . . I think that's why I was so happy there. I hated him, you see.'

'Why?'

'He was so violent. I've seen him beat Jamie to the ground with his bare fists. One night, I was lying in bed when the door burst open and my mother ran in. She had blood all over her face. He'd knocked out her teeth. I remember the way she looked at me as he dragged her through the door. Her eyes were demented with fear. I've never forgotten that.'

She reached out and squeezed his wrist. 'Don't let's talk about it,' she said, 'It's such a lovely evening, and I don't want to spoil things.'

The night wore on and soon they re-boarded the haycarts and set off back towards the village. Tully lay in the straw, his arm around Etta, the burning in his cheeks oddly diminished. He thought of what she had told him and realised that even with contact and familiarity, there was little you ever got to know about another human being. What went on inside, the dreams and hopes and fears, and all the other little things people liked to keep secret. But he had felt close to Etta for an hour or two. Closer than he had felt to anyone in his life. Which wasn't saying much, he reflected, since his life had been a miserable failure as far as personal relationships were concerned.

It was almost midnight when they got back to Etta's, and Tully sat in the parlour pulling strands of straw from his hair while Etta made coffee in the kitchen. She came through, carrying the cups on a tray. 'How's your face?' she asked.

'I'd forgotten it.'

She smiled. 'You're looking better already. Hayrides must agree with you.'

Her cheeks were flushed, and Tully thought it made her seem more beautiful than ever. Reaching out, he touched her skin running his thumb down the hollow beside her mouth. She stared back at him, her eyes smiling, and he felt a momentary spasm of guilt when he thought of how he was deceiving her. Not wickedly, he thought; not cruelly, or deliberately, or wantonly, but because he had no choice.

He stood up, slipped his arms around her, and kissed her for the first time. It had been so long since he'd held any woman. He was uncomfortably conscious of his own awkwardness.

'I thought you were never going to do that,' she whispered. 'I wanted to touch you that very first day. When you were sitting at the keyboard, I wanted to reach out and put my hand on your cheek, but I didn't dare. Do you find me attractive, Karl?'

'Don't talk crazy.'

'I want to know. Tell me.'

'Yes, I find you attractive.'

'I mean a lot.'

'A hell of a lot,' he admitted.

She smiled. 'Kiss me again,' she whispered.

The first warning surge of passion rose inside him as he pressed her hard against his body. Her lips opened, her arms slipped round his neck, and tears ran into his mouth as they kissed.

'Why are you crying?' he asked.

'This is not terribly wise, you realise that?'

'What's wisdom got to do with it?'

'But you're the enemy, Karl. A German soldier.'

'The war's practically over,' he insisted. 'We can't be enemies for ever.'

'Oh, darling,' she whispered, 'I do want you. You'll never know how much.'

Moaning deep in his throat, he slipped his hands inside her shirt and held her breasts. There was no finesse in his assault. For many months he had lived a life of total celibacy. The urges which propelled him had been too long postponed, and now his body seemed out of control.

Somehow, though he could not remember falling, they were both on the floor, and he felt her hands on his chest, pushing him back. Her eyes gleamed as she tugged her plaid shirt over her head and reached behind to unclip her brassiere. Her body looked strong and beautiful in the shadow.

Tully tore at his own clothes in a kind of fury, peeling them from his skin if their very texture had become a burden too intolerable to bear.

She turned toward him, naked, and he caught a glimpse of her breasts, and the pale sweep of her belly and hips. The blood throbbed in his throat as he felt her skin pressed against his, the softness of her hair touching his lips. His vision blurred, and he sank into a confusion of soft flesh and sweet fragrance, of curves and contours, warmth and moistness: then his thoughts lost their substance until nothing existed, only the body writhing in his arms, and the dark pulsing energy flowing in his veins.

10

For all his air of wordly weariness, Tully's experiences with women had never been more than breathless moments stolen at college, swooning encounters on crushed summer grass with the strains of Glenn Miller drifting from the campus on the other side of the river. They were fragmented affairs, brief initiations into the mysteries of femininity, and then the war had put an end to their pursuit, for Tully, during the years he'd trained in England, or the months he had spent on active service in Berlin, had never come close to a woman in the intimate sense. If he were truly honest about it, he thought, he had never been close to a woman at all, for those college liaisons had been adventures of the flesh, nothing more, a painful attempt to satisfy the gnawing hunger of youth.

He had never considered himself sexually attractive; indeed, during adolescence he had been firmly convinced he was physically repugnant, and when girls expressed an interest in him through the various body signals girls employ, he had thought it a cruel joke and despised them for it. Now, he found the attentions of the woman Etta a strangely vitalising experience. Her presence haunted him at night when he lay in the hut listening to the men snoring. In the woods by day, he thought about her constantly, held intact by the knowledge that when evening came, for two blessed hours they would be together. Their relationship remained stabilising in itself, and his entire existence focused around eventide.

Some nights they scarcely talked at all. They sat at the

piano, he playing, she listening, and he was conscious of a feeling of unity with another human being that he would not have believed possible. When they did talk, he let the conversation flow around her, for he had always been reticent by nature, and that underlying fear of disclosure, that deeply-ingrained need for secrecy drilled into him in training was now an integral part of his psyche. Still, he knew it was Etta who brought him through the rigours of the miserable lie he lived, and though he wanted her with an almost paralysing hunger, he found he wanted something more; an affiliation free of the impermanencies of the past, a union that could not be rushed, that would offer stability in a frenzied world, and, knowing this, he took what comfort he could from the brief moments in her presence, and the secret knowledge that the cravings he experienced were reflected in every touch of her hand, every movement she gave. As the days passed, he lost his air of foreboding, his nerves steadied, he began to sleep at nights. For the first time in months, the world seemed to slot satisfyingly into place.

Rising behind this new-found confidence, however, was the constant threat of Strahle. Though Strahle was not as omnipotent as Tully had first believed, he was still a formidable adversary. Unlike Steiner, Tully had done nothing wrong, which meant Strahle's assaults had to be made with strategy and reserve so as not to alienate the rest of the camp. Nevertheless, shortly after the shower incident, Tully discovered a sliver of glass nearly two inches long inserted into a slice of meatloaf he'd been eating. Almost every evening when he returned from Etta's, he found the contents of his locker scattered around the barrack-hut floor. One day, a bottle of green ink had been emptied over his bedding. Beneath the Nazi slogans scribbled in the head appeared new messages promising his mutilation and ultimate death. All this produced in Tully a feeling of constant anxiety, but even more worrying than the menace of Strahle was his failure to make any headway with Graebner. There was, he knew, no way he could justify his presence here unless he managed to breach the German's defences, but though Graebner remained friendly on the outside, Tully's attempts to gain his confidence had been repelled so vigorously that he knew any further move would only aggravate the situation. In the end, it was Strahle himself who provided Tully with a perfect solution. The idea was dangerous in the extreme, but Tully was astute enough to realise that a man like Graebner who might snarl at a lion could quite easily become benevolent towards a shorn lamb.

One morning, Tully was shaving in the latrine when Scheller, Eyke and Kruger walked in. The place was empty, and hearing their boots on the stone floor, Tully didn't bother to turn his head. The first he knew of their presence was when the razor was sent spinning from his grasp and both his arms were viciously twisted behind his back. He grunted with pain, arching his spine, but before he had a chance to speak, brutal fingers seized his neck and his face was plunged into the washbasin filled with soapy water. He struggled to hold his breath, his mouth and nose pressed flat against the porcelain bottom. The fists gripping his wrists were like metal shackles. He tried to lash out with his heels, but his legs swung futilely at thin air. He could feel his chest heaving as his lungs laboured for oxygen. The water stung his eyes and surged into his nostrils. He could see the side of the washbasin undulating strangely; it had no discernible colour, only a rippling whiteness that seemed to tunnel inside his skull.

He tried to turn his head and the grip on his neck tightened. He had to breathe. It was no use, he could hold back no longer. He sucked in, and began to buck and plunge as moisture streamed into his nasal passages.

They let him go and he pitched to the floor, gasping and spluttering, retching up water like a drowning man. They stood laughing down at him, and Scheller took his toothpaste and squeezed it out over his clothing.

'He looks a peach, don't he?' he chuckled.

Somebody kicked Tully in the ribs. He grunted with pain, and rolling on his side, began to be sick on the cold stone floor.

'This guys an actor,' Kruger said. 'He could make a fortune in the movies.'

He heard their boots scaping and the door slamming as they strode laughing into the sunlight, and for a few minutes more he lay there, trying to pull himself together. The first wave of sickness was followed by another, and he vomited again. He felt a little better when it was over, and dragging himself to his feet he scraped the toothpaste from his shirtfront and washed it off in the sink. Sluicing the bile from his lips, he studied himself critically in the glass. There were livid weals on his neck where Scheller's fingers had dug into his skin.

Then the anger started.

It was not, strangely enough, directed at Scheller or Eyke or Kruger, but at the man who had started it all in the first place, Sergeant Strahle. It was senseless putting things off any longer, he realised. One way or the other, the issue had to be settled. Strahle or himself.

That night in the bunkhouse, he talked to Willi Stroud.

'Hey, Willi,' he said, 'what do you know about duelling?'

Stroud was stretched out on his bed, reading a magazine. He looked up. 'You mean swords or pistols?'

'Swords, I guess.'

'Only what I've read in books.'

'I'm talking about the kind of duelling they'd do in a place like Heidelberg.'

'Well, that's not really duelling in the true sense,' Stroud said, 'it's more like a kind of ritual. Everything's worked out beforehand, with carefully-plotted moves and counter-moves.'

'They don't try to kill each other then?'

'Hell, no. The idea is to mark your opponent's face. You wear pads and gloves. It's not a serious affair at all. Why?'

Tully hesitated. 'I thought I'd challenge Strahle,' he said.

'You thought what?' Willi echoed, his eyes widening.

'He keeps a couple of sabres under his floorboards, doesn't he?'

'Karl, Strahle's an expert, for Christ's sake. He fought sixteen duels at university.'

'Well, he can't kill me, can he? I mean, he'll have to stick to the rules like everybody else.'

'Rules?' Stroud echoed derisively, 'What does Strahle care about rules? You know that bastard, he's after your blood. You'd be playing right into his hands.'

'Maybe,' Tully said, 'but at least with a blade in my fist, I'd have a chance to hit back.'

Next lunchtime, he crossed the compound and made his way to Hut 18. Eyke came out as he approached, and seeing Tully he began to smirk. 'Well, look who's here,' he said. 'Is this a social call?'

'Strahle in?'

Eyke's grin widened. 'He's busy.'

Tully made to enter, but Eyke blocked his way. 'I said he's busy,' he repeated.

'He'll see me,' Tully said coldly.

Eyke stared down at him, the corners of his mouth still twisting. After a moment he nodded in agreement. 'I guess he might at that,' he said. 'Wait here.'

He disappeared inside the door.'

It was raining, and Tully turned up his collar as he glanced across the compound at the lines of dripping barrack huts. An American guard sauntered by, his shoulders hunched beneath his nylon poncho.

The door opened and Eyke reappeared, still smirking.

'Okay,' he said, moving back to let Tully in.

Strahle was playing cards with Scheller, Kruger, and Wegmüller. He smiled when he saw Tully.

'Well, well,' he said, 'what have we here? An unexpected visitor. Give him a chair, somebody.'

'That's okay,' Tully grunted, 'this won't take long.'

'What's on your mind, Raderecht?'

'I thought we might have a little talk.'

'In private? I'm afraid that's impossible. We're in the middle of a game as you see, and if you want to know the truth, we don't trust each other overly much.'

'What I have to say isn't private.'

'You do sound intriguing.'

'I've come to ask you to call off your boys.'

Strahle picked up the cards and re-shuffled. His face was a picture of bewildered innocence. 'What on earth is this man talking about?' he muttered.

'Leave me alone, Strahle. It's gone far enough.'

Strahle's smile grew more cunning. He sucked thoughtfully at his cigarette, dealing the cards with crisp expertise.

'Well, now,' he said, 'what have you to offer in exchange?'

'An armistice. Mutual non-aggression.'

Strahle laughed out loud. 'Raderecht, you're as unpredict-able as ever. I thought you'd come here to beg.'

'No,' said Tully.

'Well, since I hardly regard you as a major threat, I must tell you your proposal doesn't interest me in the slightest.'

'Then I'll have to stop you by force.'

Strahle stared at him closely. 'What are you up to, Raderecht? Is this some kind of challenge?'

'Correct.'

'Let me get this straight. You are challenging me to combat?'

'You're a brave man with your torpedoes around you,' Tully said. 'Let's see how brave you feel when there's only you and me.'

Strahle smiled again. 'You've misjudged me, Raderecht. Just because my father was a stevedore doesn't mean I'm prepared to brawl like one.'

'I know that. I thought we might do it your way.'

And without hesitation, Tully stepped to the table and slapped Strahle sharply on the cheek. The smile vanished from Strahle's face. He glared up, angry and startled.

Scheller rose to his feet with a threatening growl, but Strahle caught his arm, holding him back. He stared at Tully in puzzlement. 'Do you realise what you've done?' he demanded.

Tully nodded.

''We *are* talking about the same thing, Raderecht?'

'A duel. With sabres.'

Strahle began to laugh. 'You bloody idiot. You're out of your mind. Don't you know duelling's illegal?'

'We're a long way from Germany. We make our own rules here.'

'Have you ever used a sabre before?'

'For Christ's sake, Strahle, do you accept the challenge or not?'

Strahle got up and strolled to the window. Drawing back the curtain, he peered out at the rain-soaked compound. When he looked back he seemed almost elated, as if Tully had invoked an illusion of long-forgotten grandeur.

'You damned fool,' he said, 'you've asked for it now.'

'Is it on or isn't it?'

'We'll have to wait till evening.'

'When?'

'After lights-out. In the heating plant. Appoint yourself a second.'

'What about weapons?'

'I'll supply those.'

Strahle moved back into the centre of the hut, his eyes glittering beneath his pale brow. 'I'm going to take a special pleasure in carving you into little strips, Raderecht,' he murmured.

Tully's chin stayed hard and set. 'Let's say you'll have a bloody good try,' he said.

Then he turned and strode back to his hut in the rain.

When evening came, Tully found Graebner sitting in the library. Hunched over a book, his powerful shoulders flexed, he was like a quarterback waiting for the play.

'Can I talk to you a minute?' Tully asked.

Graebner stared at him in silence. He looked as he always looked, amiable but aloof. "Go ahead,' he said.

Tully sat down. It was dusty in the library and the air was heavy with the smell of old books.

'I know this may sound a little crazy,' Tully muttered, 'but that scar on your cheek, where did it come from?'

Graebner touched the livid slash running diagonally across his face to the tip of his nose. 'Why?' he asked.

'Is it a duelling scar?'

'It might be.'

'Please, this is important.'

'Okay, then,' Graebner said, 'it's a duelling scar.'

'Did you get it at university?'

'For Christ's sake, Raderecht, what's this all about?'

'Were you a member of a duelling corps, one of the *burschen*?'

'I was.'

'So you know the rules of the Duelling Code?'

'I do.'

'I need someone to act as my second.'

Graebner swung his chair round so he could peer at Tully directly. 'Is this some kind of joke?' he demanded.

'No joke,' Tully said. 'I've just challenged Strahle. It was either that or let his hoodlums cripple me for life. We're meeting tonight in the heating plant.'

'You bloody fool. People don't fight duels in this day and age.'

'You did,' Tully insisted.

'That was a long time ago.'

Tully shrugged. He struggled to keep his face impassive. It was kind of funny when you thought about it, the way he was sitting here, pretending to be so calm and collected, when all the time his insides were quivering like a tubful of jellyfish. But at least he'd gotten Graebner interested. There was no doubt on that score.

The German was studying him intently. "Strahle's mighty handy with a blade,' Graebner breathed, 'What about you?'

'I never touched a sword in my life.'

Graebner's eyes widened. 'Then you're crazy. For Christ's sake, Strahle fought sixteen duels at university.'

'But surely this duelling's just a ceremony, a kind of ballet dance. Nobody actually gets hurt.'

'Who told you that?' Graebner growled.

Tully looked at him. Deep in his chest, he felt a momentary spasm of doubt. 'It's true, isn't it?'

'Like hell it's true. Killing your opponent isn't the point of the exercise maybe, but in my day we had fatalities all right, lots of them.'

Tully's blood went cold.

'The idea was to inflict a cut on your opponent's cheek,' Graebner explained. 'It was regarded as a mark of courage or honour. But if you accidentally killed the poor bastard, you received what was called a *consilium abeundi*. That meant you had to leave the college and continue your studies someplace else. It was more of an inconvenience than an actual crime.'

Tully realised his mouth was open. He closed it with a conscious effort, running his tongue across the front of his lips.

'I thought you wore protective clothing and stuff like that,' he whispered weakly.

'We did,' said Graebner, 'Iron spectacles to safeguard the eyes, a throat pad to cover the neck and upper chest, and heavy arm bandages. We also used a weapon called a *schläger*; that was a sword three-and-a-half feet long with a triangular blade and a ten-inch handguard that acted as a kind of shield. Even then, *burschen* still got killed. What you're talking about here is something quite different. There'll be no body-pads in Strahle's fight, and no rules either. Those weapons of his are cavalry sabres from World War One. You've handed the bastard a perfect opportunity to chop you into hamburger steak.'

Tully felt his skin crawl as he realised he had miscalculated. In an effort to impress Graebner, he had put himself in the worst position he could conceivably imagine. A duel without rules. And with a guy who wanted nothing more from life than a chance to skewer him like a kebab. Oh Jesus!

Keep a bold front on this, he thought. Don't let Graebner see you're frightened. He smiled thinly, cold bloodedly, like Conrad Veidt in *Under the Red Robe*. 'What's the difference?' he said. 'At least with a blade in my hand, I've got a chance.'

'Think so? Take my advice and call it off. Have an accident—a broken wrist, a dislocated shoulder.'

My God, don't you think I want to? Tully thought. Something simple and uncomplicated. Just bad enough to get me into the sick bay

He thought of Colonel Reiser and shook his head.

'You don't understand,' he said. 'I have to go through with it. I have to wipe the smugness off the bastard's face.'

Graebner undid the top button of his shirt, and Tully knew in that moment that in one thing he had got this just right; no longer did the German regard him as an unwanted intruder to be pacified, humoured, fenced off as quickly as possible. Graebner was intrigued. In that direction at least, he was finally making progress. All he had to do now was survive.

'I was wrong about you, Raderecht,' Graebner said, 'I

thought you were a man of intelligence. Now I realise you're merely insane.'

'Will you help me or not?'

Graebner looked at him for a moment, his face chipped and bloodless. Then he closed his book and stood up. 'Come on,' he said. 'If you're determined to fight Strahle, you might as well find out what it feels like.'

In the recreation hall Graebner selected two slats from the wall bars and, weighing each carefully in his hand, gave one to Tully.

'In the duelling corps,' he explained, 'the weapon is always held above the head, the blade diagonal to the body. The cuts are delivered with the wrist. Only at the university of Jena is the point used. That's because so many of the Jena *burschen* are theological students, and sword scars on the face bar them from the ministry. So they concentrate instead on running each other through the body. However, you'll be facing Strahle with a sabre, which is totally different from the *schläger* and in fact from any weapon you care to mention. In foil fencing, for example, you hold the sword with the fingers, keeping the wrist supple and loose. The sabre is a slashing instrument and requires a firm steady grip. That doesn't mean you have to squeeze, however. Maintain a balance between firmness and fluidity. Take up your stance.'

Feeling idiotic, Tully tried to remember how he'd seen it in the movies. He went into the on-guard position, one hand on his hip, the other wielding the slat like a truncheon.

Graebner shook his head wearily. 'That's no good at all. One sideways slash from Strahle will knock you totally off-balance. Thrust the right leg forward, bend it at the knee, and use the left as a support. Keep the toe pointing outward and slightly to the left. The secret is to maintain the body weight at the front, hips facing towards your opponent. Whatever you do, don't watch his eyes. Fix your gaze on his breastbone. That way, you'll be aware of the position of his blade. Try to imagine the sabre as an extension of your arm and wield it accordingly.'

For the next hour, they went through every defence and manoeuvre Graebner could think of, and Tully did his best to keep up, slashing, cutting, thrusting, blocking, while Graebner bludgeoned him unmercifully. It was gruelling work, and sweat streamed from Tully's skin as they clattered up and down the recreation hall, their wooden slats rattling like thunder.

At last, Graebner called a halt, wiping his face on his shirtsleeve. 'Raderecht,' he said, 'you're doomed.'

Tully looked indignant. 'I can't be that bad,' he protested.

'You're worse than bad. Take my advice and call it off. Better look a fool than end up with your face hacked to ribbons.'

'I'm not backing down,' Tully said.

'Then he'll butcher you for sure.'

Tully swallowed. Keeping his features as straight as he could, he asked in a calm voice: 'Does that mean you refuse to act as my second?'

Graebner regarded him sweatily, his eyes narrow slits beneath the cornice of his brow.

'I'll be there, don't worry,' he said, tossing the slat into a corner. 'Someone round here has to show a sense of responsibility.'

When the lights went out, Tully rose swiftly from his bed and pulled on his clothes. He padded to the door and peered outside. The camp was dark and silent, the sky heavy with cloud. He could see the elongated beam of Tower III's searchlight sliding along the rows of barrack huts. There was no sign of the sentries. He peered left and right, then trotted lightly across the compound.

He knew what he was up against. Strahle was the kind of guy who would get a kick out of killing him slowly—a psycho in every sense of the word, who was probably licking his lips this very moment at the thought of Tully's unprotected throat. It was not simply a question of facing the bastard without flinching. He had to fight Strahle to a standstill. He had to demonstrate to Graebner that he was a man to contend with, a man of substance, an ideal companion if Graebner chose to bust out of here. It was the most dangerous play he had ever made in his life, and right at this moment he wished to God he had never started it, but somehow or other he had to break this deadlock between Graebner and himself, he had to get things moving before Strahle or his henchmen finished him off altogether.

He reached the heating plant and tried the door. It was open, and he slipped inside. The room was large and cluttered with pipes hanging beneath the ceiling like strips of spaghetti. Low rumbling noises drifted inside their hollow centres. Strahle was already waiting, his companions grouped around him defensively as he tested his sabre for size and weight, slicing the air at imaginary adversaries. Flashlights jammed above the pipes cast pale beams across the floor, outlining his face in a faintly ethereal glow. He smiled as Tully entered.

'Well, well, Raderecht,' he said, right on time. You've brought someone to administer the last rites?'

The others erupted into laughter, their voices leaving a hollow echo in the confined space. Tully said: 'He'll be here in a moment.'

He wondered what would happen if Graebner failed to turn up. Was he honour-bound to continue, or was there some way, by abasing himself perhaps, by declaring his unworthiness, he could yet withdraw? Peering at Strahle's cronies, Tully doubted it. Any attempt to capitulate at this late stage would meet with the most violent response; he had no illusions about that.

He knew he had to stop staring at Strahle, because something in the guy's manner was beginning to unnerve him—that cool impervious air, that sense of utter certainty, as if an encounter like this, with such an insignificant opponent, was too trivial to command the bastard's full attention.

The door creaked as Graebner slithered in, and Tully heard the others gasp with surprise. They all felt it, even Strahle. Tully, watching, could see it in his eyes—surprise, bewilderment, even a trace of resentment, as if Graebner had, by his very presence, betrayed them in some strange way. Abruptly, three of Strahle's henchmen snapped to attention, clicking their heels on the bare stone floor. Tully blinked in astonishment. Christ Almighty! he thought wildly, they know who Graebner is.

Now it was Tully's turn to look surprised. He watched the

Germans with confusion as Graebner snapped in a harsh voice: 'Fools. Pull yourselves together.'

Guiltily, they relaxed, looking at each other with sheepish expressions.

Graebner ignored Tully and moved to the centre of the floor, his massive bulk accentuated beneath the hanging pipes and low whitewashed ceiling.

'This is madness, Strahle,' he said. 'You realise that?'

Strahle shrugged. He stood with his sabre resting casually over one shoulder. 'Why tell me?' he demanded. 'It's your man who did the challenging.'

'Raderecht is totally inexperienced in this kind of thing. He knows nothing whatever about swordsmanship.'

'Then he's a very foolish fellow,' Strahle smiled.

Graebner's face remained patient. 'Strahle, we are prisoners-of-war. If anything happens to this man, it'll backfire on everyone in camp. Hurt Raderecht, and you hurt us all.'

'Then tell him to apologise.'

Graebner turned to Tully questioningly. Tully swallowed. Graebner, in trying to save his ass, was undoing his entire plan. Keeping his face straight, he said coldy: 'Stay out of this, Graebner. It's my fight, not yours.'

'You damned idiot,' Graebner growled. 'I'm trying to bring this stupidity to a close.'

'You're my second and nothing else. Nobody asked you to butt in.'

Strahle chuckled. 'You're outnumbered, Graebner,' he said. 'Admit defeat and step aside. This is an affair of honour and outside your authority.'

Graebner glared at him. 'Don't talk to me about honour,' he snapped. 'You couldn't even spell that word.'

Strahle's smile vanished. His cheeks went paler still. He stared at Graebner for a moment as if nothing in the world would give him greater pleasure than to cleave the big man from head to chin with his sabre blade, but he made no move. It was plain, Tully realised, that Strahle was afraid of Graebner. He just stood there, looking, trying to think of something suitable to say, ending finally and, Tully thought, somewhat ineffectually with: 'Are we here to do combat or not?'

Tully agreed. He couldn't stand much more of this horsing around. If he was going to get his throat cut, he'd rather have it done quickly than stand like an idiot making heroic pronouncements he didn't really feel. 'Let's get started,' he said.

Graebner shook his head. 'You bloody fool,' he murmured. 'Whatever happens is on your own head.'

One of Strahle's henchmen produced a bucket filled with disinfectant. They could smell the acrid fumes from eight feet away. The sabre blades were carefully dipped into the reeking liquid, then wiped dry with a piece of torn rag. Tully watched as the blades were polished and handed gravely to the combatants, one to Strahle, the other to Tully. Tully's heart sank as he took hold of it. It was many times heavier than the wooden slats they'd practiced with. Its weight tugged at his arm, pulling it down. He wondered how he could be expected to wield it effectively. One wild swipe might dislocate his shoulder.

His heart pounded as he watched the others take their positions around the walls. A red-haired man in a corporal's uniform remained in the centre of the floor. His face assumed an air of grave dignity. 'In accordance with the *Code Duello* of 1777,' he said, 'the offender must either beg pardon or fight until a wound has been received by one party or the other. In an affair of this nature, between gentlemen, a verbal apology will not be deemed adequate reparation. The offender must hand a cane to the injured party to be used upon his back, or he must fight until blood is drawn. No reconciliation can take place until the challenged or the challenger has been well-blooded or disabled. You understand the rules?'

Tully nodded, his throat dry.

'When I drop my handkerchief,' the man said, 'the encounter will commence. As soon as the first blood is drawn, I shall call a halt. We will then decide if honour has been satisfied. Everyone else, please stand clear.'

Tully stared at Strahle facing him, his blade turned to the floor, his eyes glittering in the unnatural light. Tully thought: don't look at his face too much. Unlike Graebner, you always knew what Strahle was thinking, and right now Strahle was thinking murder. Tully's murder. Swift and bloody. It was going to be messy, that was the dreadful part. No quick clean death like Nelson on the poop deck—"Kiss me Hardy,' and then oblivion—but the awful bite of cold steel (a sensation Tully couldn't begin to visualise) and blood oozing all over the place, slimy, slippery, slubbery—his. He thought about Strahle's blade slicing into his quivering flesh, severing arteries, organs, soft flaccid viscera, and felt almost paralysed with fear. If he didn't quit this morbid meditating, he realised, he would break up right in front of them, and that would screw up his chances with Graebner for good. Goddammit, the Germans didn't have the monopoly on sword-fighters. What about Douglas Fairbanks? I'll show the bastard, he thought.

The handkerchief fluttered to the ground and in an instant Strahle's weapon flashed in a vicious arc, hissing through the air towards Tully's throat. Jesus! Tully thought. He leapt back, his own blade meeting Strahle's with a resounding clang, showering sparks in every direction. Desperately, he tried to remember all the things Graebner had taught him. Keeping his gaze fixed on a point just below Strahle's chin, he saw the German's sabre scything in and out, bearing down on him mercilessly. He's like a goddammed windmill coming at me from every direction, for Christ's sake. How can I fight a bastard who won't even keep still? Strahle seemed to have no subtance at all, as if his body had lost solidity and was weaving and dancing like a wraith in the darkness, impossible to touch, impossible to reach, a fantasy figure, cold and deadly, bent on Tully's destruction. Tully shuffled backwards, bumping into pillars, walls, pipes, blocking the incoming blows as best he could. He caught a glimpse of Strahle's face, the skin dead-white, the muscles rigid, the eyes filled with murderous purpose. Tully felt his stomach plunge. He wanted to rest, to breathe, he wanted a moment to reassemble his composure; he was all shaken up, for Christ's sake, the bastard had thrown him with that first brutal assault and somehow or other he hadn't been able to pull himself together.

His head clashed against one of the hanging flashlights, and stunned by the blow, he hesitated. Strahle moved forward, his sabre swishing through the air like a bird of prey. Tully felt a sting on his left cheek, and something warm splashed down the front of his shirt. For a moment, his brain failed to register, but Graebner shouted out in a terse voice, and without a word, Strahle stepped back.

Tully leaned against the wall, gasping for breath as Graebner examined him closely. The German's lips were pursed, his face creased in a heavy frown. 'Nasty cut,' he said, 'but at least you shouldn't bleed to death.'

Tully shook himself. His cheek had been severed. He could call it off now without risk or humiliation. An apology. Nothing cringing. No need for the cane, he'd already been blooded. But what good would apologies do? What had he proved? He had to impress Graebner. He had to break through that air of cautious reserve. He pushed the big man away.

'I thought we came here to fight,' he snapped.

And leaping forward, he swung his sabre wildly. Its weight almost tore it loose from his hand. Something was wrong with his left foot. He'd stepped into the bucket of disinfectant, which some idiot had left directly in his path. Now the stupid thing was jammed fast on his boot. He clattered around the floor, trying to shake it loose. The foul-smelling liquid soaked into his ankle.

Strahle didn't move an inch. He met Tully blow for blow, blocking every slash the American made, his eyes cool and calculating. Panic gathered in Tully's chest. Already he was gasping helplessly from the fury of his attack. He began to back off, sucking at the air, and with a grim relentless certainty Strahle followed, his blade whisking centimeters from the end of Tully's nose.

Around the heating plant they shuffled, Strahle advancing grimly, murderously, Tully retreating, pausing every few steps in an attempt to shake the ridiculous bucket loose as the spectators flitted from wall to wall, dodging out of their way. The clatter of steel echoed in the concrete enclosure. The air filled with the odour of sweat, and the indefinable scent of fear.

Why can't I die with some trace of dignity at least? Why does everything in my life have to end up in farce? If Strahle runs me through now, they'll find me in the morning with my innards out and my stupid foot stuck in a stupid bucket and they'll probably bury me in the stupid thing. It'll go down as my epitaph. He died with a bucket on his foot.

A flash of silver arced across Tully's eyes and he felt a stab of pain streak through his skull. For a moment his vision blurred and he almost slithered to the floor, then blood gushed over his brow, filling his left eye-socket and running into his mouth with a warm saltiness. He heard Graebner again call a halt. His brain seemed almost unhinged, as if the wound had affected his senses. His legs felt wobbly, and his arms, pressed against the wall for support, shuddered with strain and fear.

Graebner's face swung into his vision, grimacing as it studied the injury with cold professional eyes. 'I think it's time you called it a day,' he advised. 'If Strahle severs an artery, you'll be done for.'

The red-haired man came up, leaning forward to peer at Tully's face questioningly. 'Is your honour satisfied?' he murmured.

Tully spat the blood from his mouth. He wanted to quit, he wanted it more than anything in the world, but he had to impress Graebner.

'No,' he yelled.

A new feeling was in him now, a kind of fury that was welling up from deep inside, and he peered through a curtain of blood at Strahle's face, pale and determined, and felt the anger throbbing away in his vitals. Without waiting for the others to clear the floor, he reached down, tore the bucket loose, and leapt wildly in to the attack, driving Strahle back by the sheer unexpectedness of his charge. He would beat this bastard by force of will. Decades from now, experts would talk of this moment, the Last Great Duel of civilised society, how Tully, having lost first blood to the enemy, nevertheless with superb style and co-ordination finally cornered the day. He'd become a folk-hero, like Jean Lafitte.

Strahle was rattled, but only for a moment. He regained his composure and stood his ground, his sabre blocking Tully with the cool imperviousness of a seasoned professional. A wave of sickness engulfed Tully. His excitement evaporated, and he felt a tightness around his heart. Any minute now, his strength would crumble. Strahle, too, seemed aware of this, for he remained in position, content to parry Tully's strokes while his opponent blew himself out. Already, Tully's wrist was numb with strain. His right arm seemed to cease at the elbow, and he watched the blur of his blade with a kind of dazed wonder, marvelling at the way it moved, grunting imperceptibly each time Strahle's parries sent shuddering vibrations into Tully's aching shoulder. Blood blurred his vision. Strahle was little more than a dim outline on which all his fury and helplessness focused, as if he could bear the German down by the sheer power of his own terror.

Then all at once, Strahle wasn't there any more. Tully heard a heavy clunking sound and a wave of elation engulfed him as he realised it was Strahle's turn to step in the bucket. Now Strahle was clanking around the ground, struggling desperately to shake the thing loose while he, Tully, followed in vigorous pursuit. A fierce demented joy burst in Tully's chest. There was no escape for Strahle, who was cursing in an impassioned voice (a virtual stream of ingenious profanity, Tully noted) as he hobbled round the heating plant, his left foot encased in its metal cocoon, scraping and rattling on the concrete floor.

See how it feels, you bastard, Tully thought, as he followed the metallic sounds, blood streaming into his eyes. His slashes carved at thin air. He swung the sabre in a heavy arc, heard a distinct clunk as his blade contacted the heavy pipes above. There was a violent hissing noise, and steam streamed through the severed tubing, filling the room with eddying choking clouds. There seemed no end to it; the vapour just kept coming, belching out of the pipeline like a torrent of melting ice-cream. It flooded the plant from wall to wall, hissing, billowing, swirling, destroying depth and perspective, blotting out vision and reality. Everyone was coughing now, even Tully was coughing, though the intensity of his fear, coupled with the realisation that if Strahle failed to get his foot free, he might actually emerge from this the winner made him barely notice the eruptions emitting from his chest.

He saw a figure outlined in the fog and leapt toward it, swinging wildly. It was Graebner, who retreated in fright.

'It's me, you fool,' he bellowed, as Tully pursued him around the wall.

A stool got in the way and Tully leapt upon it. The stool collapsed, sending him rolling in the dirt. He clambered to his feet, lashing out in all directions. Figures darted everywhere, struggling to get out of his path.

Suddenly, Tully realised something was wrong. The sabre he had wielded with such fury had taken on a curious lightness. He peered at it, blinking with puzzlement. The blade had been sliced cleanly off at the middle, and now extended only a few inches above the handguard.

'You've broken it, you bastard,' Strahle's voice echoed.

He tumbled out of the steam, tears of rage pouring down his cheeks. 'You've broken my sword.'

Tully looked confused. 'It was an accident,' he stammered.

'You liar. You did it on purpose.'

'I didn't, I swear. It must've snapped on the wall.'

'Do you realise how much that cost, you son of a bitch?'

This is farcical, Tully thought. 'Surely your own sense will tell you I don't go around busting people's sabres for fun.'

For one mad moment he wondered if this entire episode could be no more than some nocturnal reverie from which he would soon awaken. Then Graebner came lurching towards them out of the mist, holding a handkerchief against his mouth, and Tully knew it was no dream he was experiencing, but cold hard fact.

'Look what the bastard's done,' Strahle exclaimed tearfully, holding the evidence under Graebner's chin.

'I didn't mean to,' Tully protested.

'He's a liar,' Strahle cried. 'He did it on purpose.'

'I did not,' Tully yelled. 'It was an accident. I'm sorry.'

'Sorry? What the hell does that mean, you're sorry? Where will I get another one?'

'To hell with your lousy sword,' Graebner shouted. 'Let's get out of here before we suffocate to death. Wait for me at the chapel. I'll talk to you later.'

Strahle stood for a moment, the sabre in his hand, and some of the madness seemed to die in his eyes. He breathed deeply, regaining control of himself, then lowering his weapon, he clicked his heels together. The bucket gave a metallic ring.

'Jawohl, Herr Oberst,' he said.

Followed by his henchmen, he clumped to the door,

pausing every few steps to give his leg a vigorous shake, but the bucket remained doggedly attached. Tully watched him leave with a sense of relief.

Graebner was looking at him, and for a moment Tully couldn't figure out the expression on his face; it wasn't respect, not entirely anyhow, though there was a semblance of that all right, but all at once Graebner's features started to break up, and before Tully's astonished gaze he burst out laughing. He leaned against the pillar, roaring outrageously, his rugged cheeks crimson with mirth.

For a moment Tully just stood there, then he too felt hysteria bubbling inside him, mounting swiftly, bursting from his throat in a wave of helpless hilarity. He leaned back against the wall, guffawing into the steam.

'You bloody idiot,' Graebner gasped, shaking his head. 'That was the craziest thing I've ever seen.'

Tully chuckled weakly. 'I don't think I'd care to go through it again,' he admitted.

'Strahle's an idiot, crazy as a fox, but I'm not sure that you're not even crazier.'

Graebner moved towards him, took out a handkerchief and held it against his cheek.

'Those cuts need stitches,' he said. 'I could take you up to the sick bay, but it'll mean fourteen days for being out after dark. Besides, Major Wiseman's usually pie-eyed at this time of the night. On the other hand, I can fix you up myself if you'll trust me. I used to be a doctor in civilian life.'

'You?' Tully muttered

'Sure. The escape committee keeps a medical kit hidden in the library. If we can get there without being spotted, we'll find everything we need. Think you can move?'

'I guess so.'

'Hold on to my shoulder, if you like.'

'I'll be okay,' Tully grunted.'

'Good. Let's go then.'

He hooked one hand under Tully's armpit, gripping him firmly at the waist with the other, and like a pair of music-hall drunks they lurched to the door and staggered blindly out into the night.

11

With his thumb, Graebner smoothed the sticking-plaster on Tully's cheek, then leaned back to examine his handiwork.

'How's it feel?' he asked.

'Pretty good.'

'Still stinging?'

'A little.'

'It will for a while. Nothing to shout about though. We'll take the stitches out on Friday. You won't look as pretty as you used to.'

Tully grinned painfully. 'I don't think that'll break anyone's heart.'

Graebner began packing the first-aid equipment back into its box. He switched off his flashlight and slipped it into his pocket. 'You'd be a damn sight worse if Major Wiseman had done it, I promise you that.'

Tully watched him curiously in the darkness. Graebner's shoulders looked huge outlined against the pale sheen of the library window. Without the light, the smell of old books was accentuated somehow. 'Were you really a doctor before the war?' Tully asked.

'Sure.'

'Then how come you're not in the medical corps?'

Graebner chuckled dryly. 'That's the army for you. Tell

them you're a draughtsman and they turn you into a cook. If you're a lumberjack, they send you off to officer school.'

He closed the medical chest, pulled some books from the bottom shelf, and slid the box into a hole in the back wall. Carefully, he set the books back in place. 'You were scared tonight, Raderecht,' he said softly.

'Scared?'

'Sure. Any man who'd go up against Strahle would need to have a streak of madness in him somewhere, but taking the bastard on at his own game, that was plain suicide. I could see how scared you were in your face.'

Tully sighed, resting his head against the bookshelves.

'Yes, I was scared,' he admitted.

Graebner looked at him shrewdly. 'Yet you kept going back for more. Even with your cheek slashed, even when you could have backed out without disgrace, you still went back. You were showing off. Trying to impress me. Why?'

Tully was startled. 'What are you talking about?'

'Come on, Raderecht, don't treat me like a fool. You've been busting a gut to make my acquaintance ever since you got here. I didn't think much of it at first. I put it down to an overly-developed sense of friendliness. But that duel was a deliberate gambit, and a very dangerous one at that. Now when a man's prepared to risk so much to grab my attention, I ask myself: What the hell is he up to? I'm asking that now, Raderecht. What are you up to?'

Tully leaned back, breathing deeply. A strange panic was forming inside him. He'd thought he'd done it, he'd thought he'd penetrated Graebner's armour at last, and all the time the big man had been watching every move he made, watching and appraising. He had to get this absolutely right, or everything he'd gone through would have been for nothing.

'It's true,' he admitted. 'I did want you to notice me.'

Graebner was silent. Tower II's searchbeam drifted by, lighting up the room for an instant before passing on. If only I could see his face, Tully thought, maybe I'd get a clue about what he's thinking. But the damned shadows had obliterated everything. Only the spiky peripheral of Graebner's close-cropped hair showed in the thin light from the window.

Picking his words carefully, his voice hoarse and unnatural, Tully started to explain. 'Eighteen months ago,' he said, 'I was on sentry duty at the Tirpitz Ufer in Berlin. You were there. You'd just returned from Russia, wearing the Knight's Cross and dressed in the uniform of a colonel of the Abwehr, Military Intelligence.'

Graebner sat in the darkness, his eyes fixed on Tully, his great bullet head sunk low on his trunk like a fighter waiting for the bell.

'When I arrived here and spotted you in the compound,' Tully went on, 'I thought I'd made a mistake. How could an Abwehr colonel turn up as a private in the Panzers? I asked myself. Then I saw the scar and I knew you had to be the same man. Clearly the Americans haven't tumbled you yet, and you're not going out of your way to enlighten them. Which means you must have something up your sleeve, some kind of plan.'

'Why should it mean any such thing?' Graebner asked softly. 'It's the duty of any high-ranking intelligence officer to hide his identity from the enemy.'

Tully gave him a remonstrative look. 'Now it's you who're treating me like a fool, Herr Oberst. You don't have to stay in this craphole. You could be living in comparative luxury, with your own batman, full army pay, and the respect your rank deserves. You don't have to slave your guts out in the woods like a miserable coolie, or put up with scum like Strahle. I think you've got something else in mind.'

'Like what?'

Tully hesitated. 'Busting out.'

Graebner laughed softly in the darkness. 'You think that's why I'm happy to stay here? Because it gives me a chance to escape?'

'Herr Oberst, I know damned well that's why. I knew it the minute I set eyes on you. If the Americans realised who you really are, life would be more agreeable all right, but they'd watch you like a hawk.'

Graebner rubbed his nose with his fingers. He looked so calm sitting there, so utterly at ease and sure of himself, that for a moment Tully envied him. Nothing Tully had ever done in his life had given him that kind of confidence. What are you thinking? you bastard, he wondered, knowing instinctively the question was illogical, since Graebner would never disclose what was going on inside his skull, not unless he wanted to.

'This is an interesting situation we have here,' Graebner murmured. 'You've gone to all this trouble to make friends because you think I'm on the point of breaking out, right?'

'Correct.'

'On the other hand, you could run off yourself any time you chose to. The security isn't exactly air-tight.'

'How far would I get?' Tully said. 'A mile, ten miles? No, doing it properly takes planning, organisation. A man on the run needs money, ID documents.'

'You think I can supply those?' Graebner's voice sounded amused.

'Herr Oberst, I look at it this way. As a colonel in intelligence, it's unlikely you were captured in the front line. That means you must have infiltrated your way in. Now nobody gives up his freedom voluntarily, so you must be here for a pretty good reason, and since you're doing no damned good stuck behind this wire, sooner or later you'll have to reach the other side.'

He paused as a patrol went by the window, boots crunching on the gravel path. Graebner squatted back on his heels, studying him thoughtfully, and Tully wondered for a moment if the German could see in the dark, then dismissed the idea as crazy. Graebner was clever, damned clever, but he wasn't Captain Marvel.

'What are we going to do with you, Raderecht?' Graebner said softly. 'You already know too much for your own good.'

'Buy my silence,' Tully suggested.

'How?'

'Take me with you. One extra man. Surely that's not too high a price?'

Graebner hummed softly under his breath. Again, Tully saw the spiky outline of his cropped hair framed against the window.

'My first impulse,' Graebner said reasonably, 'is to kill you.'

Tully swallowed hard, wondering what on earth he'd do if Graebner took it into his mind to get up now, this very minute, and tear his throat out. There was no doubt in Tully's mind that Graebner could do it. A man like that, built like a gorilla, who'd obviously kept himself in shape, a powerful man who'd been trained to kill with his bare hands and who, by the very virtue of his job, would be imbued with a ruthlessness Tully could never himself hope to emulate—Tully wouldn't stand a chance. That was the awful thing about violence, you never quite believed it until you were right up close, and by then it was too late, because your brain, in accepting its reality, in absorbing the realisation that you were about to get badly hurt, or killed maybe, seized up tight and quit functioning. At least, Tully's always did. With Graebner, he doubted it. Graebner looked as if he would function in an earthquake. He had that air about him, unshakable and indestructible.

'Maybe I should have let Strahle finish you off,' Graebner murmured.

'A dead man in the heating plant? You'd have had the Yanks swarming over this camp like flies. What would that have done to your escape plans?'

'You show an infuriating sense of logic, Raderecht.'

'At least admit that I'm right.'

'Very well, it's true. I do intend to escape. But not for my own sake. I'm on a mission for the Reich.'

'What kind of mission?'

Graebner's teeth flashed in the darkness. 'Raderecht, for a shrewd man you show an amazing lack of intelligence. Do you seriously expect me to tell you that? I will go this far though. It's something that could change the course of world history. I want you to understand that, because then you'll understand that if you show any likelihood of endangering my plans, I'll finish you off without a second thought.'

'Take me along,' Tully urged. 'You'll find me useful.'

Graebner leaned against the bookshelf, straightening his legs. 'Yes,' he agreed, 'you could prove something of a bonus at that. Aren't you the musician, the one who goes every night to the piano teacher's house?'

'Yes.'

'How does she feel about you?'

Tully frowned. 'What d'you mean?'

'I mean would she help you to escape?'

'I'd never ask,' Tully said hastily.

'To hell with what you'd ask, Raderecht. If it came to a pinch, would she or wouldn't she?'

Tully pursed his lips. 'I guess she might.'

'That's all I need to know. Come on.'

He straightened and rose to his feet.

'Where are we going?' Tully asked.

'I think it's time you met your new companions,' Graebner said.

The chapel was dark when they got there, having crossed the compound at a run, dodging patrols and searchlight beams. Tully felt strange as they stood in the doorway, smelling the musty odour of incense and dusty pews, experiencing the curious guilt-ridden sensation of being in church at night-time. He blinked into the gloom. He could see figures crouching in the darkness, and moving closer sensed a chill settling on his heart as he realised it was Strahle and his followers.

Strahle rose slowly to his feet. 'What the hell's he doing here?' he demanded.

'Easy, Sergeant,' Graebner said mildly, 'I've decided Raderecht could be a good man to have along.'

'Are you crazy? He's been nothing but trouble since he arrived.'

'Well, you must admit he knows how to make his presence felt.'

Strahle was almost choking with anger. 'I want him out,' he snapped furiously.

Graebner's eyebrows lifted. 'Want?' he echoed. 'What does that mean, you want? If there's any wanting to be done around here, I'll decide what it is and who does it.'

Strahle looked shaken. Tully didn't blame him. Graebner, big-shouldered and heavy-muscled, was a formidable character when he put his mind to it.

'I'm sorry, Herr Oberst,' Strahle muttered, 'but I should have cut his throat in the heating plant.'

Graebner shook his head wearily. 'That's what worries me about you, Helmuth. Three days before our break-out, you'd leave a body bleeding to death from a sabre cut. How d'you think the Americans would react to that?'

'It makes no difference,' Strahle insisted, 'it's too late for newcomers. Our plans are already finalised.'

'We can always be flexible,' Graebner smiled. 'One of the cardinal rules of warfare is—learn to adapt.'

He eased himself into a pew, calm and assured, a man who knew his power and how to wield it. 'What we have here,' he said, 'is, I believe, an impasse. Raderecht has discovered our identity. We can't kill him, because that would lead to an increase in security. We can't leave him behind, because he might not keep his mouth shut. The way I see it, we have only one alternative. Take him along. Besides, I think his presence could be beneficial.'

'How?' Strahle demanded.

'First of all, he speaks American like an American, according to the men with whom he escaped in New York.'

Strahle snorted. 'That was a catastrophe. They hadn't even the sense to get out of the city.'

'They weren't trying to,' Graebner answered evenly. 'In New York, they had no place to go. At least they succeeded in raising a little hell among their guards. However, that's not the main reason I think Raderecht's valuable. He's got a contact on the outside. The schoolteacher. She's crazy about him, isn't that right, Raderecht?'

Tully stared at him in panic. The conversation was taking a turn he didn't like at all. 'Hold on a minute,' he said, 'she has nothing to do with this.'

'She has everything to do with it. She's the reason you're still alive.'

'I told you in the library. I don't want her involved.'

'She's already involved. She's involved with you. And you'd better hope to hell she likes you a lot, because your survival depends on whether or not she's prepared to co-operate.'

'Herr Oberst, this wasn't our deal.'

'We made no deal, Raderecht. I let you live a few minutes

longer, that's all. We can extend those few minutes if you decide to be sensible, but I'm taking no chances if you don't.'

'She's an American citizen. You can't seriously expect her to help a bunch of POWs to escape?'

'Why not? Women in love are notoriously illogical.'

'She's not a traitor, Graebner.'

Graebner sighed. He hooked one arm over the pew-rest, turning his body so that he was facing Tully. There was nothing in his eyes to show what he was thinking, but somehow Tully felt his fear begin again, and he wiped a sudden sweat from his brow.

'Let me explain the situation,' Graebner said. 'When we make our break on Tuesday, our main danger will lie in the first few minutes. The problem facing any runaway is the ten miles between the camp and the main highway. We're in the middle of swamp country, so there's no sense turning east or west. There's only one way out, and that's by road. The local police can seal off that escape route tighter than a pickle jar. However, if we reach the turnpike, we can head for Cooper's Point. There's a freight train due by around 4.45, and it has to slow to a walking pace to take the grade. Nail that train and we'll be on our way to freedom, but those ten miles could be a hell of a distance to cover with Glusky's troops on our tail. Our plan was to steal a truck, but that depends on one being available at precisely the right moment. On the other hand, if your girlfriend could get us some transport . . .'

He let his voice trail away. Tully stared at him.

'You're out of your mind.'

'Why? She borrows her neighbour's, doesn't she? She brings you back in the thing every night.'

'That's a jeep.'

'It'll do. There's only eight of us.'

'Herr Oberst, you're not listening to what I'm saying. I don't want her brought into this.'

'Raderecht,' Graebner said patiently, 'we've agreed to take you along. We expect you to pay your way. Persuade her.'

'And if she refuses?'

'Make sure she doesn't.'

Tully shivered. He felt as if something had just touched the most precious thing in his life, threatening its existence for a moment before passing on.

'This is crazy,' he whispered. 'You know I can't be ready by Tuesday.'

'You must.'

'But I need more time.'

'This is a military operation, not a joyride. We have a schedule to maintain. Success or failure can depend on keeping our timings precise.'

'I'll need documents,' Tully protested, 'identification, new clothing.'

'You'll need nothing. We're here as German soldiers and we'll fight as German soldiers. We're not skulking round the countryside like a bunch of frightened convicts.'

Tully felt his resistance wilting. There was something so damned positive about Graebner, so cool and precise, you felt nothing in the world could break his composure. Then he thought about Etta, and something came over him, an intense and impossible-to-escape feeling of self-loathing. She was the first person in his entire existence who'd ever really mattered, and here he was planning to put her life on the line. Damn Reiser and his bag of dirty tricks. Why was it always the little people who suffered?

Strahle stood studying Tully in silence for a moment.

'How soon will we know?' he asked Graebner.

'Know what?'

'If Raderecht's got the truck.'

'By tomorrow night.'

'I can't do it that quickly,' Tully protested weakly.

'You can, Raderecht, and you will. We'll meet here after lights-out and make our final arrangements then. Meanwhile, for your benefit, let's go over the major details again.'

Their meeting was interrupted only once, when the midnight patrol marched by. Crouching in silence, Graebner waited for the boots to fade into the distance, then went on with his briefing. Tully scarcely listened. Depression had him in its grip, a strange dread that needled at his brain like toothache; for no matter which way he looked at it, the only fact that settled in his mind was the thought that the one person in the world he cared about was being dragged into this mess alongside him.

The discussion over, the conspirators left in groups of two. Strahle and Scheller went first, followed by Kruger and Wegmüller. In the end, only Graebner and Tully were left. The church was deathly quiet in the stillness. Graebner lay stretched on the pew, his spine propped against the seat-rest. He took out a packet of cigarettes, gave one to Tully and placed another between his lips. Tully reached for his lighter and threw it across.

'Freedom,' Graebner said. 'It's a tantalising word.'

'We're not out yet,' Tully answered darkly.

'We'll make it, don't worry.'

'Then what?'

'I've told you before, Raderecht. No questions. You'll learn everything in good time.'

'I meant after it's over. Do we stay in the United States or head for Mexico?'

'Leave me to worry about that.'

'Well,' Tully said, 'it'll feel good to be our own men again.'

Graebner chuckled. He inhaled deeply on the cigarette. 'Do you know the Rhine country, Raderecht?' he asked. 'No.'

'First time I ever took a holiday on my own, I hiked up the Rhine Valley from Mannheim to Bonn. I carried everything on my back, sleeping bag, groundsheet, cooking stove. It took me four weeks. I was thirteen years old. I remember the cherry trees on the hills above Mainz, and the way the river looked from high on the bluff, and the vine terraces crowding down to the water's edge, and castles everywhere. I remember thinking if I kept on walking, just walking, I could change the whole course of my life.'

'Did you do it?'

He smiled. 'No. I went back home.'

He drew up his knees and hooked his arms round them, his face shining with a strange light. 'You have to know something about my family,' he explained. 'We weren't like other people. My father wanted his sons to grow up cleverer than anyone else around. That was drummed into us from the age of one, the Graebners always had to come out on top.'

'The Graebners?'

'That's my real name. There were eight of us altogether, six boys, two girls. I was the youngest. Every night at dinner, the conversation would dwell on politics, music, art. My father never permitted small talk. If we didn't have something significant to say, we had to sit and not communicate at all. He was a bastard, but he certainly knew how to instill a competitive spirit. We spent our whole lives trying to outdo each other.'

'Is he still alive, your father?'

'He was, when I left. I lost my eldest brother in Russia, and one sister in a bombing raid, but the rest of the family's intact as far as I know.'

Tully looked at him curiously. He already knew Graebner's background. He had studied it in Colonel Reiser's files, but this was the first time the German had actually volunteered information about himself.

'Are you married?' Tully asked.

'Sure,' said Graebner. 'You too, isn't that right?'

Tully nodded.

'Any kids?'

'A little boy.'

'How old?'

'Just over two.'

Graebner pulled a face. 'Rotten, isn't it, being stuck in a dump like this, knowing your kids are growing up like strangers? That's what's crazy about war.'

'That, and having to work with thugs like Strahle,' Tully said.

Graebner nodded. "I know you're wondering why I chose him. If you want the truth, I had no choice. When we jump that freight train on Tuesday, we have to take it over by force. I need men, and someone to control them. In this camp, only Strahle qualifies. You can't always pick your companions in time of war.'

'He's sick in the head,' Tully said.

'But at least he's a loyal Nazi. That doesn't endear the

bastard to me particularly, but it does mean he'll obey orders. And give his life for the fatherland, if necessary.'

Graebner made as if to throw back Tully's lighter. He peered at it, the glow of his cigarette creating an orange circle across his throat and lower chin. 'Nice,' he said, 'solid gold, isn't it?'

'Yes.'

'You're lucky you've managed to keep it. These Yanks are souvenir-crazy. Get it in Mannheim?'

'Why?'

'I've seen one like this before. It's got a secret panel, hasn't it?'

Tully frowned. 'A what?' he murmured.

'Don't tell me you didn't know. There's a hidden catch someplace. Sure, here it is.'

Graebner's finger found a tiny button, and pressing it he swung open the lighter's casing with a muffled click.

Something stirred in Tully, a sense of faint unease, a subtle anger at his own stupidity, because goddammit he'd never realised that panel was there.

Graebner was studying it closely. 'That's odd,' he murmured.

'What?'

'There's an inscription engraved into the gold, in English.'

Haltingly, he read aloud: 'To J.A. Tully, with warm wishes and deep affection, from the residents of Avery, Wyoming, April 1943.'

Tully swallowed hard. Jesus Christ! he thought. All those months in Nazi Germany he'd been walking round with a bomb in his pocket. And now, at the very moment he was finally beginning to make progress with Graebner, he was about to blow everything because he hadn't had the simple basic intelligence to check out his stupid lighter.

'Where did you get this?' Graebner demanded.

'I . . . I took it off an American soldier outside St Lo.'

Graebner studied the inscription again, running his thumb over the lettering. 'Did you . . . kill the man?' he asked.

'Yes,' said Tully.

'Unfortunate. I prefer war to be impersonal. Something

like this, a name, an identity, brings it back to a human level somehow.'

Tully couldn't bring himself to speak. If only he knew what was going on in Graebner's mind, if only the German wasn't so goddammed impenetrable. Had he accepted Tully's story, or was he even now, in his bland infuriating way, playing him like a cat, waiting for the moment when he would reach out, take Tully's throat in his hands, and choke the truth from his lips?

But Graebner looked calm and unsuspecting as he stared at Tully curiously. 'You okay?' he asked. 'You're pale as a ghost. You can file the inscription off if it bothers you.'

Tully shook his head. 'It's too late,' he said, 'the man I killed, I know his name now.'

'Well, you can't bring him back to life, that's for sure. Here.'

Graebner was about to toss the lighter back, but Tully stopped him. He couldn't afford to carry the thing now. Too dangerous. Someone else might find it, someone less ready to be convinced than Graebner.

'Keep it,' he said.

'What?'

'I couldn't bear to touch it any more.'

'You're crazy. This is worth a good deal of money.'

'It's bad luck.'

Graebner chuckled in the darkness. 'You're a strange man, Raderecht. Full of moods and complexes. I can't figure you out at all.'

'Never mind about figuring me out,' said Tully, 'just as long as you trust me.'

Graebner slipped the lighter inside his pocket. His cigarette glow lit the hollows of his cheeks, casting shadows across his eyes and the corded sinews on his muscular throat.

'Who said anything about trusting you?' he laughed.

They lay together on the bed as the first shades of evening fell across the room, turning the ceiling into a plain of dusky grey. Tully smoked his cigarette, the air cool against his naked skin. Beside him, Ella turned her head on the pillow, watching him intently. Aware of her gaze, he could not bring himself to meet it.

'What's wrong, darling?' she asked.

He didn't answer.

Etta propped herself on one elbow, peering down at his face. Her hair brushed his cheek. 'You're not yourself tonight,' she whispered.

He sighed gently, taking the cigarette from his lips. 'We've got to talk,' he said. 'It's important.'

She looked at him closely for a moment, then lay back on the bed, her eyes sombre. 'I don't like the sound of that,' she murmured. 'It has a ring of finality about it.'

He took her hand, gripping the fingers fiercely. 'Etta, I want you to understand something. You're the best thing that ever happened to me in my life. That's the gospel truth.'

'Then why be sad?'

'I have a confession to make.'

Gently, she kissed his shoulder. 'What are you trying to tell me, Karl?'

'My name isn't Karl, it's John. John Anton Tully. J.A. for short.'

Her eyes looked confused. 'Is this a joke?'

'No joke. I'm not a German soldier, Etta. I'm as American as you are.'

For a moment, she didn't speak. He was filled with an unreasoning desire to crawl away and hide, as if the enormity of his lies, whatever the motives behind them, constituted a betrayal of the most unforgivable nature.

'Will you please explain to me what this is all about?' she whispered.

'You've got to understand, Etta, I couldn't tell you before for security reasons.'

'Security?'

'I'm with the OSS, Office of Strategic Services.'

'Are you trying to say that you're a spy?'

'Yes.'

Her eyes widened. 'A spy?' she echoed.

'I'm an infiltrator. There's a high-ranking German intelli-

gence officer at Camp Cannesetego, working undercover. I'm
attempting to find out what he's up to.'

'My God,' she whispered.

She peered at the ceiling, her face a pale glow in the
darkness. The strong lines of her naked body lay etched upon
the bed like alabaster. Shadows crept across her throat and the
steep curve of belly and breast.

He studied her anxiously. 'Let me get you a drink,' he said.

'No.'

'You look sort of faint.'

'Well, it takes a bit of getting used to,' she muttered. 'You
can't expect me to accept you as German one day and
American the next.'

He hesitated. 'I thought . . . well, I thought maybe
you'd be pleased.'

'Pleased?'

'I mean, discovering we're both on the same side, after
all.'

'And all those stories about your wife and little boy?'

'I made them up.'

'For God's sake!'

'I had to, Etta. They were part of my cover.'

'Couldn't you have trusted me?'

'I wanted to, I swear I did. But there was too much at
stake. You could have given me away without realising. A
chance word out shopping. A thoughtless remark at the
schoolhouse. It was safer to lie. Safer for me. Safer for you.
On Tuesday, a group of Germans are planning to escape from
Cannesetego. It's no simple break-out, Etta. There's a purpose
behind it, a deadly purpose. A military purpose. I've got to
find out what that purpose is.'

'Are you telling me I'll never see you again?'

'Of course not. My God, are you crazy? D'you think I'd
run out on the only thing I have to live for?'

'Then why the sudden confession? You felt no need to
unburden before.'

He rolled back on the pillow, groaning gently in his throat.
Why did it have to be Etta? As if lying wasn't enough.

'We need a truck,' he said.

She stared at him, her eyes clouding. 'What does that mean?'

'You've got to get it for us, Etta.'

'Me?'

She didn't believe him, and for God's sake he couldn't blame her; as far as he could see, he hadn't put a foot right since he'd started this stupid thing.

'Please listen,' he said earnestly. 'The break-out must succeed. I've put too much into this for anything to go wrong now.'

'Well, if you're really who you say you are, why don't you get one of your OSS friends to arrange it?'

'My God, don't you think I'd do that if I could? Do you really believe I want you involved? But this is war, and a hell of a lot of lives could depend on what happens next Tuesday. Please don't turn me down.'

She got up from the bed and strolled to the window, peering out at the evening sky. Her body looked strong and beautiful in the starlight. Watching her, Tully realised he had never in his life felt so low, so utterly and indescribably shameful. He felt as if he had just committed the most unspeakable act in existence, not in a moment of impetuosity, but with his eyes fully open, his brain cool and lucid and aware.

For no reason at all, his hands started trembling.

'How do I know you're not lying?' she asked without turning. 'You've lied already, how do I know you're not lying now? Maybe you really are Karl Raderecht. Maybe this whole thing is just a trick.'

'I don't blame you for thinking that,' he said. 'All I can say is, if you don't trust me by now, I guess the last few weeks have been a waste of time.'

She went on peering into the darkness, her hair forming a tangled triangle against the pale glow of her skin.

'Don't breathe a word of this to anyone else,' Tully said. 'If the Germans find out who I really am, they'll kill me without a second thought. I'm going to give you a telephone number in Washington. I want you to call it and ask for Colonel Reiser. Tell him everything, he'll know what to do. Only don't make the call until after our break-out. Whatever happens, I can't risk anything interfering with that escape, understand?'

Still she didn't answer. A wave of hopelessness filled him. Could he blame her for thinking him a liar? Surely he realised how empty and unconvincing his story sounded? He had no proof of identity, no proof of anything. He was demanding the kind of trust he had already denied her.

'I guess you don't believe me, do you?' he whispered.

Something in her voice told him she was crying. 'What difference does it make?' she said. 'What does it matter if I believe you or not? You know I'd never refuse you anything, anything in the world. Go back and tell your friends not to worry. The truck will be there.'

Three days later, they came out of the brush, running through gorse bushes, brambles, and clumps of wild sawgrass to where Etta sat parked in the battered farmtruck. Leaping over the wire fence, they scrambled into the back and Etta engaged the gear, her hand trembling. Then with a furious roar they spun off, scattering earth and dust as they thundered across the Cannesetego River Bridge and swept from sight down the rutted swamptrack.

12

It was 2.20 in the afternoon when Patrolman Mac Brady arrived at Lomstoun police-station to begin his daily shift. Glancing distastefully at the cigarette butts in the ashtrays, the mugs of half-drunk coffee on the desktops, and the screwed-up balls of paper on the floor, Brady reflected that it looked as if a tornado had just passed through. He was a tidy man by nature and had never grown used to Chief Fraser's inherent sense of disorder. A police-station should be like a military establishment, he thought. It was the hub of the community. What kind of example were they setting the people who came in here, for Christ's sake?

'Look at this place,' he said in disgust to Burt Forbes, who was sitting with his feet on the desk reading a paperback novel. 'It's like a damned garbage-can.'

Forbes eased his sweat-soaked shirt away from his skin and held the electric fan so that its current bathed his cheeks and throat.

'Makes it kind of homey,' he murmured. 'Better'n them smartass mausoleums they run in Baton Route.'

'Where's the Chief?' Brady asked.

'Where he always is this time of day. Up at Julie's.'

Brady picked up the Arrest Sheet and glanced through it. 'Anything happening?'

'Mrs Lockley's cat got stuck in a tree again.'

Brady sniffed in disgust. 'I told her she's got to stop calling us about that animal. This is a police-station, not a god-dammed cats' home.'

The telephone rang and Forbes picked up the receiver, swinging his feet to the floor. He put down the electric fan and took out a handkerchief, mopping his forehead and cheeks. 'Lomstoun Police,' he said, 'Patrolman Forbes speaking.'

He listened a few moments and Brady watched his expression freeze.

'God Almighty!' Forbes muttered, and something inside Brady involuntarily tightened.

Forbes put down the receiver and sat staring into the air.

'Shee-it!' he exclaimed, 'there goes my afternoon off. Eight of them POWs just broke out of Cannesetego and stole themselves a truck.'

'Christ!' snapped Brady, reaching for the phone. 'I'd better get Fraser right away.'

He dialled a number and a soft female voice came on the line.

'Hello?'

'Julie, this is Patrolman Brady at police-headquarters. Is the Chief there?'

'Just a moment, Patrolman Brady.'

There was a brief pause, then Fraser's voice answered, brusque and irritated. 'What's up, Mac?'

'Chief, the shit just hit the fan down here. We got a break-out at the POW camp. Eight Germans.'

There was a heavy silence at the other end. Brady waited, but all he could hear was the sound of Fraser's heavy breathing. He visualised the fleshy form of his Chief perched on the edge of Julie Gilman's bed, thinking hard. Fraser never made decisions quickly. Brady allowed that in retrospect he often turned out to be right, but he sure took hell's own time in making up his mind.

'Shall I alert state police, Chief?' Brady murmured.

'No.' Fraser's reaction was sharp and immediate. 'Keep those bastards out of it. I don't want them within sniffing distance of Lomstoun.'

'That won't be easy, Chief. This ain't no petty larceny, y'know. Them Krauts have got wheels. They stole a truck.'

'Then they'll be heading for the state highway. How many roads could they take?'

Brady consulted the area map on the opposite wall, running his finger over the complex network of highways and farm-tracks.

'Only one as far as the Craven Crossing turnpike. After that, three until they reach Morgan City.'

There was another silence at the other end. When Fraser spoke again, his voice was tense and clipped, honed by excitement into a sharp edge. 'Mac, this is an emergency,' he said. 'I want every road south of Morgan City blocked, understand? Call Anderson and tell him to get his ass over there. Whatever happens, we gotta grab them runaways before the bastards in New Orleans get wind of this.'

'Right,' Brady said quickly. And with excitement pulsing through his veins, he hung up.

It took the Germans close on two hours to cover the forty miles to Cooper's Point, leaving the swamp road at Craven Crossing, then travelling on farm-tracks and byways to avoid cruising patrol cars. As they approached the grading, they heard the shriek of a train whistle, and Graebner said thinly: 'Christ! we're cutting it fine.'

Etta stabbed the pedal and Tully's head bounced off the ceiling as the road dipped into a hollow, muddy water spraying across their windshield. They leapt up the other side, Etta working the gears like a madwoman, then they were out in the open, trees up front, swamp channels to their right, and over east, the long lazy vapour trail of the locomotive floating on the late afternoon air.

They spotted the railroad track ahead, slicing across their path, and Etta crashed gears, slowing pace. Tully marvelled at the ease with which she handled the vehicle.

As they screeched to a halt, the men in the rear scrambled out and scuttled into the underbrush.

'Okay,' Graebner snapped at Etta, 'hide this thing in the trees over there.'

Etta engaged the gear and jammed her foot on the accelerator, crashing through gorse bushes and clumps of clinging scrub. She screeched to a halt and, leaving the door swinging wildly, ran back to join them.

Tully stared frowning at the ragged trail in the underbrush which marked her route. 'They'll spot that a mile off,' he said.

'They won't be looking,' growled Graebner, 'not for an hour or two. That's all we need.'

'What about her?' Tully indicated Etta. 'How does she get back?'

'She'll have to come with us,' Graebner answered. 'I'm sorry, Raderecht, but we can't turn her loose now. She'd have the whole damned county on our heels.'

Tully's face crimsoned. 'You bastard. Once she got us to the Point you promised she could go.'

'I promised nothing,' Graebner sighed. 'I'll set her free as soon as it's practical, but until we're clear of the area, it's out of the question.'

'No,' Tully thundered.

Etta caught his arm, her fingers biting hard into his elbow.

'It's all right,' she whispered, 'I wouldn't go anyhow. I couldn't bear to be sitting at home alone, wondering if you're still alive or not.'

'There could be shooting ahead,' Tully insisted.

'I don't care as long as we're together. I'm staying, until I'm sure you are safe.'

They heard the thunderous hissing of the locomotive as it laboured up the hill towards them, then it hove into view, its blunt nose gleaming, steam from its valves belching across the iron rails. It was not one of the new diesels, but an ancient Class-F Mallet twelve-wheeler, complete with pilot light and elongated smoke funnel. They watched it lumber by, battling with the grading, followed by the freight cars, their sliding doors locked up tight and sealed with metal wire.

Tully's mind was in a turmoil. None of this was going right, he realised. He never should have brought Etta into it, never. He should have guessed from the beginning that Graebner would refuse to turn her loose when the time came. Oh, he could see the German's reasoning all right. But it left him with an added problem to consider. He had to figure a way of getting Etta out of here.

Through the steam they spotted a car with its hatch back. 'There's one,' Graebner hissed. 'Hurry.'

They trotted alongside, Strahle entering first, hauling himself over the clacketing deck. He had brought his sabre along, which he threw in ahead of him, and they heard it bounce against the opposite wall. The others followed one by one, helping each other over the wooden rim.

Tully grabbed Etta's arm and half-pushing, half-lifting, he wrestled her through the open hatchway and swiftly followed, scraping his elbows on the rough wood boards. Gasping, he crouched on the floor, surprised in the end how easy it had been. He squinted into the semi-darkness. Packs of cement lay heaped in one corner, and a dozen milk-churns stood stacked in a frame against the far wall. On the floor, staring at them in amazement, sprawled two scrawny hobos. They were dressed in threadbare dungarees and both were unmistakably drunk.

'Looks like we've got company,' Graebner murmured.

'Shall I kill them?' asked Strahle, resting the sabre across one shoulder.

Graebner stared at him. 'What in hell for?'

'They're the enemy, aren't they?'

'For Christ's sake, Strahle, you can't wipe out the whole bloody population. Leave them alone. They're not doing us any harm.'

The train was beginning to pick up speed again, and Tully felt the wheels clickety-clacking beneath his haunches, the rhythm quickening every second.

Graebner gathered them together. 'That was close,' he said, 'but stage one's successfully completed. Now it's time for stage two. We've got to take over the train.'

'What with?' Scheller asked.

Graebner nodded at the sabre in Strahle's hand. 'That,' he said. 'It's not much of a weapon, but it's all we've got. There'll be an engineer and fireman up front, and a brakeman at the rear. I'm counting on the fact that the other boxcars are sealed up tight, so let's assume there are no riders, apart from these two here.' He nodded at the hobos. 'Eyke, I want you to move to the back and disable the brakeman.'

Eyke nodded silently. Graebner peered at Strahle. 'Think you can take over the locomotive?'

'Of course,' Strahle smirked.

Graebner turned to Tully. 'You go with him,' he ordered. 'Make sure he doesn't turn violent. I don't want the engineer or fireman hurt. We need them to operate this thing.'

Tully's heart sank at the thought of moving along the carriage roofs. 'Couldn't we wait until we stop for water?' he asked.

'No time. Once the police figure out we're on this train, they'll cut us off further up the track. We've got to keep one jump ahead of the bastards. Move.'

Strahle went first, handing his sabre to Tully as he leaned out of the boxcar door and peered upwards at the roof. Two of the men seized him by the thighs and eased him gently towards the sloping canopy. Reaching out, he got his hands hooked into the rain funnel along the boxcar's rim and hauled himself to its top. Tully handed up the sabre and took his place in the open doorway, his palms hot and sweaty. The wind caught his hair, scattering it wildly. He felt strong arms seize his legs, raising him slowly upwards, and keeping one hand on the sliding door he reached as high as he could with the other and grunted with relief as his fingers found the comforting curve of the rain funnel. Strahle seized his tunic and began to tug from above, and gasping with exertion Tully wrestled his way up and over to the carriage roof.

It seemed a precarious perch as he struggled to balance on the curving canopy. They were rattling from side to side, and he had the disturbing notion that at any second one of the trees whipping by might reach down a branch and sweep them off their platform.

Strahle squinted at him, his face covered with grime from the engine smoke. 'Okay?' he yelled.

Tully nodded to signify yes. Strahle gestured towards the front, then without hesitation rose to his feet and began to trot along the carriage roof, leaping nimbly from one car to the next.

Tully took a deep breath and followed, the windstream battering his cheeks. He found it hard to breathe as he jostled forward, peering through the swirling column of smoke at the roof below. Reaching the boxcar edge, he held his breath and leapt forward, gasping with relief as his heels struck the wood-and-tarpaulin framework of the next wagon.

The smoke came belching back in a steady stream, blotting out the sky, the trees, even occasionally the narrow platform on which he scuttled, then, caught by the windstream, it swung away and he spotted the coal wagon ahead. Strahle was already scrambling over it, the sabre held across his chest.

Tully reached the edge of the front carriage and leapt, rolling awkwardly, almost falling, but saving himself in time to claw his way over the flinty chunks until he reached Strahle's side. Together, they slithered down to the locomotive platform.

A wave of intense heat belched from the open boiler. Tully saw flames leaping wildly inside the hatch. A maze of levers and dials stared down from the engine panel, and the driver and fireman, both small men, plump and sweaty, stared in undisguised amazement at the incredible sight of two German soldiers bearing down on them from the cars behind.

Strahle waved his sabre threateningly. 'Tell them to back up against the wall,' he snapped.

Tully repeated the order in English. The two men did as they were told, their faces displaying the first uncertainty of fear. Without being asked, they put their hands on their heads as if to indicate their complete willingness to be subjugated. Tully felt sorry for them. He felt sorry for anyone who had to face a bastard like Strahle. For these poor men the day would have started like any other. The war must have seemed a million miles away. Now suddenly, in the green Louisiana woodlands, violence and death had caught them up.

'Listen to me,' Tully said reasonably. 'The man holding the sabre is a highly emotional and unstable character. Whatever you do, don't try to oppose him. If he gives you an order, obey quickly and without question, understand?'

The two men nodded, completely intimidated.

'Okay,' Tully grunted. 'Now stop this thing.'

The driver did as he was told and the locomotive shuddered to a halt in a great hiss of steam.

Strahle chuckled. With his face blackened by smoke, his

shirt covered with coal dust, and his eyes lit by boiler flames, he looked, Tully thought, like a fiend out of hell.

'I'll take care of these jokers,' Strahle murmured. 'Get back to the boxcar and tell Graebner the train is ours.'

It was crowded on the footplate with Grabener, Strahle, and the two railroadmen. Tully tried to leave a gap between himself and the heat from the furnace, but there was no place to go. He pressed back against the hot wall, sweat beading his face and dripping from the end of his nose. Of all the lousy luck, he thought. Only on the most archaic freightline would they have found such an ancient engine still in operation.

Darkness had gathered round them, and Tully noticed sparks leaping out of the funnel ahead. The boiler cast an eerie circle of light across their tiny platform, giving life to their eyes and the lines on their faces. They looked, Tully thought, like creatures from another universe, the Germans filthy, covered with soot, the engineer and fireman sweaty with fear. The two railroadmen had taken off their caps, as if afraid that even those innocuous symbols of authority might be construed by their captors as a form of provocation.

Tully wondered where Graebner was going. This was no impulsive flight of panic, he realised. Graebner had worked it out detail by detail. He knew exactly what he was up to, and why.

Tully felt his pulse throbbing with excitement. It was only a matter of time now before he knew the truth. If they could somehow evade capture, he would at last find out what the whole damned riddle was all about. His job would be over. There'd be no more subterfuge. No more nightmares. Only freedom and tranquility. And—please God—Etta.

'What happens if they block the line up front?' he asked.

'I'm anticipating that,' Graebner said. 'This track's barely used, so it'll take them a little time to figure out where we've gone to. There's an old branch line two or three miles ahead. It's been lying derelict since they shut it down as unsafe ten years ago. They'll never expect us to head that way.'

He turned to the engineer and said briskly in English: 'You know the Batterman Road?'

'Through the swamp?'

'I want you to take it.'

The man's face registered disbelief. 'You're crazy. The Batterman Road crumbled into decay years ago.'

'It should be strong enough to support us if we take it slowly. We'll switch tracks at the points.'

The engineer protested, his eyes desperate with alarm.

'Mister, nobody's tried that line for close on ten years. It was built to haul out lumber when they were logging the cypress strand, but it cuts straight through the Yakamanatchee. The support posts will have rotted away. We'll never make it.'

'Just coast easy and keep your speed down. I think we'll be okay.'

Tully watched the engineer in silence for a moment, feeling a strange dread thumping inside him. Maybe he'd overplayed his hand, he thought. Maybe he'd gotten too damned smart for his own good. Instead of embarking on this ludicrous enterprise, he should have done exactly what was expected of him. Telephoned Reiser and let the OSS handle things.

'Herr Oberst,' he said, 'can I talk with you a minute?'

Graebner nodded, and they pushed their way backwards off the footplate, stepping out onto the coal-bunker and holding on tight as the slipstream plucked at their faces.

'This guy, the engineer,' Tully said, 'he's probably been riding this line since boyhood.'

'What about it?'

'If he says the Batterman Road is unsafe, I believe him.'

Smoke-blackened and streaked with sweat, Graebner's face looked unreal in the furnace glare. 'I know,' he admitted, 'I'm as worried as you are. But if we can just get through the swamp, we'll be home and dry.'

'What happens if we break down in there?'

'I'm praying that won't happen.'

Tully took a deep breath. If only the German wasn't so big, he might shake some sense into that thick Prussian skull. But the idea of grabbing Graebner was like dancing down the middle of Fifth Avenue in the rush hour. He'd mow Tully down like a tank.

'I think we should leave the train here,' Tully declared.

'Find ourselves an automobile someplace. We'd be less conspicuous and less vulnerable.'

Graebner shook his head. 'They'll have every road up to Baton Rouge sealed up tight. The train's the only way.'

'But not through the swamp, for Christ's sake. We're asking for it.'

Graebner squeezed his arm. He looked sympathetic. 'If I could think of another route, believe me I would. But right at this moment our only hope is to put as much distance between us and Cannesetego as we possibly can. I reckon they'll have blocked the line by now, but one thing they'll never believe is that we'd be crazy enough to take the Batterman Road. We've got to try it.'

'What about the girl?'

Graebner's face clouded. 'I'm sorry about that, Raderecht, I didn't want to bring her along.'

'You never intended to let her go from the beginning, did you?'

'You're wrong. As soon as we're safe, I'll turn her loose, I promise.'

'I'm holding you responsible if anything happens to her,' Tully said coldly.

Graebner squeezed his arm again. 'Quit worrying, will you,' he whispered. 'Nothing will happen. Nothing.'

He moved back to the footplate, leaving Tully still clinging to the coal-bunker. Tully felt the wind whipping at his cheeks and throat. He held his face to its current, savouring the cool revitalising slipstream.

He had to get Etta away from here, he thought. If the army headed them off, Graebner would use her as a hostage, he had no doubts on that score. But helping her escape was one thing. Keeping his cover was another. He'd have to do it cleverly. He couldn't afford to botch this up now, not when he was so close to success. Another few hours at the most and he would know everything. The realisation made him dizzy with excitement.

He saw Strahle staring at him from the locomotive footplate, then Strahle stepped across to the coal-bunker, his pale face smeared with grime, his eyes glittering in the furnace light.

'Feeling jumpy?' he asked.

'Aren't you?'

'Not me, Raderecht. I'm having a good time.'

His thin lips twisted into a humourless grin. 'How's the face?' he grunted.

Instinctively, Tully touched the dressings on his cheeks. Graebner had changed them before the escape bid, but he had noticed during the run along the boxcar that one of the dressings was wet with blood.

'I've still got the stitches in,' he said.

Strahle's grin widened. 'You'll never live to have them out.'

'What the hell are you talking about?'

Strahle hooked his elbow over the bunker rim. His eyes flashed with a crazy light. 'We need each other for the moment, you and me, Raderecht. This mission is too important to jeopardise with personal enmities, but once it's over, the very minute Graebner tells us we're free men again, I think you should know something. I'm going to kill you.'

Tully shook his head resignedly. 'Strahle, you're a sick man, d'you realise that?'

'I mean it, Raderecht.'

'I know you do, you poor bastard. That's what makes you so goddammed sad.'

He felt his spirits drop. As if he hadn't enough to worry about. Now he'd have to keep an eye on Strahle as well.

They spotted the fork in the track ahead, and the engineer slowed, applying his brakes as the great locomotive hissed smoothly to a halt. With Strahle's sabre at his neck, the fireman clambered down and switched the points by hand. The rails altered position with a muffled click and the fireman slotted the lever into 'lock', fastening it steady with a metal chain.

Belching black smoke, the locomotive eased gently forward. The line was built up on wooden trestles rising out of the swamp water. Tully could see mud and slime glistening in the starlight. Cypresses clustered in like the bars of some immense prison cage.

'It's a bit crowded here,' Tully called to Graebner. 'I'm going back to the boxcar.'

The German nodded wordlessly.

The trip back along the carriage roofs was easier now the train had slowed. Tully reached the freight-wagon without incident and lowered himself in through the open doorway.

The two hobos were asleep in the corner. Scheller, Wegmüller and the others lay stretched wearily on the boxcar floor. Tully looked at Etta. 'How're you feeling?' he whispered.

'Okay.'

'Try and sleep.'

'I couldn't. I'm too tense.'

'Well, nothing's going to happen for the next hour or so. We're in the swamp.'

'Is that why we've slowed down?'

'Yes.'

Etta joined him in the doorway, staring out at the stars glimmering above the trees. Tully found it hard to believe this was the same sky he had looked at only the night before, locked in the comparative safety of the prison camp.

'Smells soggy,' Etta said, as an odour of rank humidity reached their nostrils. Peering down, Tully saw water glistening in the darkness. The track was raised several feet above its surface, running along a wooden causeway built on stilts. Tully wondered how long those support posts had been left uninspected. Shuddering, he slipped his arm around Etta's waist and pulled her close.

'What's going to happen, darling?' she whispered.

'Christ knows.'

'I get so scared when you leave me.'

He leaned forward and kissed her in the darkness, and somewhere far off an owl hooted, its voice soft and mournful on the still air.

'When we get out of this,' he said, 'I promise I'll never leave you again.'

As evening fell over the makeshift control room at Lomstoun police-station, an air of furious activity took place. Uniformed officers manned the telephones. Tiny flags dotted the wall map, denoting the deployment of national guard trucks.

Chief Fraser, small, sweaty, heavy-jowled, watched this invasion of his privacy with undisguised disgust. He had held out for as long as he could, sitting on the roadblocks at Craven Crossing, but when it had become clear the POWs had eluded him he'd had no choice but to contact the authorities in New Orleans. So far, no-one had commented on the fact that he'd disobeyed regulations, but he knew the captain of state police, Price, was simply biding his time. If their luck didn't break soon, there was going to be one hell of an explosion. Price had that air about him, the air of a man who believed in playing by the rules and despised anyone who didn't.

Captain Price was lean and sinewy, with very black hair and bushy eyebrows that came together over the bridge of his nose. He walked up and down across the floor, sipping aimlessly at a mug of coffee prepared by Brady. His eyes looked tired and worried. He was not by nature an impatient man, but it seemed incredible to him that eight POWs still wearing German uniforms could vanish without trace into a countryside filled with people. He knew damned well if Fraser had had the sense to contact him the minute the alarm had sounded, they'd have had the escapees safely behind barbed wire by now.

'It doesn't make sense,' he said. 'We've got the entire area sealed off. Morgan City, New Iberia, Thibodaux, Houma. They can't have got out without somebody spotting them.'

'Maybe they're not on the move at all,' Fraser suggested. 'Maybe they headed into the swamp.'

'We've got a bunch of Cajun trappers checking the channels out now,' Price said. 'If they're in there, you can bet your ass them Cajuns'll find them.'

He glared at Fraser coldly. 'If you'd contacted us like you should've, we could have saved ourselves three precious hours.'

Chief Fraser sighed. 'Okay, I made a decision and it was a wrong one,' he said. 'What do you want me to do, cut off my arm?'

Captain Price didn't answer. He was staring at the wall map with a kind of dull fury. 'They must be someplace,' he muttered. 'Hiding, waiting. A farm maybe, a derelict barn.

They can't have left the vicinity. There's just no way, unless . . .'

He hesitated a moment, then leaned forward, studying the map intently. 'What's this?' he asked, stabbing at the complex diagram with his forefinger.

'That's the freight line to New Iberia,' Fraser said. 'It ain't used too often these days, but they still run trains a few times a month.'

'What about today?'

'I could check,' Fraser grunted.

He made a quick telephone call. When he hung up, he looked excited. 'A freight went through Cooper's Point around 4.40 this afternoon,' he said. 'That would just about give them runaways time to board it.'

'I wonder,' Price breathed. He thought for a moment. 'Is there any way of stopping it before it gets to New Iberia?'

'It generally takes on water at Soames.'

Price made up his mind quickly. 'Let's get some men there and block off the track. Make sure they're well-armed. And Fraser,' he added, looking at the Chief intently, 'tell them to check the undersides of the boxcars. Those prisoners could be riding the frame-brace to avoid detection.'

'Okay,' said Fraser, hitching up his pants.

He moved to the telephones, his brain working quickly. If Price was right, if the Nazis really were on that train, then afterwards everyone would remember it was he, Fraser, who'd made the phone call, not Captain Price. He would come out of this clean as a baby. Price's word wouldn't be worth a damn.

He dialled a number and waited for a voice to answer.

'This is Chief Fraser at Lomstoun police-station,' he said briskly. 'I just figured out where them Krauts is hiding.'

Tully knew something was different the moment he woke up. He glanced at Etta sleeping soundlessly on the boxcar floor, then turned and peered through the hatchway at the stars beyond. The train had stopped. They were standing motionless, with only the purring of insects breaking the stillness of the swamp night. He slithered to the door and dropped outside. Poised on stilts above the water, the track looked like a causeway to nowhere, sliding between the cypresses to vanish into a veil of mist.

Tully stumbled along the line of boxcars until he reached the locomotive, where Graebner stood arguing with the engineer.

'What's up?' Tully demanded.

'The river cuts through the swamp ahead,' Graebner said. 'The engineer thinks the bridge is unsafe.'

The little railroadman nodded vigorously. 'Mister, nobody's been near that bridge in almost ten years. It was deteriorating bad when they shut the track down.'

Tully looked at Graebner. 'Maybe he's right.'

'What do you suggest we do, turn back?'

Tully thought for a moment. 'How far is it out of here?' he asked the driver.

'Eight miles maybe.'

'Couldn't we leave the train where it is and go the rest of the way on foot?'

'I thought of that,' Graebner said. 'It's no good. Eight miles could take us a good two hours, maybe more in this light. By then, some smartass cop at police headquarters might figure out where we've vanished to. Our only hope is to move fast and stay in front. Besides, I think the engineer is wrong. I think the bridge will hold.'

'You think!' Tully exclaimed. 'What the hell does that mean, you think? Herr Oberst, if that bridge cracks, we'll end up going no place at all. I think we should consider this very carefully.'

'I have considered it, Karl. I've thought of nothing else for the past eight weeks. You think the weight of one miserable train is going to bring the bridge down?'

'At least let's uncouple some of the boxcars, for Christ's sake. Give ourselves a fighting chance.'

'There's no time, goddammit. Just standing here arguing is wasting precious seconds. I've told you the bridge is safe. We've got to move *now*. At the moment, the Americans probably think we've faded into thin air. Even if they remember the swampline, they'll still only be guessing. But leave those boxcars behind and they'll nail us for sure. The train must remain intact to cover our escape. We'll take the bridge as slowly as we can, and you and I will check the rails up front, then wave the engineer on as we go. If we spot any sign of danger, we can holler out a warning.'

Tully sighed. There was no arguing with Graebner when his mind was made up. He was as intransigent as a tank.

They stepped out in front of the locomotive, moving slowly, their boots clumping on the timbered struts. Tully saw the point where the trees ended and the broad river came streaming by. Its current nudged the curtain of scum which coated the stagnant swamp water, thrusting it back to leave a silvery arc slicing through the jungle below. He breathed deeply, savouring the night air, peering at the stars. It seemed unreal, this fragmentary moment in time; the locomotive quietly hissing, the night sounds of the swamp stirring around them, and Graebner's chunky outline moving at his side, stamping at the track as he tested the bridge for firmness and reliability.

Tully toed at the timber. A piece broke away and dropped into the current below. Not too stable, he thought worriedly; that locomotive would weigh God knew how many tons. The engineer was right. This bridge was a dubious prospect indeed.

'How's it look?' Graebner called.

'Like matchwood,' Tully said. 'I guess the damp's got at it. This is crazy, Graebner.'

Graebner ignored him and turned to wave the train on. Nothing in the world seemed to stop the man.

The locomotive inched slowly towards them, and they walked forward, the engine following at a snail's pace like some incredible monster brought to heel. Its nostrils heaved out steam and fire as it trailed obediently in their wake.

Tully kicked at the wood, checking its solidity. It was rotten to the core, having been drenched a million times over the past ten years. For all they knew, it was probably riddled with some kind of bug or other. At any second, he expected to see the whole damned lot go crashing into the darkness. He peered through the gloom, trying to spot the line of trees that would signify the opposite side, but only the night hung maddeningly before him, an ethereal curtain shutting off sight, hope and reason.

'How far does this reach, for Christ's sake?' Tully muttered.

'It's a wide river,' Graebner said, 'but if the timber gets no worse, I think we'll be okay.'

They were crazy coming into the swamp like this, Tully thought. And he was even crazier to think he could outwit Graebner simply by joining forces with the man. Now here he was on this crazy railroad bridge in the middle of this stupid swamp and he was still no closer to understanding what it was all about than he had been back in France. Where the hell were they going? Why was Graebner so prepared to take almost any risk to avoid recapture? Who had given him the information on the old logging branch line, and what would be waiting when they reached the other end? Well, he would find out sooner or later, he told himself, and then he would fix Graebner for good. Which was kind of unfortunate, since he realised he quite liked Graebner, but he was going to fix him nevertheless. Then he thought: to hell with Graebner. Quit worrying about Graebner. Start worrying about yourself, for a change, you and Etta.

Ahead, the shadows seemed to merge together, taking on form and solidity. In the misty starlight, Tully spotted the ragged outline of trees poised against the sky and felt relief flooding his limbs. They were almost across.

And then, as the first tremors of jubilation began to rise inside him, he heard a sound that sent a shudder down his spine. It was a low, gentle, creaking noise, an almost indiscernible rumble that grew steadily in volume, like thunder rolling through a range of distant mountains.

'What's that?' Graebner said.

'It's the bridge, for Christ's sake. It's trembling.'

'My God.'

Graebner's face went pale. They stopped, staring at each other in alarm. The noise picked up force as the seconds ticked by, growing and intensifying. Tully felt the framework vibrating beneath his feet.

'Graebner, the struts are giving way.'

Graebner waved his arms at the engineer. 'Back up,' he bellowed. 'Move her back, for Christ's sake.'

It was too late. There was a thunderous screech, a tortured ripping noise that split the air like the death shriek of a dying animal, and Tully, turning, saw the great locomotive tilt helplessly to the left as the bridge sagged and bent, sections of its timbers breaking loose and dropping to the current below. He felt himself slip, and, crouching, grabbed the metal rail for support.

'Look at the train,' he yelled at Graebner. 'We've got to get the people out.'

'Stay where you are, man.'

'If it goes, they'll be killed.'

'Stay where you are, for Christ's sake, it's going now.'

Tully saw the engine rolling wildly, its funnel belting out steam in angry protest. For a second, it seemed to hover there, defying space, balance, gravity, and then, as Tully watched spellbound, its massive flanks heeled over and with a blood-curdling roar it plunged into the curtain of darkness. The loco hit the water in a welter of spray and hissing steam and the boxcars rocketed down on top of it, pitching helplessly into the swirling current, hurling carpets and foodstuffs, furniture and farm machinery, into the sleekly-moving river.

'Etta,' Tully screamed. But before he had time to assimilate his horror, the bridge sagged again and he heard Graebner shout:

'Raderecht, hold fast, we're going too.'

Tully felt the timbers buckle beneath them, pushing downwards and outwards until the entire world had gone out of control, then he was falling, his brain lost in an awesome void; he hit the water and began to spin, caught by the boiling wash. For a few desperate moments he could not determine the way to the surface, then his head broke clear and he felt cool air against his cheeks. He sucked hard, drawing oxygen into his lungs as the timber roared and showered around him.

Etta, he thought wildly, I've got to find her. He began to swim, picking his way through the floating wreckage, trying not to listen to the ominous splashes as missiles dropped from the bridge above, skimming perilously close to his unprotected skull. The locomotive had come to rest on the river's bed, its footplate perched above the surface like some incongruous growth belched up from the bowels of the earth. The boxcars lay in disarray behind it, some submerged, others resting clear, propped sideways or upside down on the backs of the ones in front.

Tully spotted Strahle clambering over the footplate. He had lost his sabre and his pale face looked rigid with shock, but he appeared otherwise unhurt.

The fireman had not been so lucky. He was floating beside the boiler, his face frozen into the blank implacability of death. The lower half of his body was sliced cleanly away, and blood and viscera mingled with the mud and debris, spreading outwards as the current cast it into a macabre scarlet starburst.

Tully reached the first of the boxcars and scrambled up its side, slithering as his toes slipped on the wet surface.

'Etta,' he shouted, his voice almost unrecognisable in the tumult.

He spotted Wegmüller and Scheller dragging Eyke between them, splashing dazedly toward the locomotive through the chest-high water. Eyke's face was covered with blood, and there was a jagged tear on the front of his skull.

Tully grabbed Scheller by his tunic. 'Where's the girl?' he snapped. 'Where is she, for Christ's sake.'

Scheller seemed to have trouble focusing on Tully's face. He tried weakly to say something, but his voice was inaudible. Tully let him go with a snort of disgust.

He peered through the gloom, struggling to define the bobbing shapes in the river; it was impossible to identify them in the dark—were they human heads or bits of useless debris?

He began to crawl again, balancing on the slippery boxcar walls, dragging himself along with something akin to hysteria. Please God let her be all right. Take anybody else You like, take me if You have to, but let her be all right.

Unexpectedly, he slipped and plunged into the river, gasping as its muddy coolness closed about his head. He broke the surface, spluttering. Above, the bridge had stopped breaking up and now hovered menacingly above them, threatening to collapse at any minute. Tully felt chilled, and a

spasm of trembling shook his battered body. Then he heard
Etta's voice calling through the darkness and a sob of relief
burst from his throat.

He stumbled towards the sound and spotted the boxcar with
its hatch half-open, its front wheels propped on the wagon in
front. Moaning, he reached the doorway and hauled himself
inside. Etta was crouched against the back wall with Kruger,
holding one of the hobos across her knees. Tully didn't need to
look twice to see that the man was done for. There was a
gaping hole in his chest, and his eyes were glassy, imbued with
the blue-marbled milkiness of approaching death.

He peered anxiously at Etta. 'Are you okay?'

'I'm fine,' she said weakly.

'You're not hurt?'

'No.'

'Thank God.'

He looked again at the little hobo. Blood was pulsing down
the man's flanks and an unpleasant odour reached Tully's
nostrils as gas escaped through the hole in his chest.

'What happened?' Tully asked.

'He got crushed by the milkchurns,' Kruger said. 'He's
bleeding bad.'

'We've got to get him to dry land,' Etta whispered.

'Let's try the opposite bank,' Tully said. 'It can't be far.
What about his friend?'

'Dead,' Kruger grunted. 'His skull got busted.'

'Can't we stem the poor man's bleeding?' Etta asked
urgently.

Tully hesitated. On an impulse, he took off his drenched
shirt and tied it as tightly as he could around the hobo's torso. It
was little more than a gesture, he knew, for no dressing in the
world could staunch the terrible outflow from that shattered
ribcage, but he felt he had to do something, anything at all that
might, just for a moment or two, slow down the inexorable
seeping away of the man's life-force.

'Will it hold?' asked Etta.

'Who knows?' Tully said. 'But it's all we've got.'

He nodded at Kruger. 'Grab his other arm.'

Together, they manoeuvred the moaning hobo across the

boxcar floor and into the swirling water. His eyes rolled backwards in his skull and his thick lips hung open wordlessly, emitting low bleating whimpers that struck straight into Tully's heart.

Struggling for balance, his feet fumbled beneath the waterline. Slowly, cagily, they began to inch their way toward the front of the train. Etta followed, holding on to the cars for support. Once Tully fell, and the three of them, Kruger, the hobo and himself, tumbled beneath the surface, their heads completely submerged until Tully found his feet again. Coughing and spluttering, they struggled on, inching car by car towards the great shadowy phalanx of the upturned locomotive.

Despite their dilemma, he was filled with relief that Etta, by some incredible miracle, had managed to survive that terrible plunge. He reached back towards her with his free arm. 'Let me help you,' he offered.

'I'm all right, really,' she said. Her face was a pale oval in the darkness.

Tully spotted a figure battling towards them through the current and recognised Graebner. The German had a charmed life, it seemed. It was little short of remarkable that both of them could have survived that fall, but Graebner it indisputably was, his face blackened, his clothes in tatters, and a livid weal running from his forehead to the tip of his jaw.

'Who's hurt?' he croaked.

'One of the bums from the boxcar,' Tully said. 'The other one's dead.'

Graebner stared at him. 'You okay?'

'Sure.'

'The girl?'

'She's fine.'

Graebner waved into the darkness. 'You'll find a line of duck-blinds just beyond the trees up front. They'll give us someplace dry we can rest until daybreak.'

'What about you?' Tully asked.

'Eyke left the brakeman tied up in the rear van. I guess he's probably dead by now, but I've got to check. I'll follow you over there.'

Gasping and heaving, they struggled across the river, the injured man between them. Tully spotted the cypress trees ahead, then the duck-blinds rose into view, their brush-covered rims butting from the water like tiny floating islands. There were four in all, but only one was still unoccupied. Strahle and the others had taken over the rest.

Tully helped Etta into the final barrel, and then he and Kruger, working together, eased the little hobo over the rim and into the shadowy interior. Tully and the German followed quickly, glad to be out of the water at last, glad to be anywhere at all that offered a hint of sanctuary. The blind was barely big enough to contain them all, but they were able to crouch on its bottom, water streaming from their saturated clothing.

'What is this thing?' Kruger demanded.

'It's a hide,' Tully said. 'Hunters use it for duck-shooting. Looks like it's been occupied recently, too.'

He leaned forward to examine the hobo's wound and realised that the shirt he had strapped so carefully around the man's chest had been washed away by the current. Blood was now flowing in alarming quantities down the front of the emaciated trunk.

'What are we going to do?' Etta whispered.

'Little we can do,' Tully admitted. 'He'll be dead before morning.'

She glared at him furiously. 'We can't just sit here and let him die without trying. There must be something, for God's sake.'

Tully looked at Kruger. 'Take off your shirt,' he ordered.

The man hesitated a moment, then without a word unbuttoned the garment and slipped it off. This time, instead of strapping it round the hobo's chest, Tully bunched it into a little ball, and jammed it against the open hole. Blood soaked into the sodden material, but some of the outflow seemed to ease.

'We'll take turns holding it in place,' Tully said. 'Come daylight, we'll be able to judge how bad it is.'

There was the sound of water rippling, then Graebner popped his head above the rim. 'Room for one more in there?' he asked.

'Sure, if we all squeeze along,' Tully said.

Graebner slithered in and they crowded back, their shoulders jammed fiercely together. Tully felt Etta pressed up hard against him.

'Find the brakeman?' he asked Graebner.

The German grunted. 'Part of him anyhow,' he said. 'The rest was squashed by the car in front. The fireman and the other hobo got it in the crash, and we lost Schultz, which brings us down to seven, excluding the girl and the engineer. Eyke's hurt, but we can't tell at this stage how badly. He can still walk, which is a blessing. And of course, there's him.'

He nodded at the hobo, bleeding on the floor. 'How bad is he?'

'Dying, I think,' Tully said.

Graebner pursed his lips. Gloomily, he rubbed both cheeks with his fingers and peered round the duck-blind's interior.

'Not too comfortable,' he muttered, 'but at least it's dry.'

'And it's been used lately,' Tully observed.

'That's right. Which means there must be human habitation someplace near. In the morning we'll try and find it.'

Tully frowned at him. 'The people who live in this swamp will be hunters and trappers,' he said. 'They'll be armed.'

'I know. But at least we'll have surprise on our side.'

'Then what?'

'Steal a boat. Find our way out of here.'

'Herr Oberst,' Tully said patiently, 'we're badly shaken and we've two injured men on our hands. Long before morning, the Americans will realise we're in this swamp. It's over, can't you see that? We've gone as far as we're going, this trip.'

Graebner glared at him in the darkness. He looked affronted, as if Tully had let him down in some unforgivable way. 'If we're finished, so is Germany,' he snapped. 'As long as there's breath left in our bodies, we've got to keep trying.'

He sighed, and Tully saw the weariness riven into his face.

'Get some sleep,' Graebner added curtly. 'We'll need all our strength for tomorrow.'

13

Morning came with a greyness that infused them all with dark dismay. It was Tully's turn to hold the bunched-up shirt against the hobo's chest, and as the first streaks of sunlight drifted through the trees he saw that the man was dead. The ravaged face was thrown back, the eyes open, staring sightlessly at some point beyond the duck-blind's rim.

Tully sat up straight, dropping the blood-soaked shirt over the edge. He had slept little during the night, for the horror of the crash and the discomfort of crouching, drenched, in the cramped little barrel had turned the few hours before dawn into an ordeal none of them cared to repeat.

'What now?' he asked Graebner.

'Check our gear and move off. That way, I think.' The German nodded through the cypress trees.

'Wouldn't we be better following the railroad track?'

'Safer, maybe, but that branch line will be the first place they'll look. Our best bet is to get as far from this spot as we can.'

'Through the swamp?'

'We'll hit dry land eventually. People.'

'What about Eyke?'

Graebner frowned worriedly. He had climbed out at the first glimpse of daylight to examine Eyke more closely. 'He's bad,' he admitted. 'Could be a fractured skull. He's got some kind of abdominal injury too. I've tried to patch it up, but he may be bleeding internally.'

'He shouldn't be moved in that condition,' Tully said.

'I know, but we have no choice.'

Graebner clambered out of the duck-blind and gathered the survivors around him. He studied each in turn, peering for signs of exhaustion and defeat. The livid weal on his face had turned purple during the night, and now he looked the most bizarre figure of them all, his tunic in tatters, his skin coated with mud and dried blood.

Tully helped Etta into the water. 'We'll have to wade for a while, I'm afraid.'

'That's all right,' she said, 'I'll manage.'

'I'm sorry, darling.'

'For what?'

'Bringing you along. I never wanted you involved, never.'

She smiled faintly. 'Stop apologising. I'd rather be here than worrying at home alone.'

Graebner was busy examining Eyke, who was standing with his arms around Kruger and Wegmüller's shoulders, sagging helplessly like a sack of potatoes. His face looked blank and stupid.

'He's wandering in his mind, Herr Oberst,' Wegmüller said.

'Can he still walk?'

'I think so.'

'Then we'll take turns helping him along.'

Graebner's cropped hair was plastered smooth against his skull. Only his eyes seemed alive, peering out from the dirt caking his skin. They were all like that, Tully thought; not like people at all any more, but like some grotesque swamp creatures struggling for survival.

'Somebody's missing,' Graebner stated.

No-one said anything. Tully saw Wegmüller glance at Scheller, and something in their faces made his senses tense.

'We're one short,' Graebner repeated.

He looked round, counting heads. 'The engineer, what happened to the engineer?'

Strahle shifted uncomfortably in the water. 'He didn't make it,' he said.

Graebner frowned at him. 'What does that mean, he didn't make it?'

'He had a seizure.'

'He was okay just a few hours ago.'

Strahle smiled thinly. 'Delayed reaction,' he grunted.

Graebner stared at him in silence for a moment, then waded to Strahle's duck-blind and peered inside. When he came back, his eyes were hot with fury. 'That man's been strangled.'

Strahle shrugged. 'He was old. He was useful no longer.'

Scheller interrupted. 'He wanted to do the same to Eyke, Herr Oberst.'

Tully pursed his lips. Even Strahle's followers were beginning to baulk at his brutality.

'That engineer would only have held us back,' Strahle declared. 'It's the same with Eyke. Look at him, for God's sake. He's finished, any fool can see that. We should kill him now, swiftly and cleanly. Better for him, better for us.'

Without a word, Graebner hit him between the eyes. He used his fist hammer fashion, and Strahle crashed backwards into the water threshing wildly. His boots emerged, kicking at the air, then he came to the surface, coughing and spluttering, blood pulsing from his swollen nostrils.

'You damn near bust my nose,' he yelled.

Graebner took Strahle's throat in his massive hands and shook him like a rat. 'That little man didn't ask to be here,' he growled. 'He wasn't doing us any harm. When the Americans find his body, it won't be back to Cannesetego we'll go, it'll be to a prison cell and a hangman's noose.'

Strahle's eyes bulged, and through the blood streaming from his nostrils, Tully saw his tongue stabbing at the air.

He put his hand on Graebner's shoulder. 'We need Strahle, Herr Oberst,' he said gently. 'You'd better turn him loose before you break his neck. The engineer's dead, we can't help that now.'

With an almost physical reluctance, Graebner released his

grip and Strahle stood gasping hoarsely, sucking oxygen into his lungs.

'Listen to me,' Graebner said in a dangerous voice. I'm going to tell you this once and once only. If you so much as spit in somebody's direction without a specific order from me, you'll never leave this swamp alive, do you understand?'

'Yes, Herr Oberst,' Strahle muttered, holding on to his throat.

Graebner nodded grimly. 'Okay, let's go.'

They moved off through the swamp, their clothes clinging icily to their bodies, bearing away from the railroad track but moving without any true sense of direction since none of them had a compass. For more than an hour the country repeated itself, an endless sprawl of waist-high water, tall trees reaching straight out of the scummy surface, and occasional islands cluttered with foliage and dense underbrush.

Tully pressed forward in a daze, one arm locked around Etta as if to help her along, though he knew it was a gesture, nothing more. Her will alone kept her on her feet.

The swamp closed around them, dense and frightening, and out of the overlocking branches shutting off the sky and sun came the chorus of a million birds.

Tufted outcrops of land loomed in the stillness. There were buttressed cypresses with branches dripping Spanish moss. There was custard apple, pop ash, swamp fern, and water lettuce. Lily pads floated on the water's surface. Steam filled their nostrils with the odour of rotting vegetation, imbuing the scene with a curious primitiveness, as if the world had reverted to the very beginnings of creation.

Tully's limbs felt numb beneath his crotch; constant immersion had chilled his nerve ends so that now his flesh moved by instinct, his legs functioning with no direct awareness lodging in his brain. Underfoot, the mud sucked at his boots until each step became a private struggle between the bog and himself. Soon, the idea settled in his skull that to pause even for an instant might immobilise him for ever; feet stuck fast, he would sink slowly and inexorably into this unspeakable sludge.

They were strung out in a ragged line, Graebner up front,

his big shoulders hunched in an attitude of dogged determination, his head thrust forward as if to force the pace, though even he seemed to find difficulty in pushing through this irritating quagmire. From time to time, Tully thought about alligators, but he thrust the image from his mind as quickly as it appeared, for the simple strain of placing one foot in front of the other was bad enough, without having the horrors of his imagination to contend with as well.

They reached a sliver of dry land with water channels slicing through the trees on either side, and began to follow it, the ground marshy and uneven. Tully was filled with the terrifying conviction that they were stumbling about in circles, that these soggy trunks were the same they'd passed over an hour ago, that they were doomed to flounder on forever, passing continually back on themselves until one by one they sank with exhaustion.

Suddenly Kruger, trailing behind with Eyke, gave a shout. He was standing in the mud, struggling to hold Eyke upright. The injured man seemed to have lost control of his legs, and was sagging in Kruger's arms like a rubber toy.

They eased him into a patch of swamp grass where, shaking noticeably, he began to vomit, spewing out bile that trickled down the grassy sward to mingle with the slime oozing from his body.

'I'm cold,' he whispered. 'Jesus! it's so cold.'

'He's running a fever,' Graebner said.

He looked at the underbrush. 'If we could light a fire, it would help to keep him warm.'

'Somebody must have matches,' muttered Scheller.

Graebner pulled a face. 'Lot of good they'll be after wading through that mess.'

He fumbled in his pocket and drew out Tully's lighter, flicking it with his thumb two or three times. Nothing happened.

'Damn thing's saturated.' He slipped the lighter back. 'Maybe it's just as well. Woodsmoke would give our position away. He'll have to sweat it out the best way he can. Pass over all the spare clothing. We'll try and conserve his body heat.'

They stretched out in silence, watching Eyke fight his

lonely battle for survival. Tully felt overcome with weariness. He looked at the reeds and the great curtains of hanging moss and tried to will life back into his aching limbs.

Strahle, he noticed with interest, was doing the rounds of his followers, attempting to re-establish some of the authority he had lost earlier in the day. And not getting far either, by the look of things. Something had happened during the last few hours, something that had changed their attitudes entirely. Probably Strahle's desire to finish Eyke off, Tully thought. That would turn his men against him, if anything would. Alienated, they ignored Strahle's overtures with expressions of open contempt.

At length, To Tully's amazement, Strahle shuffled to his side and lay down in the grass. 'Raderecht?' he whispered.

Tully looked at him. 'What d'you want, Strahle?'

'Do you think Eyke's done for?'

There was no hostility in Strahle's tone. His voice was flat and neutral.

'I don't know,' Tully said.

Strahle thought for a moment, then nodded gravely. 'I think so. I think he's done for. We should have left him behind at the duck-blinds.'

'Like the engineer?' Tully asked dryly.

Strahle spat in the grass. 'If you were Eyke, which would you prefer? A quick death, fast and painless, or sweating your life out in this miserable sewer? He's finished. You can see it in his face.'

Tully didn't answer. He wanted to draw away, as if Strahle was contaminated with some unspeakable disease.

'You think I'm a ruthless bastard, don't you, Raderecht?' Strahle said.

'Yes.'

'You're wrong. I look at what's expedient, that's all. For God's sake, Eyke was my friend, I don't want to see him die, but that's no reason to let him kill the rest of us, which is what will happen if the Americans catch up.'

'Thanks to you,'' Tully said coldly.

Strahle glared at him. 'That engineer would have turned us

in, first chance he got. There was only one sensible decision to take and I took it.'

'Strahle, can I ask you a question? Why are you talking to me?'

'It's time we settled our differences, Raderecht. We're in a jam.'

'Last night you wanted to kill me.'

'I've changed my mind. I think we should join forces and get the hell out of here.'

'Just the two of us?'

'Bring the girl if you want to.'

Tully sat up straight as Strahle's reasoning dawned on him. Shunned by his friends, he was turning for support to his enemy.

'You mean the three of us should just take off? Now?'

'No damned sense in waiting for Eyke,' Strahle insisted. 'How far d'you think we've travelled since we left that railroad bridge? I'll tell you how far. Two miles, if we're lucky. Once the Yanks figure out where we are, they'll be through this swamp like hornets. Every minute we delay is cutting down our chances of escape.'

'What about Graebner?'

'For Christ's sake, what about him? What is this mission that's so damned important? Only Graebner knows, and he's not telling. If you want my opinion, I think he's a little soft in the head.'

He eased himself forward on his knees, peering intently into Tully's face. 'Raderecht, all I ever wanted was for us to be friends.'

Tully touched the mudstained dressings on his cheek.

'I still have a few mementoes of your friendship,' he said dryly.

'The duel was your idea.'

'It was a question of survival, Strahle.'

'I wish you'd forgive me for that, Raderecht. What's past is past. Now we need each other.'

He fumbled inside his shirt and dropped something into Tully's lap. It was a small leathery purse, its surface gleaming like dull copper.

'As a sign of good faith, I'll give you this. I've kept it hidden for months at Cannesetego.'

Tully picked it up and studied it curiously. 'A tobacco pouch?'

'I took it off a Jew in Pruszhow. It's the most treasured possession I have in the world.'

'What? Some poor Jew's tobacco pouch?'

'Not his pouch, you idiot. His testicles.'

Strahle's pale features looked flushed around his cheek-bones.

'Took me three solid months to clean out the insides, salt the skin, and cure it in the sun. Look at its texture, see how pliable it feels.'

Tully was filled with a sense of disgust and fury. It was as if the mere act of talking to Strahle had, in some curious way, turned him into an accessory. He hurled the pouch in the German's face and rose to his feet, moving to the other side of the clearing. 'Keep away from me, you bastard,' he snapped. 'Just having you near makes me feel unclean.'

Some time toward evening, it rained briefly. There was no longer any doubt that Eyke was deteriorating. They waited in silence as, shaking convulsively, he went through his slow ritual of death. It took nearly six hours in all, and when at last the shivering stopped, they were filled with bitter relief.

Tully peered at the corpse wonderingly. He had never liked the man, but seeing him lying in the scrub, his features frozen into a glassy mask, Tully was filled with a strange sense of sadness.

Graebner took off Eyke's shirt and pulled it on to replace his own. It was too small to encompass his massive shoulders, and he had to leave the buttons undone, the two sides forming a soggy V that framed the thick hair on his chest. 'We've got to move on,' he told them shortly. 'The longer we stay here the more dangerous it gets.'

Wearily, they rose to their feet and moved off in single file, Graebner in the lead. Tully wondered how much longer he could stay in motion, and felt a sense of quiet pride as he looked at Etta stumbling along in front. She was holding up

better than any of the men, and he wanted to hug her close in
sheer delight. Not once had she admonished him for getting
her into this mess, and not once had he heard a murmur of
complaint pass her lips. He really did believe she would still be
moving when he, Strahle, Graebner, and the others had walked
themselves to a standstill.

It was amazing, he thought, how much Graebner knew
about this area; the branch line, the swamp, he knew
everything. Either he had studied it for months, or somebody
else had, somebody who belonged here, somebody who had
given him the information. The realisation made Tully feel
strange.

Suddenly, Scheller paused, pointing into the thicket.

'Look,' he cried.

Reaching away in front of them, slicing through the brush
in a parallel line, was a wooden fence. It was rough-hewn with
the bark still on it, and staring, Tully felt his senses jump. A
fence had to mean something. A boundary. Human habitation.

'I can smell woodsmoke,' Kruger whispered.

They sniffed furiously at the air, not daring to believe the
truth. There was no mistake. Mingled with the odour of rotting
vegetation was the scent of something burning.

'People,' Strahle said hoarsely.

Graebner held up his hand. 'Let's take this easy. This
swamp is swarming with trappers and their families, and
they'll be armed. Our only chance is to catch them by surprise,
so move slowly and stay hidden.'

They pushed forward with renewed energy, the woodsmoke filling their limbs with a fresh sense of purpose. Tully
saw the trees ahead taking on substance, gathering into a dark
hump that rose from the ground like the prow of an ancient
galleon. As they drew closer, they spotted a shack hunched
among the underbrush. Tully almost shouted aloud with relief.

A dog, sensing their approach, began to yelp, and a woman
came on to the porch to quieten it, peering intently into the
swamp to see what had set it off. She was medium-sized, very
thin, her face seamed with the rigours of hard work. Her body
looked tough and angular beneath her cotton dress. Her age
might have been anything. Life had imposed its own stamp of

durability, and young or old she carried the enigmatic air of the swamp creature.

After a moment, she moved back inside, and they trotted on, not bothering this time when the hound started to yelp, but scuttling swiftly across an open yard where raccoon pelts stretched drying in the sun.

Plunging through the door they stood blinking in the shack's interior. The air was hot and muggy. A few spindly bits of furniture had been knocked together with an almost contemptuous disregard for the comforts of life. The woman they had just seen stood cooking at the far end of the room, where a blackened stove cast a circle of heat across the earthen floor. Her long hair was bound into a single braid which hung casually over one shoulder like a length of thick rope. Her skin was dark, her cheekbones high, and she stared at their unexpected entrance with no hint of surprise or alarm.

Smells from the cooking pot stirred Tully's senses. For the first time, he realised they had not eaten since the previous day, and the ravages of hunger gnawed at his stomach. The woman began to move toward the opposite wall, but Graebner beat her to it. Pushing her aside, he reached behind the closet and drew out a long-barrelled shotgun. Going down on all fours, he scooped a handful of cartridges from a box on the floor and loaded it. 'Spread out,' he ordered. 'The woman can't be alone. There'll be rifles around the place somewhere.'

Tully felt strangely guilty rummaging through the family's shoddy possessions. He opened drawers, peered under beds, scoured closets. Everything he touched seemed shabby beyond belief. The woman watched in silence. Her poverty was like an enemy crouching in the heat.

It was Strahle who found the rifle. He held it aloft with a whoop. Scouting through the larder, he discovered three boxes of ammunition.

'Where are your menfolk?' Graebner asked the woman in English.

She gave no answer. Her face was moulded into a blob of stubborn defiance.

Strahle peered around the shack with exasperation. 'Jesus Christ!' he exclaimed, 'how can people live like this?'

'They're Cajuns,' Graebner murmured. 'They move out of the bayou villages to hunt muskrat and raccoon. They know how to live off the land, how to use the swamp to furnish their needs.'

Outside, Kruger uncovered a narrow skiff bobbing at the water's edge. It was twenty feet long, its hull hollowed out of a giant cypress tree.

'As least we're through walking,' Kruger grunted.

Graebner seemed unimpressed. 'They'll have something better. A power boat maybe. I guess the men are using it to check the trapline.'

'What the hell,' Kruger told him. 'We'd have to fight for the power boat. This we can get for free.'

'We can't afford to leave those men mobile,' Graebner explained. 'They could overtake us if they'd a mind to, or cruise out of the swamp and warn the authorities.

Kruger hesitated. 'You mean we should wait?'

'We'll have to. They'll be back before sunset. We'll take it in turns to keep watch while the others eat what's in that cooking pot. At least we'll have food inside our bellies.'

Tully found a line of dungarees and workshirts hanging behind a curtain, and tried some on for size. They fitted perfectly. Threadbare and workworn, they were still better than his tattered uniform, and he struggled into the unfamiliar garments with a feeling of relief.

The others too tried to find scraps of clothing, but only Strahle was successful. He forced on a pair of denim pants and a mackinaw jacket, while his companions, with their heavy shoulders and muscular bodies, were obliged to stick to their German battle-dress.

They took turns eating at the crude wooden table, and Tully felt better after supper. He sat with Etta, drinking coffee as tremors of life returned to his aching limbs. She looked, he had to admit, almost unrecognisable—scratches all over her splendid face, mudsplashes on her cheeks, her hair tangled into a thick unruly web—but there was still that light in her eyes, that gleam of strength and determination he'd seen before, and again he felt a flush of pride.

'My arms are cut to ribbons,' she said. 'How far d'you think we walked today? Feels like a hundred miles.'

'Four, if we're lucky,' he told her.

'What happens now?'

'Only Graebner knows that.'

'We shouldn't have let this happen, darling. We should have warned the authorities before the escape took place. Seven men have died for nothing.'

'It was the only way,' he insisted. 'I had to get Graebner to trust me. He's finished now, and he knows it. Boat or no boat, it's only a matter of time before the army catches up.'

'So it's been pointless, hasn't it? You're no better off than you were before. It's still only Graebner who knows what we're up to.'

'That's why we've got to convince him it's time to start talking.'

'How?'

'I haven't figured that out yet. But we must try. It's our only hope.'

'And then what? After it's over?'

'They'll probably send me back to Europe.'

'I couldn't stand that.'

She reached across the table and squeezed his hand.

'Whatever happens,' she said, 'I don't want to risk losing you again.'

He felt his heart jump looking at her. Sitting there smeared with dirt and grime, she seemed more divine, more perfect than anything he could have imagined. "Is it important to live in Louisiana?' he asked.

She shrugged. 'Not important at all. I wanted to get out of Baltimore. There were too many memories for me there.'

'The place I come from—Avery, Wyoming—isn't a bit like this. It's wide open and full of distance. Gets colder'n hell in wintertime, and in summer the sun scorches your butt off, but there's no place I'd rather be right at this moment.'

He turned his hand so he could hold hers and squeezed her fingers, smiling at her gently. 'They're going to love you in Avery, Wyoming,' he said.

It was late in the evening when they heard the chug-chug of

the power boat. Graebner cocked his shotgun and peered through the window. 'Keep an eye on the woman,' he ordered. 'Shut her mouth in case she cries out.'

Tully smiled an apology and placed his palm across the woman's lips. She made no attempt to struggle, and he was uncomfortably aware of her eyes regarding him calmly over the top of his thumb.

The engine noise grew louder, the voices drifted towards them on the still night air. The dog was barking furiously, not in warning, as it had on their own approach, but with welcome and excitement. There was a muffled clunk as the boat nudged the jetty. They heard the sound of men moving about, their boots scraping on the damp wood. Their metal traps clanked as they tossed them onto the foreshore.

Footsteps moved towards the cabin. The door swung open and a man stood there, his chin covered by a thick dark beard. He stared in dumb surprise at the sight of the armed intruders, Etta seated at the table, Tully with his hand on the woman's lips, Graebner facing him, the shotgun pointing unerringly at his skull.

'Keep quite still,' Graebner warned in English. 'We don't want to hurt you, but if you make any move that isn't exactly as I order, you'll never breathe again. Do you understand?'

The man's face looked gaunt and ravaged. Like his wife, it was difficult to determine his age. The lines etched into his skin came more from hard work and privation than from the passing of the years.

'Tell me if you understand?' Graebner repeated.

The man nodded.

They heard fresh footsteps moving towards the doorway, and without taking his gaze from Graebner's face, the man said in a loud voice: 'Get out of here, Noah. Run boy, fast as you c'n.'

Graebner swore, and lowering the shotgun, hit the man in the stomach with its butt. The trapper doubled over, his breath exhaling in an exclamation of surprise and pain.

Tully let the woman go and dived for the door, but already Strahle and Kruger had burst from the underbrush to grab the boy on the boat-landing. Now the three of them were wrestling furiously. The boy was fifteen or sixteen years old, dressed in dungarees and a workshirt identical to the ones Tully was wearing. He lashed wildly at Strahle's shins with his feet, struggling to reach the precious power boat. The Germans dragged him, still kicking and punching, back towards the shack. When he saw his father crouched on the floor, the boy stopped fighting and stood panting heavily, staring at their faces. 'What you done to him?' he gasped in a high voice.

'He's okay. He's got a touch of stomach cramp, that's all.'

'What d'you wnat?'

There was no fear in the boy's eyes; though he was very young, he looked as uncompromising as his father, and Tully was glad it was they who held the guns.

'We need your boat,' Graebner said shortly.

'That power boat is all we own,' the boy grunted. 'We can't check the trapline without it.'

'You'll get it back,' Graebner promised. 'We'll leave it out where somebody will find it.'

He hesitated. 'We're taking some provisions too. We've left you enough so you won't starve.'

He glanced at Kruger. 'Go outside and smash the skiff,' he ordered. 'Use the felling axe and make sure it can't be patched up again. Be as quick as you can. We've wasted enough time already.'

Fifteen minutes later, they chugged away from the jetty, slicing through the curtain of scum that coated the coffee-black water. The two men and the woman watched from the shoreline, their sombre frames outlined against the hanging moss, their faces touched with an impassivity as old as time itself. It was born out of hard experience and endless disappointment. Tully looked back from the rear of the power boat, keeping them in sight until they were nothing more than smudges against the feathery foliage.

Then the swamp closed around them, and he looked no more.

In the control room at Lomstoun police-station, Captain Price was into his second night of vigil. The air smelled stale, and the clatter of typewriter keys filled the room as he opened his eyes and realised with a start that he had been dozing.

He peered across at Patrolman Brady. 'What time is it?'

'Ten minutes later than the last time you asked.'

'Christ! I'm pooped. Was I sleeping?'

'Like a baby.'

'You should of woke me.'

'You can do the same for me some time,' Brady said. 'Like in an hour maybe.'

Captain Price gave a thin smile as he stood up. He liked Brady. For Price's money, Brady should have been in charge here. He was cool-headed and conscientious, not at all like that idiot Chief of Police, Fraser.

'Any news?' Price asked.

Brady's face looked weary and strained, and there was a coating of beard stubble on his cheeks. 'Well, we figured out what happened to the train,' he said. 'They took the old branch line through the swamp.'

'So you were right?'

'Only route they could have gone. Freight trains don't usually vanish into thin air.'

'Think they'll be okay?'

'No, sir. Those trestle beams are old and sagging. If you want my opinion, they'll be lucky to make it.'

'Have we got the track sealed off?'

'Like a drum. We're checking it out this very minute.'

The radioman took off his headset and called to Price from the other side of the room. 'Cap'n?'

'Yeah?'

'They found the freight train in the Yakamanatchee River, what's left of it. The bridge done give way.'

'Jesus Christ!' exclaimed Price. 'What about the prisoners?'

'They're looking for survivors now, Cap'n.'

Price felt a surge of quick excitement. 'If they're in that swamp, then we've got 'em cold.'

Brady looked dubious. 'It's a hell of a big area, Captain. There's two hundred miles of channel in there. We'll need guides, boats, all the help we can get. I think it's time we contacted the army.'

Afterwards Price could never understand how it happened, how he'd managed to be taken so completely by surprise, but suddenly a voice cut across the room, sharp and authoritative: 'It's okay, officer, the army's already here.'

Startled, Price glared at the three figures standing in the doorway. They were dressed in military uniforms. The faces of two were young and clean-shaven. The third was plump and middle-aged, with a nose that had clearly been broken at least twice.

Price felt confused. After nearly two days of waiting, he experienced a sense of unreasonable annoyance at this unexpected interruption.

'Police-station's closed,' he announced coldly. 'If you have an enquiry, see the sergeant at the desk outside.'

The older man smiled. 'We've already made the acquaintance of the sergeant,' he said.

His chin bulged over the starched rim of his shirt collar as he reached into his tunic and drew out an ID card. 'Colonel Theodore Reiser, Office of Strategic Services,' he announced.

'Is this some kind of joke?'

'Nothing for you to worry about, Captain.'

'Colonel Reiser, we have an emergency on at the moment. I'd appreciate if it you'd leave any business you might have until the morning.'

'Can't do that, son. Your emergency is what we've come about. I understand you've had a break from Camp Cannesetego?'

'That's right.'

'Have the prisoners been recaptured?'

'Not exactly,' Price said, 'but we have their position pinpointed to within a few square miles. The train they were riding crashed on the Yakamanatchee River. We figure they're somewhere in the swamp without a boat. We're getting a search party organised now. We'll have them back inside the pen before morning.'

The colonel looked unimpressed. 'Do you have a list of the escapees, Captain?'

'A list, yes, sir.'

'Tell me, does it include the names Raderecht and Graebner?'

Price hesitated. 'Why, I believe it does, Colonel.'

Reiser exchanged looks with the two men accompanying him, and something in his face seemed to change. It hardened visibly, the muscles tightening, the eyes narrowing. 'Call off your men, Captain,' Reiser ordered.

Price was taken aback for a moment. 'I beg your pardon?'

'I want you to drop out of this and leave things to us.'

'You're crazy.'

'We've been expecting this escape for quite some time. To tell you the truth, we've been waiting for it.'

A sense of indignation rose in Price's chest. He said curtly: 'Colonel Reiser, we have a responsibility to the American public. We're willing to co-operate with you people any way we can, but not when it means allowing enemy soldiers to go raping and murdering across the countryside.'

The colonel's face looked patient. 'There'll be no raping or murdering, I give you my word on that.'

Price felt his temper beginning to crack. He was not, he knew, an unreasonable man, but goddammit he needed sleep badly, and who wouldn't feel a little crabby at one o'clock in the morning after working flat out since the previous lunchtime? He was not about to be pushed around by a total stranger, colonel or not.

'Colonel,' he said, 'we've been engaged on this break-out for close on thirty-six hours. I'm pretty tired, and I know my men are tired. I don't figure on dragging this out any longer'n I have to. What's more, I'm not taking chances with the civilian lives of this county. Now will you please leave, and let us get on with our job?'

The colonel stared at him with what seemed to Price an air of amusement. For the first time he sensed the inherent toughness of the man.

'I don't think you quite understand, Captain. It's not a request I'm making. It's an order.'

Price felt momentarily uncertain. 'Order?' he echoed.

The colonel took an envelope from inside his tunic.

Opening it, he removed a letter with an official heading, and handed it to Price.

'I'm assuming command of this operation on the authority of the President of the United States,' he said.

'Jesus God!' Price whispered, staring at the letterhead.

'Tell your men to stand down,' Reiser instructed. 'There will be no further pursuit of the prisoners. As of this moment, as far as you are concerned, they have ceased to exist.'

'Where now?' Graebner asked, his face a pale blur in the moonlight. They had been cruising around for hours, chugging between butterfly orchids, strangler figs, and shrouds of ghostly Spanish moss. The boat cast ripples across the swamp water.

'Christ knows,' Tully said. 'Left or right, it makes no difference.'

Kruger spat over the side. 'See that tree over there? We passed it more than an hour ago. We must be trundling around in circles.'

'Maybe we should rest up till morning,' Tully suggested. 'At least with daybreak we might pick up our bearings. This way, we're just eating up gasoline.'

Graebner reflected for a moment. 'How many hours have we left, d'you reckon?'

Tully calculated swiftly. 'Should be around one o'clock, I guess. Four, maybe. We could all do with a sleep. We're dead on our feet.'

'Okay, let's do it your way. We'll find some place we can anchor.'

A shadowy hump of dry land loomed to their left, and Graebner steered into it, shutting off the engine as the bow nudged tangled vegetable growth and twisted tree roots. Tully clambered forward and tied the line fast to the bank. He turned to smile at Etta, who was sprawled in the hull, her eyes blank with exhaustion. He realised they were all like that now. The survivors (seven, if you counted Etta) were hunched in attitudes of weariness and despair.

The swamp seemed to close about them as Tully found himself a seat, peering out across the lily pads to where a distant ripple sliced the slimy surface; a watersnake or alligator maybe. Instinctively, he shuddered. He hated the swamp by day, but at night its terrors grew, became distorted.

He peered at Etta, who seemed lost in reverie. She had cleaned her face at the shack, but there was no way of wiping the fatigue from her features. Watching her, he felt a sense of tenderness and sudden warmth.

He stared at Graebner, who had closed his eyes and was leaning back, his shoulders against the hull, one arm stretched along the bow. Tully knew he couldn't go on fooling himself any longer. He was no nearer to cracking Graebner's infuriating reserve than he had been at the camp—unless Graebner had taken such a beating he was ready for anything now, questions, explorations. Maybe his guard was down at last.

It was worth a try.

'We're not going to make it, you know,' Tully said softly.

Graebner opened his eyes and looked at him. 'You're a power of comfort, Raderecht.'

'Just a realist. If something bad's going to happen, I like to face it and be ready. When dawn breaks, there'll be American soldiers all over this place.'

Graebner sighed. 'The train crash finished us,' he admitted. 'That damned bridge. If we'd got out of the swamp, we'd have been clear across the country by now.'

Tully's heart thumped.

This was the moment, he knew it with absolute certainty. The buzzing of crickets thundered in his eardrums.

'Herr Oberst?'

'What?'

'Where were we going?'

Graebner looked puzzled. 'Huh?'

'Do you realise seven men have died already, and so far, only you know why. If we're about to get ourselves captured, I'd kind of like to feel it's somehow been worthwhile.'

'He's right, Herr Oberst,' Kruger said suddenly. 'We're not going any place, not any more. We have a right to know.'

There was a stirring in the boat as the others eased themselves upright, peering expectantly at Graebner through the darkness.

'Supposing you'd been killed back at the train,'' Tully said.
'The mission would have been over, because nobody except
you knew what the hell it was all about. Don't you think you
owe us that much?'

Graebner chuckled wearily. 'You have a point, Raderecht.
There's little sense in keeping the thing secret any longer. But
you're not going to like what I have to say.'

Tully felt a sense of triumph. Graebner had bought it. After
all this time, the sonofabitch had finally bought it.

Graebner folded his hands in his lap and eased back against
the hull. He stared at them in silence for a moment, then
cleared his throat noisily. 'How many of you, apart from
Raderecht, come from Berlin?'

Scheller raised his right hand.

'Is your family still there?'

'Yes, sir.'

'Then I'm sorry.'

Scheller looked at the others in puzzlement. 'I don't
understand, Herr Oberst.'

Graebner's big-muscled body looked shapeless in the
darkness. Tully could see the V of his open shirtfront framing a
tangle of hair. His sleeves were drawn back to reveal strong
muscular forearms. Shadows hung across his features.

'If the bridge hadn't collapsed,' he said, 'we'd have been
on our way to Roanoke, Virginia, to see a man called Harvey
Menotti. Menotti is a research scientist, and an extremely
gifted one at that—or at least, he was. He's retired now. Before
the war, he visited the Kaiser Wilhelm Institute in Berlin and
worked with some of our biological experts there. I had the
pleasure of meeting him at the Tirpitz Ufer. A charming man.'

'Is he an American traitor?' Tully asked.

'Not at all,' Graebner said. 'But in 1937 he took part,
along with a number of German scientists, in a series of
experiments aimed at developing a substance known, for
simplification purposes, as SSG 300.'

Something crashed through the underbrush on the bank
above, and they heard the squeal of a small animal, faint and
indistinct. Graebner ignored it, stretching his legs out in front
of him.

'You have to understand something about biological warfare,' he explained. 'It has a major disadvantage. Because it affects living organisms, its germs can be carried by birds, insects, and people to areas far removed from the battlefield. In other words, it can end up killing off soldiers and civilians on the wrong side. SSG 300 is a toxin, a chemical produced by a form of bacteria known as Sarenthynthrax. It's a million times more effective than, say, the nerve and mustard gases employed during World War One, and it has the added advantage of being unable to multiply, so it's possible to wipe out all life forms within a certain area in the secure knowledge that inside twenty-four hours the toxin will have safely evaporated.'

Tully frowned. 'What's all this leading up to?'

'Menotti and his associates failed to perfect the toxin back in 1937, but German scientists reached a major breakthrough early last year. They discovered that by allowing the bacteria to incubate in living organisms, the toxin could be produced at an extremely rapid rate. In fact, enough SSG 300 now exists to wipe out the entire population of Europe. It was manufactured in Belgium and shipped to Berlin in cargoes of tulip bulbs.'

'But for what reason?'

Graebner moistened his lips, staring at them silently, and for a moment Tully thought he detected in his eyes an unwillingness to proceed, as if what he had to say filled him with both disgust and shame.

'When the first Allied armies enter Berlin,' he announced in a flat voice, 'SSG 300 will be released into the atmosphere from strategically-placed stockpiles between Spandau and Köpenick. There is no known antidote. Within two hours, all life in the city and the surrounding area will have ceased to exist.'

Silence fell over the little power boat. Somewhere in the trees, a bird shrieked shrilly, its voice rising above the hum of the crickets. Tully felt disbelief rising in his chest.

'You're insane,' he breathed.

'You're wrong. I'm the only rational factor in the whole stinking set-up. The SSG 300 idea was formulated by the Führer himself as a last-ditch suicide bid if everything else failed. I've been trying to contact Menotti ever since my arrival. Only he knows the real horror of SSG 300. If I can convince him we have it, it may be possible, even at this late stage, to negotiate an honourable peace.'

'For God's sake, Graebner,' Tully exploded, 'why didn't you just take your story straight to Colonel Glusky?'

'Glusky wouldn't have believed me, nor would the Joint Chiefs of Staff. They've got victory in their nostrils, and they're determined to settle for nothing less than unconditional surrender. If I went to the military with a story like that, they'd throw me out on my ear. They've been receiving overtures for months now from the German High Command offering all kinds of inducements in return for a negotiated settlement. Their answer is always the same. No deals. I've got to get to Menotti. He knows me and he knows the toxin. He'll realise I'm not bluffing.'

'Go to the army, you idiot,' Tully cried. 'Tell them you want to see Menotti. Whether they believe you or not, they won't fool around with a story like that.'

Graebner gave a tired smile. 'My dear Raderecht, it's not so simple. I can't afford to be interrogated. I might be persuaded, through no fault of my own, to disclose the locations of the stockpiles. Forewarned, the US army could defuse the situation. Part of my deal with Menotti must be that he helps me disappear while negotiations are taking place.'

Scheller interrupted. His face had gone deadly pale in the darkness. 'Let me see if I understand this correctly, Herr Oberst,' he said. 'When the enemy enters Berlin, this deadly toxin will be released into the air. Please explain to me exactly what effect that will have.'

'They'll be wiped out to a man. SSG 300 will kill more Allied soldiers in the space of two hours than our armies will have managed in the entire war.'

'And the civilians?'

Graebner hesitated. 'I said I was sorry, Scheller.'

'Herr Oberst, they're our own people. My wife, my child . . .'

'If it makes any difference, I want you to know that I vehemently opposed the use of SSG 300 when it was first suggested.'

Tully felt anger stirring inside him. 'Graebner,' he said coldly, 'do you realise what you've done?'

'Not me, Raderecht. I'm trying to prevent it.'

'But you've bungled, you imbecile. You've squatted around on your ass wasting precious days, precious hours, while for all we know, the Allied armies could be marching into Berlin this very minute.'

Graebner's face looked pale, and for the first time Tully sensed a moment of indecision as the German floundered for an answer. Then suddenly through the swamp sounds they heard a strange disorientating noise. Tully paused, his brain reeling wildly, trying to grasp the meaning of this new intrusion. It was the drone of an automobile, growing steadily louder. They peered at each other in disbelief. Graebner's words momentarily forgotten.

There was no mistake. The noise rose to a crescendo as the car thundered by less than thirty yards distant. The glow of its headlamps cast a pale sheen through the trees.

For a moment they sat in silence, frozen by surprise, then with one accord they tumbled out of the power boat and began to flounder through the prickly underbrush, scrambling up the bank.

The thicket ended as they burst, gasping, onto a stretch of open highway, its dark surface slicing through the trees in a ribbon of hazy moonlight. Tully could scarcely believe it. He looked at Etta, who was standing, both arms locked across her chest, biting her lip.

Beyond the first bend, they could see the amber glow of a town or village reflected in the sky. 'How far is it, d'you reckon?' Graebner asked.

'A mile,' Strahle said, 'maybe two.'

Something like triumph shone in Graebner's eyes. In the midst of defeat, he was already sensing victory. 'We're not done yet,' he declared. 'We can steal food, clothing, some kind of transport to get us out of here.'

Scheller's face was grim and insistent. 'I think we should give ourselves up, Herr Oberst.'

'You're mad.'

'Tell the Americans what you've told us. They'll listen, I know they will.'

'You know nothing, Scheller. The Americans are blind with victory. Menotti's the only man we can trust.'

Wegmüller spat on the ground. 'How can we go in there in this mess?' he growled. 'They'll grab us for sure.'

'It's the middle of the night,' Graebner said. 'There can't be too many people around.'

'But we're still in uniform, for Christ's sake.'

Graebner hesitated. He looked at himself dubiously.

'You're right. It'll have to be Raderecht and Strahle. They're the only ones in civvies.'

With a quick sideways motion, he plucked the rifle from Strahle's grasp. Strahle looked affronted. 'What's that for?' he demanded.

'You won't need this.'

'Maybe we'll run into trouble,' Strahle protested.

'That's what I'm afraid of. You're too damn ready to use this thing for my liking.'

Tully was silent. In a flush of anxiety, he looked at Etta. Her big eyes regarded him wordlessly. He felt a moment of sudden pain. He couldn't leave her here, he thought wildly. On the other hand, he couldn't afford not to. He had to tell somebody. He had to get a warning to the proper authorities. There was too much at stake and too little time. If he moved at all, it had to be now.

'Where will you be?' he asked Graebner.

'Right here by the road.'

'And the girl?'

'She stays with me.' Graebner smiled gently. 'Don't worry, she'll be safe enough.'

'We'll be as quick as we can,' Tully promised.

Graebner nodded in agreement. 'Good luck,' he said.

14

Tully felt strange walking into town with Strahle at his side. For almost a mile, neither of them spoke, each thinking in his own private way of the discord between them. No cars passed, which was a blessing, and they watched the swamp fall away and green fields begin to filter through on each side of the road, with little houses peeking among the pasture folds.

Tully felt uncertain. He couldn't for the life of him see how he was going to get his news to Colonel Reiser unless (and the idea seemed unlikely) he managed to convince Strahle, his old enemy and duelling partner, that the time had come to put aside personal considerations and begin thinking about humanity.

Unexpectedly, Strahle began to chuckle. 'There's a certain irony in this, Raderecht,' he grunted. 'Though you spurned my offer of an alliance, we've ended up depending upon each other, nevertheless.'

'Is that all you can think about? Didn't you listen to what Graebner said back there?'

'I listened.'

'And you don't care?'

'My dear fellow, what can I do?'

'We're talking about the deaths of millions of people, Strahle. Not just a few battalions, but an entire population. Civilians, women and children, the sick, the elderly.'

Strahle's boots scraped on the blacktop roadway. He peered

at the first scattered buildings of the little town, their timbered roofs gleaming like panels of snow in the moonlight.

'Raderecht,' he said, 'there's a war on. Civilians have been dying since 1939.'

'The war's practically over, and you know it. Germany is defeated.'

'A few weeks ago, I broke a man's leg for a statement like that.'

'To hell with what you did a few weeks ago. What are you going to do now? We can't let the Führer annihilate Berlin.'

'How can we stop it?'

'By giving ourselves up.'

Strahle lurched to a halt. 'I must be hearing things,' he breathed.

'I mean it, Strahle. We've got to warn the Americans.'

'I should have killed you that night in the heating plant.'

'But you didn't, Strahle. And now I'm here. And I'm telling you it's time we put an end to this madness.'

Strahle started to walk again, his movements quickening as if by some subconscious instinct he realised he had to put as much distance between himself and Tully as he could.

The town began to build up as Tully hurried after him. 'You think you could live with yourself afterwards, if it really happened?' Tully demanded.

'Death doesn't worry me, Raderecht. You can't measure death by numbers. It's too intrinsic, too individual. Does it make any difference if a million people die in an earthquake in Africa? Does it affect the progress of the human race? Of course not. Did the Great Plague put an end to European civilisation? Multiplying death by numbers only makes it more communal, less remote. Besides,' he added, 'I'll tell you what I think. I think it's a bluff.'

'You mean Graebner's lying?'

'I mean the Führer would never stoop to such a thing.'

'Like hell he wouldn't. Who knows what madness men are capable of when they're backed against a wall.'

'For God's sake, we're out of the swamp, we're on our way to freedom. I say we should stick with Graebner until we find this man Menotti.'

'That's good, that's pretty damned good. Just a few hours ago, you were trying to persuade me to desert.'

'A few hours ago, I thought Graebner was crazy.'

'So what happened to change your mind?'

Strahle turned and glared at him, and in the glow of the streetlamps Tully saw the hatred in his face. It was no middle-of-the-road run-of-the-mill hatred, but an emotion so strong Tully could feel its venom like a physical force.

'Don't try to influence me, you snivelling bastard,' Strahle growled. 'I gave you your chance in the swamp. Just remember what we've come for. Food, clothes, transport. We can settle our personal differences later.'

Tully fell silent. He realised he was alone, as he had been from the beginning. If he wanted to contact Reiser, somehow or other he would have to ditch Strahle. And he would have to do it subtly, since he very much doubted if he could overpower the German physically.

They passed a courthouse and entered a wide square surrounded by plane trees. In the middle of the lawn stood the statue of a Confederate army officer, his sabre upraised, his walrus moustache quivering with stony righteousness as he turned his gaze towards heaven. A plaque at his feet proclaimed: 'To the glorious men of Chaumont, who fell in the great war between the States.'

They left the square and followed a street strung with overhanging lights. Tully spotted a delicatessen on the opposite corner. 'Store over there.'

Strahle looked at it and shook his head. 'Too open. It's under the lamps.' His voice was neutral, neither friendly nor hostile.

They turned up an alley-way and discovered at the far end a little foodshop set back from the sidewalk, its frontage masked by an overhanging canopy. 'This'll do,' Strahle whispered, and tried the latch. It was locked.

'We'll need to bust the glass,' he said.

'What if there's an alarm?'

'Have to chance it.'

Tully found a piece of charred wood in a garbage can and

wrapped it in his sodden handkerchief. He began to tap tentatively at the glass panel.

'Harder,' Strahle hissed.

Tully increased his pressure. The noise seemed to echo across the darkened sidewalk.

'For Christ's sake,' Strahle snapped, grabbing the wood from his hand.

He smashed it violently against the glass and the pane shattered, scattering fragments in all directions. Tully held his breath. No lights flashed, no doors opened. The town remained as peaceful as ever.

Strahle slipped his hand through the opening and undid the latch.

They crossed the threshold and stood inhaling the smell of coffee beans and margarine. Strahle chuckled triumphantly.

'Like Aladdin's cave,' he said, 'everything we need.'

Tully stared at the shelves, all bountifully-provisioned, then pulled open the cash register. There were still a few coins inside. He waited till Strahle was looking the other way and slipped a nickel into his pocket.

'Why don't you gather this stuff together?' he suggested. 'I'll see if I can find us an automobile.'

Strahle peered at him suspiciously. 'Let's both gather the stuff together. We can find the car later.'

'We'd be wasting precious seconds, Strahle. We must operate as a team.'

'You're sure that's all you've got in mind? You're not still thinking of turning yourself in?'

'Alone? Not on your life.'

'I hope you mean that.'

'For Christ's sake, Strahle, we don't have time for this.'

Strahle nodded slowly in agreement. 'Okay, you get the car. I'll be out in a minute or two.'

Tully ran down the street, his heart furiously pounding. A phone booth, he had to find a phone booth. It was two o'clock in the morning, Reiser would be at home, not at his office. Still, he could phone OSS headquarters. Somebody had to be on duty. A security guard, a caretaker. Anyone at all.

He found a booth two blocks down and shut himself inside.

Lifting the receiver, he slipped the nickel into the slot and called the operator. In a fever of impatience he waited as the line purred maddeningly. There was a click and a voice said:

'Number please?'

Tully took a deep breath. 'Lady, I want you to listen very carefully. I only have a moment. I must call OSS headquarters in Washington.'

'Who is this?'

'Please. I want to talk to Colonel Theodore Reiser, or to one of his aides. Have you got that?'

'Do you have the money for this call, mister?'

'Make it collect, for God's sake.'

'May I remind you there is a war on?'

'Please, lady, please do as I ask. Give them my name, J.A. Tully. They'll pay, I promise.'

'I hope you are not deceiving me.'

'I swear I'm not.'

'One moment.'

The line went dead, and Tully waited, sweating profusely. Maybe it wasn't such a good idea after all, telephoning Reiser, because Reiser was up there in Washington, D.C. and he was down here in Louisiana, and Etta was two miles up the road with a bunch of enemy soldiers who were just desperate enough to kill her if things got really rough. When he thought about Etta, his insides seemed to melt, and he promised himself grimly: if Graebner touches one hair on her head, I'll rip out his guts with my bare hands.

But Graebner wouldn't do that, he reasoned; he was, above all else, a decent fellow, a humane man despite his ruthlessness, and with capture inevitable, surely even Graebner would see that hurting the girl would achieve nothing, would only compound his villainy.

(Where the hell was that telephone operator? Did she think he had all night?)

First, a message to Reiser just to keep things on the level— Reiser would get the word to the War Department or the White House or wherever the hell it went to reach the Allied forces in Europe, and then he, Tully, would find a police-station someplace (there had to be a cop in this one-horse town, there had to be *somebody* in authority) and maybe get some action on freeing Etta.

Graebner would be reasonable, he thought; a show of strength would do it, and maybe Tully could go in ahead and explain how he'd called the military and told them the whole business, and how everybody appreciated that Graebner had done his best in the circumstances, had done his duty in the very highest tradition, but now it was all over, so if Graebner would just deliver up his hostage, he could go back to Cannesetego in peace and wait fdor repatriation.

Would Graebner do it? Tully wondered; or was he, like Strahle, just crazy enough to make one last bid for freedom? Were they all tarred with the same brush, fanatics to the core?

Where the hell was that telephone call?

A shadow fell across his vision and he glanced up, his muscles tightening. Outside, his face pressed against the glass, stood Strahle. Oh God, the bastard followed me.

Strahle's eyes looked madder than ever. 'What the hell do you think you're doing?' he hissed.

'I was just . . . I was just trying to find out where we are.'

'You liar. You're calling the police.'

'No, no,' Tully cried helplessly.

'You're blowing the whistle on us, you traitorous bastard.'

Strahle was smiling, as if this betrayal provided him with some curious fulfilment. He dragged open the door. 'Come out of there.'

Tully slapped the phone back on its hook. He held up his palms defensively, inching out of the narrow booth.

'Remember what we came for,' he whispered, 'remember Graebner.'

But Strahle was beyond remembering. Perspiration was pouring down his skin and there was a strange exultation in his face as in one fluid motion he grabbed for Tully's throat. Tully sensed him coming and dove outwards, rolling swiftly, but before he hit the sidewalk Strahle was upon him, his muscular body bearing Tully to the ground. Tully, in that moment of panic, that first awful second when their two frames locked together, realised that he was no match for Strahle. The hard lean body, the superior height, counted for too much. As long as Strahle had him on the ground, Tully hadn't a chance in hell. Fear pumping adrenaline into his veins, he knew he had to get to his feet and run, shout for help, make a disturbance, a commotion, anything at all that would get people here.

But Strahle's forearm was locked across his windpipe, and it was all Tully could do to gasp a lungful of air now and then, and the more he struggled the more Strahle's grip tightened, till he could smell the German's breath in his nostrils as they rolled around the sidewalk, kicking and twisting, bending and straining. And then, blindly, Tully lashed out with his fist and felt the blow connect solidly with Strahle's open mouth. Seeing the tall man flinch he thought: that one hurt, you bastard, and as the forearm across his throat shifted slightly, he dragged himself loose and started to rise.

He was running now, wanting to shout but needing the air to keep his legs in motion, and somewhere at his rear, boots clattered on the concrete as Strahle followed in hot pursuit. (Goddammit, was there no stopping the man?) He was gaining already, and Tully, fixing his gaze on the storefronts opposite, knew in his heart he would never get there. Something hurtled into his back, a piledriving weight that stunned his spine, and suddenly he was in the gutter with Strahle straddling his chest. The big hands seized Tully by the neck and squeezed hard, shutting off his windpipe with murderous intent. Tully drove his heels against the road in a desperate effort to fling the German clear. He saw the pale, demented face, the eyes glittering ecstatically, and thought in a moment of incongruous logic: I was right all the time, the bastard *is* insane.

Tully started to gasp. His vision blurred, his brain drifted, his lungs shuddered dangerously. He was losing consciousness. It was the stupidest moment of his whole stupid life. He was dying at the moment of victory, killed by a German soldier in the middle of an American street. The world was tilting, losing substance, and Jesus, if something didn't happen soon, it would all be over, they would find him in the morning, limp and lifeless, an enigmatic figure in somebody's cast-off dungarees, and maybe, after he'd lain around the mortuary slab for a few days, somebody would work out who he was,

Lieutenant J.A. Tully of the OSS. Only by then it wouldn't matter a damn, because by then the Allied armies and all the people who huddled among the shattered remnants of the Berlin tenements would be just as dead as he was.

He reached out with both hands, feeling along the roadway. If only there'd been a brick or something, anything at all he could use as a weapon. But the concrete was bare against his fingers.

Then his right hand hooked over a bar at the kerbside. The sewer grating. He gave it a tug, and it budged.

With a sudden wild exultation, he heaved with all his might. The iron grid reared in his fist, swinging sideways under its own momentum hard against the side of Strahle's skull. The blow was not strong enough to knock Strahle out, but it shook him momentarily, and as his grip relaxed a fraction, Tully broke free.

He began to roll, Strahle toppling over, sliding from his chest and, with the breath rasping in his throat, Tully clambered to his knees and swung the grating in another vicious circle. This time he caught Strahle full in the face and watched, with a kind of wonder, as the pale brow caved inwards like a dented can. He swung again, once, twice, three times until he realised Strahle was moving no longer, and peering down at the bloodstained corpse he heard the sound of doors opening, voices murmuring, feet scraping, and when at last he pulled himself together and staggered painfully to his feet, he saw with no sense of surprise or alarm that the street had filled with people.

'Well, son,' the sheriff said, 'that's quite a story.'

He nodded his head two or three times as if in emphasis, a big man, heavy-shouldered, with a massive paunch that sagged outwards alarmingly as if he had a load of potatoes stuffed inside his shirt. His eyes were a vivid blue, and he wore a moustache that hung down both sides of his mouth, completely obscuring the upper lip.

'Yes, sir,' he added thoughtfully, 'quite a story.'

'You can check it easily enough,' Tully said. 'One phone call. OSS headquarters, Washington. Ask for Colonel Reiser.'

'I didn't say I didn't believe you,' the sheriff said, crossing his legs and tilting back the chair until Tully felt sure it would crash beneath his weight.

The office was almost empty in the early hours of the morning. A solitary sergeant sat behind the desk, typing out his report. He'd been sleeping when the sheriff had brought Tully in, and now his face held a faintly indignant air, as if no crime in the world could be more heinous than one committed outside working hours.

'Where is it you reckon them Germans is hiding?' the sheriff asked again.

Tully hesitated. He was not feeling too good, he realised, and his hands, for some reason, just wouldn't stop shaking. He couldn't get the memory of Strahle out of his mind—the pale face smashed beyond recognition, the road strewn with bone fragments and bits of human hair, the sewer grating coated with blood and brain. With a faint surprise, Tully realised Strahle was the only man he'd killed in this entire war.

'They're two miles out of town,' he said, 'on the swamp road.'

'And they've escaped from Camp Cannesetego?'

'Officer,' Tully pleaded, spacing his words for the utmost effect, 'the important thing is to waste no time here. We've got to get word to the Allied forces in Europe.'

The sheriff nodded sagely, his blue eyes shrewd and wise.

'Oh yeah, I almost forgot. They're gonna wipe out the whole goddam army, you say?'

'Sheriff, I'm not asking you to believe me. Just make the phone call. Please.'

The sheriff sighed. 'Well, son, you see it's like this. It's true we had a warning about a break-out from Cannesetego, but word come through a couple of hours ago that all the runaways had been recaptured. Now what is this story you're handing me here? You say we got some more down the road apiece?'

'Sheriff, believe me, I've got no reason to lie.'

'Why, that ain't so, boy. You got every reason in the whole damned world. You just murdered a man in cold blood, right out there on the main street.'

'That man was a German soldier. He was trying to prevent me raising the alarm.'

'That so?'

The sheriff nodded a few times more, and Tully felt his heart sink.

'I ain't sayin' you ain't right,' the sheriff grunted, 'but I ain't sticking my neck on the line neither. I'm taking you out this minute, and handing you over to the army.'

Tully looked at him in surprise. 'The army?'

'Sure. We got a bunch of them soldier boys camped in a field on the edge of town. Recruits mostly, training in the swamp for jungle warfare. I guess I'll let them decide whether you're telling the truth or not. That's what they're paid for.'

He rose briskly. 'Turn round,' he ordered.

Tully felt the cool touch of metal cuffs being slapped on his wrists.

'Not that I don't trust you, boy,' the sheriff said, 'but I feel a whole lot more comfortable with you wearing bracelets.'

This is crazy, Tully's brain screamed. Convince the army and you might save Etta, but what about Reiser? Remember what you know. An hour's delay could make all the difference.

'Sheriff,' he said urgently, 'before we leave, let me ask you one more time; please call Washington.'

He stared at the police officer as intently as he dared, trying to will some kind of integrity into his face. It wasn't easy, he thought, with these stupid dressings on his cheek.

'Please,' he added softly.

The sheriff studied him for a moment in silence.

'Linus?' he snapped across the room.

The sergeant glanced up from his desk. 'Yeah?'

'Call OSS headquarters in Washington and ask for Colonel Theodore Reiser. Tell him what's been happening here. See if he knows a guy by the name of J.A. Tully.'

Tully felt his heart lighten with relief.

'Where'll you be, Chief?' the sergeant asked.

The sheriff glared at him. 'Where the hell d'you think I'll be? Winning the goddammed war in Europe, that's where.'

He took Tully's arm. 'Let's go, Cousin.'

The ride in the jeep took no more than ten minutes, and as

they drove out of town, heading north, Tully saw the pale blue of tents taking shape in the darkness. He was feeling better now, a little more secure with the knowledge that Reiser was being brought into this. Now maybe he could get out of here, leave behind this crazy lie he'd been living for so many months.

He'd tucked the memory of Strahle into the dimmest corner of his brain, concentrating instead on Etta, thinking of ways to spirit her free. Maybe the sheriff was right. A job like this belonged to the army. He just hoped they'd handle it with tact and diplomacy, that was all.

The sheriff jerked the jeep to a halt at an open field gate, and a sentry furtively smoking a cigarette behind the fence leapt to his feet. The man cupped the cigarette in his hand, but when he saw who the visitor was, he relaxed visibly. 'Hello, sheriff,' he grinned.

'Lieutenant about?' the policeman asked.

'Well, sir, he was an hour ago. They been doing a little celebrating on account of Sergeant Camero's wife having a baby son and all. They're in the mess tent.'

'What, at 3.30 in the morning?'

'It's been quite a celebration, sir.'

Tully had to be helped from the jeep. With his wrists cuffed behind him, he found any movement awkward and unstabilising.

The earth was soft underfoot, and he followed the sheriff between rows of neatly-spaced bell-tents until they reached one lit from inside by a hurricane lamp.

The sheriff pulled back the flap and motioned Tully to enter. Tully had to duck his head beneath the sagging roof.

There were two men sitting at a clapboard table, a bottle of booze between them. Three more bottles, all empty, had been tossed on the floor.

One of the men had sallow cheeks and a thick moustache. He wore a sergeant's stripes on his sleeve. The other was very young, twenty-two or three, and very good-looking, with crewcut hair and the kind of face Tully always hated because it looked so even, so beautifully symmetrical (and because, secretly, he'd always dreamed of looking like that himself) except for one thing—the guy's eyes, which were pale grey and strangely empty, as if nothing existed inside his skull.

The young man, the crewcut, rose to his feet as they entered, and lifting his arms, cried in a slurred voice: 'My God, we've been raided. Get your hands in the air, sergeant. The big bad sheriff is coming to arrest us.'

The sheriff smiled thinly. 'You'll have a swell head in the morning, Scotty.'

The young man chuckled, reaching for his tunic, and Tully's heart sank as he realised this was the officer in command. The man was plainly pie-eyed. 'What are you doing here, Blech?' the lieutenant asked. 'Don't you cops go to sleep at nights?'

'I brung you a visitor,' said the sheriff.

The lieutenant frowned at Tully. He seemed to have difficulty focusing. 'Why's he in handcuffs?'

'He just done killed a man,' the sheriff said.

'God-DAMN! You're kidding.'

'Smashed in his skull with a sewer grate.'

'Nice people,' the sergeant grunted dryly.

The sheriff moved further under the tent's apex so he could stand upright. 'The thing is,' he murmured, 'he claims he's working for the OSS. He says the guy he poleaxed was a German soldier. He says there're four more German soldiers hiding out along the swamp road right now, waiting for him to steal them a truck.'

The lieutenant's eyes widened as the sheriff went through Tully's story from beginning to end. He missed nothing, not even the business about SSG 300, and Tully could have hugged him for that, since if anyone should see the significance of such information it would surely be a lieutenant in the United States army. Except that this particular lieutenant, Tully realised, as well as being three-parts drunk, was clearly a simpleton, and as the sheriff's voice droned on, Tully watched the handsome young face grow increasingly flushed.

When the sheriff had finished, the lieutenant calmly buttoned up his tunic, looking outwardly cool and in control of himself. Tully knew, however, that he was holding on to his excitement with an effort. 'Sergeant,' the lieutenant ordered crisply, 'get the unit out of the sack and ready for action. Carbine and twenty rounds of ammunition per man, plus the machine-gun and anti-tank weapons.'

My God, Tully thought, he thinks he's General Patton.

'Lieutenant,' he said hastily, 'these Germans have only a rifle and one shotgun between them.'

The lieutenant glared at him. 'Shut up, Kraut.'

'What?'

'I said shut up. You might have fooled the sheriff here, but you haven't fooled me.'

'I'm an OSS officer,' Tully insisted.

'Sure you are, buddy. And I'm Abraham Lincoln.'

The sergeant hurried from the tent. Outside, Tully could hear his voice bellowing shrilly, and the muffled curses of men being roused from their rest. The rattle of rifles and accoutrements rose on the air as the unit stirred into motion.

The lieutenant tugged on a combat jacket and a domed helmet with camouflage netting. His young face was gleaming with exhilaration. 'God-DAMN!' he hissed, 'I thought I was gonna miss this war.'

'Lieutenant,' Tully whispered anxiously, 'remember there's an American woman with those prisoners.'

'Listen, you Nazi sonofabitch, open your mouth once more without being spoken to, and I'm gonna blast the top of your greasy head off.'

The lieutenant moved to the door, and the sheriff asked: 'What about the bracelets?'

'Leave 'em on, for Chrissake. I wouldn't trust this bastard further than I could spit.'

They rode back into town in a heavy army truck, the troops in the rear, hidden discreetly beneath its canvas awning. Christ, Tully thought, of all the lieutenants in the USA, he'd landed himself a meatball. Handsome as a film star, but with the brain of Frankenstein's monster. Worst of all, ambitious into the bargain.

What about Etta? Supposing this dummy lost his head, a possibility Tully found increasingly probable? She could get hurt, killed even. My God! he couldn't bear to think about that. Imagine if he'd finally found the one thing in the world worth staying alive for, only to have it destroyed by some cocky young fool who hadn't learned how to control his liquor. If anything happened to Etta, he'd see the lieutenant regretted it till the day he died.

Tully bounced about on the passenger seat as they headed along the swamp road. He was jammed between the lieutenant and the sheriff, and with his arms firmly fastened behind him, seemed to lurch helplessly with every vibration the truck gave. No attempt was made to question him, and when Tully tried to volunteer information, the lieutenant snapped him into silence.

For a moment, Tully toyed with the idea of saying he'd been lying—it was all a joke, fellas, a little merriment to brighten up the drabness of your dreary lives—but that still left Etta in Graebner's hands, and by the time Reiser arrived, she could have been spirited any place in the country.

'How much further?' the lieutenant snapped.

'Another fifty yards,' Tully whispered, 'over by that blasted cypress there.'

The driver slithered to a halt and switched off both engine and lights. The road looked dark and empty. Against the sky, the swamp loomed in a tangle of murky grey.

Tully's heart was thumping and he tried desperately to swallow. Had he got the right place? he wondered, or had the Germans, for reasons known only to themselves, drifted back into that interminable swampland to vanish forever like the Pied Piper?

He couldn't be wrong. He'd marked the spot indelibly in his brain. This had to be it.

'No-one in sight,' the lieutenant hissed.

'What the hell do you expect?' Tully said. 'This is an army truck, for Christ's sake. They'll be hiding in the underbrush someplace.'

'You'd better not be bullshitting me. If this is a hoax, buddy, you'll wish to God you'd never been born.'

Tully ignored the threat. All he could think of was Etta. He hoped to God this maniac knew what he was doing, which Tully very much doubted.

'Keep your men under control,' he muttered. 'Just remember they've got a woman with them, and she's one of ours.'

The lieutenant leaned over and opened the door. 'Get out,' he ordered. 'Stand up front where they can see you. Give them a holler.'

The sheriff held Tully's arm as he clambered awkwardly down. He moved ahead of the truck, standing clear in the moonlight, peering at the swamp. There was nothing to see but black shadow. Even the contours had been wiped out by the sheer profusion of foliage.

'Graebner,' Tully called tremulously. 'Graebner, it's me.'

For a moment, nothing happened.

Then he heard branches rustling, and five figures emerged into the moonlight. Tully's heart raced as he recognised Etta.

Graebner was staring at him, puzzled. 'What kept you, Raderecht? What is this thing, it looks like an army truck?'

'It *is* an army truck.'

'What happened to Strahle?'

'The soldiers got him.'

Graebner's eyes narrowed, his face tilting suspiciously, and in that instant, the driver switched on his headlamps. Frozen in astonishment, the Germans stood caught in the dazzling glare like captured salmon. Tully saw the leaves behind them flapping gently in the wind, he saw the tall spars of the cypresses and the clay bank beyond. Don't try to resist, he thought pleadingly, you haven't a chance in hell.

It was Graebner who recovered first. 'What is this, Raderecht?'

'It's over, Herr Oberst. The truck's full of American GIs.'

'You've betrayed us, you bastard.'

Tully opened his mouth to protest, and in that moment Graebner moved. Swinging up the rifle, he fired a shot at the nearest headlamp. There was a tinkle of glass as the beam went out, but it was a futile gesture; they were still caught in the second beam, and the chances of Graebner hitting that one too were too remote to contemplate.

For a fraction of a second, nothing happened. Tully waited, holding his breath, and then he heard the young lieutenant's voice bellow crisply: 'Give the bastards hell.'

'No,' Tully shouted.

The canvas awning on the truck rear was thrust back and

the night erupted with the rat-tat-tat-tat-tat-tat of machine-gun fire.

Tully yelled out loud in dismay. It was all happening with an almost pre-ordained inevitability; there was no sense to it, no sense at all, and if there was anything left to surprise him, it was simply his own inherent belief that events could have followed some different course.

He saw a fountain of blood burst from Wegmüller's lips and splash down the front of his sweat-soaked shirt. Wegmüller's eyes bulged in glassy astonishment, and in what seemed an almost leisurely motion, he toppled sideways into the under-brush.

Tully dropped to his knees as he heard the soft swish of incoming bullets and the flat rhythmic stutter of the machine-gun scything around him in a deadly tattoo. Scheller and Kruger were scrambling furiously back through the shrubbery, their movements jerky and uncoordinated as they fled for cover. In that instant, watching them, Tully knew they wouldn't make it. Before his eyes, Kruger's skull seemed to disappear, not in a clear concise way, but in short rapid bursts as bits of bone and flesh flew off in every direction, and then Kruger too was sprawled in the dirt, kicking out the last remnants of his life in a frantic dance of death.

The machine-gun took Scheller low in the spine, tossing him into the air so that he plunged, his body torn almost in half, into the muddy swamp water.

Then suddenly and abruptly, the machine-gun faded into silence, and Tully crouched, sobbing under his breath, peering into the dark.

'Etta,' he shouted in a despairing voice. 'Etta?'

Something rustled among the branches and he spotted two figures scrambling through the brush. One was Graebner, the rifle still clutched fiercely in his right hand, his left arm hooked around Etta's waist, dragging her along. Tully saw her face, a pale glow framed by her tangled hair, as she slipped and slithered on the slimy bank.

'Etta?' he shouted again.

Hearing his voice, Graebner turned and saw him kneeling at the roadside. Cursing softly, the German swung the rifle to his hip. Tully watched him take aim and thought with no sense of fear or alarm: the bastard's going to kill me.

With a muffled sob, Etta hurled herself on Graebner's arm, and the rifle clattered into the mud. Graebner left the gun where it was, and seizing Etta by the wrist, slid madly down the bank and disappeared from view.

Tully closed his eyes, breathing deeply. Suddenly the world was full of jostling men as the troops tumbled out of the truck and spread across the roadway. She's still alive, he thought. By some miracle, the machine-gun had missed her. Thank God, thank God.

Somewhere close, the roar of an engine split the air. A soldier came running back, his face sticky with sweat. 'The Kraut's got a power boat, Lieutenant.'

The lieutenant looked like a man possessed. His face radiated destruction as he cupped both hands to his mouth and bellowed: 'Bring that Bazooka over here.'

'No,' Tully shouted. 'For Christ's sake, no.'

He saw the pale gleam in the darkness as the power boat headed across the swamp water. He saw Graebner standing in its rear, holding on to the tiller. He saw the three-man Bazooka crew kneel down at the roadside, steadying the blunt ugly tube across their shoulders. He saw the primer slot the shell into place.

'No,' he yelled again, and rising to his feet ran towards them, his wrists still manacled.

The lieutenant stuck out his foot and Tully tripped, hitting the ground with a solid thump. Please God, no, he thought. Please God, not Etta.

The boat bobbed in the headlamps' beam. Framed in the light, it offered a perfect target. He heard the sharp cough of the Bazooka firing and the heavy, stomach-shuddering swoosh of the shell, then the night erupted into dazzling day as crimson flames belched skyward and the boat disintegrated in a ball of fire. The air reverberated with a deafening explosion, and Tully's brain lost focus. Stricken with anguish, he closed his eyes and sank into merciful oblivion.

* * *

It was raining slightly when the sheriff swung the jeep to a halt outside a sign which said: 'Chaumont Happy Valley Social Club.'

Sitting in the passenger seat, Reiser felt a cool wind blowing from the swamp, carrying with it the scent of rotting vegetation and the almost indiscernible odour of burning timber. He shivered, folding his arms across his chest. The haunting strains of piano music drifted through the clubhouse windows, striking a chill into Reiser's heart.

'That's him playing, Colonel,' the sheriff murmured. 'He's been pounding that keyboard for close on six hours now. Seems like nothing in the world will get him to quit.'

Reiser nodded. He had never in his life heard music so full of pain. He climbed wearily to the ground, his body stiff and aching. It was a dismal day, the sky heavy as roofslate, draining the colour from the drab little sidestreet. The day and the music seemed to go together.

'I'd like to be alone with him for a while,' he said.

'I understand, sir,' the sheriff answered.

Reiser entered the clubhouse through the open doorway. The daylight scarcely penetrated the dismal interior. Around the room, chairs and tables had been stacked on top of each other. At the opposite end, the bar was shuttered.

Tully was seated at the piano, playing softly. It was music of a kind Reiser had never heard before, and listening to it something lodged in Reiser's chest, a lump that wouldn't go away. When his shadow fell across the keyboard, Tully stopped abruptly. He did not look up. He simply sat on the stool, his eyes staring into space.

Reiser cleared his throat. He tried to make his voice lighthearted. 'You've led us quite a dance these last couple of days, you and Graebner,' he said. 'I don't mind admitting you had me worried for a while there. When no word came through, I thought maybe they'd blown your cover and dumped you in the swamp. I should've known better, I guess.'

Tully didn't answer. He looked, Reiser reflected, like a corpse. The bony face was haggard and drawn, and there were two soiled dressings on the cheek and forehead.

Staring into the vacant eyes, Reiser thought: he's been hurt so much, I don't know if he's still functioning any more, or if he's operating by numbers only; it's like talking to a machine.

'We got your message,' he said with forced cheeriness. 'The sheriff passed it on to Washington and they radio'd me at Lomstoun police-station. We checked out this Menotti guy in Roanoke. He died last November from natural causes. We talked to Menotti's wife, and to his assistant Rita Penchant, who'd worked with him before his retirement, but neither ever heard him mention SSG 300. We've gone through his records and all his personal papers and can find no reference to any kind of toxin. It could be a trick. The Nazis have been pulling every stunt in the book these last few weeks, trying to swing an armistice. Anyhow, we're taking no chances. The President's been informed. He'll take all the precautions necessary.'

A shaft of watery sunlight fell across Tully's glazed eyes, and Reiser hesitated. Christ, how he hated this job. The worst thing in the world, even worse than going into combat, was sending out some other poor bastard to get his ass shot off, then watching him come back and try to pick up the miserable pieces of his life again.

'You've done a good job, Lieutenant, I want you to know that. The President sends his personal congratulations. We found the bodies of the Germans. The couple on the power boat were pretty well blown to bits—unrecognisable, I'm afraid—there were flesh fragments all over the place. The lieutenant had no right to take things into his own hands. He's under arrest, and I intend to see he's severely punished.'

A fly settled on Tully's wrist. He gave no reaction.

Reiser took a deep breath. 'I know what you've been through son,' he murmured, fumbling for the right sentence. 'I just want to say . . . well, I'd just like to say that we're grateful, that's all. For you, it's over. You'll never have to go behind enemy lines again. I'm transferring you to Washington. I need a good translator up there. Some of those bastards they send me from language school still speak German with a Brooklyn accent. I want you to know also that I'm going to get you the highest decoration I can. Years from now, when you look back on all this, you'll be able to tell your grandchildren you saved the lives of the whole US army.'

He grinned. 'Who knows, your name could even go down in history.'

No emotion showed on Tully's face.

Reiser wanted to shout: 'Do something, for Christ's sake, show me you're alive. Spit in my eye, fracture my jaw, curse, holler, laugh, cry.'

He had seen men crumble before, slowly, from the inside out, but never so utterly and completely. It was pointless going on. He was talking to a statue.

'They told me about the girl,' he said. 'I had no idea.'

He patted Tully's shoulder sympathetically. 'Sorry it turned out this way, son,' he added. 'I'm really, truly sorry.'

As he reached the door, the music started again, full of sorrow and desolation. Reiser hesitated a moment, and turning, peered across the stacked tables. Tully's body was immobile. Only his arms moved as his fingers danced over the keyboard.

Slowly, sadly, Reiser shook his head, then putting on his hat, he walked back to the jeep in the rain.

15

Tully sat looking at the lighter for a very long time as the Paris street sounds drifted through the open window. He barely heard the door open until Thiedeck's voice brought him back to the present with a start. 'Stapius is here.'

Tully sighed. He slipped the lighter inside his pocket, and stood up. For the first time in his life, he suddenly felt very old. Thiedeck reached for the light switch, but Tully raised his hand. 'Don't,' he whispered.

He couldn't stand the brilliance. He needed time to compose his features.

Thiedeck moved to the window. "You'd better prepare yourself for a shock,' he whispered.

Tully nodded. 'I think I already know.'

They walked together along the marble corridor, the traffic sounds outside mingling with the clicking of their feet beneath the high ornate ceiling.

On the second floor, Leyton met them at the elevator. There was no expression on his face. 'Stapius would like to see you in private,' he told Tully. 'You've got thirty minutes.'

They had given Stapius the reception room used for visiting diplomats and their wives. It had once been the Embassy library, and the walls were still lined with bookshelves, though now they contained porcelain, china, and ivory ornaments from all corners of the world. Elegant pictures offered a restful contrast to the almost crudely-designed furniture. In the corner, by the window, stood a grand piano.

Tully's senses were racing as he stepped through the door and closed it gently behind him. He felt naked. Bare all over, bare inside. In a curious way, it seemed he had always, in some dark corner of his mind, been waiting for this moment.

The figure which rose to greet him looked much as he remembered. Even the ravages of age had been kind over the years.

For a moment, he stood in silence, his heart thumping. Then, in a voice he scarcely recognised he said softly: 'Hello Etta.'

She smiled. Her skin looked pale and transparent, plunging from her cheekbones into the dark hollows on each side of her mouth. In the harsh light of the crystal chandelier, the lines at her eyes seemed deeply pronounced. Yet she was still a very beautiful woman. Nothing in the world, Tully realised, could interfere with that.

Something caught in his throat, and for a moment he couldn't speak.

'Hello, Karl,' she whispered softly, her eyes shining. 'You don't mind if I call you Karl?'

He swallowed. 'I don't mind.'

'I thought you'd be surprised.'

'Are you disappointed?'

'No,' she said, 'relieved. You haven't changed a bit.'

His lips twitched, and with his fingertips he touched the livid scars marking his cheek and chin. 'A little more shopworn, I guess.'

'Not so you'd notice.'

She nodded at the armchair next to her. 'Come and sit beside me,' she murmured.

Tully crossed the floor, his limbs strangely unsteady. This was the enemy he was facing here, he thought. It was Etta, true, but the enemy nevertheless. He had to handle this just right. He had to maintain some semblance of dignity. By God, she was dignified all right.

They settled in the armchairs, caught in a flurry of shyness and uncertainty. Now they were close, he saw that her hair wasn't dark as he'd first supposed, but flecked with grey, and the lines at her eyes were deeper than he'd imagined, and her chin looked delicate and frail like a piece of exquisitely-carved china; but her beauty had never been an outward thing, he told himself. It came from something deep inside.

'Are you really Stapius?' he asked.

'Does it shock you?'

He shook his head. 'When I saw the lighter, I knew it had to be you. I'd glimpsed Graebner in the power boat. You never did get on that thing, did you?'

'No. Graebner did it alone. He gave me the lighter as a keepsake when you and Strahle went into Chaumont. He was a very brave man.'

'But how did you get away?'

'It was easy. There was so much confusion after the shooting. People came out from the town, then the state police arrived, and the ambulance brigade. I rode into Chaumont with a tobacco farmer after the crowd broke up.'

He flexed his hands, trying his best to look calm and composed. It wasn't easy, he thought. Not every day of the week did a man come face to face with his past in palpable fleshly form. 'It's crazy finding you alive, after all these years.'

'Well, you look pretty cool about it.'

'You're kidding. I'm shaking like a leaf.'

He hesitated, almost afraid to ask the question that was thundering in his brain. 'Why did you do it?' he whispered. 'You were an American citizen.'

'Naturalised only. I wasn't born in the United States.'

'But you were Swedish. Why did you choose the Germans' side?'

'No, Karl,' she whispered, 'I wasn't Swedish. I lied.'

'Then what . . . ?'

'I was born in Russia.'

'Russia?'

'It was never a German operation,' she said bluntly. 'It was formulated in the Soviet Union.'

Tully sank back in his chair, rubbing his cheekbones with his fingertips. 'Forgive me if I look a little dazed,' he said. 'I mean, first I discover you're not dead, after all. And now you're telling me the Soviets gave a deadly toxin to Hitler in the Second World War. You have to admit it does have a touch of fantasy about it.'

'It was Stalin's idea,' Etta said.

'Stalin?'

'He was obsessed with the Russians seizing Berlin.'

'That was always understood. Both Churchill and Roosevelt agreed at the Yalta Conference the Russians should be the ones to take the city.'

'Stalin never believed his Western allies. He was a wily old fox. And in the end, it turned out he was right. On 27 March 1945, Soviet Intelligence intercepted a telegram from Montgomery to Brooke outlining his intention to drive hard for the Elbe and then via the autobahn to Berlin, taking it before the Russians got there.'

'Hold on a minute,' Tully protested. 'Are you saying Russian scientists gave the toxin SSG 300 to Hitler to halt a British and American invasion?'

'There's no such thing as SSG 300,' she said quietly. 'There never was.'

'What are you talking about?'

'It was a hoax. It didn't exist.'

For the first time she turned away from him and he had to be content with her profile (which wasn't such a chore, he thought wryly, since whichever way you looked at it, it was an impeccable profile), but he knew by her manner that she wasn't lying.

His voice was almost inaudible as he whispered: 'Why?'

She crossed her legs, speaking in a monotone as if she was reciting some carefully-rehearsed declamation. 'By 3 February that year,' she said, 'the Soviet army had established the Oder bridgehead near Kuestrin, just thirty-five miles from the German capital. All Stalin had to do was allow Marshall Zhukov to launch his troops in a spearhead attack. But Stalin never forgot the lesson of the Red Army's assault upon Warsaw in 1920, when a reckless advance turned victory into disaster. Even at that late stage, he was wary of the German war machine. He knew if he moved too fast, the Allies could well reach the west bank of the Oder and leave him with nothing more satisfying than East Prussia. So he decided to fight on an extended front, safer in the long run but slower and more laborious. Of course, the British and Americans had promised him first bite at the capital, but Stalin was an arch-intriguer, and he'd survived the most turbulent period in his nation's history by learning never to trust a soul. He decided to take out a little insurance.'

'You mean he deliberately created the illusion of SSG 300?'

Etta nodded. 'Of course, it had to be done delicately. The idea was too preposterous to expect the British and Americans to accept it at face value. We allowed references to the toxin to be filtered through your intelligence network in a way that would arouse curiosity. Nothing concrete. A hint here, a hint there. And from widely diverse sources, so there'd be no suspicion of trickery. Graebner was supposed to be the final key. However, like so many complex operations, it didn't work out quite the way we'd intended. We expected the Americans to recognise Graebner in France and interrogate him at once. He'd been programmed to divulge information in scraps so US intelligence would believe they'd uncovered the plot for themselves. But Colonel Reiser decided to play it differently. When Graebner was shipped to the United States, I have to admit it threw us for a while. We knew that sooner or later the Americans would send in an infiltrator, but we were afraid we'd run out of time.'

Tully looked at her helplessly. 'For God's sake, you knew who I was from the beginning?'

'Almost, but not quite. That first day, when you came to help me with the piano, I took you for just another German soldier. It nearly ruined everything. You see, my job was to co-ordinate the operation from outside the camp. I used to meet in secret with Graebner, and by the time he'd figured out that you were the man we were waiting for, I was too emotionally involved to believe it. Correction. I refused to allow myself to believe it. Isn't it silly how easily we blind ourselves to the things we don't wish to see? The night you told me the truth came as quite a shock.'

'And the break-out?'

'Part of the deception. We knew Menotti had died the previous year. Oh, it was true he'd once studied at the Kaiser Wilhelm Institute in Berlin, but never in the field of dangerous toxins. However, who could prove it? What worried us more was the flimsiness of Graebner's story. You see, our original plan had aborted. We'd been forced to improvise. The question was, would you believe Graebner would go to so much trouble just to contact an obscure American scientist? We needed the break-out to convince you.'

'So we were never intended to get out of the swamp?'

'No. The train crash was a mistake, but one way or another the result would have been the same.'

Tully felt his stomach tighten. 'You used me,' he accused.

'Yes, but with justification. Stalin was right. His allies *were* planning a double-cross. While we were in that swamp, Montgomery's Twenty-First Army Group was already sprinting like hellfire toward the Baltic, hoping to take Berlin on the way.'

'So what happened?'

'Six hours after you'd reported your discovery about SSG 300, Eisenhower telegraphed the Soviets that he considered the German capital had lost its strategic importance and he now intended to make his main thrust along the Leipzig-Dresden axis. There was no mention of a dangerous toxin. Oh, I don't think the Allies swallowed the story entirely, but they were wary enough to let the Russians take the consequences if it turned out to be true. The Russian army captured Berlin on 1 May 1945, and thereby cemented the Soviet presence in Eastern Europe.'

'My God,' Tully hissed.

He sank back in his chair, a sense of unreality seeping through his limbs. 'But Graebner was a patriot, dedicated to Germany's survival. He'd never agree to work with the Russians.'

'Graebner was a realist. He knew the Nazis were finished. He was recruited by Soviet Intelligence during the German retreat.'

'And the others, Scheller, Eyke, Strahle?'

'They believed, as you did, that they were working for the fatherland.'

'It's the craziest thing I ever heard in my life. You're asking me to accept that, consciously or not, I've been responsible for changing the geography of the world.'

She smiled. 'My poor darling, it must come as quite a shock, after all these years. But it wasn't Graebner who was the real head of that operation. It was me. My first command.'

Tully glared at her. 'How could you lie with such utter conviction?''

'Aren't you forgetting something?'

'I only lied at the beginning.'

'You still lied.'

Suddenly, Tully felt cold, despite the warmth of the room. She was right, he thought, you couldn't escape it. In the world of purity and goodness people attempted to fashion for themselves, their very foundations were steeped in mendacity.

'Don't look so doomridden,' Etta smiled. 'I thought you'd be happy to see me.'

He felt a sharp unreasoning anger. 'Do you realise all this time I've held myself responsible for your death?' he cried. 'Can you imagine what I went through?'

Her face was calm. 'I don't blame you for getting mad, but you're not the only one who suffered, Karl. You're not the only one capable of feeling pain. You were lucky. You believed me gone forever. In my case, I knew you were still alive.'

'What the hell difference does that make?'

'Think about it for a moment. Try to imagine what it took to go back to my homeland knowing you were still in the United States. Knowing I'd betrayed you.'

'I'll bet you found a way to get over it,' he said bitterly.

'The only one I knew,' she whispered. 'I threw myself into my work. I lived for nothing else. But how often I've asked myself since: has it been worth it?'

He felt his anger fade. How beautiful she looked, he mused. He didn't fool himself into thinking he was hard-boiled and purposeful enough to be unmoved by her presence. And yet, you couldn't turn your back on a lifetime and pretend nothing had happened in-between. Nevertheless, sitting there, he felt again the lightness of youth, as if past and present had somehow separated, creating a strange division of loyalties.

'I loved you once,' he admitted gently.

'I never doubted it for an instant.'

'But I'm married now.'

'Yes.' she smiled, 'with two sons. One a lawyer in Abilene, Texas, the other a doctor in California. We have a file on you at MfS Headquarters. I always insist it's kept up-to-date.'

'And you?'

She shrugged. 'For me, there was only one man in my life. You thought I was dead, so I threw myself into my career. As a young communist, I'd always been taught that the function of the state was far more important than the individual anyhow. It took me a long time to realise what an absurd lie that is. I used to keep up-to-date on your progress through our operatives in America. It made it seem . . . I don't know, almost as if you were away on some kind of business trip. I think I actually believed that for a while, that it was just a temporary separation, and pretty soon we'd be together again. When I heard you'd married, I was terribly upset. I had to be hospitalised for a time. Emotional overstrain, they called it. They said I'd been working too hard.'

She smiled. 'It's funny really. Back in Berlin, I have a reputation for being ice-cold and untouchable.'

The smile imbued her face with an almost mystical, faintly ethereal air. 'How well you look, Karl,' she said.

'You too,' he admitted. 'You're as beautiful as ever.'

'How's the music?'

'I still play. Every morning.'

'I'd always hoped . . .'

She gave a sad little laugh. 'There I go again.'

'It's the nature of reality,' he said. 'Nobody ever gets quite what they hoped for.'

'You had such a remarkable talent, Karl. You could have been a musician of real distinction.'

'Maybe,' Tully said. He hesitated. 'Maybe I didn't want that. If I'm honest, it's been a good life. I retire on Friday. We're moving out to California.'

'I know,' she whispered.

'I want to relax a while, take stock of things. Sure, I could have been a good musician, maybe even a great one. But you know what that takes? Dedication, sacrifice, ruthlessness. It's not enough to have talent, you need the drive to go with it. You must be prepared to put everything and everyone else in second place. A great philosophy, but don't expect it to make you happy.'

'Are you happy, Karl?' she said.

'I used to think not. Now I'm no longer sure.'

Her face clouded, and for a terrible moment he thought she was going to cry. Then the danger passed and he breathed more easily.

He stared at the features he had once loved so much.

'You know,' he said, 'there's one thing you still haven't told me.'

'What's that?'

'After all these years, why choose now to defect?'

Her face didn't alter. 'I'm dying,' she said.

Oh, God, he thought, was this the final irony in the whole sorry joke?

'Don't look so sombre,' she smiled. 'Life is meaningless when you devote it to work. I've lived in a self-made prison for so many years. When the doctors told me the truth, I realised that more than anything in the world, I wanted to see you, just once more.'

Tully found he couldn't speak. There was a tight constricting pain round his chest.

Her eyes were tender as she looked at him. 'May I ask you something?' she whispered.

Weakly, he cleared his throat. 'What is it?'

She nodded at the piano. 'Will you play for me? For the last time?'

Tully felt as if the spark of life had grown heavy in his stomach. And yet, in a curious and perverse way, he seemed terribly calm. Let the future take care of itself, he thought. For this solitary moment, there was only the past.

He rose and crossed the floor. In the silence of the room, witih the window shuttered, he sat at the piano and she moved beside him, her body soft and lithe against his shoulder. Her fingers played in his hair.

Somewhere a truck rumbled by, its radio disturbing the soft Parisian evening, engaging their senses for a moment before fading into silence.

Then Tully lifted his hands and started to play.

That Friday, Tully sat with his wife Louisa at his retirement dinner in Washington. He had flown back from Paris ill and drained, fatigue lying heavily in his limbs. It was not the natural fatigue of flesh and muscle, but a weariness of the spirit, an awareness of his own mortality, a feeling of decomposition, as if his body, rather than wait for death, was ready to anticipate it, decaying away inside him as he went through the motions of day-to-day living. For almost forty years he had sustained himself with a memory. To find that memory tainted by deceit, corrupted by betrayal, filled him with dismay.

Nevertheless, he managed to disguise his feelings at the dinner, nodding to acquaintances, smiling at friends, exchanging wisecracks with the subtle ease of a born diplomat. It was while Abel Brennan was rising to make his presentation speech that Charles Schulman, head of the Foreign Operations Co-Ordination Board, entered briskly and walked over to kneel at Tully's side.

'I thought you'd want to know at once,' he whispered hoarsely. 'Stapius is dead.'

Tully's coffee tasted bitter in his mouth. He breathed, filling his lungs with air in an effort to clear his mind.

'She was alive just two days ago,' he hissed.

'She took some damn pill or other. Christ knows where she'd hidden it. Death was instantaneous.'

God Almighty, was there anything else?

Tully listened to the flatteries issuing from the speaker's lips, and tried to keep his face composed. He had to remember he was the guest of honour. Others might be watching.

'What about the debriefing?' he murmured.

'She told us nothing, not a damned thing. The only good

point about the entire exercise is that we've got her out of our hair at last. I thought you'd want to know, Jack.'

'Thank you. You're quite right.'

He went through the next few minutes in a daze, rising politely as the speaker finished his speech, accepting the gold-plated retirement cup to thunderous applause, thanking everyone wittily and abundantly, and strolling back to his table with the air of a man who knew precisely what he was doing.

Louisa smiled at him as he sat down, her thin face creased with pride. Watching her, Tully felt his heart melt. Everything he cared about, every good thing that had happened in his life was there in the sunbrowned skin, the gentle eyes, and the beloved features of this woman in front of him. For years, he had filled his soul with something that didn't exist, yearning for something that had been empty of reality. Great loves were transient things, he realised. The business of living together provided the true essence of existence. It was a culture in itself, with its own subtleties of language and communication, its own traditions, customs, etiquette. He loved Louisa. They had been happy together. What more could any man ask?

She reached out and took his hand. 'I never realised you were sentimental, Jack,' she said.

'What are you talking about?'

She chuckled lightly, and in the glare from the chandeliers, her eyes seemed to sparkle with a secret understanding.

'Why, darling,' she whispered, 'you're crying.'

ABOUT THE AUTHOR

Bob Langley, the popular presenter of "Pebble Mill at One" and "Saturday Night at the Mill," joined the British Broadcasting Corporation in 1969. Apart from his television career, he has written ten action-packed novels of adventure, including *Autumn Tiger*, *Falklands Gambit*, *The Churchill Diamonds*, *The War of the Running Fox*, and *East of Everest*— each to considerable acclaim in both Great Britain and the United States.

Born in Newcastle, in northern England, Langley and his wife Pat live in a cozy cottage in the picturesque Lake District where he spends as much time as possible outdoors, hiking and planning his tales of adventure.

RELAX!
SIT DOWN
and Catch Up On Your Reading!

☐	25432	**THE OCTOBER CIRCLE** by Robert Littell	$3.95
☐	24172	**NATHANIEL** by John Saul	$3.95
☐	27148	**LINES AND SHADOWS** by Joseph Wambaugh	$4.95
☐	27386	**THE DELTA STAR** by Joseph Wambaugh	$4.95
☐	27259	**GLITTER DOME** by Joseph Wambaugh	$4.95
☐	24646	**THE LITTLE DRUMMER GIRL** by John Le Carré	$4.50
☐	26705	**SUSPECTS** by William J. Cavnitz	$4.50
☐	26733	**VENDETTA** by Steve Shagan	$4.50
☐	26657	**THE UNWANTED** by John Saul	$4.50
☐	26658	**A GRAND PASSION** by Mary Mackey	$4.50
☐	26572	**110 SHANGHAI ROAD** by Monica Highland	$4.50
☐	26499	**LAST OF THE BREED** by Louis L'Amour	$4.50
☐	27430	**SECRETS OF HARRY BRIGHT** by Joseph Wambaugh	$4.95

Prices and availability subject to change without notice.

Buy them at your local bookstore or use this convenient coupon for ordering:

Special Offer
Buy a Bantam Book
for only 50¢.

Now you can have Bantam's catalog filled with hundreds of titles plus take advantage of our unique and exciting bonus book offer. A special offer which gives you the opportunity to purchase a Bantam book for only 50¢. Here's how!

By ordering any five books at the regular price per order, you can also choose any other single book listed (up to a $5.95 value) for just 50¢. Some restrictions do apply, but for further details why not send for Bantam's catalog of titles today!

Just send us your name and address and we will send you a catalog!